"SHHH, WEE BABE," CROONED THE WOMAN.

Her fair head, sprinkled with twigs and leaves, bent over the infant as they rode. Whoever this woman was, she had endured a great deal in the past few days—enough to be willing to challenge an armed knight with nothing more than a small dirk and a tigress' maternal instincts. "Hush now, my love."

But the babe's squalling didn't cease. It grated on Boden's well-honed sense of survival. "What seems to be amiss?" he asked gruffly.

"He is hungry."

Boden found no words as the thought of what that meant came home to him. He knew an infant this young was sustained by mother's milk alone. The idea of cradling this woman between his thighs while she bared her breasts sent all his blood pumping from his heart to more intimate organs. He forced himself not to squirm in the saddle.

"Then feed him."

"I canna," she protested.

He saw her cheeks flush a wild-cherry red. Her eyes were wide, and seeing her with the babe in her arms stirred sharp, defensive feelings in Boden.

Feelings he would have sworn were long dead.

Highland Brides

THE LADY AND THE KNIGHT

LOIS GREIMAN

AVON BOOKS ◆ NEW YORK

AVON BOOKS
A division of
The Hearst Corporation
1350 Avenue of the Americas
New York, New York 10019

Copyright © 1997 by Lois Greiman
Inside cover author photo by Barbara Ridenous
Published by arrangement with the author
Visit our website at **http://www.AvonBooks.com**
Library of Congress Catalog Card Number: 97-93751
ISBN: 0-380-79433-0

First Avon Books Printing: December 1997

AVON TRADEMARK REG. U.S. PAT. OFF. AND IN OTHER COUNTRIES, MARCA REGISTRADA, HECHO EN U.S.A.

Printed in the U.S.A.

WCD   10   9   8   7   6   5   4   3   2   1

To Gail Swenson

THE LADY AND THE KNIGHT

Prologue

Burn Creag Castle
Year of our Lord 1509

Lightning forked across the inky sky, illuminating the curved walls of the tower room. Shadows flickered and undulated like the ghosts of people long dead. Silence echoed for a moment until lightning crackled again. Suddenly a tiny spot of red fire winked from the center of Rachel's small palm.

"Dragonheart!" Shona gasped, recognizing the amulet even in the fickle light. "You stole it from—"

Thunder crashed like a giant's wicked fist against the tower, shaking the very stones around them and startling the three girls who crouched on the floor in the wavering candlelight. The noise rolled slowly away, leaving the air taut in its aftermath.

"You stole it from Liam?" Shona finished breathlessly. She was the youngest of the three, barely nine years old and trembling in her voluminous white nightgown.

"Aye." Rachel pursed her lips. Her face looked pale against the wild frame of her dark hair. "I took it whilst he slept."

"'Tis magic," Shona whispered, transfixed by the sil-

1

ver dragon that looked docile but indomitable against her cousin's palm.

"It canna be magic," Sara corrected, still holding Shona's small trembling hand in her own. "Tis but stone and metal."

"But Liam said twas," Shona whispered.

"Tis the very reason I doubted," Rachel said, her voice barely audible in the high storage room. "But even Liam must tell the truth sometimes, I suppose. And twas the truth he said when he told me of our great-grandmother."

"*Our* great-grandmother?" Sara asked. "But how does *he* know about our ancestry?"

"I canna say for certain," Rachel admitted, glancing from one girl to the next. "But this is the story he spewed.

"Long ago there lived a lass in this very castle. Her name was Ula. Small she was like me, with Shona's fiery hair and Sara's kindness. Her mother died when she was but a bairn, and she was scared to be left alone at night. Sometimes she would cry out."

"And her father would come and tell her outlandish stories to make her laugh?" Shona suggested.

"Aye." Rachel smiled. Shona's father, Roderic, had told them all more than a few wild tales in the wee hours of the morning. "Aye, he would tell her stories. But still she was afraid. So he called on the best mason in the land to craft a magical stone dragon near her room to protect her."

"He must have loved her so," Sara whispered, more to herself than to the others.

"They built the dragon out on the roof to overlook the land about," Rachel said. "Now the lass felt safe in the comfort of her quarters. But her father worried that something might happen to him and Glen Creag would fall into the hands of the Dark Wizard. Then wee Ula would be left alone. He knew if such was the case she would be forced to leave her home, and he wished for her to be bold enough to make the journey. So he beseeched a good sorcerer to craft a silver amulet for her. A magical pendant it was, graced with gems taken from the enchanted water of Loch Ness.''

"Where Nessie lives?"

"Aye. That amulet would protect Ula wherever she went.''

"And this is that very amulet?"

"Aye."

"But Rachel," Sara said, "though I dunna understand it, ye never believe a thing Liam says. Why do ye trust him in this?"

Rachel closed her fingers over the dragon. It felt warm and heavy in her hand, almost as if it had a life of its own. "Come here," she whispered, and stepped toward the window. The three clustered together like mischievous fairies, tilting their heads close. Auburn hair sparked against flaxen and black. "Look out there."

"Where?"

"Tis dark," Shona said, but suddenly a fork of lightning slashed across the sky.

"There!"

"A dragon!" Sara gasped, seeing the stone statue illumined in sharp relief upon the ancient roof. "How did it get there?"

Rachel drew the amulet closer to her chest. "It must have been there for many long years, but ye canna see it from most points, only from here and from that room beside it."

"Ula's room," Shona whispered.

"Tis truly magic, then," murmured Sara.

"Aye," said Rachel, "and tonight we will bend its magic to our will."

"We will?" asked Shona, eyes as wide as eggs.

"Aye. We will. For tomorrow Sara will return to her home. And shortly after ye will go back ta Dun Ard. Tis impossible to know when we shall be together again."

The tower room fell silent.

"I will miss ye," Sara whispered.

"And I ye," Rachel said, reaching out to take her cousin's hand in her own. "Ye are the sisters of my heart."

"We will see ye soon, surely," Shona said. She tightened her grip on Sara's hand. Brothers she had aplenty. But sisters were a rare and precious thing. "When the weather warms . . ."

"One of us will surely be betrothed soon. In fact, the MacMurt has asked for my hand in marriage and—" Rachel stopped abruptly, glancing quickly at the barrels stacked along the curved wall. "What was that noise?"

Each girl held her breath and listened.

Behind the barrels, Liam did the same, careful to make no sound as frustration screamed through his soul. Betrothed! Surely the girls could not be promised at such tender ages—bartered off like so many sheep. Not his wee little lassies. Of course, they could take Rachel. He cared little if she married someone as old as sin and ugly as a troll. After all, Rachel was vain and aloof and when she laughed her eyes danced like . . .

She was nothing but a silly girl, he reminded himself. She'd believed his ridiculous stories about magic. She'd actually thought him asleep when she'd snatched his amulet! God's balls, she was a terrible thief! Still, he shouldn't have duped the other two bonny lasses.

"It must have been a mouse," Sara said, then turned her gaze back to Rachel. "Promise ye'll not move far from us."

"I'm not going to move away," said Shona fiercely. "I will marry Liam and live forever at Dun Ard."

"Liam!" Rachel scoffed. "Not that wild rogue. Ye will marry a great laird as will we all."

A sliver of noise issued from behind the barrels again.

"The mice are certainly restless," Shona murmured, glancing nervously behind her.

"Please dunna leave us," Sara whispered again.

"That's why I asked ye to come to the tower," Rachel

said. "If the dragon is truly magical it can grant us our fondest desires and bind us together. We will each touch the amulet and make a vow to take care of the others."

"But if we're far apart how will we know when we're needed?" Sara asked.

Rachel scowled, drawing her dark brows together over eyes as bright as amethyst. "The dragon will know," she improvised. "He will make certain we are safe or he will send help."

Sara thought a moment, then nodded. Her expression was somber, but she shivered with excitement as they formed a circle. "We shall all touch it together."

They did so now. Piling their small hands atop the amulet, they closed their eyes in unison.

"My fondest desire is to be a great healer like my mother," Rachel began.

Thunder boomed again, making Shona jump.

"I wish to be bold!" she chirped. "Like Father and the Flame."

Rachel squeezed Sara's hand. The room fell silent.

"Your turn," Shona whispered.

"I but wish for my own family to care for," Sara said softly. "My own bairns by my own hearth. Nothing more."

Silence fell upon the room.

"Now we must make a solemn vow," Rachel said. "Forever and always we shall be friends. Neither time nor distance shall separate us. When one is in need another shall come and assist her, for we that are gathered in this room are bound together for eternity."

All the world seemed suddenly to be utterly still.

"Now we must swear to it," whispered Sara.

"I swear," they said.

Thunder crashed like a cannon in their ears. The candle was snuffed out, pitching them into blackness. Wild energy crackled through the room, shooting up the girls' fingers.

They shrieked in unison, dropped the amulet, and raced as one toward the door.

The portal slammed open. Bare feet pattered down the stairs. The room fell silent. Behind the barrels, Liam lay sprawled against the wall, limp as a skewered hare.

Mother of God, what had just happened? It must have been the storm, of course. An errant stroke of lightning let loose in the tower. It must have been, and those silly girls had surely dropped his amulet in their fright.

He should go find it—shift through the rushes and retrieve it—but his limbs felt weak and his mind strangely boggled.

He'd best leave this place. Now! he decided, and launching himself from the floor, fled down the stairs after the girls.

Silence ruled the world. A crescent moon crept from behind a tattered cloud to smile on the earth below. And deep in the rushes, Dragonheart waited.

Chapter 1

Year of our Lord 1516

"I will leave tonight," said Boden.

Lord Haldane nodded from his sickbed. He looked drawn and thin, a pale remnant of the robust man Boden had served for many years. Above the mantel hung a portrait of him in his younger days. His thick, golden hair was uncovered. In one strong fist he held a shield that bore his crest—the black adder and the olive branch. It might seem a strange combination to some perhaps, but not to the duke of Rosenhurst. "I cannot allow Caroline to stay at Holly House if she feels unsafe. She fears for the child's life there." The duke stared out his night-blackened window. "Or so she says," he murmured. "Brigands broke into the house, her missive said. But I think, rather, it was a quarrel with her current lover. I am not as blind as she thinks me. But she was pure when she first laid with me, of that I am sure. And so I owe her a good deal. Another of an old man's follies— seeking my youth in a young maid's arms." There was silence for a moment, except for the sound of the wind outside the solid brownstone walls. "How fresh and lovely she looked when she abided here—such innocence. But mayhap she was not so naive even then. Cer-

7

tainly she knew the advantages of producing a duke's heir. I think now that was all she wanted. God knows she was happy enough to leave my company once she knew she carried my child in her belly. A comely face can hide a host of secrets. That, at least, I should have learned long ago.''

Silence again, followed by his quiet words. ''Tis said, the flattery of maidens is sweeter than wine, and some temptations I shall never outgrow, no matter how long I live. She knew just what to say, just how to watch me through her lashes.'' He sighed, deep in his own thoughts. ''Another sin to add to my lot, I suppose. But that sin granted me a son at least. So was it sin or was it wisdom?'' His voice was low, as if he spoke to himself. ''I would bring the babe to Knolltop to be with me, but it would be too cruel to put him under the same roof with my wife. Tis surely not Elizabeth's fault that she cannot bear a live child. Perhaps it would be no sin but a kindness to release her from this marriage. Perhaps another man could give her a child, and I would be free. Free to follow my heart.''

His voice had faded nearly to silence, his thoughts rambling.

''I will leave then, my lord, if there is nothing else,'' said Boden.

''There is something else,'' said the duke. He paused, still staring out the window. ''Lady Sara. What of her? Surely I cannot bring her here, flaunt her under Elizabeth's nose. Had I known her years ago I would have wed for love instead of for gain. Then surely I would have felt no need to stray to another's bed. My heirs would be legitimate. My line ensured. My happiness complete.''

Lord Haldane's fingers curled on the deep blue blanket that covered his bed. ''But I did not meet her until two years ago—on the eve of her wedding to William's son Stephen. I had already taken vows with Lady Elizabeth, but I knew immediately. Sara was meant to be mine—

the fairest flower in all of Scotland, she was, dressed in her red plaid with her hair bright as gold,'' he murmured. ''Stephen never knew what he had in her. He cared more for his hunting, for his ale. Twas just that he die by the hunt.'' His fingers curled into a tight fist. ''Twould that I had not been there. But I could not keep myself away. Like a besotted fool I would travel to Baileywood just to catch a glimpse of her, to spend a few minutes in her company.''

The wind gusted outside, scraping a branch against the stone wall.

''He was never worthy of her,'' Haldane whispered. ''Love personified she is. Like sunlight in my hand.'' His palm fell open as if he imagined his fingers against her flesh. For a moment he closed his eyes. ''With Stephen gone and a decent mourning time behind her, she could be mine. Not only in the flesh, but in name also. Surely she deserves better than she had, and I could give her all she desires if only . . .''

Boden cleared his throat, wanting to hear no more. Twas neither his place nor his wish to listen to his lord's innermost thoughts.

''My apologies,'' said the duke, drawing himself from his reverie and raising his voice. ''I have too much to occupy my mind and too little to occupy my hands these days.'' He scowled, remembering their conversation. ''Twill be a long journey for you, Boden. But at least this mission will surely involve no bloodshed. Still, I am loathe to send you so soon after that trouble with the Welsh. How is your knee?''

''Tis fine, my lord.''

The duke watched him for a moment, then grinned, looking more like the powerful duke Boden had served for so long. ''Had you used your crossbow on the brigand your words might well be true.''

''He was but a farmer with a scythe,'' Boden reminded him.

''Tis a well-known fact that when taxes are due a tight-fisted Welshman can do more damage with simple farming implements than most men can do with a cannon and battering ram. I would have thought you'd learned that from your first encounter with the Welsh.''

Boden tilted his head in concession to his lord's words. ''I fear I am a slow learner, Your Grace.''

Haldane watched him closely. ''But had you learned it earlier you would not have changed your course. Tis one of the reasons I send you now, Boden. I can trust you not to spill blood unless a battle is unavoidable. Perhaps Caroline's fear is well warranted. But I do not think so. Either way, you are not one to look for trouble.''

Hardly that, Boden thought dryly. ''For one good reason only,'' he said. ''I find I rarely spill another's blood without forfeiting some of my own.''

Haldane smiled. ''I've known you too long to believe you and need you too much to argue,'' he said. ''I merely ask that you do this task for me.''

Boden nodded. ''I will see your babe and his mother safely to Cinderhall, my lord. If that is all . . . ?''

''And the Lady Sara,'' Haldane said.

Boden tensed. Was he to escort both of the duke's mistresses to the same abode? That seemed neither prudent nor healthy. He had met Caroline, and she didn't seem the type to appreciate competition. ''Sara?'' Boden asked, pretending he hadn't heard Haldane's murmurings from only minutes before.

''Aye. She is Caroline's companion.''

Boden forced his expression to remain stoic. Lord Haldane had always had a selection of mistresses, but thus far Boden had never been asked to become involved with any of them. And he preferred it that way, for he was not good at resisting temptation.

''She and Caroline became aquainted at Baileywood before Stephen's death,'' the duke explained. ''Sara journeyed to London to be at her friend's side during my son's birth. She has not left since. Strong on loyalty is my Sara.''

"So you would have me bring her to Cinderhall with the mother and child?"

"For the time being. You must afford her every courtesy, see to her every need until I can do so in person." He paused. The wind gusted. "For in truth, Boden, it is she I cherish above all others."

Boden glanced toward the door, hoping the duke's wife was well out of hearing. Theirs was no more than a marriage of convenience of course, but surely there was no reason for the duchess to know her husband had bedded not just one, but both of the women he had sent to London. Certainly Lady Elizabeth had known enough pain with the stillborn death of her children.

"Do you understand my words, sir?"

"I do, my lord," said Boden, turning his attention back to the duke.

"Good," said Haldane, his tone becoming brusque. "There is none other I would send in your stead."

"My thanks for your faith in me. I will try not to disappoint you, my lord."

The duke smiled. "You are like a son to me."

Boden's eyebrows rose. This was indeed a day of surprises. The duke had never been short of women he cared for, but words of sentiment for his knights were few and far between.

Haldane laughed out loud. "I am neither as young nor as healthy as I once was. I have no wish to die with things left unsaid."

"You must not speak like that," Boden said. The duke of Rosenhurst had as many faults as the next man, but in a score of years, he had never been unfair to Boden. Twas a fact for which Boden would be eternally grateful. Worry coursed through him as he stepped toward the bed. "Tis not your time to die, my lord."

Haldane smiled again. "Are you certain or are you but hopeful?" he asked.

"I am both."

"Well spoken." Haldane reached up to clasp Boden's

hand. "You have my thanks for agreeing to go."

"You failed to tell me I had a choice."

Haldane chuckled and released his hand. "Return the lady safely to my side, Sir Blackblade, and you will be justly rewarded."

Boden nodded, not for a moment doubting of whom Haldane spoke. Then he left. The hallway down which Boden hurried was lit by a single sconce.

"Sir Blackblade."

Boden turned quickly at the quiet voice. "My lady."

Lady Elizabeth rushed toward him, her white nightrail billowing behind her. Boden took a cautious step backward. Never did Elizabeth realize her allure. It was no different now it seemed, because she reached for his hand with both of hers. They felt warm and soft as rose petals against his.

"He is sending you away," she said, her voice breathless.

"Aye, my lady."

"Please do not go."

Boden stared in open surprise. Much younger than her husband, she was both beautiful and regal. But now she had abandoned her lofty demeanor. Her dark hair was unbound, making her look young and innocent. Gone was her costly gown, replaced by this touchable bit of linen, as if she'd just left her bed.

"I've had a frightful dream and I worry for your life," she continued, leaning closer.

"My life?" he asked. She smelled of lavender and sweet wine. He was not a man accustomed to the company of women, but one thought stood out clearly in his mind—she was his lord's wife, regardless of the duke's philandering.

"Aye, good sir," she said. "My husband does not sometimes realize your worth, I think. You are the best of his knights. And though I know . . ." She paused, her eyes very sad. "I know he is not always faithful to me.

But he is still my husband, and I would have what is best for him.''

''What do you mean?''

''I fear for his life,'' she said, her voice sounding urgent. ''He is not strong these days. And London is such a far way. What if you do not return in time.''

''Lady, you shouldn't speak of such things.''

''But I must,'' she said, squeezing his hand imploringly. ''You must not leave him now. Won't you come to my chambers and discuss this with me at the least?''

Her chambers! He may not be accustomed to the company of women, but at least he knew the limitations of his self-control, and that was far beyond them.

''I . . . I must not,'' he said, and pulling his hand from her grasp, rushed away.

Boden's hurried journey to London had been long and fruitless, for when he'd arrived at Holly House, he'd been told that the women for whom he searched were gone.

Gone! It had taken all of Boden's control not to shake the little servant that elevated his nose as if Boden's scent of fermenting horse sweat somehow offended his sensibilities. Gone where?

The ladies had not deigned to share that information with *him*, the house servant replied. And it was not his job to ask, but only to see the packing done well and efficiently.

Packing?

Yes, for a long and arduous journey, judging by the lady's demands. Caroline had been well spooked after the brigands broke into the house, though her personal guards had bested the villains and secured the house.

Boden shifted his weight in the saddle as he mulled over his thoughts. It had been five days since he'd left London and he hadn't had a decent meal since. The sun shifted irrevocably toward the horizon, reminding him he would go to bed hungry again. He wasn't one to complain, but his arse hurt. It looked like it might rain again.

His knee still ached from its meeting with the Welshman's scythe. He had a headache, he was weary to the
bone, and his chain mail was beginning to rust.

Beneath him, the dapple-gray destrier called Mettle
cocked a hip and heaved a martyred sigh. Theirs had *been*
a long and arduous journey, and they were ready for it
to end. But as of yet Boden had found no trace of the
mistress or her entourage, though he had followed every
available lead.

They were heading north, that much he knew, and
though he would like to believe they were returning to
Lord Haldane under their own power, Boden's luck had
never been what one might call colossal. Thus, here he
was, in the midst of nowhere, trying to imagine what had
happened to the women for whom he searched.

Dusk was settling softly around him. Twould be another night spent on the soggy earth, and while that fate
was not unusual, neither was it much appreciated. There
would be little reason to hurry to his bed tonight. So he
would follow Caroline's trail and hope to shorten his
quest before morning.

Mettle stepped forward at a touch of Boden's spurs.
Daylight slipped away, fading to a pearlescent luster.
Quiet pervaded the earth, disturbed only by Mettle's solid
footfalls against the dirt road. They rounded a corner, but
suddenly the stallion stopped abruptly. His dark-tipped
ears flicked forward above the black metal champfrein
that armored his head.

Boden nudged him. The horse remained immobile but
for a twitch of his tensed muscles.

"'Tis no time for one of your moods," Boden murmured. He pricked the stallion's sides again. Mettle
shook his head in irritation, but finally moved forward,
his gait trappy and jarring now, his huge body tense.

They'd not gone more than ten rods when Boden saw
the scrap of crimson cloth. It was draped messily over a
branch. But in a moment he saw that the fabric was not
intended to be red. No, it was blood that made it so.

Bile rose in Boden's throat. Sweet sainted Mary, please, not more death, he prayed. But his pleas went unanswered, for not thirty feet into the woods, he found the first bloated body.

Boden closed his eyes for a moment, willing this to be a nightmare. But it was not, and there was nothing he could do but force himself to dismount and face the truth. His legs felt wooden as he approached the corpse. Memories of a dozen past battles haunted him—sightless eyes, torn limbs, the wails of the wounded.

But this was worse still, for this was a woman. Caroline. His lord's mistress. He remembered how Haldane had spoken of her freshness, her innocence. The thought twisted his insides into a painful knot, forcing out the contents of his stomach.

He wretched and wretched again, then stumbled backward, ready to run away like the coward he was. But the next body was only a few yards away. It was a man. His shirt and boots were gone and his chest grotesquely swollen.

The next corpse was that of another woman. It lay just outside a collapsed tent. A red plaid shawl was twisted about her. Her blond hair was matted with blood and her face half gone. Boden's stomach lurched viciously, but now only bile spewed. It was bitter and galling, and accompanied by the wild ferocity that had seen through dozens of nightmarish battles.

A ferocity that would exact justice—and take lives.

Sara whimpered in her sleep. Lord Haldane was going to kill her. She knew it, but she couldn't move, couldn't escape. And suddenly his face changed, darkening, hardening into one she had never seen. His wicked grin was a white slash against his granite features and in his hand he held the hilt of a sword entwined with the image of a black snake. The blade rose. Terror welled up inside her. She couldn't die. Not now. She screamed, and awoke with a start, still gripping the dragon pendant that hung from her neck.

Bracken rustled beneath her. Beside her, the feeding gourd and pouch still hung from her belt. Glancing up, she saw that the sun hung low in the sky. Inside his makeshift sling against Sara's breast, Caroline's child bumped to awareness. Thomas, sweet Thomas. Sara stroked his head, assuring herself he was safe as she collected her thoughts. It was only a dream—just another of the eerie nightmares that visited her of late.

Where was she?

She glanced about, steadying her breathing and remembering.

It had been Sara's idea to return to the Highlands. They would be safe there, she'd told Caroline. But the journey north had been anything but safe.

It had started well enough. The weather had been warm and sunny. For two days they had traveled unmolested, singing songs and passing Thomas amongst the three women in the carriage. Though Anne of Boneau seldom cared for the babe except to nurse him, she seemed attached to the child. She'd taken a liking to Sara's red plaid shawl and in a moment of playful sisterhood, they'd made an exchange—the plaid for the nursemaid's leather pouch.

Caroline had laughed as Sara stashed a few items into the bag, a needle, a few vials of herbs that Fiona had given her—her witchy concoctions as Caroline called them. Sara had laughed back and attached the pouch to her girdle, saying she now had all she needed to care for them in any eventuality.

Their comradery had lasted longer than the good weather.

The rain began midafternoon, slowing their progress. By evening they realized they would not reach the next inn before dusk. They'd been forced to spend the night in the wilds and they had prepared for that.

But nothing could have prepared them for the brig-

ands. Nothing but the dreams that had awakened Sara.
Even before the first sign of trouble, she had gathered
Thomas into her arms. Frantic, and not knowing why,
she had tried to warn the women. But Caroline was not
in the tent and Anne only rolled over with a sleepy groan.

Sara scurried into the darkness.

From the woods she thought she heard Caroline giggle.
She rushed toward the noise. Behind her, a guard shouted
a warning. It was cut off mid-cry.

Terror streaked through her, accented by battle cries.
There was nothing she could do but run. Run and hide
from the screams that ripped through the night.

By morning all was quiet. Sara slunk from her hole.
Loyalty and uncertainty brought her back toward their
camp.

She found Caroline lying on her side not far from the
body of her favored guard. Dried blood soaked her bodice, but she still breathed and her eyes were strangely
peaceful.

"You have Thomas." The words were no more than
a whisper. "I knew you did, prayed you did. Waited to
make certain."

Sara reached for her, but the other woman shook her
head.

"Let me talk. Just a few words left." She paused,
fighting for breath. "Haldane."

Sara searched for meaning. "What?"

"Haldane's snake." She nodded weakly toward the
ground not far from her hand. A black piece of metal lay
there, wrought into the shape of an adder and broken off
of a larger piece. "Sword . . . sent . . ."

She spasmed, then relaxed.

"Caroline!" Sara gasped.

"Protect him," she whispered through stiffening lips.
"From them."

"From who?"

"Promise me."

"I promise. I promise I will!" vowed Sara, but Caroline was already gone, slipping quietly into death.

The days since had been hideous, the nights terrifying. But somehow, miraculously, they had survived this long.

Twas only another wicked dream that haunted Sara now, and yet it seemed so real.

But there was no time to consider that now, for her dreams were eerily premonitory of late. Perhaps they were warning her of some nearby evil. Or perhaps not.

Fear coiled in her belly. Sara pushed herself to her feet.

A noise rustled in the underbrush! Fear sharpened to terror. She spun away, but suddenly a brigand leaped from her nightmares. His face was dark, and in his hand he held the black blade from her dreams.

She screamed and yanked out her dirk.

He reached for her. She slashed. The blade skittered across his mail and sliced into his arm. She heard his hiss of pain and drew back to strike again. But already he was behind her, one arm across her throat, the other grabbing her wrist.

She couldn't breathe, couldn't move. She had to protect Thomas. But the grip on her arm was ungodly tight. Her fingers went numb and she dropped the dirk like a leaf to the forest floor.

"Do you wish to die now?" hissed the villain.

She shook her head jerkily, barely able to breathe. Fear froze her muscles. Her heart crashed against Thomas's sling.

"Move. And don't make a sound." He gave her a shove. Her legs buckled and she almost fell, but his hand on her arm held her up. They hurried through the woods. How had he found her? She had hidden them carefully and well. Why was he alone? Where were the others and where was he taking her?

She stumbled along for an eternity. A stream appeared before them. It was narrow and swift flowing. Behind it was a tangled mass of foliage, then a cliff that rose more than twenty feet above her head.

He pressed her into the water. It sloshed cold and rapid

against her feet and soaked her gown. They were across in a moment. He pushed her into the gorse bushes on the opposite side. The branches closed behind them. A root snared her foot. She stumbled again and he let her fall.

"Where are the others?" he asked, his eyes hard as obsidian and looking absolutely mad.

It took forever for her to find her voice, and when she did, it shook. "What others?"

He smiled. The expression was brittle. "Why did you kill them?"

She shook her head, trying to make sense of the madness.

"If all you wanted was the child, you could have let them live. Is it ransom you're after? Who sent you? Where are your accomplices?"

"Accomplices? I have none!"

"There's little reason to lie. Already I've killed one of them. I heard your cry. Tis what helped me find you. Did they think to cut you out of the profit? Is that why you screamed?" He leaned toward her, his teeth gritted in anger.

She cowered back. "Twas naught but a bad dream that haunted me!"

"Surely you can think of a better lie than that."

She scrambled to her feet, steadying the babe as she did so. "Tis not a lie. I swear tis true."

For a moment, he stared at her as if her brain was made of pudding. Then he turned back to scan the woods. "You must think me daft indeed," he said, then more softly, as if to himself, "Where are her friends? And how many? Our backs are safe. They'll come straight at us. Are you hungry, Black Adder?" he asked, helfing his sword.

Fear mixed with hope. So there was someone out there, someone who could save her, she thought, but if they came for her, this man before her would surely slaughter them.

A rustle of noise sounded off to the side. Quick as

thought, his right hand covered her mouth. His attention snapped to the underbrush nearby. Above his mail shirt, the tendons in his dark throat stood out sharp and rigid.

Sara stared at him, unable to move for the fear that engulfed her. What was he afraid of? From whom was he hiding?

A fawn rose from its bed in the bracket and darted away.

The brigand released a heavy breath and dropped his hand from her. His eyes were slightly less wild.

She stumbled back a pace. "If ye let us go . . ." She paused, searching for the romanticized courage of the Highlander, the courage that had never been hers. "I will pay ye."

He narrowed his eyes. A scar slanted through the right corner of his lips, making it almost look as if he smiled. "Pay me?"

"Aye." She had seen him and his sword in her dreams—the sword with the snake wrapped about the hilt, the same metal viper that had lain so near Caroline as she lay dying. Whoever had killed her had carried the same type of weapon.

"And why would you pay me?" he asked.

"I have no wish to die."

He laughed. The sound was deep and humorless. It curled into her belly in new waves of terror. "Why would I want to kill a pretty thing like you? Except of course that you're a murderer."

She shook her head, but knew her denial would do little good. "I'll give ye . . ." Her voice trembled and her knees felt as if they might spill her to the earth. What could she give him? In truth, she had nothing, nothing but . . . She moved her cloak aside with a trembling hand. The dragon amulet winked in an errant shaft of evening light. "I'll give ye Dragonheart."

His gaze pinned on the silver pendant that hung just above the square bodice of her tattered gown. He reached for it. She jerked shakily back, and he grinned—the expression a white slash against his dark skin.

"Tis a pretty bauble," he said.

"Bauble!" She tried to laugh, but the sound was raspy. "Tis far more than a bauble. Tis a magic token."

He tilted his head at her, still holding his dark sword. But its tip pointed down now. "Magic?"

"Aye. Twas made long ago when the earth was still young. Crafted by an all-powerful sorcerer, it was."

One corner of his mouth lifted, causing the fine scar on his lips to dance. He was laughing at her, letting her ramble on while he planned evil things. She had to escape! There was no hope of outrunning him, but she had stashed Caroline's knife inside her cloak. If she could only reach it, this time she wouldn't be so foolish as to stab at his protected chest, for his throat was exposed.

"Indeed," she said, forcing herself to concentrate, to keep her gaze on his eyes and not on the pulse that throbbed at the base of his broad jaw. "If the pendant is freely given to ye, ye will have . . . twice your usual strength and cunning. Surely that would be useful for a— for a man such as yourself."

The brigand lowered his gaze to his wounded arm. A muscle jumped angrily in his jaw, and when he raised his eyes they looked primitive and only half sane. "It seems a small scratch for one with twice her usual strength."

"Nay." She shook her head. "Ye dunna understand. Dragonheart does not give the same gifts to each person. It but enhances those ye already possess." The words were ridiculous, a blatant lie, and yet they seemed to come of their own accord. Perhaps if she blathered on, he would underestimate her, relax, and give her an opportunity to escape.

He took a step forward. Dear Lord, he was a big man. She would have no chance against him in a battle of strength. Surprise would be her only hope.

"And what gifts do you possess, pretty one?"

She stepped back an abbreviated pace, stumbled on the

bushes behind her, and fell to a sitting position in the gorse. "Kindness." The single word sounded like a plea for mercy.

"Kindness!" he growled, and swung his sword wildly to the side. She cowered away, but he made no move to approach her. "I am surrounded by death. Is this an example of your kindness?" he snarled and reached for her.

She shrieked in terror. Her hand whipped out holding the knife in her fist. She stabbed and the blade bit into the side of his neck. He roared in pain and stumbled back.

Sara scrambled away, clawing at the bushes as she ran. Branches grabbed her. Mud sucked at her feet. Waves dragged at her gown, but she was across the water and away, running wildly, her lungs burning.

Hide! She must hide! But already she could hear her pursuer, could hear his curses and rasping breath.

Dear God save her! She must not look back. He was closing in! She heard him grunt as he leaped, felt his fingers scrape her back, and suddenly she was snatched from her feet and crashed on the ground.

Thomas howled. She tried to steady him against her breast, tried to scramble away. But already the villain was atop her, pinning her down.

"A fine example of a woman's kindness!" he rasped.

Sara bucked against him, trying to break free, struggling for survival.

"Cease!" he ordered, pressing her to the earth. "Cease or I'll repay your kindness with your own brand."

Sara went still and found his eyes with her own. They were dark and enraged. Blood dripped from his neck and onto her gown. She swallowed the bile in her throat and closed her eyes. Fear tasted bitter and harsh. Death waited with hungry jaws.

"Please," she whispered. The word sounded small and pathetic to her own ears, but she was far past caring. "Spare us for mercy's sake."

"You dare beg for mercy! After what you have done?" he growled. She shut her eyes, certain death would come. But suddenly he stood up and yanked her to her feet.

She gasped, snapping her eyes open.

"I have no mercy," he said. "No more than you. Tell me, what kind of ransom did you think you would get for the child?"

"Ransom!"

He shook her. "Don't think me too kind to kill you here and now. Why did you take the babe?"

"I did no such thing. What do you mean? Who are you?"

He narrowed his eyes at her. A muscle jerked in his jaw. "I am Sir Boden Blackblade, come to return what is Lord Haldane's."

Haldane! She shook her head, trying to clear it, to make some sense of this nightmare. Had Lord Haldane sent this huge warrior to kill her? But why? It made no sense.

"Please let me go," she pleaded.

"Go?" He laughed. The noise sounded maniacal. "Tell me, have you ever seen a woman after the wild animals have gotten to her? With her face half gone?"

Sara scrunched her eyes shut and cowered away.

Blackblade tightened his grip and yanked her back toward him. "Tis not a sight for your pretty eyes. There was little enough left of them by the time I got there. Still, the signs were clear. The carriage had stopped before the brigands attacked. Why? Did you stop for *you*? Did you stand in the trail and feign some injury? Pretty as you are, you would have little trouble distracting the guards." Releasing her arm, he ran a finger along her jaw. "But you would not be so comely if you were left to bleed to death in the woods."

She leaned away from him, terror knotting her stomach. "You're mad."

"Mayhap . . ." He paused, watching her eyes as he pulled a narrow blade from a sheath by his side. "And mayhap if you give me the names of the people involved in this crime I will not prolong your death. I've no stomach for torturing women.''

''Please!'' Her hands shook. She couldn't think, could barely stand. Was he accusing her of the murder of her friends? ''I dunna know what you're talking about. I swear it.''

He watched her, then glanced at the clearing again, his brow knotted in thought. A modicum of sanity shone in his eyes now. ''Are you saying you had no part in the murders? That you knew nothing of their plan?''

''I've done no one any harm.''

''So you were just hired to nurse the babe?''

''Hired?'' She shook her head wildly, desperately searching for a way to save herself and the babe. Surely her best bet was to distance herself from this entire nightmare. ''I dunna know what you're talking about. I was not hired. The babe is mine.''

''You lie!''

''Nay!'' she whispered, scrunching back.

The woods were silent. ''You are in leige with the men who killed the child's mother,'' he accused.

''Nay, I am not,'' she rasped. ''My name is Bernadette, late of Shrewsbury.'' Her mind spun. ''I was but traveling to Edinburgh to my father's house.''

''You lie,'' he said again, but his tone was softer now. ''No woman would be in the wilds of England alone.''

''I was not alone. My husband . . .'' A sob came from somewhere, bidden or not, she wasn't sure. ''My William died some months ago. Killed he was by a wild boar. I have no family here, so I had determined to return to my homeland. My maid was with me, and a small retinue of guards.'' He looked as if he would speak, but she rushed on, committed to this fanciful tale that might save her life and that of the babe she'd vowed to protect. ''We were attacked by brigands. Mayhap even the same band that killed those women of whom you speak. That is the truth. I swear it.'' She sobbed again. Thomas squirmed in the security of his pouch. ''I swear it!'' she repeated and fell to her knees to drop her face into her hands and cry.

Minutes ticked by. She continued to sob, softly, not trying to stem the flow, but thinking, planning.

Looking between her spread fingers, she watched him sheath his sword. His legs were covered in dark hose and his feet in high, leather boots. Nearby there was a rock the size of her fist. If he didn't believe her story, she would slam it into his knee and pray for strength.

He cleared his throat. She watched his feet shift slightly, as if he were uncomfortable with her tears.

He cleared his throat again. "Were they all killed?" His tone was still gruff, but there was uncertainty in it now.

"I dunna think so. My maid, Shona . . ." Not Shona! She shouldn't have used her cousin's name, for if this man knew of Caroline and the bairn, mayhap he knew something of *her* family, too. But it was too late to change her words now. "Shona's mount came up lame. We had to stop. Twas just afore dusk two days since when we were attacked. There were so many of them. They were all around us. I canna . . ." She hiccuped. Behind him was a hill. She would have a better chance against his greater bulk if she ran uphill, especially if his knee was broken. But that was a last resort. "I canna blame the guards for running off."

His fists tightened again. "Your guards left you?"

Glancing up, she saw his scar dance as his mouth quirked. But the insanity had left his eyes.

"They tried to fight. Edward, poor Edward fell, and then I . . . I'm so ashamed . . ."

"What happened?" His tone was flat, his expression inscrutable.

"I grabbed John and hid in the woods. I told myself . . ." Hiccup. "I told myself I had to save my child, but . . . But I know twas pure cowardice. And in the face of such bravery."

"Bravery?"

"Shona! Always so clever she is . . . was," she corrected softly. "She led them away from us."

He waited in silence.

"My steed was the faster. She had the best chance of leading the brigands afield if she rode Reul."

"She took your horse?" His voice was deep as he tried to assimilate her garbled story.

"Aye. And she hasn't returned. I'm so afraid for her. She may be dead or worse." Glancing up at his face, she grasped his sleeve. "Could ye . . . Could ye go find her?"

"Lady, I—"

"Please. My father is not a poor man." She stared up at him from her knees. It was a long ways up. "He will pay. Wee John loved her. She's so selfless and—"

"Aye." He scanned the clearing again, then whistled softly—one long note and one short. "She has probably selflessly sold your steed by now and is living well off the proceeds as you and your babe perish in the woods."

She raised her chin slightly as she wiped the tears from her cheek with the back of her hand. "Shona would do no such thing."

He stared at her as he cradled his wounded arm against his chest. "And you are all kindness and caring."

"I must go find her." She hoped with all her might that he would believe her and let her go, because the chances of breaking his knee before he killed her were slim.

But in a moment he had caught her arm and dragged her to her feet, leaving the rock well out of reach.

"You'll do no such thing," he insisted.

Chapter 2

The woman called Bernadette tugged, trying to break free of Boden's grip on her arm. He supposed she had some right to fear him. After all, he *had* threatened her life. But the death craze was fading now. Reality was settling in, dulling the memories of the horrors he had seen in the woods. She'd had nothing to do with Caroline's death. Or so she said. And though he may be a fool, he believed her. If she were part of a plan to abduct Lord Haldane's child, she would surely be with her accomplices now and well on her way to demanding ransom for the child.

He had not been thinking clearly since he'd found the women's dead bodies, that much was certain. Had he been lucid he would have questioned the brigand he found, instead of killing him outright.

Bernadette's scream had done nothing to steady his thinking. Hope had surged through him. Perhaps someone had survived the attack, he'd thought. But the woman had not seen him as a savior but as a villain, and had attacked *him*. Once again he'd been given no time to think, but only to react, to assume, and to act on those assumptions. And he'd been trained to assume the worst. Thus, in his mind, the woman had become an abductor. The theory held some logic. After all, he'd never found

27

the baby's body, only scraps of cloth and patches of blood.

A noise crackled behind him. Survival instincts crashed to the fore. In an instant, his sword was in his hand and he was facing the onslaught. But his horse Mettle was the only menace that charged from the woods.

Boden released a shaky breath and returned Black Adder to its place at his side. "No need to fear," he said. Reaching into the pouch that hung from his belt, he brought forth a chunk of dark bread for the horse. There was little hope the great, dappled charger would come when called, and no hope that he would make such a spectacular entrance if a treat wasn't forthcoming. Little wonder he was so damned fat.

Boden turned his attention back to Bernadette. She stopped her backward retreat abruptly, her eyes wide. "Your ride is here," she said. "I'll just be on my way."

Boden almost grinned as he grasped Mettle's trailing reins. "You'll come with me, lady."

"I've done nothing wrong."

"So you've said. But you are a woman. Of that I am fairly certain. Tis my duty to protect you."

"Protect me? Is that what ye've been doing?"

He chuckled. "Surely a scrapper like you wouldn't let a few idle threats worry her," he said. "After all, you got in more than your share of licks." He grimaced at the blood on his arm and tried not to think how his neck must look.

She winced as her gaze followed his. "They are . . . only flesh wounds," she assured him.

"True," he said. "But tis *my* flesh and I rather like to keep it intact whenever possible. Still, you're a woman and I'm a knight."

"A—a knight?"

He turned to see that her expression looked as surprised as her voice sounded. "Aye. And sworn to protect the . . . weak and the mild."

Her gaze swept to his bloodied arm again. Darkness

had settled in with only the last remnants of dusk clinging to the western sky.

"You're a knight?" she repeated.

He frowned at her surprise. Surely it wasn't warranted. His sleeveless mail shirt evidenced fine Oriental craftsmanship. His sword was made of Spanish steel, his steed bred for a king. Without knowing the circumstances of his birth, why would she be shocked by his title? "Aye," he said, peeved by the thought. "Come. You'll ride in front."

"I . . . fear I must decline." She took a step back and shook her head, but he was fresh out of patience and snatched her to him.

"Come," he gritted through his teeth and pushed her and the child aboard the gray. "I owe you a kindness."

She perched with both legs on one side while he mounted behind her. Her body felt stiff against his. The saddle was too small for them both, but he dare not stay afoot much longer, for the memory of decaying bodies sat heavy in his stomach. The fact that two of them had been women had only made his anger greater. Admittedly, it had also made his reasoning less than sound.

After his initial shock, he had hoped the baby might have survived somehow. Even if the babe had been taken for ransom, it would have been a blessing. But such was not the case. The duke's heir must have perished and been dragged from his mother by a wild animal.

The baby cried suddenly, startling Boden from his thoughts. "Keep him quiet," he warned. He had seen only one brigand, but he had no reason to think others weren't close by. His motto was—keep your head down and don't court trouble. Twas a coward's motto, he knew, but so far as he could tell it was the only thing that had kept his neck between his head and his shoulders this long.

"Shhh, wee babe," crooned the woman, gently jostling the child in his strange sling. Her fair head was sprinkled with twigs and leaves and bent over the infant.

Whoever this woman was, she had endured a great deal in the past few days, enough to be willing to challenge an armed knight with nothing more than a small dirk and a tigress's maternal instincts. "Hush now, my love."

But the squalling didn't cease and grated on Boden's well-honed sense of survival. "What seems to be amiss?" he asked gruffly.

"He is hungry."

Boden found no words as the thought of what that meant came home to him. He wasn't the kind of man who was comfortable amidst women or the babes they nursed. But he knew enough to realize an infant this young was sustained by mother's milk alone. The idea of cradling this woman between his thighs while she bared her breasts sent all his blood pumping from his heart to more intimate regions. Regions best left forgotten until this woman was deposited somewhere safe. And yet, he could hardly allow the babe to go on squalling.

He forced himself not to squirm in the saddle. "Then feed him."

"I canna."

So whoever she was, she was still modest enough to be embarrassed by such circumstances.

The babe yelled louder. Looking over Bernadette's shoulder, Boden could see a small fist waving wildly in time with the screams.

"Tis not the place for feminine sensibilities," he said. "Such ungodly racket will draw every blackguard from here to the ends of Christendom. Feed the child."

"I canna," she repeated, then straightened even more, but the movement pushed her off balance. She gasped as she slipped, babe and all, toward the ground.

Dropping the reins, Boden grabbed her by the arm and dragged her back up. Pain ripped through his battered body.

"Sit up proper!" he growled, and reaching about her, grabbed one thigh to pull it over the saddle's pommel. She straightened with her backside dead center against his hardening member. The pain in his arm was immediately forgotten as he ground his teeth and grappled to retain his senses.

For a moment she had grasped his sleeve and turned toward him in alarm. Her cheeks were flushed a wild-cherry red. Her eyes were wide and lovely, stirring sharp, defensive feelings Boden would have sworn were long dead. Her bottom, however, pressed firm and round against his nether parts, evoked feelings that had nothing whatsoever to do with defenses and everything to do with the kind of raging desires that could get a careless man killed.

The noise from the babe had not abated a whit.

"Feed him," he repeated, his tone somewhat hoarse.

"I told ye, I canna." Her voice was no more than a softly burred whisper, making him lean closer to hear.

He scowled down at her. "I think it would be *kinder* to consider the babe's needs than your own misplaced discomfort. I swear I won't look."

The silence lay heavy around them, but for the muffled clop of Mettle's iron-shod hooves.

"I do not have milk." She said the words in a rush without turning toward him.

He scowled. "So twas more refined to pay another than to see to the task yourself?" he asked.

Silence again, then, "I had no milk to give him."

He scowled at the back of her head, thinking. "So this Shona that stole your mount, she fed the babe in your stead?"

"She did not steal Reul," Sara corrected, peeved against her better judgment. "She was Scots and thus loyal to her death. She but went for help. And aye, she was wee John's nursemaid." She lifted the child, sling and all, to her shoulder, patting him gently. The squawks turned to whimpers.

Boden grimaced as he turned his attention to the top of the child's head so near his own. It was bald except for a few wisps of blond hair that scraggled out at odd angles. His face was a puckered, angry red, and just above his left ear there was an ugly splotch the size and color of a plum. Good Lord, he was a homely thing. He guessed it would not be wise to share that opinion with the mother. His arm and neck were already pierced, best not to induce her to try for his heart.

"How long since you've eaten?" he asked instead.

"He's had naught but water since the day afore last," she said.

But that hadn't been what he'd asked. "And you?" he said.

"I found some watercress this morning."

Watercress and nothing else for two days. Could she be lying? But no. She had felt as light as lily petals when he'd lifted her onto Mettle's back.

Reaching behind him, Boden opened his saddle pack and withdrew a chunk of bread wrapped in linen. He pushed it toward her. "Eat this. Tis all I can offer for now."

She glanced up at him. An errant slash of sunlight found its way through the leaves beside the trail, and in it he saw that her eyes were an unearthly blue. "What do ye plan to do with us?" she asked.

What did he plan, or what did he wish to do with her? They were far different things. But he guessed she would not appreciate his advances, for there was still fear in her eyes.

"Why are you afraid of me?" He asked the question out loud, though he hadn't meant to.

She was silent for a moment, then. "Twas it na ye who accused me of abduction and worse?"

"Well . . ." He scowled, feeling guilty.

"Wasn't it ye who ran me down as if I were a rabid hound, who threatened me with death?"

"Aye, but . . ." He winced as he shrugged. "I'm granting you a ride on Mettle now." The statement sounded lame even to his own ears.

She turned to face forward. "What are ye planning for us?"

"I'm not planning murder or ravishment if that's your worry," he told her. "Eat this."

"It seems I am already in your debt."

"'Tis good of you to notice," he said irritably.

"I but thought ye were one of the brigands," she explained.

"You can be certain in the future I'll declare my intentions clearly before rescuing any damsels in distress."

Her gaze skimmed to his arm. She grimaced. "I am sorry about your wounds."

"Not nearly so sorry as I, I'll wager."

Her expression became even more contrite. "I canna take your bread," she said. Her profile was almost painfully perfect, her nose dusted with just a sprinkling of pale freckles.

"The last thing I need is for you to faint dead away," he said. "'Tis bad enough supporting you when you're awake."

She centered herself immediately, leaning her slight weight out of his arms, and he smiled at the back of her head. Whoever this woman was, she was far too conscientious.

"Eat the bread," he said. "I'll hunt soon."

"Nay." Her voice sounded panicked. "The babe canna last much longer. We mustn't stop until we find milk."

Boden scowled at the top of the infant's head again. He'd heard that some women yearned endlessly for such a helpless babe to nurse. Looking at this one, it seemed difficult to believe. Still, twas his duty to protect. He had taken an oath.

"Take this," he demanded, lifting the bread toward her again. "You'll do the child little good if you're dead."

She finally did, slowly, though her hand shook, proving the depth of her need. She took a bite while he

watched. Mettle turned and laid back his ears. The steed
had a weakness for bread. Boden ignored his histrionics.

"Will the babe take water?"

"Aye."

Boden abruptly realized she had ripped the bottom portion of her green linen cloak in half to make the baby's
sling. She pushed the remainder of the garment aside
now, showing him a strange, hollowed gourd that hung
from a strip of cloth. At the bottom it had a small growth
perhaps the size of his little finger.

"Each day he's taken a bit of water from the tip of
the gourd, but he needs milk badly," she said.

"Nursemaids are hard to find in the midst of nowhere," Boden warned.

"But I must." She raised her eyes again. There was
panic there and pleading. "I must not stop until I do."

He should hunt, let Mettle rest, see to his wounds, which,
by the by, hurt like hell. But her eyes were very blue,
and the thought of refusing her never crossed his mind.

"The roads may be watched," he said.

"Watched?"

"What did they want? The brigands who attacked
you."

"I dunna know. The usual, I suspect. Coin, jewels."

"And the villains that attacked Caroline's party, what
of them? What did they want?"

"I couldn't say."

Boden glanced down at her. Her response had been
very quick, almost as if she were hiding something. His
musings had been to himself, for rarely did he ride with
a companion of any sort, other than Mettle. Although the
charger was like a wildcat in a pinch, he wasn't much of
a conversationalist. And in a thunderstorm he was little
more than a damned nuisance.

"What time of day did you say you were attacked?"
Boden asked.

"Evening. Twas the day afore yesterday."

"How many brigands would you guess?"

"Ten? But mayhap fear multiplied their number."

"Did they attack from the woods as you passed, or had you stopped for some reason?"

"We stopped, as I told ye. Shona's mount had gone lame."

"How?"

"I dunna know."

"How many guards did you have with you?"

She paused.

"Four."

"Why so few?"

"They dunna work for naught."

"But you said your father is wealthy. Surely he would help you pay."

"But I—"

"What's your father's name?"

"Gregor—MacDuff."

"A Scot?"

"Aye."

"But Bernadette is a French name."

"My mother is French."

"I thought she was dead."

She stopped. Was there panic in her eyes? "I did not say she was dead."

He still watched her, trying to read her thoughts. "I must have gotten the wrong impression."

"Ye think I lie," she deduced.

"Nay," he said. They'd come to a road, a gray ribbon of trail that wound between the trees into the gathering night. He urged Mettle into a high-stepping canter. "Why would a lady lie?"

Sara laughed. She was with Liam and her cousins— clever Rachel, fiery Shona. They were en route to a fair, bouncing along on the hay in a wagon, braiding wild- flower wreaths and laughing at Liam's tricks.

The weather was idyllic, the sky an indigo blue, dotted with puffy clouds that threatened nothing more dire than tickling the imagination. Beside them the countryside rolled away in verdant shades. A river wound along the road, and there, just to their right, was a single boulder, shaped like a great white shell. If they went past the boulder and up the hill they would find a crofter's cottage, she knew. But they would not. They would proceed on to the fair and the revelers there. Maybe her father would buy her a trinket. A silver mirror perhaps, or—

Lightning shattered her world. A voice shook the earth. Eerie, opaque eyes glared at her from a wizened face.

She awoke with a cry of alarm.

"Easy."

The voice startled her and she jumped, straining away to stare at the man behind her.

"Who are you?"

"It matters little how long you sleep, I'll still be the same man," said Blackblade.

"Oh." Reality was settling in, and though she knew her circumstances were grim, they weren't so bad as she had dreamed. Could she really have slept through the night? she wondered, seeing the sun's first rays sweep over the trees ahead. She gripped Thomas to her, suddenly afraid she would find him gone. But he was there, fast asleep in his makeshift cocoon. Her breathing came easier. "I must have fallen asleep."

"Tis a possibility," he said, and flexed his arm, as if to stretch the stiffness from it.

"I am sorry. I did not mean to be a burden."

He watched her face for a moment, making her blush. Time and silence stretched between them. "Perhaps you shouldn't have stabbed me then." He paused. "Twice."

"I am truly sorry." She fingered Dragonheart. It felt warm where it lay against her skin. "I thought ye were a brigand."

"So you've said. And now that you know better?"

She watched him as she searched for words. His eyes were dark, his brows black, his skin tanned. His jaw was strong and stubbled by several days' growth. A stranger's face, and yet it was hauntingly familiar. The face from her dreams. "I know not what to think when . . .

"Look!" She jerked her gaze to the left where a white, shell-shaped boulder lay near a rolling stream. "The rock! The rock by the crofter's cottage."

He stopped his steed with the slightest of motions. "You've been here before?"

Messages blurred in her mind. Time sagged. Reality wavered, then firmed.

"No," she murmured. "No I have not." She could feel his deep gaze on her face. "But it seemed . . . so familiar somehow. My dream. We were in a wagon. Liam had filched Rachel's hair for ribbons and turned them into bluebells while Shona and I told riddles." She stopped abruptly, noticing his gaze hadn't shifted for the briefest of moments from her face. "Ye think I am daft."

"The possibility has crossed my mind," he said, his deep voice barely audible in the stillness, his body pressed up against hers so that she could feel his warmth, the strength of his arms around her.

"And are ye in the habit of humoring daft women that ye find in the woods?" she asked breathlessly.

"That depends."

"On what?"

"On whether they have any more knives stashed away on their person."

She shivered a little, but whether it was from fear, or a chill, or the gravelly feel of his voice on her ears, she couldn't tell. "I'm fresh out of knives," she whispered.

The corner of his mouth lifted slightly. "What did you have in mind?"

"Over the hillock and down, might it not be a likely place for a farm?"

"Tis a long way from nowhere, with little defense."

A warrior's logic, she thought. "My wee babe canna go much farther. He must have milk."

The knight's eyes were piercing. For a moment she thought he would insist on continuing on, but finally he lifted his hand and turned the stallion from the road.

Chapter 3

The countryside was bumpy with tussocks of springy, green grasses and flat, gray rocks. The charger struggled over them, breathing hard. Sara leaned forward, placing a hand on his muscled neck and gazing breathlessly over his armored poll. There had to be a farm up ahead. There had to be something. She and Thomas had survived against the odds this long. Surely God didn't intend for them to die now.

They topped the hillock, weaved through a stand of gnarled elders, and stopped.

"There!" she cried, seeing the small crofter's cottage through the trees. "God be blessed. There it is."

"How did you know?" Boden asked, sitting very still behind her.

"I did not know. I but hoped."

"But how could you guess there might be a farm here?"

How indeed? She had no answers, and feared voicing her own questions. "There is no time to spare, sir," she said. "The child needs milk and he needs it soon. Please."

"There's little hope of finding a nursemaid this far afield," he said, but he cued the stallion to move forward. Mettle, however, remained as he was. "There might be mares," Boden murmured and kicked him more soundly.

38

The steed flickered his ears back, remained still for a moment as if in thought, then arched his neck and pranced forward. They moved with cadenced grace now, through the woods, past a lean-to to a squat, dark cottage.

There was a bang and clatter from the hovel, then, "Hold still ya damned bitch!" someone roared.

Sara started at the noise. Mettle stopped, dropping his big head and champing his bit.

With the slant of the morning sun, they could see well into the house.

A white-haired man stood in a bandy-legged stance with his back to the door. A fawn colored goat leaped from the table, trailing a frayed rope behind her. Three others skidded out the door. The man cursed again, then turning, saw his visitors and jerked in surprise. But in a moment, he'd collected himself and grabbed a pitchfork from outside the door.

"Off with ya!" he yelled. He stood, scrawny legs spread as he brandished the weapon. "Off with ya, if ya hope to see the full light of day."

Boden sat very still. Could it be that some years from now he would be in just this situation? He could imagine himself standing splay-footed, armed with nothing but a two-tined wooden fork as he defended himself against an armored knight on horseback. It seemed a distinct possibility, since he had failed this all-important mission. But as things stood, he was not so lucky as to have a hovel like this to call his own. The thought was almost depressing enough to make him beg the old man to run him through with the fork.

"We've not come to harm you," he said instead. "The babe is in need of milk. We hoped there might be a nursemaid about to aid us."

"What?" The old man turned his head sharply to the side in an attempt to hear better.

"Might there be a maid hereabouts that could nurse the babe?" Boden asked, raising his voice.

"Huh?" A blue-veined hand raised to an oversized ear.

"Do you know of a nursemaid in these parts?" Boden roared.

"A nursemaid?" The old man lowered the fork slightly.

"Aye."

"A young woman to suckle the babe?" the codger shouted.

"Aye," repeated Boden. "The babe cannot last much longer without sustenance."

"Well, twould seem that luck be with ya this day," the old man yelled and cackled. "My Mabel twould be the one for the job. Mabel. Mabel," he croaked.

Boden felt Sara stiffen with breathless hope.

Then, through the doorway an old woman tottered. She was a hundred if she was a day.

"Mabel," rasped the old fellow, "these good people need a maid to suckle their babe. I told them ya'd be up to the task."

The old couple looked at each other, then burst into cackling laughter.

Sara drooped in Boden's arms like a plucked daffodil left too long in the sun. Anger ran through him, and for an instant, he considered rapping the old codger on the head just for sport. But he stifled that ungentlemanly impulse and settled for a scowl.

"Mayhap you know of a maid nearby that might be better equipped," Boden said, but this suggestion only spurred the couple to greater hilarity.

"Where do ya think ya be?" gasped the old man as he set his fork aside, "at bloody court? Nay. I've no idea where—"

"A goat!" Sara gasped.

The codger's guffaws quieted. "What?"

"You have a milch goat," she said, her tone rife with excitement.

The old man scowled, cliffing his brows over his watery eyes. "Aye, we have that, but I don't see what good that will do you."

Sara lifted her gaze to Boden's for one quick instant. St. Peter's ears, her eyes were blue and entrancing as a summer sky! But Boden managed to wrench himself back to the business at hand.

"Might we purchase a goat?" he asked.

"Ya need a mother's breast to feed a babe," the woman said, letting her chuckles subside as she squinted against the sun at them.

"We've no choice," said Sara. "If the babe does not get milk soon, he will surely die. Please help us."

"Well!" The old man shifted his bird-bright gaze to his wife who met it and reflected the same fierce gleam. "Tilly could fulfill their need."

"Aye. Tilly could." The old crone shifted her gaze to the pair on the horse and back to her husband. "But nay! They'll not have my Tilly."

"There now," soothed the codger, creaking forward to pat his wife's humped back. "Tis for the babe."

"Nay," croaked the woman, grasping her husband's sleeve with gnarled fingers. "Twould break my heart to part with our dear Tilly."

"There there." He patted her hand and shouted the words. "Think of our David. When he was small."

The old woman's face twisted into what might be called a reminiscent smile. "Such a sweet babe."

"Aye, aye. Remember how he would cough?"

The crone nodded. "David. Aye. He did cough."

"Robert's daughter brought by a potent."

"Such a sweet lass."

"Aye, she was, and surely saved our David's life."

The wife scraped a weathered finger below her eye as if wiping away a tear they could not see. She sniffled once. "But to give up our Tilly . . ."

"Tis our Christian duty."

She sniffled again, then turned, twisted her husband's tunic in her hands and wailed loudly into it.

"There there." He patted her back as he shouted condolences. "There there."

She continued to cry, loud, hacking noises that echoed in the open space. He patted her again.

She lifted her face, sniffed. He patted.

"Twould not be Christian to—" he began, but suddenly the wife wailed with renewed vigor.

The old man scowled and patted harder. "There there!" he said, more forcefully this time.

"We will pay, of course," Boden said, watching them closely.

The old man nodded, seeming to have no trouble hearing those words. "We would not accept payment, but . . ." He paused and sniffed as if he, too, might join in his wife's piteous outburst. "We'll have to replace her—"

"Replace Tilly!" the wife sobbed, looking up at them. "It cannot be done."

"I am sorry." Sara's words were little more than a whisper. "If our need were not so great I would not ask."

"Nay." The old woman waved a bent hand. "Ya must do what ya must for the child."

"Aye," her husband agreed quickly. "What'll ya give us for her?"

Boden watched the man for a moment, then opened a pouch behind his saddle and drew out a woolen blanket.

But the old man was already shaking his head as he hobbled forward. "I've got blankets aplenty. What else have you got in there?"

Frowning, Boden draped the blanket over Mettle's rump and pulled out a tightly wrapped bundle of soft hide. "Tis fine leather," he said. "Carefully tanned and dyed."

"What is it?" the codger asked loudly.

"Tis leather," Boden said. "Ready to be crafted into whatever you need."

"Crafted! Do I look like a bloody tanner? Nay. By the time I got it made into something useful I'd be in the ground. What else have you got?'' he asked, dipping his papery hand into the pouch and pulling out another bundle of leather. When he drew it out it fell open to reveal a finely tooled doublet.

The old man smiled toothlessly up at Boden. ''Ain't much to ask for the life of a child, I suppose. But it'll do.''

Boden scowled at the elderly couple. ''I'd rather not part with that.''

''Have ya got three pounds instead?'' shouted the old man.

Boden leaned back in his saddle. ''Might this Tilly be embossed with gold?''

The old man stiffened as if immediately affronted. ''If ya don't want her, tis fine by me!''

''Nay!'' Sara gasped and turned her pleading eyes up to Boden's. They smote him like twin flames of blue. ''Please!'' she whispered. ''He will surely die else.''

Three pounds! Boden had paid only a little more than that for Mettle as a colt. Surely a goat could not be worth such a fortune. But when he glanced down at the woman cradled between his thighs, he knew he could no more refuse her than cut off his own arm.

''We'll try the milk first,'' Boden said. ''If the babe doesn't drink it there will be little reason to take your Tilly from you.''

The old woman's gaze shifted quickly to her husband's. He stared back, then jumped as though zapped by some phenomenal idea. ''We've already milked her. Come inside.''

Boden dismounted, then turned to assist Sara. The baby awoke and set to crying.

''Here. Here.'' The old man shouted as he motioned to them. ''Come along.''

They did so. The ceiling beams were low and sooty, the room unlit but for the open door and the hole in the roof where the smoke from their cookfire was meant to escape but didn't. A wooden bucket filled with frothy milk sat atop a table, and a steaming kettle was suspended from a hook near the failing embers.

Sara eased the makeshift sling from her neck. The baby swung erratically, his screaming becoming high-pitched. She soothed, cuddling him against her shoulder. It did little to quiet him, Boden noticed.

"Hold him," she said, pushing the child, sling and all, toward him.

Boden backed quickly away.

The old woman chortled. "Here then. Give the child to me," she said.

Sara did so reluctantly, then untied the gourd from her girdle. Covering the tiny hole with her finger, she ladled a bit of the warm, creamy milk into the receptacle.

Boden watched as she prepared to take the babe back. "Have you fed a child this way before?" he asked.

"Nay." Sara raised her gaze to his. "Why?"

"In the spring, when the grasses come in fresh, Mettle will rush out into the meadow." He eyed the rich milk. She eyed him. "There's rarely been a time when he hasn't become sick. It seems as if the same might happen with the babe."

"Ye think I should dilute the milk?" she asked.

Boden shrugged. He was far out of his realm, yet it seemed likely that what was good for a colt was good for a babe. "I don't see how it could hurt."

She nodded. Boden took the kettle from its hook near the fire and added a few drops of hot water to the milk.

Sara stirred it in, then, biting her lip, retrieved the screaming child and placed the gourd to his mouth.

How, Boden wondered, could anyone tolerate such a cacophony? And how could such a tiny creature create such noise? He waited, breath held, hoping the sound would cease, but when he looked into the lady's face, he wondered if she even noticed the racket. Emotion was written on her face—a love so deep it stole his breath away.

The child turned away from the gourd, screaming

louder still if such was possible. A droplet of milk spilled onto his cheek, seeming unearthly white against his scrunched red face.

"Please drink," Sara whispered, but he would not, so finally she handed the gourd to Boden and eased the child to her shoulder.

She had taken off her truncated cloak. The dragon amulet winked in the early morning light as she turned, swaying gently. Slowly, quietly, she began to sing.

Boden covered the gourd's hole and remained still and silent as the melody built in the small room. Somewhere in the back of his mind, he realized the language was none he recognized. And yet the words seemed to matter not at all, for the magic of her voice was everything.

Gradually the cries turned to sniffles, the sniffles to silence, and finally, she slipped the babe from her shoulder and onto his back. Still swaying, still singing softly, she motioned for Boden to give her the gourd. He broke out of his trance with a start and handed her the milk.

The baby whimpered. She slipped the impromptu nipple into his mouth, and though her song was still haunting and sweet, Boden saw the worry in her eyes as she waited.

The babe gnawed, scowled, then took one suck on the gourd. His fair brows converged, puckering over his midnight blue eyes as though he were contemplating some great, universal mystery. He paused. Not a soul in the cottage breathed, until finally he sucked again. Milk bubbled from the sides of his mouth as he turned his face away and stuck out his tiny tongue, tasting. And then, like a miracle, he twisted his head back and began to suckle in earnest. Smacking sounds filled the hut. He curled his tiny fist up tight against his chest. The angry color faded from his face. Looking into the mother's eyes, Boden saw tears sparkle in the sunlight.

Something knotted hard and fast in his chest. This woman had stabbed him. Had run from him. Possibly she had lied to him and was lying still. He had no loyalty for this woman. He had no *feelings* for this woman, he reminded himself.

But what would it be like to feel her fingers soft as morning against his skin? To hear her whisper to him in that satiny voice? The questions caught him by surprise. He was a knight, and therefore nothing more than a soldier of fortune, no matter how romanticized the title might be. Surely softness was the last thing he needed. But her expression was so tender, her voice so entrancing, her eyes so damn blue.

"Where's the goat?" he asked, and turned away.

Twas a fairly certain thing, Boden thought. The goat had won, and *he* had been rooked by an ancient pair of crofters who could conjure false tears like a magician might conjure golden coins out of an ear.

Replace Tilly. It cannot be done, the old crone had moaned.

True enough. It could *not* be done, unless you could find a demon-possessed bag of bones with horns like a battering ram, and a kick that would intimidate a fortress.

The old couple had produced a rope, surprisingly free of charge, with which to lead the bony beast. The problem was, as Boden soon learned, the goat wouldn't be led, no matter what he did. She would rather lie down and be dragged like so much timber down the trail, a fate Lady Bernadette was quite distressed to see.

How the hell had he gotten himself into such a predicament?

He stepped down from Mettle, simultaneously glaring at the stinky goat that was tied across his proud destrier's ample arse. Tilly glared back, her marbled eyes eerie in the evening light.

"Is she quite well?" Bernadette asked as she slid back from the high pommel.

"I hate goats," Boden said, seeing no reason to reassure her. "They have bad dispositions and bad body odor."

She stared at him as if thinking the same could be said of him.

He scowled. "I'm usually in better humor." Silence. He cleared his throat. "Tis not me that you smell. Tis . . . the horse."

Mettle irritably flicked back an ear.

A fleeting smile lifted Bernadette's lips as Boden turned to help her dismount, but she refused to look into his eyes. Hell, he'd bought the damn goat, given up his best doublet for her—even told the old codger how fine he looked in the soft hide jacket that hung like an empty sack nearly to his knees. Couldn't she, perhaps, after all that, trust him a wee bit by now?

"Ye could have left me at the crofters' cottage," she said.

And there was another thing. Why did she wish to be left behind? There was something she wasn't telling. And he would be damned if he'd leave her before he knew what it was.

"You said you want to return to Scotland," he said. "Tis my duty to grant your wish."

The nanny thrashed behind the saddle's cantle. Mettle shifted his feet, rolling white-rimmed eyes toward his unlikely baggage.

"If ye'll get Tilly down, I'll feed John," she said.

Boden grunted noncommittally and untied the goat. The beast thrashed more wildly, and though Boden tried to catch her, she slipped over Mettle's rump and fell from view with an irritable bleat. The stallion skittered nervously to the side.

"And you call yourself a warhorse," Boden scoffed. He drew back on the reins, pulling Mettle in a tight half circle as Tilly bounded to her feet. "St. Dismas's cold arse, you'd think the bony beast was going to—" It was pure bad luck that when Tilly charged, she thumped directly into Boden's wounded knee. Pain shot up his leg like slivers of fire. Tilly backed away, and Mettle jumped sideways, pulling Boden with him. He fell with a curse, finally releasing the reins and grabbing his knee.

"Sir Blackblade."

Boden opened his eyes to see Bernadette bending over him. Sometime during the day, she'd braided her hair. The messy plait hung well past her shoulder.

"What?" he growled.

She grasped the braid in one hand and backed off a step. "Is there ought I can do for ye?"

"Other than killing the goat?"

"Aye. Other than that." The flicker of a smile crossed her face again. It did nothing to improve his mood.

"Nay."

"But your knee—"

"I'm fine!" he snapped.

She opened her mouth, then nodded pertly and re-treated another step, her eyes bright with the humor she wisely kept to herself. "Then I will see to the goat."

"Aye," he grumbled. "And when you're done with her I'll make myself a fine leather purse."

There was little enough to do once the baby was fed, so Sara wrapped them both in her shortened cloak and settled down on a trampled stand of bracken for the night.

It took only moments for sleep to take her, and not much longer for the dreams to follow. They were pretty dreams, deep and quiet.

Sunlight sparkled off the silvery waves of the chuckling burn. From its edge two boys laughed in unison. They were bare to the waist, one broad and one skinny, with their hose pulled up high and their calves pink from the chilling waves that washed past.

The skinny one splashed, chasing a fish, and the other lad laughed as he watched. The sound blended musically with the burble of the waters.

From somewhere far away, Sara watched too. She knew she didn't belong in this pastoral scene. Yet, she couldn't look away, for the children were so beautiful in their innocent play. The husky boy laughed again, then glanced to his right, and there, upon the shiny pebbles of the far shore, was a black sword.

A chill washed over Sara. The boy turned, mesmerized by the weapon as he made his way through the deepening water. Dark clouds suddenly raced like mounted steeds toward the sword, swirling from the sky, ready to engulf the boy.

The skinny lad turned, terror in his eyes.

"Go back!" Sara screamed. "Go back!" But no one heard her.

The boy touched the blade. The clouds turned to dark, gnarled faces. And the river turned to blood.

"Nay!" Sara shrieked. She woke with a start. Evil approached. She felt it in her heart, and in wild desperation, snatched up a branch from the fire.

Her scream ripped Boden into wakefulness. He grabbed for his sword and slashed even as he leapt to his feet.

Shadows sprang toward him through the darkness. Boden slashed again, catching the nearest man across the belly. He screamed and crumpled to the ground, but there was no time to think. The first brigand was felled, but there was another behind him, shrieking a battle cry. He dove from a nightmare, hefting his sword as he came.

Boden ducked, stabbed, and ducked again. Blood spurted into the night air. A man fell with a gurgling cry. Another came on.

Where was the woman? Was she dead?

Boden slashed again, then felt the bite of steel against his arm. The hiss of pain was his own, but his opponent fell, and now he could see the woman. She stood with a blazing brand in her hand while a villain lunged at her.

She screamed, but in the same instant she swung. An arc of sparks sprayed outward, lighting the villain's hideous expression. Wood met steel and the wood was severed. The villain laughed as he sprang forward.

Boden lunged toward them. A mace swung from the darkness. He leaped sideways, but not soon enough.

Thunder echoed in his head and he staggered. The world
slowed. Reality trembled as a brigand screamed a battle
cry. The sound echoed in Boden's mind. He turned, disoriented, dulled. Someone leapt toward him. He reacted
by instinct. His arm lifted, blocked, parried, and suddenly
the villain was impaled on his sword.

The man fell, dragging Boden's blade with him. He
staggered sideways, pulling Adder free and searching for
Bernadette. Did she still stand? He turned, trying to fo-
cus.

She was there. The flaming end had been severed from
her brand, but she stood with her legs apart, nearly atop
the child she so desperately tried to protect. The villain
laughed again and lunged toward her, but in the wavering
shadows of the failing fire, he tripped, and in that instant
she swung wildly. The club connected with his skull and
he fell to his knees.

Bernadette stumbled backward. The baby cried. She
reached down, scooping him into her arms, but in that
instant the brigand rose with a roar.

Darkness swirled around Boden. He grappled with it,
yanking it aside as he struggled through the tattered webs
of his failing consciousness toward her.

The brigand lunged. Bernadette raised an arm, trying
to shield the baby.

A battle cry ripped, unbidden, from Boden's throat.
Adder swept upward and suddenly, like black magic, it
was embedded deep and ugly in the villain's back.

Boden watched the sword drop from the other's hand,
watched his body reach skyward and stiffen before it
crashed to the earth.

Then there was silence. Boden listened to it for a moment, nodded to the woman, and then he, too, slumped
into darkness.

The music and the dream became one, cushioning him
like a lover's arm, easing his aches, drawing him gently
toward consciousness.

Still, the two young boys played on in his mind. One was dark, with a crooked smile, the other fair. A golden-haired woman with ethereal eyes and the face of an angel stood nearby. A river flowed over his feet and away into happiness.

Boden drank in the feelings, let them swirl around him, fill him. There was peace here, happiness, a soft cocoon between him and life's harsh realities. A man smiled, and suddenly he realized it was himself. The woman laughed and he reached for her hand. Warmth washed over him.

He opened his eyes slowly, and he saw her. Bernadette. The woman with the heavenly eyes. It seemed right somehow, predictable, fated.

"Can you stay?" he asked, still wrapped in the soft cocoon of his dream.

Her eyes were very wide and shone dark in the light of the fire behind him. He could see a pulse beating in her throat just below her jaw. "I thought ye had left us," she said, not answering his question.

No. He had not, for this place was too filled with beauty and peace. This place so difficult to find—until now. Until he was with her.

He held her gaze as a thousand soft emotions washed over him.

She shifted her eyes away. "You've been wounded. I feared ye might not come to."

Reality bloomed suddenly in his head. There was no peace. Dear Lord! They were under attack! Memories swarmed in. He jerked upright, trying to clear his head, to find his sword.

"Nay. Dunna," she pleaded and pressed him back down.

He tried to push her aside, but there was no strength in his arms. Terror seized him. Vulnerability threatened. He struggled harder, but she merely tucked away his hands and eased him onto his back.

"Quiet! Lie still! Ye are safe. Shush now."

But the brigands! He must fight. Yet he could not. Panic welled up.

"Ye are safe," she said again.

He forced himself to relax, remembering his dream, the feel of her slim hand in his. "Tell me, lady," he murmured. "Are you an angel?"

"Hardly that, sir."

"Then are you a witch?"

"Nay," she denied, drawing back. "Why would ye say such a thing?"

He lay still, drawing in perceptions. Her hair was the color of spun gold, her skin like fine ivory, and when she turned her eyes on him, his heart felt somehow too heavy for his chest. "You make me feel things I've not felt before. To dream dreams I've not dreamt."

She glanced momentarily sideways, then hurried her gaze back to his. "Tis the battle. Not me."

The battle. Possibly. Boden tried to concentrate on the events just past. Brigands had swarmed out of the darkness. How many? Five? Six? He had slashed and swung by rote, the familiar terror making him act. A man had fallen, then another and another. Boden had ducked but not quickly enough, and he had been struck.

He shifted his eyes to glance sideways. A half dozen bodies lay strewn on the ground about them. The earth was dark with their blood. So the battle was over. Once again the maniac inside him had been loosed, and once again he had survived. Nausea twisted his stomach, replacing the panic as it always did. He turned his attention back to the woman and saw that her gaze had followed his own.

Her body was stiff, and in her eyes he saw the shock he had missed before.

"There's no need to worry," he said, though his own pulse was just now slowing again.

A shudder racked her fragile form. She turned her gaze to his face. "They are dead," she whispered.

The statement almost made him laugh. Pain and the

possibility of death always made his mood unpredictable. "Aye," he said, managing to keep his tone subdued. "They're dead. They'll not hurt you." But even as he said the words, her eyes told him he spoke a lie, for their deaths already haunted her. When had it ever been that a death did not scar the living?

He watched her face, lit only by the firelight's golden glow. A million thoughts were reflected there. A million emotions in her eyes. They worried him, scratching at his soul. The feeling was uncomfortable, so he pushed it aside, concentrating on what he knew. Survival.

"What woke you?" he asked.

"I was dreaming," she whispered.

Her answer seemed nonsensical, and he saw now that she was struggling to keep her gaze from straying onto the field of battle. He'd seen young squires look the same. Boys who had thought war would be bold and glorious had found the ravaged, horrifying truth far different from their expectations. Many emptied their stomachs after the sight of their first skirmish. But only a weak-kneed few were nauseated after every battle. Boden tried to ignore his queasiness.

"A soldier sleeps lightly by necessity, lest he sleep forever," Boden said, holding her gaze with his own and willing hers not to stray to the gore beyond the fire's brightest glow. "I heard nothing to wake me. What alerted you?"

She lifted her gaze, looking dazed, but now he found the strength to grip her arm and hold her attention with his eyes.

"How did you know they had come?" he asked again.

"Twas the dream," she said, clutching the silver dragon in her fist.

Premonition laid its cold hand on Boden's shoulder. "What dream?"

She didn't answer immediately, but stared at him as if she were entranced. "Of two boys by a river. One was stout, the other small with dark hair and a crooked smile.''

His own dream! "What woke you?" he asked again, his tone raspy, his heart racing.

Still she stared at him. "I dreamed he was in danger."

St. Adrian's arse! What was she doing dreaming his dream? Boden wondered. But he gave himself a mental shake. It was purely coincidental that their dreams were similar. Nothing but coincidence. He pressed his mind on to other matters. "What did they want?" he asked, turning toward the dead bodies.

She tried to pull from his grasp, but he had found a modicum of his strength and held her steady. "I dunna know," she said.

The fire sparked once, then fell silent.

"I think you lie," he said.

"Nay. I dunna know what they wanted. Coin, I suspect. Plunder."

He watched her face. He'd learned long ago that if one was openly trusting, he was likely to find himself parted from his head at a tender age. And he'd grown rather attached to his head.

So it seemed worth his while to try to sort the truth from fantasy, especially since the truth had brought on a half dozen men with big, nasty weapons. What had they been after?

"I dunna," she repeated, then drew a deep, shuddering breath. Her eyes, wide and haunted, shifted sideways. "They're dead," she whispered, and a tear, bright as citrine in the firelight, slid down her cheek.

Dear Lord! He scowled as he watched the tear glide along the curve of her delicate jaw. He might *hurl* on the enemy, but he never *cried* over them.

"Get the child," he said, stuffing his emotions quickly away. "We leave this place."

They rode for several hours, moving quietly through the darkness.

"You were singing in French."

Sara started from her reverie, but God knew it was foolish to jump from this man, for she was, once again, cradled in his arms like a lover as they rode along.

Tilly was tethered behind them. Perhaps it was the smell of blood at their campsite that had made her decide to follow docilely behind.

"Lady," Boden said, interrupting her thoughts with his low voice.

"Ye are mistaken. I dunna speak French," she said. Despite the darkness that still surrounded them, she could sense his gaze on her face, could feel the tautness of his chest against her back.

"It seems unlikely you could *sing* in French when you do not speak it. And singing you were. Twas the words from my youth that brought me to consciousness."

Sara felt her heart thumping in her chest. She *had* sung in French. But how? She did not know that language. Where had the words come from? Why did she dream such frightening dreams? Why did Dragonheart seem so warm against her flesh at times? Was she going mad?

He was staring at her.

She didn't turn toward him. There was no need for that. She knew how he would look. She knew his face, for she had seen it before ever meeting him. She had seen it in a dream. She had seen it, his sword, his childhood! Dear God!

"Your mother is French," he said, breaking into her frantic thoughts. "Yet she does not speak her native language?"

Sara caught her breath. She had forgotten her lies. "Nay, Mother does speak the language, but I dunna."

"Yet you were singing in that tongue just this night."

She twisted about, desperately catching his gaze. "I was not. I dunna know that language."

"Perhaps the amulet spoke it to you," he said, his expression dark, his tone the same. "Perhaps singing is one of your fine attributes that the pendant 'enhances.'

Was that not the word you used?'' His eyes smote her. He was very close. So close she could feel his breath fan her cheek, could feel his forbidden allure.

She forgot to breathe as she fought his dark appeal and the swirling confusion. She could not afford to trust him. She had made up lies about Dragonheart's powers, pure lies, to save her life.

"Ye were unconscious," she said, trying to quiet the thrum of her heart. "Ye dreamed it."

"You were not singing?"

Perhaps insanity had truly gripped her for a while, for yes, as the dead men had lain in their hideous positions upon the ground, she had cradled Thomas to her chest and sung. "Nay I *was* singing."

For one crazed moment she was tempted to reach out and touch his arm, to beg him to protect her from the insanity that surrounded her, to tell her that all was well and normal. But all was not well and things were definitely not normal.

How had she known where to find the farm? Where had she seen his face before?

She remained as she was, staring into his eyes, lost in uncertainty, and fighting the inexplicable desire to touch him.

The horse had stopped.

"Twas a song from my boyhood you sang. A song that soothed me when I was small," he said. His voice was very soft, but deep, like the quiet babble of rapid waters. "Twas French."

"Nay." She shook her head. "I swear, I dunna speak French. Twas Gaelic words I sang."

The world stilled as he searched for truth in her eyes, but suddenly he grabbed her arm in a tight frustration.

"Why do you lie?" he rasped, leaning closer.

"I dunna."

"You do. Who are you?"

"I am Bernadette."

"You lie!" he snarled, and slipped onto the earth in a heap.

He felt her presence like a ray of warmth the moment he awoke. Daylight had come. He lay on his back on a swath of green beneath a bent oak. The sunlight streaked between the branches overhead and glistened on her gilded hair. Her face was turned sideways, showing her delicate profile.

"Why did you stay?" he asked.

She started, her eyes going wide as she swung her attention to him. But in a moment she steadied herself. "How do ye feel?" she asked.

Like he had been skewered by a meat hook and concussed by a battering ram. "I feel well," he said.

She stared at him and for a moment he saw the flicker of a smile on her face. "Ye dunna look well," she said, her tone relaxed now.

How was it that even with her hair littered with leaves and her gown torn and soiled, she seemed like an angel? Perhaps she had not lied about the dragon's abilities. Perhaps it had enhanced her feminine charms, for surely no woman could be so entrancing.

"Why did you stay?" he asked again, frowning at the lush ridiculousness of his thoughts.

"I wanted to leave you," she said, settling back on her heels. "Actually, twas the babe who thought we should remain."

"Indeed?" Boden asked, studying her face. The gamine angel, with sunlight at her back and magic in her voice. "And his opinion carries more weight than your own?"

"Nay. Twas Mettle that broke the tie. He said we must stay."

"So you *are* a witch," Boden said.

She stiffened immediately. "I am not."

"Forgive me." Twas not unusual for him to insult when he meant to amuse. "I fear the brigand's mace did little to improve my sense of humor. I meant the words as a jest."

She relaxed marginally, and he hurried on, hoping to put her more at ease. "If every person who spoke to a steed was accused of witchery I fear I would have been staked and burned long ago."

"Tis when they begin talking back ye need to worry," she said.

"And do you speak from experience, bonny Bernadette?"

For a moment, he thought she might answer, might speak of the worry he saw in her eyes, but she did not. "I examined the wound on your head," she said instead.

He wished he could call back her more relaxed nature, but in lieu of any better plan, he opted for levity. "And am I destined for the graveyard?"

"Eventually, but not from that wound."

"More's the pity?" he asked.

Again, she didn't answer, but gestured toward his upper body. "I was about to have a look at your arm when ye awoke."

He lifted the mentioned limb. Pain stabbed through his flesh, ripping him from shoulder to wrist. "Tis fine." He lied, but with a certain degree of panache, he thought.

She canted her head slightly. The wink of a smile mesmerized him. "It burns like hellfire," she countered.

"And why would you assume that?" he asked, hoping he looked stern, yet wondering if he only managed to appear cantankerous.

"Because my father would oft say the same when I knew in truth that he was badly wounded."

"Your father," he said, and suddenly he saw her as a child, smiling up at him with raspberry-stained lips and eyes that glowed like sparkling blue waters. A bright mixture of sunshine and laughter.

St. Polycarp, he was getting sappy. He was not the kind to think of children, fondly or otherwise.

"Was your sire a knight?" he asked, forcing his mind to the matter at hand.

"Nay." She turned away, and he saw now that she had built a small fire and placed his kettle in the rocks near it. Wrapping her hand in a cloth, she lifted it from its spot near the flame. "He was the laird of a small castle."

"Was?" Had he caught her in a lie? "He is dead? I thought you wished to return to him."

"There have been times I wished I could be with him," she said softly and poured a bit of water into the pearlescent hollow of a shell. "He died in a skirmish with the border lords."

But she'd said she lived near Edinburgh. "You lived on the border?"

"Ye must remove your mail and tunic if I am to see to your wounds."

"Tis just my arm that's cut," he said, surprised by her words. "Dare I hope this is some ploy to view more personal parts of my anatomy?"

She blushed, and he grinned.

"Ye may be more appealing if you staunch the flow of blood," she said, her voice stern, but her cheeks still pink.

"What?"

"There is blood seeping through your armor."

"Nay," he argued, but glancing down he saw that she was right. Damn it all, he didn't wrap himself in rusty mail for fun. Twas supposed to keep his torso safe. "Probably just from my arm."

"I had best check."

"I told you, I am fine."

"Aye," she interrupted, "and I told ye I'm accustomed to brave lies. Take them off."

Boden considered arguing with her, but it would take a good deal of energy, and she looked quite insistent. At times she seemed such a delicate thing, but not at the moment.

He managed to sit up, but not without her help. Disrobing was going to be the devil's own fun, he thought, and he was right.

Removing the chain ring mail was difficult enough, but removing the tunic sent waves of pain splintering off in every direction. For several moments after he gritted his teeth and staunchly refused to faint again. Surely he'd impressed her enough with his ability to swoon already.

"So . . ." He drew breath through his teeth and stared straight ahead, refusing to look at the wounds. "Ye lived in the border country?"

"It looks as if the brigand's sword didn't actually cut ye," she said, lifting a rag from the kettle of hot water. "But the force of the blow against the metal rings scraped off some flesh. There's a good deal of bruising, but it does not look to be too serious. Your arm, however—"

"Is fine," he interrupted.

Her eyes softened. "Ye've little need to pretend it doesn't hurt, sir. I've seen grown men cry for less grievous wounds."

"Cry!" Good Lord! He'd rather die of the clap right here and now. Boden concentrated hard and came up with a respectable glare. "Need I remind you that I'm a knight, lady. I don't pretend. Nor do I lie. If I say I am fine, I am fine."

"Oh. Well . . ." she said and tipping her hand over, dropped the hot cloth against his wound.

Jesus, God! Boden jerked up with a mental roar of pain. Fire seared his arm, consuming his mind. She was trying to maim him! Dismember him! Kill him! But no. Reality settled slowly back in like dust motes on an abandoned path. He dropped from the balls of his feet back into a flat-footed stance.

She'd stood up with him. Still holding the cloth to his arm, she stared dead center into his eyes. "My apologies," she murmured. "Did that hurt?"

It was nearly impossible to breathe. But he managed

to draw in one shallow inhalation and said, "Nay." She *was* a witch. "Not atall."

To his utter surprise she chuckled. The sound surely should have irritated him, but somehow it did the opposite.

"Regardless of what ye think, I am not a witch," she said.

"Nay?" he managed from between his teeth.

"Nay. I be but an evil woman bent on vengeance."

He turned his eyes to her, nervously watching as she removed the cloth, rinsed it in warm water and replaced it on the wound.

"Revenge for saving your life?" he asked.

Her gaze rose swiftly to his. "Revenge for threatening to take it."

"I did no such thing."

"I am Bernadette," she said. "Your badgering will do nothing to change the facts."

He drew another deep breath. Pain shot through his torso. "My apologies," he said. "Being skewered and clubbed always seems to put me out of sorts."

"That does not change who I am," she said. "Nor will it."

From somewhere unseen she produced a needle. He eyed it nervously, reminding himself not to run screaming into the woods. After all, he *was* a knight, but St. Boniface's butt, he hated needles. Far better to suffer untouched. "What are you planning to do with that thing?"

"I will stitch your wound for ye," she said.

He said nothing for a moment, but couldn't remain silent for long. "If I apologize again would it change your mind?"

"'Tis my duty," she said, smiling a little.

"If I apologize to the goat?" he asked.

She laughed aloud. "I would give ye spirits to help ease the pain if I had any."

"Leaving me alone will ease me enough," he said.

"Do ye forget that I owe ye for saving my life?"

"I would have done it for anyone. Even the goat, if she but smelled a bit sweeter. Tis in the time-honored vows of the knighthood."

"Truly?"

"Aye."

"What a hero ye are."

"Tis good you've noticed."

She nodded. "Cold water will bring down the swelling."

"What?"

"Twould help if ye would soak your arm in the burn."

"The burn?"

"The river," she said, translating from Gaelic to English.

He turned toward the rapidly flowing stream, then back to her. "It surprises me that a face like yours could hide such a cruel heart. That's not water. Tis ice that flows."

She propped her hands on her hips. "Is whining a part of your training, knight?"

"I don't whine."

"Then get yourself in the burn, afore the swelling worsens."

He glanced at the stream. It was fast-flowing, shallow, strewn with rocks the size of his fists.

The night had been bad. It looked as if the day would show little improvement.

Chapter 4

◯◯◯◯

S he should have left him. Sara stared at Sir Blackblade as he lay on the rocky shoreline with his
torso draped in the racing water. His back was dark-
skinned, criss-crossed with a myriad of scars and muscles, and very broad. She had been a fool to think he
couldn't care for himself. She owed him nothing. Her
loyalty was to Thomas; he was hers now. Her heart
twisted as she glanced at the babe, then back to the
knight.

She should have taken Mettle and left while Blackblade was still unconscious. Hadn't she learned anything
from her haunting dreams? She couldn't trust this man,
and yet he drew her to him. He had the smile of a rogue
and the wit of a jester. Against her will, against her better
judgment, these things intrigued her. Which made it even
more imperative that she leave.

Blackblade moved, drawing his arm from the water
and rising to his feet. Sara yanked her gaze away from
him and onto the items she had laid out on her cape on
the ground—the needle, several hairs from Mettle's tail,
and strips of cloth torn from her much-abused underskirt.

Boden came toward her, and though she could sense
his approach, she refused to look up. True, she was a
widow, and therefore somewhat accustomed to the sight
of a man's body. But it seemed there could be vast dif-

ferences in men's bodies, and this one made her heart race and her skin flush.

He stopped not far from her cape. She stared at his boots. "Was it cold?" she asked.

"Nay. Not atall," he said, but she thought she heard his teeth chatter on the last word.

She hid a smile and motioned for him to sit down. When he didn't comply, she was forced to glance upward. It was like looking up the face of a mountain.

"I am ready," she said.

"For what?"

She motioned toward the cape and her paraphernalia set upon it. "'Tis obvious, I think."

He narrowed his eyes at her. They were dark eyes, nearly matching the color of his hair which was tied back behind the broad width of his sun-darkened neck. "Ye said I should soak in the stream instead of stitching it."

"I said no such thing. Sit down."

He raised his chin and thrust out his chest. It was a mammoth chest, mounded with muscle and tipped by ruddy-colored nipples that stood erect from their time in the freezing burn. She turned her gaze rapidly away.

"I am a knight," he said. "I do not, nor have I ever, taken orders from a woman."

"'Tis fine with me then," she said. "But I wonder how a one-armed knight will fare. Of course, ye are probably the heir to a fine estate. Mayhap ye've but to rest on your laurels and await your father's death."

She waited in silence. In a moment he sat down, cross-legged before her.

"Have you any skills as a physic?" he asked.

"Did I not tell ye? My aunt is the great healer?"

He scowled at her. "And my horse can outrun a stag for a hundred rods. It doesn't mean I can do the same."

She stared at him.

"Not to say I am slow," he corrected.

She forced herself not to laugh. "'Tis your choice,"

she said. "But ye'd look rather unbalanced with only one arm."

A muscle jumped in his jaw. "Tell me, Lady Bernadette, have you always been so cruel?"

"Aye," she said, and threaded the needle with aplomb. "Those who know me call me the butcher of the border."

"I fear your sense of humor is lacking."

"I did not say I was jesting," she said, gripping his arm in her left hand.

She felt his muscles tense and for a moment she thought he would yank his arm from her grasp.

"Just stitch it up," he said instead.

But she didn't want to. If the truth be told, she was no healer. True, she had watched Fiona work on any number of injuries. Her uncle's wife could sew and patch, medicate and soothe, all with a confidence and kindness that could not help but reassure her patients. But Sara knew only the rudiments of healing. At best, her skills and assurance were adequate, but now, after long days of terror and deprivation, she felt her hand shake.

The knight turned his face toward her and lifted a brow. "Are you going to start, or shall we wait for the next band of brigands to come along and finish what they already began."

"I won't stitch the lower wound," she said.

"The one *you* gave me, you mean?"

She cleared her throat. "Aye. It's ahh, it's not terribly bad, but the one higher up . . ." She paused, lifting her gaze to his biceps. His upper arms were as big around as her neck. Surely it was a sin to mar such beautiful muscle.

She sat immobile until she felt his gaze bore into her. Lifting her gaze to his, she reddened, and then, steadying her fingers against his arm, pushed the needle into his flesh.

An eternity later the angel-witch tied off the last stitch

and settled back on her heels. Probably she wanted to see how much pain she had managed to inflict. It was his duty as a knight not to let her know, but he thought perhaps the rivers of sweat flowing down his forehead might give her a clue to the truth.

"Finished," she said, her tone breathless, drawing his attention to her lips. St. Thomas's teeth, no witch should have lips like that. "I am sorry if I hurt ye."

He noticed she looked pale.

"You didn't," he said, and was quite proud that his voice trembled only a little.

"I've but to wrap it now."

"Wrap it!" he said, then winced at the squeak in his voice. He cleared his throat and made a point to lower his eyebrows to a well-honed look of irritation. "I'm certain tis fine as it is."

"It willna hurt," she promised.

How the hell would she know? It hurt right now. Like the devil was stabbing him with his fiery pitchfork.

"I've seen more battles than I can count, lady," he said. "Think you that your touch would frighten me?"

"I think as a child ye did not spend enough time with your mother," she suggested.

"Wrap it," he said, and looked away.

He could feel her gaze on his face, but after a moment, she began to bandage. Upon completion, he tested her handiwork. The clothes were snug, but not too tight, allowing his muscles to flex with only enough pain to leave him this side of consciousness.

"I owe you my thanks," he said finally.

She didn't look up as she gathered what was left of her medicinal items. "Twould be best for ye to continue to use your arm a bit to discourage swelling, but I would not suggest any more battles for a couple of days."

"I'll try to remember."

Their gazes locked. Silence settled between them.

"I am sorry about your mother."

He started at her words. "What about my mother?"

She bit the inside of her lip as her fair brows drew together. "I dunna know," she murmured, looking shaken.

Premonition prickled eerily up Boden's spine. He pushed it away. If he allowed himself to believe she could read his mind what would come next? Ghosts and goblins?

"We'd best be moving," he said. "I'd not wish to defy my physician's orders by killing more brigands so soon after her efforts."

Sara sat absolutely still. Once again, she was cradled between the massive, oaken thighs of Sir Boden Blackblade. Trying to avoid the disturbing intimacy of this position, she had insisted on riding sidesaddle, but he refused, saying her balance would be compromised.

Tilly had followed docilely along behind for some miles, but finally she had lain down and refused to get up. She was now tied behind the saddle like an ungainly sack of feed.

In retrospect, Sara, thought, her own position could be worse.

"We'll spend the night here," Boden said.

Sara nodded and prepared to dismount, but before she did so, Boden was on foot and assisting her.

"I am not helpless," she said. "Ye are wounded, ye should rest."

"I am a knight," he argued, and turning back toward Mettle, remounted.

"Where are ye going?" Despite her words of independence, despite the fact that she knew she could not trust this man, the thought of him leaving sent terror spurting through her.

Reaching behind his saddle, he withdrew the sword he'd obtained at the last battle. "Take this while I search for food."

The blade felt heavy in her hand. "I know nothing of swordplay."

"I saw what you can do with a branch," he said. "Think about your child. The brigands will be lucky to leave with their heads above their shoulders."

Despite her better judgment, she reached past sleeping Thomas to touch his thigh. The muscle there was hard and broad. Warmth spread up her arm. She pulled her hand nervously away. "Ye will be careful?"

His expression changed slightly. Although she doubted he would have wanted her to realize it, there was, perhaps, a modicum of softness in his expression. "I've a fondness for life, lady. Rest assured that I will be cautious."

The rabbit gave off a tempting aroma as it roasted over the fire. Boden had skewered several pieces and turned them again to roast the opposite side. To his left, Sara sang to the babe. Her voice was soft and dusky and conjured up a strange sort of peace in his soul.

Peace! He rose abruptly to his feet. The last thing he should be feeling was peace. He was far from civilization, had failed his lord's mission, and even now might be stalked by brigands whose reasons he could not fathom. He should have examined the men he had killed. Perhaps they could have given him some clue as to why they had attacked. But the lady had seemed so fragile just then. He glanced at her standing in the shadows, her face tilted toward the child, her lips slanted slightly upward—not in a smile exactly, but in an expression of such soft beauty that it made his heart ache.

He turned rapidly away. Mayhap he *should* have left her at the crofter's cottage, but such had not seemed right. She was a lady. He was a knight, and even though he had oft scorned the rules of knightly chivalry, he had no choice but to protect her, to take her where she wished to go. But what of Caroline and Lord Haldane's babe? They were dead, and yet he didn't even have the child's body for his lord to mourn over.

Boden ground his teeth. He may be an irreverent bastard in most regards, but never had he failed Haldane before, and he didn't like the feel of it now. Twould be best to hurry back and admit his defeat.

But that didn't feel right either. There was nothing he could do but follow his war-honed instincts, and those instincts told him to keep Lady Bernadette close to hand.

Logic, on the other hand, said he should leave this witchy angel-woman and run like hell. He glanced at her. The babe was rarely awake, but he saw now that one tiny fist waved above the blankets that usually bound his arms tightly to his sides.

The widow laughed softly and bending lower, kissed the babe's cheek. For a moment her face was limed by firelight, the soft curve of her cheek, the blush of her lips. Time ceased to be as Boden held his breath.

Dear God, she was beautiful.

No. He would not leave the mother and he would not leave the child, though perhaps his reasons had less to do with battle instincts than his instincts of another kind. When he looked at her, his body felt strangely heavy and his head somehow useless. Twas not a good thing for a knight to experience, since if he did not use his head he was likely to lose it soon enough.

"Your pardon?" She looked up suddenly, catching Boden off guard.

Had he spoken? Panic rose, but in an instant, he assured himself he had remained silent. A witch!

"The meat is ready," he said.

She carried the babe with her to the fire and sat down on a log. Boden sliced off a piece of steaming rabbit and handed it to her, still speared by his knife.

"I'll let you keep the blade if you promise not to stab me with it."

The hint of a smile crossed her face. "Not until after supper leastways," she said, and taking the meat, rocked the babe gently in her lap. The deep melody of her humming seemed somehow to fill the wood, his mind, his soul.

From where he stood, Boden could see the child's face. His mouth was open, toothless, and lifted into a silly smile as the mother rocked him.

The child giggled once. Twas a strange sound, a sound Boden had never heard before. He sliced off a chunk of meat for himself and stepped closer.

Firelight cast a golden light on the pair. The babe clenched his tiny fist. The way he held it tripped some vague memory in Boden's mind. The child looked almost like a balding warrior, well past his prime, clenching his fist and defying his age. Not unlike Lord Haldane.

Boden remained perfectly still, forgetting his meal. There was something more important here, some mystery he had failed to unravel, but he would fail no more. Today he would learn the truth, and neither her heavenly eyes nor her angelic voice would sway him from that quest.

In his mind, he carefully added up the facts one by one. Haldane's heir had been in that woods. The child's body had never been found. Was it not strange that this woman, with a babe of the same approximate age, would be in the same woods at the same time? And the mother—she had no milk for the child. Why? Wasn't it likely she was not the infant's mother at all? Wasn't it far more likely that this was Lord Haldane's heir?

Bernadette glanced up suddenly, catching his gaze with her own. The smile dropped from her lips. Her eyes went wide like a doe's at the sound of a footfall. "Did ye need something?"

He remained silent for a moment as he devised a plan to learn the truth. "Seeing you thus," he said finally, "made me realize how difficult it will be to tell my lord that his child is dead."

Sorrow and empathy softened her eyes. "You were sent to bring his babe to him?"

"Aye. The babe and the women who cared for him. But all is lost now, for they are dead."

She drew a deep breath. "You found their bodies?"

"The women and their guards. But not the child."

"Then mayhap he is not dead," she said softly. "Mayhap he is safe and well somewhere."

Boden shook his head. "There is no hope for a child to survive on his own."

"Perhaps there was another in the party. Someone who is now caring for the babe."

He watched her for a moment, but finally shook his head. "I fear I cannot share your optimism. The world is rarely kind to the young and infirm."

Silence settled in. The fire crackled. "Do ye speak from experience, Sir Boden?"

He paused for a moment, then, "Nay," he said. "I am amongst the noble few. What have I to worry about? Twas the poor babe I was referring to. Although . . ." He sighed. "Had he lived he would have wanted for naught."

"Truly?" Her gaze never left his face. "The father had feelings for the baby then?"

"What father doesn't care for his only heir?"

"I did not mean that kind of feeling," she said. "An heir is an entirely different entity than a baby."

"I thought they could be one and the same."

"And what of the mother?" she asked. "Did the duke have feelings for her, too?"

Silence settled in as he stared at her. "I didn't say my lord was a duke."

He watched her mouth open soundlessly, then, "I only assumed . . ."

"Nay," he countered softly. "You know because you were hired to care for the babe until a ransom could be paid to get him back."

"Nay." She stumbled to her feet. The babe had fallen asleep and made no protest.

Boden watched her without moving. "I would accuse you of worse, but after the past few days I believe you incapable of murder. I think you did not know they planned to kill the women and their guards.'' He rose to his feet. "Is that not so."

"Nay." She stepped back an additional pace. "I don't know what you're talking about."

"Did you run from them after you realized their cruelty? I see the love in your eyes when you look at the child, and I think you could not bear to give him up to such men."

"I am Bernadette."

"Why do you lie?" He had sworn he would not lose his temper. But suddenly he was certain he was right, and angry that she would not admit the truth. "You've nothing to fear from me." He lowered his voice slightly and took a step forward. "Tell me the truth and I will see that you are kept safe. Give me the names of the men and perhaps there will even be a reward."

She retreated a pace, bumped into a tree, and was brought up short. "I am not who you think I am."

"Truly?" He stepped up close enough to look into the baby's sleeping face. His head was uncovered, his lips slightly parted as he breathed softly through them. "Then say farewell to the child."

"What?" She pulled the babe hard against her breasts and her eyes went wide.

He watched her in silence for a moment, then crossed his arms against his chest and explained. "Some years ago Lord Haldane was wounded in a skirmish with the Welsh. What they lacked in training and weaponry, they made up for in cunning. We thought we had won the day, but as my lord surveyed the battleground he was attacked by a band of farmers bearing forks. One managed to strike him on the head. We soon came to his rescue, but since there was no one around to tend Haldane, I saw to the wound myself. When I clipped away his hair I found a mark the exact same shape as the babe's."

"What an astounding coincidence," she said, but the words were breathy.

"Nay," he countered roughly. "The child is Haldane's heir. You know it as well as I."

"Nay!"

He grabbed her arm. "Tell me the truth or I will take the child here and now," he said, and releasing her arm, snatched the baby from her.

She tried to pull the babe from his grasp. The child awoke with a start and a whimper.

"Ye canna take him!"

"You misjudge me, lady. I have no loyalty but to myself and my future. And my future demands that I take the child to Knolltop, so take him I will. Just as easily without you if you refuse to cooperate."

She tried to pull Thomas from Boden's grip, but he held on, not moving his gaze from her face. The baby's eyes were wide, his bottom lip protruding.

"Ye cannot take him from me," she said.

"He is Haldane's child."

"Give him back." Her voice trembled. "He needs me."

"I'm a knight, trained in every manner of battle and survival, I think myself capable of caring for one small child," Boden said.

The babe eyed him for one instant, then sniffled, gasped, and suddenly began to wail, filling the woods with a god-awful cacophony.

Boden shuffled his weight from foot to foot as his every muscle tightened. "What's wrong with him?" he asked, staring into the child's brick-red face.

Glancing at Sara, Boden thought for a moment she might try to snatch the child back, but finally she shook her head and formed her hands into fists. "You're the knight," she said. "I'm certain you're capable of caring for one small child."

Chapter 5

Sara hugged herself and refused to move. But she couldn't manage to force her gaze from Thomas. She'd vowed to protect him, and if the truth be known she loved him like her own.

"What troubles him?" Boden asked.

Everything in her screamed to snatch Thomas back, but she kept her arms folded against her chest. Force would do her little good here. She must think.

"Mayhap he is hungry," she said.

Sir Boden glanced at the goat, the babe, the goat. His eyes narrowed. "The child is Lord Haldane's," he said, as if that one statement would set everything right.

Thomas howled louder.

The knight stiffly shifted the babe in his arms, tentatively trying a rocking motion as he had seen her do.

Thomas shrieked like a full moon banshee. Blackblade's gaze skimmed to Sara, turning his expression from one of anger to something akin to panic. "He is Thomas, Haldane's heir," Boden said. "Admit the truth and I'll give him back to you."

She forced herself to remain immobile but could manage no more—no denials, no witty explanations.

"Deny it," he said, barely heard above the baby's squall, "and I'll take him alone." He grimaced, glancing at the howling infant. "No matter how onerous the task I swear I'll do it."

Panic roiled through Sara. Would he take the babe? Nay. His loyalty was to his lord. He could not risk the child's life by trying to care for him alone. But just then the knight stepped toward his mount, taking the infant with him.

"He is Thomas!" she gasped, then rushed toward them. Blackblade turned, happily relinquishing the child. She drew the baby into her arms with flooding relief.

"He is Lord Haldane's child," Boden said.

"Caroline's." Sara drew herself from her reverie with an effort. "He is Caroline's child," she murmured.

The knight glowered at her, his uncertainty obvious. "Who are you?"

She didn't answer. Didn't dare.

"Who are you?" His voice, always low, seemed deeper than the night now.

Memories welled up out of the nightmarish past, reminding Sara to be cautious. But other memories jostled them aside. More than once this knight had risked his life to save hers, and for no reason but that there was goodness in him.

"What do you want?" she whispered.

"The truth."

"I'll not hurt the babe," she vowed. "Let us go. Please."

"Let you go?" His tone was incredulous, and suddenly he stepped forward, gripping her arm and shaking her. "Who the hell are you?"

She cowered away. "Berna—"

"The truth," he gritted. "For once."

"I am Sara of the Forbes."

"Caroline's companion?" He dropped her arm and stepped back a pace. "But she is dead. I saw her body. Wrapped in a red plaid, it was."

"'Twas Anne's body you saw." Sara could barely force out the words. "She took a liking to my shawl."

"So you are Sara? But—" He shook his head. "Then why did you fight me when you knew I was Haldane's man?"

She glanced at his sword. Her heart told her to trust him with the truth. Her mind told her otherwise. "'Tis hard to differentiate between one man who threatens me and the next," she said. "What are your plans for the babe?"

"He is my lord's only son. Does it not seem credible to you that Haldane would want him at his side?"

"Nay. It does not seem credible. Not when he sent the mother from his sight after learning of her condition."

"'Twas for her own good," Blackblade said. "And out of respect for his lady wife."

"Respect," she scoffed, feeling her temper rise. "Is it respect you call it then? Mayhap he should have considered that respect before seducing a young girl overawed by his lordly manner and rich garb."

Blackblade stepped up close to her, his dark face inscrutable. "And would that young girl be you?"

She drew back with a start. "Nay!" she said.

Boden watched her as if trying to read her mind, but finally he turned the conversation aside. "You were the only one to survive?"

She drew a deep breath. Harsh memories crowded in. She pressed them desperately back. "So far as I know."

"It would seem you could have been somewhat more appreciative of my rescue, if such is the case."

"Rescue? How was I to know you planned a rescue? In the past three weeks I and my party have been attacked and attacked again. I know neither why nor by whom. How was I to know ye did not mean to do the same?" Indeed, how did she know now?

"The fact that you still live should give you some indication," he said. "I could have killed you in the first moment had I been of a mind."

"Mayhap had ye seen your friends killed and your life

threatened, ye would be in no hurry to trust, either,'' she said.

His eyes looked flat, and suddenly she wondered what memories haunted *his* sleep. When he'd removed his tunic, she could not help but notice the scars that marred the rolling muscles of his back. Scars did not come without pain. It was likely indeed that he *had* seen his friends killed and his life threatened.

But that was not her concern, she reminded herself. She had the baby to think of now.

''What do ye plan to do with us?'' she asked.

''I will return you to Lord Haldane, of course.''

''And if I do not want to go? As a knight is it not your duty to grant the wishes of a lady?''

His expression showed his surprise. ''What lady would not wish to be the mistress of a duke? He is not only powerful. But wealthy, and not ungenerous with his women.'' Boden tilted his head. ''True, he may no longer have the virility of a young man, but I would think you could overlook that shortcoming, considering what you would gain after his death.''

Sara's temper rose as she absorbed his meaning. So he thought her to be Haldane's mistress, and a greedy witch at that. ''Ye, Sir Knight, are an ass.''

There was some satisfaction in seeing his look of surprise. Could it be he hadn't tried to insult her?

''Are you saying you don't care about his money?'' he asked.

''I am saying ye are an ass,'' she said tightly. ''I would have thought that quite clear.''

His brows lowered again, as though he tried and failed to understand her. ''My lord wants you at his side,'' he said, as if in the end that was all that matters.

''He wants his heir, ye mean,'' she countered.

Silence again as he watched her in thought. ''Ahh. So there lies your concern.'' He nodded and crossed his huge arms over his mailed chest. ''You think he has no feelings for you.'' Something sparked in his eyes. ''You

can rest your mind on that account, lady. For my lord
bade me keep you safe and well until you are back at his
side.''

Damn him. She was not Haldane's mistress. Nor
would she ever be. But perhaps that information was best
kept to herself. Perhaps Boden meant her and Thomas no
harm, but someone did, and her dreams told her that
someone was connected with Haldane, if it was not the
duke himself. She dare not go to Knolltop. But surely
her chances of escaping would be greatly improved if she
pretended to be soothed by Boden's words. If she pretended to be content to accompany him to the duke like
a lamb to the slaughter.

"So my lord spoke of me?" she asked, making her
tone soft and dreamy.

"Aye, he did." Boden scowled as if trying to follow
the change in her mood. "He said I should give you
whatever your heart desires."

She desired to be safely in the Highlands with her baby
in her arms and peace in her heart. Guilt crowded in. He
was not *her* baby after all. But Caroline's, and if Caroline
was alive, she would still be alone. Sara forced the
thought from her mind, and hugged Thomas to her as if
she were holding Haldane's words against her heart.
"Did my lord . . . Did he perhaps say anything else regarding me?" she asked.

A muscle jumped in Blackblade's jaw. His scowl deepened. "Aye. He said I should make certain you eat, because you're too damned skinny as it is."

She couldn't disavow her angry blush. All she could
do was hope it would seem that the thought of her love
made her flushed. Forcing a giggle, she said, "He always
teases me about my figure." She turned away, still
flushed.

"Eat something," he said.

She flashed him a smile over her shoulder, hoping its
brilliance would strike him dead. "Oh, I could not pos-

sibly eat anything now. I'll just sleep and hope I dream of . . .'' She sighed. *"Him."*

The night was long. Many times Sara awoke, listening, contemplating. Should she try to escape again? she wondered. But each time she glanced at Sir Blackblade, she saw him staring back at her, his eyes just visible in the darkness.

Morning found her tired and sore. She was not accustomed to sleeping on the ground. The dampness seemed to have seeped into her very bones, and the thick fog that enveloped them added a layer of depression to her mood.

Sir Blackblade, on the other hand, seemed little affected by either the weather or the night.

They broke the fast with the rabbit still warm from supper. Boden wrapped the remaining pieces in strips of linen and placed them in the pouches behind his saddle.

Despite Sara's singing and pleading, Tilly stamped and kicked, upsetting the small kettle and causing a good deal of racket. Finally Boden abandoned his chores to come to her assistance. He held the nanny by the horns until Sara had finally coaxed out enough milk to feed the babe.

Thomas fed hungrily, burped, and true to his agreeable nature, settled in for another nap in the sling against Sara's breast.

"Are you ready?" Boden asked. He had tied Tilly's rope to the back of the saddle in the hopes she would follow for some miles without undue trouble. He stood now, tightening Mettle's girth and not turning toward Sara as he spoke.

"Aye." She glanced about their small camp. The fog was as thick as bread pudding. Twould be a perfect opportunity to escape. But would it not be wiser to wait until they were farther north? Despite her uncertainties, Sara was fairly sure Boden meant to deliver her safely to Lord Haldane. So why not accept his protection until then?

Or was she insane? Were all her reasonings and musings without base? Nothing made sense.

He turned toward her as she approached his horse. "I'll give you a leg up," he said, cupping his palms near Mettle's elbow.

Placing a hand on the charger's withers, Sara put her foot in Boden's grip. He boosted her upward, but just as she was about to swing her leg over the cantle, Tilly threw her weight against the rope. Caught off guard, Mettle grunted and sidestepped.

Sara teetered. Thomas slept, and Boden, steady as a rock, settled his palm against her buttocks and boosted her into the saddle. She turned her face away as she sank into the deep leather seat. He'd removed his hand, replacing it on her thigh. Even so, the heat of his touch seared through her.

"Are you all right?" he asked.

She could feel his gaze on her face, but refused to look at him. "Aye," she said, staring at the top of Thomas's head. The warmth of his fingers confused her. "Aye. I am fine."

He drew his hand slowly away. She watched him turn the stirrup sideways and crouched forward, intending to make room for him. But instead of mounting, he grasped her ankle and placed her foot in the iron.

"Are ye not riding?" She raised her gaze to his face, then silently caught her breath. His eyes were dark, hooded, as deep as forever.

"Nay," he said, and taking Mettle's reins, led them northward.

Sometime before noon they stopped at a fast-flowing stream. Mettle drank his fill. Tilly, miraculously, had walked the whole way and now pawed the water with her sharp, split hooves.

Sara slipped Thomas's sling from her neck and set him on a soft bed of bracken before kneeling upstream from the horse. After dipping her cupped hands in the water, she raised them to her lips. Droplets raced along her chin and down her delicate throat. Boden watched her pink tongue dart out to catch them. And then, like a doe caught napping, she raised her startled gaze to his. He turned away, driving his thoughts from her.

The sun had burned the fog from the morning, leaving the day warm and humid. They rested in the shade of a tilted willow, ate more rabbit, and drank again as Thomas slept on his back beside the garrulous waters.

Sara watched the waves roll by, and Boden watched her. She had plaited her flaxen hair into a long, chunky braid that fell down the middle of her back, but still it seemed untamed, as though such a task was beyond mortal man. Twas a strange thought, because for the most part she seemed the epitome of genteel womanhood, and yet there was something about her that suggested she was much more, much deeper than the shallow confines conventionality would allow.

She toyed with a blade of grass for a while, then, ''Tis a bonny spot,'' she commented finally.

He said nothing. What kind of a woman could be attacked by brigands, forced to travel alone with an unknown man through the wilds of England, and still appreciate the beauty of the countryside? There was a slight blush on her cheeks that accentuated the light sprinkling of freckles that frosted her nose. ''I oft played in a place much like this as a child.''

And what was she now? he wondered. If not a child, surely she had just left that stage behind, for she looked so untouched, except for her eyes. Sometimes, when he looked into her eyes, he could see a glimpse of a formidable past, of pain conquered but not forgotten.

''We would make tiny ships of bark and sail them to strange and wondrous new lands,'' she said. There was silence for a moment, broken only by the chattering waves. ''Shona, she was the youngest of the three cousins, yet hers always made it the farthest. She had an uncanny ability to keep them afloat. Mayhap Rachel and I overfilled ours, though we sometimes accused her of sneaking out at night to find the best bits of bark . . . in anticipation of the next day's adventures.''

Downstream, a small fish splashed, silvery in the bright light. She turned toward it. "Say something," she said.

The water rattled on.

"Why?"

She turned slowly toward him, finally lifting her gaze to his. "Your silence makes me nervous."

He didn't answer right away, but lifted a stone, turned it in his fingers once, then skipped it over the waves. "I've seen you fight brigands with nothing more than a flaming brand," he said. "I thought mayhap, nothing made you nervous."

She laughed softly. "Ye know little of me, Sir Knight. Many things make me nervous."

"Does Lord Haldane?"

"What?" Her eyes got very wide.

Boden cursed himself in silence. He shouldn't have broached the subject of her relationship to Haldane? Twas none of his affair. His task was to return her and the babe to Knolltop. Nothing else. Neither her youth nor her feelings had anything to do with that mission.

Nevertheless, the question gnawed at him.

"We'd best move on," he said, rising quickly to his feet. "Every hour we delay will make your love worry more."

Chapter 6

I t was almost dusk when they drew near a small lochan. Sara slipped from the saddle. After the nooning, Boden had mounted behind her, and thus they had ridden for endless hours. Her legs and back ached from remaining immobile for so long—trying, and failing, to keep a respectable distance between her and the huge knight that rode behind. But no matter what she did it seemed she could feel his nearness—if not his hands, at least his gaze.

Sara heard him dismount behind her. Thomas had been awake for more than an hour during the ride, and slept again now, secure in his pouch, his face scrunched against the soft fabric. Slipping the carrier off her shoulders, Sara turned her neck in an effort to ease the tension caused by the baby's weight. The discomfort remained, so she glanced about, looking for a safe place to settle the child. It wasn't difficult to find a branch suitable for her purposes, for an oak tree grew nearby. It was a venerable old tree, weathered by years and untouched by the transient problems of man. Its branches grew as thick as her waist, horizontal to the ground and just above her head. Twas a simple task to secure Thomas's sling to a sturdy portion of it. She watched him for a moment. He was undisturbed by this position so similar to his place against her heart. A gentle breeze wafted through the trees, setting the sling to sway slightly and soothing the baby even more with the tranquil motion.

Stretching her aching muscles, Sara walked down to the water's edge. The shoreline was sandy, and along the serpentine coast, prickly bushes grew in profusion. She knelt beside the lake, drinking her fill before washing her face with the sun-warmed waves.

She rose to her feet. Her stomach grumbled a complaint, and as Boden led Mettle down to the water, she wandered off, noticing that some of the thorny plants were raspberry bushes that twisted and twined up in profusion. Here and there she could see a small cluster of red. She picked what she could of the seedy berries. They tasted indescribably, almost painfully sweet as she savored them and moved on, searching for more.

Supper would be modest. But they had a bit of rabbit left. Perhaps if she were lucky, she might find something to use in a stew and boil up what little meat they had left.

She wandered on. The raspberries gave out. But in a quiet sheltered spot, where the sun still slanted kind and soft through the woods, she found a patch of wild potatoes. Breaking off a dead branch, she dug up the small tubers and put them in a pile. She noticed, too, a cluster of tiny, pink blossoms drooping beneath soft, green leaves. Comfrey, she thought, and smiled as memories of quiet evenings at Glen Creag soothed her. Fiona would often send the girls to bed with mugs of comfrey tea. Twas good for "what ails ye," she would say, and would launch into a litany of specifics. Most of that knowledge had bypassed Sara, but she remembered well that a poultice could be made from the roots and used to heal wounds or mend bones. Twas more than once that her father had sought out Fiona for just such a purpose.

Carefully pulling the plant up by the roots, Sara added it to her treasury.

Then, through a maze of brambles, she saw the straight, shiny tops of what looked to be scallions. She hurried through the woods. Perhaps it was her excitement over the thought of her stew that made her careless. But whatever the reason, she failed to notice the wild boar until she heard its disgruntled snort.

She turned, and froze. The boar lumbered to his feet, its beady eyes trained on her, its tusks protruding half a hand's length from its lower jaw. One side of the animal was covered in drying mud, but the flies still tormented it. It switched its bristly tail, then rutted up a patch of turf and tossed it at its back.

The flies buzzed and settled again. The boar grunted, then angry at the insects that bedeviled it, threw its head back to chase them away.

The movement startled Sara, and she jumped. The boar started, stared, and then, without warning, charged.

Sara screamed and pivoted away. The woods were thick, her skirts long. Terror thundered through her as the boar crashed after her. A low-growing elm loomed ahead. If she could reach it she could scramble onto the bottom branch.

But suddenly tusks ripped at her skirt. Shrieking, she darted toward a broad-based oak, her heart in her throat. But the boar was gaining on her. She felt the rip of her skirts again and lunged for the tree trunk. But just then the beast's tusks caught the flesh of her calf.

Pain ripped up Sara's leg. She shrieked in agony as she fell and rolled, shielding her face with her hands. The pig came on, trampling her legs, head lowered.

She screamed again. Death swept down upon her.

But in that moment there was a squeal of rage. Blood sprayed into the air. The boar twisted away. His tusks skimmed past her face, and then, like a felled fir, his body crashed to the earth beside her.

She was frozen to the ground, her gaze locked on the grizzly sight of a black sword protruding from between the beast's ribs.

For a few moments there was no sound but for the

ragged rasp of her breathing, then, "Dead?" she asked on a breathy whisper.

"Aye." The answer came from her right. She turned shakily in that direction and watched Boden shove his dagger back into the top of his high boot. He looked casual and relaxed, as if he saved foolish maids from wild boars every day before breakfast.

Sara pushed herself to her elbows. Her stomach roiled, but she refused to gag, not with this giant warrior standing over her looking bored. True, she thought, he was a knight, and thus had seen much worse than this little drama. Still, it wouldn't have killed him to look worried.

Willing her stomach into submission, she tried to draw her legs up beneath her.

"Lie back." He was beside her in an instant, and the moment his hands touched her shoulders, she felt like she might cry.

She twisted her neck, refused to acknowledge her weakness, and tried to peer around him. "You're certain? You're certain it's dead?"

"Aye." His voice was steady and deep, his scowl dark. He pulled his hands quickly away. "Lie back."

"Thomas!" She tried to sit back up as she remembered the child, but he pushed her down again.

"The babe could sleep through the crusades. Not a knight in the making, I'm thinking."

She remained on her elbows, trying to ignore the pain in her leg at least until her queasiness retreated. "I suppose ye were saving damsels in distress afore ye learned to stand."

"I was *born* standing," Boden said and pressed her shoulders to the earth with stubborn hands.

In a moment, she felt him push her skirt past her knees. "And most probably ordering people about, I suspect," she said. Idle conversation seemed a good bet. Fear was not. Yet, she could feel her heart thumping wild and hard against her ribs. Her head felt strangely light.

"Giving orders with a sword in one hand and my

crossbow in the other,'' he said, his voice deep.

"So ye were born a knight,'' she deduced, staring at the sky.

"Aye. They took one glance at my manly face and decided to bypass the formalities. Roll over.''

"How bad is it?'' Her voice shook when she asked.

"It's still attached. Roll over.''

She did so, and found that her hands were shaking. The earth smelled musty beneath her. Her twisted braid lay littered with leaves beside her head. Why, after more than a score of years could she not plait her hair into a respectable braid? "*Such a pale little sparrow*,'' Mairi, her father's mistress, would say. "*Ye think yer father will ever wish to come home to such an untidy child?*''

"Sir—'' she said, her tone shaky.

"Call me Boden.''

"I was about to.''

"No 'sir,' '' he said, "just Boden.''

"Such informality hardly seems proper with a man who departed the womb already knighted.''

"I can afford to be magnanimous,'' he said.

His touch felt gentle and warm against her calf— strange for such large and calloused hands. For a moment she thought she felt them tremble? But that was silly, of course. Twas her own body that shook with fear.

She bit her lip. Tears prickled her eyes. "How bad?''

"Twill need stitches.''

"Nay!'' She twisted rapidly about and found his eyes with her frantic gaze.

He smiled. It lifted the corners of his dusky mouth into an expression that momentarily stopped her heart. "I jest,'' he said. "It's jagged and long, but not deep. Though these wounds can heal grievously slow, it should mend on its own. Tis a good thing too, for I fear my stitchery is not much coveted.''

She turned over with a wince. "Being born a knight, I imagine ye have little need for the feminine skills.''

His hand remained on her leg, bumping up her heart rate, warming her flesh.

"Tis true of course," he said. "I have my hands full rescuing fair princesses from dragons and whatnot."

"Tis sorry I am to take up yer time from the royalty," she said. But that was far from the truth. His nearness only made her want to move closer to him, to feel the strength of his arms around her.

Their gazes met. "Fair damsels of any station are well worth my time."

Forbidden hope twisted in her gut—hope that he might feel a modicum of the desire she felt. The pain had momentarily eased in her leg, but her heart felt strangely tight. "I fear ye've been at battle too long if ye think me a fair damsel, sir."

"I *have* been at battle too long."

She couldn't hold his gaze, but lowered her eyes quickly. Shona was the bonny one. Or Rachel. Or Mairi. But not her. She was Sara—the little mother. "I am an old woman, married and since widowed."

"Truly?" His voice was husky and low. A corner of his mouth lifted into a slash of a smile. "And how old are you, lady?"

"Tis two and a score years I've seen."

His smile deepened. Twin grooves stretched down along the sides of his mouth. "St. Notburga's nose! Tis a miracle you've survived to such antiquity."

He was laughing at her boast of old age. Scowling, she tried to rise to her feet, but he pushed her back down again. She should have been relieved that he'd moved his hand from her ankle. But still her skin tingled from his touch.

"Rest a while, lass."

"I am hardly a lass," she said, wanting more than anything to push her unwanted emotions aside.

"Rest, then, old hag."

She deepened her scowl. "There seems no need to insult me."

"'Tis strange," he said, "you object just as strenuously when I call you fair as when I call you hag."

The forest was very quiet. She should ignore his words, should turn away, should at least keep up the inane banter, but she could not. "Think you that I am fair?"

There was surprise in her voice. Boden stared at her. Could it be that this woman didn't realize her allure, didn't know that he longed for even her simplest touch? Could she not know that she consumed his thoughts, that her voice was as kind as a song, her skin as smooth as fine satin, her eyes so—

Dear lord! What was he thinking? This woman, widow or not, was not for him. Hardly that! In fact, he had been ordered to bring her home to Lord Haldane, and although Haldane was generous with his knights, he was not the type to take kindly to the seduction of his favored mistress. And not for an instant had the duke pretended she was anything else.

Boden had known Haldane for many years, had fought for him, respected him, argued with him. And although Boden had never met Sara, he had known from only a few words the value Haldane placed on the Scottish lass.

Boden pushed those thoughts to the back of his mind. Twas his job to return her to Knolltop, and he would do his job. "Can you stand?" he asked, reaching for her hand.

"Aye," she said, and ignoring his offer of help, pushed herself to her feet.

Boden knew the moment she would fall, for he had seen a hundred warriors overestimate their abilities in just the same way. He caught her in his arms as she went down.

Her gasp of pain whisked against his face. Her hands clutched his arms as his encircled the taut diameter of her waist.

For a moment he could find no words, for unlike the

hundred seasoned warriors, her body was as alluring as forbidden fruit, as soft as a lover's sigh.

"Are you well, lass?" he asked, finding his voice, and aching at the touch of her fingers on his arm.

"Aye." Her tone was breathy. She looked embarrassed and pained, but in a moment, she righted herself. "I am simply . . ."

Her words faded away. What would happen if he kissed her? Just once. Just to taste the sweetness of her lips.

What was wrong with him? He had to start thinking. And not about *her*—at least not in that way. "Simply what?" he asked, scrambling for some foolish words to calm the too-rapid beat of his heart. Settling her on her feet, he tried to find some coherent thought, but his voice sounded rusty, his sense of humor, sorely taxed. Her heavenly blue gaze settled on him. "Surely it is your old age that caused the fall."

Apparently his words made her forget her infirmity because she took a tentative step. Was her expression grateful? Had she, too, felt the impact of their touch? Did she, too, know the folly of reacting?

"Methinks it is unbecoming for one so nobly borne to bait an old woman," she said.

The last rays of sunlight shone through the branches, setting something akin to a halo aglow over her head. He could not help but notice how it gleamed off her flaxen hair, liming her fragile profile, setting blue flame to the depths of her indigo eyes.

"Can you make it back to the babe on your own, venerable one, or shall I carry you?" The thought of holding her in his arms was almost overwhelming.

But she shook her head and turned away.

"I fear in your senility you've forgotten your way. The lake lies yonder," he said nodding to the side.

She limped a little farther and finally bent to retrieve a small pile of something from the ground. It took him but a moment to realize they were potatoes. It had been some days since he'd enjoyed a decent meal, and taters would go a long way toward improving his lot, but it would not do nearly as much good as a night in her arms.

She hurried farther away, but soon she stopped and bent again.

He followed her, seeming unable to do anything else. "Here. Let me," he said, bending too.

"I can get it," she said, but just then their fingers brushed together along the smooth, green tube of a scallion. Her breath hissed softly between her teeth. A shiver ran up Boden's arm. They were so close he could feel her warmth. But in a moment, she straightened.

"I can do this," she murmured, and all he could do was nod and turn away before it was too late.

It was dark by the time Boden reached camp. The onerous task of butchering the boar had given him time to think, to catch his breath, to reprimand himself. She was his lord's, and not for the likes of him. From now on he would treat her as he would a sister. He could do that.

Sara had built a fire upon the sand. It burned orange and bright and smokeless in the surrounding darkness. The aroma wafting from the low, hanging pot made his gaze skim hopefully in that direction.

"Shall I save the pork for tomorrow?" he asked.

"I am cooking the rabbit," she said, looking up from where she chopped something on a flat log. "But more meat would only improve the taste. If ye like I will add it to the broth." She prepared to rise, but he noticed her stiffness and motioned her back down.

"I am not unaccustomed to cooking," he said, and slicing the meat in strips, tossed them into the pot. "How is your leg?"

"Tis fine," she said.

He watched her eyes. Even by firelight, they looked unearthly blue. "I've heard better lies from monks."

"I dunna lie."

"Not well at least," he admitted. "Your leg needs washing and bandaging."

"I'll see to it in a moment."

"See to it now, lass."

"The scallions—"

"Can wait," he said, and stepping forward, took her arm and steered her toward the lake.

"Rather pushy for a callow youth," she said.

He settled one hand around her waist, steadying her. Surely he would do the same for a sister. "'Tis the advantage of being knighted at birth. Instantaneous respect."

He thought he saw her smile, and suddenly wished with a terrible longing to see it more, to hear her rasp his name in the middle of the night, to feel her hands, soft as velvet on his skin.

Sister! He was going to treat her like a sister.

They had reached the water's edge. She stared across the glassy, moon-bright surface. He tried to pull his hand from her waist but couldn't quite manage it.

"Thank ye. I will be fine now."

"The night is warm," he said. What a clever statement. And so brotherly.

St. Edward. Her waist felt as slim as a reed beneath his hand.

"Twould be a fine night to bathe." His lips said the words long before he could recall them.

Her gaze darted to his face, her eyes bright as sapphires in the moonlight.

"And wash your clothing," he added. Well hell, he'd say the same to his sister. "There is blood on your gown. And mud."

She opened her mouth to speak, but he hurried on.

"I have a spare tunic and a cape. You could borrow them while your garments dry." Why did he do this? Did he have a need to feel the spur of desire bite him even deeper? Even knowing that her eyes were bluer than the heavens, her voice softer than a song? Suddenly he found himself wanting to beg. Although he wasn't certain for what, he knew he wanted far more than a sisterly kiss.

Her tongue darted out, wetting her lips. He watched and felt his brain go limp.

"If I bathe do ye promise not to look?"

Was she out of her mind? There was no reason to try to convince her to bathe if he couldn't watch. He wasn't, after all, a complete idiot. He'd learned early to take what this world had to offer, whether it be coin or opportunity or women. But damn, her eyes were blue, and he was a knight, and somehow that foolish title must have afflicted his mind, for he heard himself say, "I will keep the babe safe."

"A bath would be most welcome," she said.

It took him a moment to decipher her words, for all he was aware of was the slow, mesmerizing movement of her lips. But finally her meaning settled into his brain. "I'll fetch my cape and tunic," he said, and forcing his hands from her waist, jerked away.

He was back in a matter of moments. Placing the garments on the sand, he stared down into her eyes again and offered her a small sliver of soap. "Do you need any further assistance?"

She stared into his eyes. It was safer to watch him under cover of darkness, for surely her emotions wouldn't be so easily read now. "Nay. I shall be fine. Thank ye."

He nodded once and slipped away into the night.

Maybe she trusted him far more than she knew, or maybe, she thought as she let her gown slip down around her ankles, maybe she was such a wanton that she didn't care if he saw her. Her undergarments followed her gown. The night air felt soft and gentle as a lover's touch. But truly, how would she know how a lover's touch would feel? The only man who had touched her had been her husband.

Her breath felt tight in her throat. She glanced over

her shoulder, but she could see nothing of the knight who guarded her.

For one wild moment she thought of screaming to draw his attention. After all, there might be any kind of danger in these English waters. But the idea left her with a nagging feeling of guilt. She waded quickly into the lake, past her knees, up to her thighs, and then she slipped farther in, letting the tender waves seep over her shoulders and soothe her aching muscles. The water was surprisingly warm, still heated by the sun and trapped in the tranquil peace of the silent hills that surrounded them. Unlike most of her peers, she and her cousins and siblings had been taught to swim. Thus she swam for a while, letting her hair caress her shoulders and arms in silken waves. At times it would flick soft as goose feathers against her buttocks and thighs. She searched for any sight of Sir Boden, but he was nowhere to be seen. Swimming toward shore, she touched her feet to the sand and walked to the beach to retrieve the soap he'd given her. It smelled like nothing more than its basic components, tallow and beech ash, but reminded her, strangely enough, of this man. She closed her eyes for a moment, savoring the scent that conjured up feelings of large, strong hands on her waist, of a whisky soft voice against her ear, of an almost smile, tilting up the corners of a sardonic mouth—so near she could almost—

This had to cease! Turning hastily, Sara slid back into the water until it lapped at her waist. There, she leaned back, letting her hair float in the waves until it was saturated and slick as seal skin. She shampooed it, rinsed it, shampooed again. Then, rubbing the bar between her palms, she urged forth a hard-won lather and soaped her body from her shoulders on down. Her breasts felt strangely sensitive, her nipples erect. And dead center between them, Dragonheart felt warm and heavy.

Finally, her bath finished, she hastened to shore, donned the tunic Boden had left her and quickly soaked and scrubbed her clothing. Wringing them out without soiling them again was a bit of a struggle, but she managed. In a short while, she threw the cape over her shoulders as much for modesty as for warmth, and hurried back to camp.

Boden was resting with his back to a log, but instead of facing the fire, he was looking away, into the darkness.

Sara slowed her steps as she entered the wavering ring of light. She cleared her throat, then, "My thanks," she said. Never had she felt more ill at ease. Never had each nerve been stretched so tight, each desire been so stark.

"The water was warm?" he asked, rising to his feet.

"Aye." Their gazes met. "Aye, it was warm." She turned away, fiddling with her gown and finally striding to a branch where she could spread the garment on the limb. "And Thomas? He has been quiet?"

"Aye," Boden said quickly. Her feet peeked from beneath the hem of his cape, he noticed. They were narrow, pale, delicate—and bare. Dear Lord! "And your leg?"

"Fine!" she said rapidly. She turned to face him, seeming to forget she still held the gown scrunched carelessly in her fists. "Tis fine."

"I had best bandage it."

"Nay!" She said the word very fast. "Nay. That willna be necessary. Ye were right, I'm certain. Twill heal on its own. And too, I have my amulet."

She lifted the pendant from her chest, and somehow, as if by some magical force, the chain came free from her neck to lie in her hand. The dragon's eye winked ruby bright in the firelight.

"Good luck is it?" he asked, stepping closer. Dammit! He was forgetting to breathe again. But this time he would remember not to touch her, for when he did so he could not think.

She didn't raise her gaze to his, but studied the clasp. It seemed unbroken. How had it come free? And why? "Aye. Tis lucky," she said distractedly. "So Liam tells me."

"Liam?" He felt emotion rise in his throat. But it

could not be jealousy, for such would make no sense.

"A friend," she said, her voice soft as air in the darkness. "Twas his long ago. Then it was lost. But just before I left for London he rediscovered it at the bottom of Burn Creag. Like magic it was, he said. As if it had come just to be with me."

"He gave you the amulet?"

"Aye. He said it would keep me safe."

Who was this Liam to her? he wondered. It was a foolish question and none of his concern. Yet, he could no more stop his wondering than he could stop his hand from straying toward her. Nevertheless, he diverted his fingers just in time, turning them aside to touch the pendant in her hand.

"Then we'd best take no chances," he said. "For surely luck is needed until we reach Knolltop." The silver felt strangely warm against his fingers, the chain as supple as a serpent when he stepped behind her.

Gathering her hair in both hands, she moved it aside, baring her slim, pale neck. Boden's breath caught in his throat. He'd be a fool to touch her. A fool to take that risk.

But he'd been called a fool before.

His knuckles seemed to burn where they touched her neck.

"Lady, I . . ." For a moment he forgot every word he had ever learned, like a knock-kneed boy caught stealing a peek through a brothel's open door. "I . . ." Dear Lord! He slipped his hand from her neck. "I need a bath," he said, and pivoting on his heel, hurried toward the water.

Sara turned more slowly, clutched the dragon in her hand, and drew a deep, cleansing breath as she watched him go.

Dear God, what was wrong with her? Why did she feel such hot, foolish emotions? She was no giddy maid, but a widow with responsibilities and vows she must keep.

She should check on Thomas. She should stir the stew. She should see to Tilly.

But one truth stuck in her mind like a burr caught in wool. *She* had never promised not to watch *him* bathe.

Chapter 7

⎯⎯⎯✦⎯⎯⎯

Sara was heading toward the water and just managed to stop herself in time. What was she thinking? She couldn't follow him like some hound on a hot scent. She was Sara of the Forbes, sensible, kind, caring.

Pivoting swiftly on her bare heel, she paced toward Thomas. He remained as she had left him, blithely asleep, his body snugly wrapped in his narrow cocoon, his face pressed against the soft cloth.

He didn't need her. She fingered her wet gown again, and then spread it upon the branch not far from Thomas's impromptu swing. After, she wrapped Boden's bulky cloak closely about her. It smelled of pine and leather. She closed her eyes and breathed in the scent, then shook her head and hurried to the fire to check the stew. But there was little to be done there. It was cooking well on its own, its fragrance rich and full. She stirred it once, then remembered Tilly and tied her in a spot where there was more browse available.

She could milk the goat now, but by the time Thomas awoke the milk might well be cold. So she fidgeted again and scowled toward the water. Mayhap she should tell Boden it was time to sup. After all, twould be best to eat before wee Thomas awoke.

It was logical. And too, he'd been gone some time now. Several seconds at least. Would it not be prudent to check on him? After all, he *was* wounded.

Yes! He was, she thought, and turned toward the lake.

Her heart was beating very fast, but her feet seemed inordinately slow. Perhaps she shouldn't be doing this. Perhaps it was ridiculous to think she could nurture a seasoned warrior. Her father had been wont to tell her that she couldn't be responsible for all of Christendom. But if that was true, didn't someone have to be responsible for her? Yes. It was Sir Boden's job to protect her, and surely he couldn't do so from the lake.

Feeling better for her logic, Sara straightened her back and quickened her stride. She was doing nothing wrong, merely calling him for a meal. She would not tarry. Indeed, she would state her business and if he was within view, which was doubtful, considering the darkness, she would avert her eyes and leave.

Overhead, the fat, round moon grinned at her through tattered clouds. "Sir Boden," she called, but the name was barely audible to her own ears. For heaven's sake, what was wrong with her? "Sir Boden," she said again, clutching a gnarled branch. But still there was no answer.

Surely there was no need to panic, she told herself, and yet she could not help the shiver of worry that hurried up her spine.

"Sir Boden," she called, but just then something leapt from the water near shore.

She stumbled into the bushes with a gasp.

What was it? A sea monster! But it wasn't a sea!

Boden!

The truth drained into her mind. It was Boden, just lifting his head from beneath the water's surface. Sara closed her eyes and placed a shaky hand over her heart.

Twas not like her to be so jittery. There was nothing to fear. Sir Boden squatted in the water, which reached just past his hips. Bathed in moonlight, his hair shone blue-black. Silver-gilded water rolled down his face. She saw him scoop his hands up his cheeks and over his hair, wringing it out so that it settled against his powerful shoulders.

One slick, tidy strand remained on the tight mound of his right pectoral. It nearly reached his dusky nipple. He straightened, revealing the rippled muscle of his abdomen, the flat expanse of his belly.

"Boden!" She called his name, trying to stop him before it was too late, but the word came out as nothing more than a pathetic squeak of sound, easily drowned by the lap of waves against sand. And suddenly he was standing, and the water barely reached his calves. She tried to close her eyes, but it was the strangest thing—they wouldn't shut and she found herself staring like a naughty, mesmerized child.

He was hard. All of him. She swallowed. The least she could do was look away, but she could not. Her gaze slid down his body and caught on his manhood. It pointed toward the moon as his thighs, wide as oaken boughs, the left one scarred high up, shifted back and forth, bearing him toward shore and causing the light to gleam off a thousand moon-kissed muscles.

He stopped, and suddenly she realized he had left the water behind. She forgot to breathe as he bent over. The moon shone on the hard curve of his buttocks, the broad expanse of his back. His arms flexed as he retrieved his tunic. Running the garment over his chest, he stared up at the sky. The moon smiled down on him.

Dear Lord! She was beginning to sweat.

He slipped the tunic lower, over the hillocks of his abdomen, across the mounds of his hips, down the endless length of his legs. And then he straightened, naked as an egg and just as unconcerned. Finally, he picked up the remainder of his garments. Suddenly it dawned on Sara that he would now return to camp. And she wasn't there!

Her mind whimpered a small cry of defense. How could she possibly explain her whereabouts?

Perhaps if she circled around. No! Pretended she'd not

seen him! Sweet Jesus! She could cause a distraction, she thought, but just then he turned and headed down the shoreline, naked as a babe, sculpted as a warrior.

With desperate relief, Sara slipped from the bushes and sprinted toward camp.

Boden stepped into the wayward light of the fire. He wore only his hose and boots, for his tunic was still wet from its washing, and he couldn't quite force himself to wear his mail without something to protect his skin from its chafing.

He tried, for a moment, to keep himself from staring at Sara, but the firelight illuminated her face—his lord's *mistress's* face, he reminded himself. She sat on a rock with his own tunic and cape wrapped close about her. The garments were large and enveloping, exposing nothing more than her bare feet and a bit of ankle. Still, the sight made his heart beat speed up a bit.

His lord's mistress! His lord's mistress, he reminded himself. He averted his eyes, ladled a bit of stew into a shallow wooden bowl and concentrated on the taste.

But she was singing, softly, in that way she had. In that ethereal, moon-soft manner that made his gut clench and his brain go soft. What kind of woman could live out here without complaint, prepare a meal from fresh-killed boar and salvaged potatoes, then nurture another woman's babe as if this was her heart's full desire?

She turned suddenly toward him. Her gaze, bright as the firelight, caught his. "She was my friend," she murmured.

He forced himself to remain still as he watched her. But in that moment, just when she seemed most ethereal, he imagined her naked, as she would have been not long before, caressed by the moon, revered by the stars. Dear lord! She belonged to Haldane.

But if that bit of truth didn't worry him, he could at least be concerned with the fact that she seemed to have the uncanny ability to read his mind. He snapped his attention back to his previous thoughts.

"Caroline was your friend?" he asked, though he knew that's what she had meant.

"Aye."

She had plaited her hair and somehow managed to confine it to the top of her head. It left the long, pale length of her throat perfectly bare. Bare feet and a bare throat. St. Bruno's butt, it was more than any man should be expected to resist.

"She was Lord Haldane's ward." Sara paused and glanced at the baby. A slight frown marred her smooth brow. "It was more than a year ago that she came to live with us. Lord Haldane would often visit. When he learned she was expecting his child, he sent her to London. Baileywood seemed very quiet without her."

"Baileywood is your home?"

"My husband's home," she said quickly, then hurried her gaze back to the babe. He wondered if her cheeks were red, but twas a hard thing to tell by the fickle firelight.

He waited a moment for her to continue. But she did not. Reticence would be a wise course here, he knew. And yet her words intrigued him. "Twas it not your home also?"

"I only meant to say Baileywood was not mine by birth," she said, but her voice was too soft to be believed.

"Baileywood is in England?"

"Aye. Stephen considered himself English. Though his mother was part Scots."

He watched her face. "I am sorry for his death." It was the proper thing to say. Wasn't it? Or were knights not allowed to lie even when spouting platitudes.

"Aye." Her voice was barely discernible. He tried to read the nuances. There was a pause. "Thank ye."

"He was good to you?"

Her gaze snapped to his, her eyes wide with surprise. Apparently that wasn't a knightly kind of thing to say.

But hell, he wasn't a knightly kind of man.

"He was . . ." She paused again, and for a moment he wondered if she was holding her breath. "He was from a good family."

So was that all that mattered to her? The heritage of a man? "He treated you well then?" he asked again, beyond caring that it was not the proper words to speak to a lady.

"He wished for an heir." She paused and looked down at the child again.

"Your pardon?"

"I canna bear children."

The night was very quiet, broken only by the mournful call of a distant tawny owl. Boden waited.

"He was impatient for an heir. My failure to produce one was certainly a disappointment to him," she said finally.

Though Haldane had given him some details of Stephen's death, Boden longed to learn more. "How did he die?" he asked.

Her eyes again, large as a speckled fawn's. Was there mourning in those eyes or was it another emotion?

"Twas a hunting accident."

Boden remembered Haldane had said that it was just that the hunt had killed him. What did that mean? "I'm sorry," he said. That lie again. And a gentle man would question her no further, but rarely had he been mistaken for one of those, even when he tried. "Was he killed by another archer?"

"Nay. Twas a buck. He had wounded it. It went down. He thought himself a great hunter." She bit her lip. "He was a great hunter. He went to kill the beast, but it rose up. Lord Haldane said he died immediately. There was nothing he could do to save him."

Boden pushed away his dark thoughts. Haldane had his faults but he was no murderer, regardless of how much he might have coveted another man's wife, and Boden would not allow himself to consider it. The duke of Rosenhurst had been more of a father to him than any other he had known.

"The duke was a friend to Stephen's father." She said it in way of explanation. But it seemed to open a wealth of questions that he didn't want to consider.

So Haldane was a friend of the father, but was he a friend of the son? The duke had said he'd become enamored with Sara the first moment he'd seen her, and the duke was accustomed to getting what he wanted.

Boden shut off those disloyal thoughts and turned the subject aside.

"Why did you leave your husband's house after his death?" Haldane had said her husband hadn't deserved her, but did any man? "Surely you inherited some of the property."

"The usual amount," she said, then looked into the darkness that surrounded them. "But in truth, I wanted nothing of Baileywood."

"Why?"

For a moment he thought she wouldn't answer.

"I missed my homeland."

"But you soon left your homeland again, when you went to live with Caroline, did you not?"

"Caroline was afraid to bear her child. She needed my help. And too, my father died while I lived at Baileywood. With him gone, Nettlemore did not hold the same appeal."

"You spent a good deal of time there during his burial?"

She paused. "My duties didna allow me to return for his burial."

"Damn him!" Boden said, leaping to his feet.

Her eyes went wide. She leaned away, hugging the child to her breast.

Boden stopped his motion with an effort. He clenched his fists and drew a steadying breath. "He did not even allow you to return for your father's funeral!"

"I didna say that."

No. She had not. But twas the truth. He knew it. "Lord Haldane was right. Twas just that he die by the hunt. He was not worthy of you." The woods were silent for a moment. "I lied," he said. "I am not sorry he is dead."

"Nor am I," she whispered.

Boden took a step toward her, but suddenly she was on her feet and backing away. Every emotion that plagued him shone in her fire-bright eyes. But she was stronger, for she was the one retreating, holding him at bay.

"Nay. Please. Dunna come any closer. Twould surely not be right to betray Lord Haldane's trust. We must not."

Boden stopped, clenching his teeth and his fists simultaneously. "Have you feelings for him?"

"Feelings? For . . . the babe?" she asked, knowing her question was foolish, but needing time to think, to sort out her emotions.

"Haldane!" Boden growled. "Do you care for him?" Against his will and his better judgment, Boden moved toward her again.

"Aye!" she burst out, then steadied her voice and tried again, trying to push him away with that one word. "Aye. I care for him."

Boden remained as he was, trying to read her thoughts, to judge her feelings, but he was out of his depth. Retrieving his sword, he strode into the darkness.

The night lay soft as a down blanket against Sara's skin. She woke slowly, languidly, not certain what had disturbed her sleep. It almost felt as if someone had touched her face, kissed her throat. A hand seemed to be caressing her thigh, slipping her tunic upward.

Against her better judgment, she bent her leg and moaned. She felt wet and hot, alive with an eagerness that could only be caused by the dream. But this was foolishness. She blushed at her own feelings and opened her eyes.

Boden leaned over her. His dark hair lay spread across his endless shoulders, and his face looked shadowed and sculpted in the flickering firelight.

"Boden!" His name escaped her lips like a solemn prayer.

"Aye, lass. And the answer is yes," he said. His kiss was like liquid fire on her face, her throat, her shoulder. Her nerves jangled. Her heart raced like horses at dawn. Mists roiled in her mind.

"The answer to what?" she whispered.

"I think ye are fair." His eyes were as deep as forever. "Though I try to deny it. Though I fight to keep my distance. You call to me, for you are far more than fair. As golden as the sunrise after a long night, as sweet as wine to a parched man." And suddenly he was kissing her lips.

She wrapped her arms about his back. It was bare, criss-crossed with muscle and as broad as a stallion's. His arms were tight about her, his fingers warm and strong as they slipped through her hair. Shivers raced up her spine. She moaned again.

One hand pushed her tunic higher. "We don't need this, lass," he murmured, and there was naught she could do but agree.

Her clothing disappeared.

"Sweet Mary, how I need you," he whispered. She could see the fevered light in his eyes, could feel the tremble of his hands as they smoothed up her waist and over her breasts.

She wanted him. Like never before in her life, she wanted a man. Gone was the little girl who had hoped for nothing more than children and a hearth of her own. Gone was the woman who would be content with another's family to foster. She wanted this man. And she wanted him now.

He kissed her again. The heat seared her senses, scalded her thoughts. "I need you," he whispered, his voice husky. "This moment!"

"Aye," she moaned. His erection was hard and hot. She gasped as he pressed against her.

And suddenly, she woke up!

Sara sat up with a start, her heart pounding, her hand closed about Dragonheart. Across the fire from her, Sir Boden rose, too. The blanket fell away from his bare torso. His hair, still damp from his bath, was slicked back from his sharply sculpted face, and his eyes were fierce and dark.

"Are you well?" he asked, his tone husky.

"Aye." What had she said in her sleep? How much did he guess and how much could he read in her face? she wondered. But just then her gaze caught on his bare chest. He was so close, almost near enough to touch, to run her hands down the dramatic strength of his arms, over the undulating muscle of his abdomen. Every coherent thought evaporated like fog in the sun.

"A dream," he whispered.

"Aye," she said, but in a moment she realized it had been a statement and not a question at all.

It was then that she saw that his breathing raced along in rhythm with her own. His muscles were as taut as bowstrings, and his jaw like granite as he watched her.

"It was . . ." Dear God, what was it? A dream, yes. But so real she could still feel his fingers against her skin, could hear his words reverberate in her soul. What was wrong with her? Never had she set store by a man's looks, never had she needed the physical. "It was . . . distressing," she whispered.

He didn't agree to this, but watched her as a falcon might study a hare.

She could think of nothing to say, nothing to do but stare into his eyes. "Tis sorry I am to have wakened ye."

"Twas not you that awakened me," he murmured. "Twas the dream."

No. They could not have shared a dream again. Twas too eerie, too frightening. She shouldn't acknowledge his words, and she certainly shouldn't look at him, for with every moment that passed, the fantasy only seemed more real.

"There was a maid with golden hair and eyes so blue they challenged the brightness of the heavens. Soft as satin was she in my hands. Warm as sunshine."

She swallowed, lost in his words, the deep timbre of his voice, the depths of his eyes.

"Lass," he breathed, rising to his knees. "What was your dream?"

"I dreamed of a dark man, a man like none other. Strong he was, but kind, with eyes as deep as forever and hands that promised heaven."

"Sara," he whispered.

But in that moment the goat bleated. Reality flooded back, and with it a harsh reminder of her responsibilities. "Tilly!" She jumped to her feet. "I dreamed she had gotten into some poisonous yew and become sick. I—I must check on her," she croaked, and spinning gracelessly away, scrambled into the brush.

Chapter 8

Morning dawned gray and still. Mists blanketed the world. Every serrated leaf was wet, every coiled frond heavy with moisture, bowing toward the earth.

Sara awoke to Thomas's morning squeals. Pushing back the flap that covered his face, she drew him gently to her. He smiled toothlessly, but her thoughts were elsewhere. Once again, she had made a fool of herself, she thought, glancing toward Boden's empty pallet. But wee Thomas brought her attention back to him with a gurgle. She smiled, offering her little finger. He curled his fist around it and cooed.

"Good morningtide, bonny Tommy," she murmured. His grin increased.

"Are ye hungry this day?"

His arms waved wildly and his legs joined in. Although twas the practice to swaddle babes tightly to teach them to walk upright instead of on all fours like the beasts, Sara's circumstances had negated that dubious practice, allowing his limbs to wave freely.

"Poor bonny babe," she crooned, leaning closer still. "Left alone in this world with only a strange Scot to care for ye. And her riddled with unimaginable dreams and unforgivable fantasies. But I should not trouble ye with my problems, for surely ye be ready to break the fast."

"Twill not be so simple."

Sara yanked to a sitting position. Boden stood only inches away. The mists shaded him like a curtain of silver, but even so, she could see that his chest was still bare.

How much had he heard? She tried to see through the fog to make out his expression, but there was little hope of that.

"How long have you been standing there?" she asked.

"Long enough to imagine your dreams and forgive your fantasies."

She was on her feet in a moment. "You misunderstand. The dreams—"

"Are the same as mine," he interrupted. "And I wonder, are they caused by the amulet, or by something deeper?"

She found, to her dismay, that she was clutching Dragonheart in her hand again. Loosening her fingers, she let it fall against her chest. "They are caused by fatigue. Nothing more."

"Are you certain, lady?"

"Aye," she lied. Even now she wanted nothing more than to go to him, to feel the warmth of his skin against hers. But hardly could she give in to such insane fantasies. For if she went to him once, she would never have the strength to leave him.

"I would gladly let you rest to prove you wrong," he said, his tone resigned. "But I fear there will be little enough time for that, for the goat has disappeared."

"Tilly? It cannot be," Sara said, reeling from one crisis to the next. "Thomas needs her."

"And she has taken your gown and my own garments with her."

"What?"

"Twas either the goat, or the fairies have absconded with our clothing for their own amusement."

Sara turned to pick up the babe who had begun to fuss. "Tilly took my clothes?"

"You don't believe in the little folk?" he asked. "I thought twas your Scottish duty."

Sara ignored his jibe. For God's sake, she was dressed in nothing but his tunic and cloak. She needed her clothing. "But how did she get loose? I tied her myself."

"And a fine knot it was," Boden said, lifting a damp, frayed piece of rope for her to see. "Twas no easy task for me to untie it."

"She chewed through it."

"Aye."

"What shall we do now? Thomas needs milk."

Boden scowled in return. "Were she a normal beast I would think it likely that she would tire of a full udder and look to be milked."

"Ye dunna suppose someone stole her!"

Boden's expression was wry. "Even the fair folk would see no fun in that."

Sara turned, searching the mists. "I must find her," she said. But just as she was about to take a step forward, Tilly bounded out of the mists and into their camp.

Sara stumbled backward.

Boden yanked his sword from its scabbard, then seeing no immediate threat, raised his brows in wonder. "You've a knack for this goat finding, lady."

"You've come back," Sara said, squatting down to stroke Tilly's bony head. The goat bleated once, gazing up at the lady with round, marbleized eyes. Sara stroked her again. "Did ye mayhap miss our wee Thomas, Tilly?"

"Saint Ephraem's ear!" Boden muttered. "More likely she missed kicking me in the shins. Secure the beast before she eats my cape."

Thomas whimpered and kicked again, his movements agitated now.

Sara reached for the jagged end of rope dragging from Tilly's neck and rose to her feet. "If ye'll hold the babe I will see to the milking."

Boden's brows lowered quickly. He glanced toward

the surrounding, mist-shrouded woods as if wondering which way to run. "The babe?"

"Aye. Twill only be for a short time. Unless you would rather milk Tilly."

His brows lowered still more. "There are many things I would like to do to that goat. Milking her is not amongst them."

Sara chuckled. So what if her gown was missing? Thomas was well and Tilly had returned. "Take the babe," she said, extending him toward the knight.

For a moment, Sara thought the brave Sir Boden Blackblade might run for cover.

She drew Thomas back a few careful inches. "You're not afraid of him, are ye?"

"Me?" Boden scowled even darker, looking huge and forbidding in the misty morn. "Lady, I am a knight, trained, true, and trusted."

She laughed again and pressed the babe into his arms. "Tell wee Thomas all about it. I won't be but a minute," she said, and hurried off in search of the kettle.

Boden shifted the babe uncomfortably about as he stared into the infant's eyes. They were midnight blue and very intense. Utterly solemn he was as he curled a tiny fist tight against his swaddled chest. The two studied each in silence as the seconds ticked away, but twas not a comfortable silence for the knight.

Finally, feeling disconcerted under the babe's scowl, Boden cleared his throat. "Yer moth—ahh—Lady Sara has but gone to gain your meal."

The babe's brows lowered a bit more, cliffing in pale, irregular lines over his eyes.

"Twill only be a moment I'm sure."

The babe's bottom lip protruded slightly. It was pink and bowed, and might seem comical if this were a humorous situation.

Boden drew a deep breath. How had he gotten himself into such a situation? He had come to do his lord's bidding. A simple task, really—to escort a pair of ladies and one small babe to Cinderhall. That one task, and he would be well rewarded. What had gone wrong?

The babe's lip began to quiver. Panic welled in Boden's chest. "Don't cry!" he ordered.

But perhaps he used the wrong tone, for the babe drew a deep breath and sent out a sharp squawk.

In desperation, Boden tilted the baby up, bouncing him slightly. "She'll be back soon. Tis true," he babbled. "She said as much, and she wouldn't lie. Not to you."

Thomas inhaled again.

Boden bounced more rapidly. Thomas's head jostled slightly. "Truly. Though I see little to admire in you, she seems to cherish—"

But suddenly all hell broke loose, and the baby erupted into a cacophony of discontent. His face turned brick red and scrunched up like a sausage left too long in the sun. His arms waved wildly and his legs kicked like a mule gone mad.

At a loss, Boden held the babe at arm's length and forced himself not to drop him and run.

"What's all this?" Sara asked, approaching from behind.

Boden pivoted about. His panic was too sharp to allow him to wonder if there was laughter in her voice. "Take him. Take him," he ordered, shoving the child toward her.

"Well . . ." Sara said, trying to shuffle aside the milk bowl and feeding gourd. Finally, she was forced to set them upon the ground as Thomas was pushed into her hands. "Am I to take this to mean that ye two didna get on?"

"He just . . . He doesn't . . ." Boden began, searching hopelessly for words. "I am no nursemaid."

She laughed. "Nay," she said, dipping her gaze momentarily to Boden's chest. Thanks to Tilly, the demon-possessed goat, it was still bare. He almost flushed under her quick perusal. "Ye are no nursemaid. But surely even a knight must care for children sometimes."

"Why?" The question sounded more panicked than he had intended it to, but—did knights really have to care for children sometime during their careers? he wondered. And if so, was it too late to become a wainwright?

Her gaze met his and she laughed again. "If for no other reason, surely ye will wish to sire an heir," she said.

"An heir?" To what, he wondered.

"Aye." She had put the babe to her shoulder and rocked side to side in a movement that could have put Boden himself to sleep given the chance. "A man like yourself . . ." she began, then shifted her gaze momentarily to his bare torso, before snapping it back to his face.

Was there a flush on her cheeks? Boden wondered, and realized suddenly that his heart was beating overtime, and his muscles were tense "A man like me what?" Boden asked, knowing he shouldn't, that a nobly borne man would back off and leave it alone.

Her gaze lifted to his, striking him with its sapphire beauty. "A man like ye should sire children," she said, and awkwardly retrieving the milk and gourd, hurried into the mist.

The morning slipped slowly away. Boden said nothing, but rode in silence. Sara, searching for a more comfortable position, had twisted slightly in the saddle in front of him. One leg was bent over the pommel and her face was turned slightly toward the side.

That wasn't good, because the sight of her made it hard for him to think . . . or sit . . . or breathe.

They'd never found the clothing Tilly had absconded with, his mail shirt included. Thus, Sara still wore the garments he had lent her. But they were traitorous things. His cape kept slipping open and his tunic was, in general, a lecherous garment that continuously slunk up her legs toward parts better left unthought of.

She had no gown. He had no shirt. And his hands were beginning to sweat. God help him!

But things could be worse, he assured himself. They'd had no signs of brigands for some days. Fresh water had been plentiful, and Tilly, perhaps thinking she had caused enough trouble for one day, was following peaceably along behind.

What the hell had she done with their clothes? he wondered, trying to fix his mind on something that didn't involve yards of soft, silken skin. The goat would make a fine purse, or a milk bladder. But then, if he made her into a milk bladder, there would be no milk. He glanced behind him, making certain Tilly still followed. She twisted her neck to stare at him with her eerie, marble eyes. Her lips were turned up slightly as if she were laughing and waiting to see what would happen next.

What indeed? Boden turned forward again, glancing over Sara's shoulder. Saint Patrick's pate! Her leg was bare again, even to the knee. Sweat popped out on his forehead.

She was not for him! She was not for him! He closed his eyes. Sweet heaven. He was not a disciplined man, regardless of the image he managed to portray to the general populace.

He opened his eyes and tried to stare straight ahead. She was a lady, a lord's daughter, and a *duke's* mistress. Yet, she was so much more. Her nearness did odd, frightening things to his heart. The sight of her face in the firelight made his knees strangely weak and his head quite light. He didn't need her kind of trouble. But her knee was bare and damn it if her hair, soft as morning, wasn't pressed against his bare chest and burning its way into his heart.

Reaching out, he yanked his cape over her knee. His knuckles brushed the satiny skin of her calf. A shiver, fine as gold gossamer, ran up his arm.

She roused, drawing away from him, pulling the heaven from his heart. "My apologies," she murmured, looking momentarily disoriented, as if she had slept in the arms of love and awakened in a strange bed.

Dear God! Why did he let himself think of that?

"I fear I fell asleep again," she said, blushing, like rose petals on ivory, as beautiful as springtime. "'Tis sorry I am to burden ye so."

Her gentleness scorched his heart. He ached to touch her cheek. What if he begged for her favors?

She drew his cape firmly about her and refused to meet his eyes.

"What did you mean about siring children?" His emotions were so unsettled, he knew he should not ask *that* question, but was unable to resist.

"I should not have spoken about such a personal matter," she murmured. Her words were barely audible, and for one wild moment, he wondered if he might use that excuse to lean closer still, to press his chest more firmly against the kitten-soft length of her hair.

"What did you mean?" The words came of their own accord, certainly without thought, for it seemed all his concentration was directed at her lips. They were so full, delicate, begging.

"Ye are a good man, Sir Boden," she said without looking at him.

Never before had he thought simple words could wound his heart, but hell, his armor had disappeared. "You know little of what kind of man I am," he said, trying to make sure he kept breathing. In and out. In and out. "In fact, you met me only a week ago."

"But it has been a long week."

And soon she would be returned to Haldane. God, his chest hurt. "You know little of me," he said, wishing he could replace his armor.

She turned slightly, looking into his eyes, and suddenly he felt as if her very gaze had pierced his heart.

"Ye dunna believe ye are good?" she asked.

"I'm a knight and therefore you are safe with me. I merely meant that you're too trusting, for you've not known me long enough to judge whether I am good or bad.''

"Indeed?" she asked.

"Aye."

She smiled, just a corner of a smile as she faced forward again. "Then mayhap I merely meant yer physical attributes should not be wasted."

Did that mean what he thought it meant? Sweat rolled down his back.

"Ye are a great swordsman, sir," she said.

Oh. She was speaking of his swordsmanship.

"And ye defend those who are weaker than yourself," she continued. "Tis no small feat."

It was not his lot to be modest, but her words pricked his conscience. If she had seen into his lurid dreams last night she would not think so highly of him. "A monkey can hold a sword," he assured her.

"Ye found me," she said softly. "Though I tried to leave no trail, to lose all those who might follow, ye found me."

"Any hound can follow a trail."

"Ye protected wee Thomas."

"He's my lord's son."

"Ye bought the goat."

"But I dream of drowning her."

A smile flirted with her lips. "You are kind to your horse." Reaching forward, she placed a small, slim hand on Mettle's neck. The charger snorted and shook his head, setting his mane to wagging.

"A steed is a valuable animal," Boden said, scowling at Mettle's comment. "Only a fool would treat him poorly."

"Ye loaned me your clothing," she countered.

Memories flooded over him. Her small bare feet, peeking out from beneath his garments. Her hair like molten gold, slick as golden ermine as she came into camp. Her legs bare as she rode before him, her cheek soft as a dream against his chest.

''Twas for my own protection I gave you the garments,'' he said. ''Tis in my best interest to keep as many layers as possible upon your back.''

She turned toward him. Their faces were only inches apart. Their breath mingled.

''And how am I to protect myself?'' she whispered.

''I will protect you,'' he said, but who would protect him from her beauty?

''Ye cannot be with me every moment.''

''Aye, I can.''

She shook her head. She was breathing fast, her berry-bright lips parted. ''I would not have ye scarred again. One more near miss and ye might well lose your leg.''

Her words were very soft. Her lips so near. But suddenly her meaning permeated his mind. ''What?''

''What?'' She sat very straight suddenly, and her eyes went wide.

''How did you know of my leg wound?''

''I . . . dreamt it.''

''You dreamt I had a leg wound?'' But he had seen her dreams, and none of them involved a leg wound.

''Aye.'' She blinked.

''Oh.'' He nodded once. She nodded back and turned abruptly away, her cheeks red as summer apples.

Sweet Saint Simeon! His body was stiff with rank desire. She'd watched him bathe in the nude!

Chapter 9

ara hummed quietly as she rocked Thomas in her
arms. He was sleepy and limp, a still weight that
filled her arms and her heart. He stared up at her, lids
droopy over his dark, wise eyes. The sun sank over a
world just as full and just as sleepy.

She sang a few words, humming and rocking until his
eyelids slipped lower, covering the midnight blue win-
dows to the freshness of his soul. Finding a sheltered spot
on a bed of dry bracken, she laid Thomas upon it and
stood, staring over the water that rustled and bustled past
her. So fast. Where was it going? And what of her with
wee Thomas? What lay ahead? Downstream, Boden watered Mettle, then turned the steed loose.

What kind of man possessed that kind of loyalty from
a steed, that he could trust him to come when needed?
What kind of man would walk naked with the starlight
shining like diamonds upon his wet skin?

Dear God, he was a thing of beauty. Suddenly she saw
them walking together in the moonlight, their bodies
bare, their fingers entwined. She lifted her face to his and
he leaned close to kiss her—

"The babe is asleep?"

"Ack!" She jumped backward when Boden spoke,
crashing into a tree and feeling for all the world as if he
had risen out of the earth in front of her feet.

He remained perfectly still, his dark face impassive. "Are you well?"

"Aye! Aye!" Except her heart had stopped and her lungs refused to draw a normal breath. "I just . . ." What the devil was wrong with her? What was she thinking, becoming so entranced with her lurid imaginings that she would forget the here and now—forget even to guard wee Thomas as he slept? "You startled me."

"Really?" His lips cocked upward a notch as he continued to watch her. "You didn't see me at the water's edge?"

Of course she had seen him, but suddenly he had disappeared into the realm of her imagination and she had joined him there. What was wrong with her? Her hands were sweaty, her knees knocked like chimes in the wind, and she felt very warm, as if Dragonheart was melting a hole in her chest. She placed a hand to it, steadying herself. "Aye. I saw ye," she said. "I was simply thinking of other things." Please don't ask what those other things are, she silently pleaded. The heat from her chest crept upward, coloring her face with her risque thoughts.

"Tis hot," he said.

Dear God! Yes it was. "Aye."

He turned slightly away, showing her his profile, and for a shattered moment, she wondered if he did so to allow her time to collect her wits. Mayhap he was accustomed to rattling women so. "As a lad, I would swim with . . ." He stopped, looking across the narrow stream and seeming to see something she did not.

"Ye would swim with who?" she asked, and found for some inexplicable reason that she was holding her breath.

He glanced at her. For a moment it almost seemed as if she saw into his soul, but then the moment was gone. "I would swim alone," he said.

But he was a liar, and suddenly she knew it. "Who would ye swim with?" she asked again.

She watched him narrow his eyes and draw a breath.

"My brother's name was Edward. Sometimes we would swim together."

"A brother," she said, and in her mind's eye she could see both boys, just as they had appeared in her dream not so many nights before. Boden was there, but he was not the man of brawn and bravery she now desired. Instead, he was a boy that she would have cherished. A small, sun-darkened lad with a wayward lock of midnight hair and an amber gleam in his mischievous eyes.

"Older than ye, is he?" she said softly, no longer ashamed of her prior thoughts of him, but immersed in his memories.

For a moment, she thought he might turn his back on her, but instead, he squatted to lift a broken shell from the shore. "Aye. Older he was."

Was! She remained silent for a moment, reading the nuances, the picture in his mind. "He is dead?" she asked softly.

"Aye." He didn't look up at her, but kept his gaze on the quicksilver tips of the rushing water as he tossed the shell into the soft waves. "Twas a wager we made. Who could swim beneath the water's surface to the far side of the river. He had taught me to swim himself. Not many could, you know, and we were quite proud. He was stronger than I—a right stout lad, as Tanner was wont to say."

"Tanner?"

Their gazes met. A muscle flexed in his jaw. He turned back toward the water. "Edward was a strong swimmer," he repeated softly. "Stronger than I."

His tone was pensive, deep, making her want to reach out against her good sense and touch him. But she kept her hands firmly at her side. "I am sorry," she said.

"Twas long ago and far away. And of little consequence now." He said the dark words dismissively and tossed another shattered shell to the waves.

But in her mind she saw the truth—a young boy upon the shore. He was breathing hard and fast. At first he grinned down at the water, waiting for his brother to surface, waiting to rejoice his victory. Dear God, she could see him in her mind, waiting long minutes, until he was chilled and scared and running like a frantic puppy up and down the shore, calling.

"I am sorry." Her voice caught. Tears burned her eyes, and one spilled, hot and painful down her cheek.

"Lady." He breathed the word as he stood and caught her tear on his knuckle. "You cry for Edward?"

"Nay." She closed her eyes and though she knew she should retreat, she could not help but brush her cheek against his hand. "I cry for a boy alone."

"Independence breeds strength," he said.

"Your parents?" Dragonheart felt warm beneath her fingers. When had she clasped it? "They were gone too?"

He drew a deep breath. "In truth, lass, I did not long mourn my father's death. Twould be a far stretch to say I was his favorite."

His fingers felt like a bit of velvet heaven against her cheek, igniting a small, warm flame beneath her skin. "But ye were yer mother's," she murmured, for surely no woman could disavow the boy's irresistible charm.

"I'd best see to a meal," he said.

But she reached out, touching his arm. "What of your mother?"

He tightened his jaw, then relaxed marginally and shrugged. "I fear I wasn't very brave when I learned she had left. Edward was the brave one."

"Nay," Sara said in absolute disbelief. "She didna leave ye. No woman could leave such a bonny lad."

His face was tense, as if he, too, felt the pulse of her emotion. "Why do you think I was a bonny lad?" he whispered.

Time hung suspended.

"I watched ye by the water in the moonlight," she whispered. "Never have I seen anything more beautiful."

So he'd been right. She admitted it. But now he wished she hadn't, for there hadn't been a moment of the afternoon when he had thought of anything else, when he had not fantasized about her standing on the sand, watching him.

"I am sorry," she whispered, and he couldn't help but draw her into his arms.

For a moment he did nothing but hold her. She leaned against him, snug in his arms, her tears hot against his chest.

"Don't cry, lady," he said and gently, ever so gently, he kissed the top of her head.

She felt narrow and soft in his arms, slim and fragile, and when she lifted her face, he could do nothing but kiss her.

Emotion seared. Thoughts strained. Every element of earth and sky stood still as their lips met and their souls swirled—as if all of nature had held its breath waiting for this moment. His hand slipped beneath the thistle-down weight of her hair, scooping about her neck, pulling her closer. She felt like sunlight against his bare chest. She smelled like heaven. The cape fell away, baring the smooth, glassy length of her neck. He kissed her there, drinking in her flesh, and she clung to him, needy, needed. Warm and cool, and strong and delicate.

Her fingers splayed across his back, pulling him closer still. He found her mouth again. Need roared through him, tightening every muscle, punctuating each movement. Desire consumed him, driving him on. His hands trembled lower, down her legs. Her waist was taut and narrow and her buttocks, when he cupped them, were firm and round.

He should stop! He must stop! But suddenly he felt her hands on his back, pulling him closer. Their lips met again in a clashing kiss. Fire screamed between them.

She wanted him. Dear lord, he didn't know how this could be, but she did. Her kiss seared his soul. Her hands were quick and eager. But his own feelings were far be-

yond that—beyond want and well into the realm of ir-
repressible need.

Dear Lord, he would surely sear to ashes if—

"Thomas!" She ended the kiss with a gasp, and suddenly, as if the child were in another world, he realized
that the babe was squawking. "He is crying!"

So? he wanted to ask, but suddenly she wrenched herself from his arms and sprinted across the turf to lift the
baby into her arms.

Somehow Boden managed to control his body, to remain where he was, to do nothing but watch her. In his
mind, he knew it was best that she called a halt. He may
think chivalrous love an idiotic thing. He may think pin-
ing for a lady from afar, crafting poems to her beauty,
dreaming hopelessly of her in his sleep, was foolishness.
But it was far smarter than the alternative. Only a dolt
would lay with his lord's mistress. Only a *suicidal* dolt.

And yet death might be worth the heaven she could
give him. Mayhap twas time to admit what he was—not
a gentleman at all.

"Twas naught but a bit of a belly ache," she interrupted abruptly, patting the babe's back and rocking
slightly. "He will be well soon."

"Sara." Boden's voice sounded pleading to his own
ears.

"Please! Dunna say it. Tis my own fault. I dunna . . ."
She paused for a moment. "I dunna know what is wrong
with me. I can but apologize."

"Apologize?" He let out a careful breath, trying to
relax. "And me, I was thinking of falling on my knees
and thanking you."

She smiled, though she didn't look at him. "You must
think me wanton."

"Hardly that," he said, and took a step toward her.

But she lifted a hand, and in that moment, he realized
it shook. With what? Fear? Passion?

Dear God, it would be nice to think it was passion.

"I am sorry," she said, and turning away, hurried into the woods.

The night was endless. Every noise disturbed him, and every time he woke it was to look across the embers of the fire into Sara's eyes.

He hurt. Not his arm, where she had stabbed him, not his leg, where the Welshman had wounded him. But his heart, and his soul and every muscle that screamed to take her back in his arms.

What the hell was the matter with him? He may not be a well-educated man, but life had taught him a few things. First and foremost, he knew he would be a fool to cross his lord. Especially when it came to this woman, who the duke thought himself in love with. Such an action could get a man killed—or worse.

He laid back down, still watching her. He knew she wasn't asleep, and yet it made no difference. She had declared her intentions loud and clear. She would remain loyal to Haldane, and if he was any kind of a man, he would accept that. But . . .

St. William's wick! If the sun would just rise, he could be on his way—heading north, getting closer to being rid of her. The thought of every moment, with her sitting astride in front of him, her bottom pressed tight and warm against . . .

Where was that damned sun?

An eternity later, and only shortly after Boden had finally found sleep, it rose, rousing him with the pink glow of its first light.

Sara sat up. Her hair was disheveled and her borrowed tunic tilted on her delicate shoulder, as though, if she moved, it might slip like morning dew from her body.

It took Boden a moment to realize he was neglecting to breathe. She stared back at him. He inhaled finally, and found he felt no better for it. "A gown."

The words sounded nonsensical even to him. She

stared, her flaxen hair a wild halo, her heavenly eyes wide. "Yer pardon."

"I said . . ." He managed to rise to his feet and was rather proud of that fact, considering his current lack of control. "Today I will buy you a new gown."

"Are we near a village?" she asked, sitting straighter. The tunic slid sideways.

His every muscle tensed. She stared at him, and then self-consciously pulled the humble garment close about her neck.

He drew himself from his trance with a start. "It matters little," he assured her, his voice a rusty grunt. "I'll find a village."

And he did.

Sara hugged his cloak closer to her body as she felt eyes scour her. They were indeed a strange menagerie. A bare-chested knight, a bedraggled woman in an oversized tunic, a baby in a sling, and a goat. Poor Boden, she thought, but when she dared turn to glance into his face, his expression was impassive, as if he had spent the entirety of his life in just such circumstances and felt not the least bit embarrassed about it. For a moment, she let her gaze linger on his face—for after today she would not be seeing him again.

Her chest ached suddenly, but she ignored it. She had no choice. She had known from the beginning that she would have to leave his protection. Now, after last night, she could wait no longer, for somehow she had become obsessed with him.

His gaze lowered to hers. She skittered hers away, feeling her heart bump along its rapid course in her chest, and refusing to look at him again.

Mettle pranced on, his steps high and cadenced as if he carried the crowned king of England instead of this motley crew. In a moment, Boden pulled on the reins. Their forward movement slowed, but didn't stop until they were even with a white mare that stood beside a ironsmith's open hearth.

With one foreleg held between the smithy's brawny knees, the mare cocked a disinterested ear at them. Mettle tossed his head and minced more dramatically yet. Boden mumbled something under his breath. Mettle snorted in return, but finally his hooves stilled. He arched his great neck into a regal posture and slanted a gaze toward the bored mare.

"Your pardon," Boden said, his voice low. "Might you tell me where we can obtain some new garments?"

The smithy glanced up. He was a young man with a jaw almost as wide as the anvil beside the hearth. But his mouth was open, and his eyes held that vacant expression seen in the very dull.

"Yer askin' the wrong 'un there, mate," said a middle-aged woman just passing by. She carried a pole across her back and a wooden bucket at the end of each. "Ol' Chapman was dropped on 'is 'ead when 'e weren't more than a babe. 'E ain't never been a big talker."

"Might you be able to help us, then?"

"Yer lookin' for clothes, y' say?" she asked, her gaze brazen and steady on his bare chest. "For yourself?"

"Aye, and—"

"Twould surely be a sin and crime for me to answer then," she said.

"Ach, and what your thinkin' would be a greater sin," countered the man who strode up to the hearth. "Now get yourself gone, Molly, afore I tell your man what you've been up to."

The woman laughed, and swaying her generous hips, gave Boden a leer as she continued on.

Sara felt her cheeks warm and refused to look at the man behind her. His chest felt hard and powerful against her back, and she had to leave.

"Pay Molly no mind," said the newcomer. He was a big fellow, similar in looks to the younger man, but full through the waist, with his sleeves rolled up above meaty forearms. "There be a widow just down the way what can help you."

After a few more questions, Boden cued Mettle to move forward at a high-stepping trot that all but rattled his riders' bones.

The widow's cottage was small, windowless, and dark. The door stood open.

Boden dismounted first, then helped Sara down.

"Good day," called a woman as she stepped out, drying her hands.

"I was told you could supply us with garments," Boden said.

The widow was a homely woman with pale eyes and a bold, winning smile. "And it looks like you be in dire need."

Was she, too, eyeing Boden's chest? Sara wondered. But at least this woman had the decency to pretend she was not.

"Can you help us?"

"Aye," said the woman, motioning them inside. "That I can."

Two small girls sat near the door, studiously stitching what looked to be stockings. The widow absently stroked one's hair as she passed.

"And what might you be wantin'?" she asked, glancing at Sara before diverting her attention back to Boden.

"A gown for the lady and a tunic for myself."

"As Molly might say, it would seem a shame to—"

"We've already spoken with the milk maid," Sara interrupted, then felt herself blush as Boden turned to stare at her. His expression seemed unchanged, and yet there was something in his eyes . . . Curiosity? Laughter?

"Ahhh," the woman laughed. The sound was clear and bright, but she kept her thoughts to herself. "Well. My name is Fran, and if you'll tell me your wishes I'll try to oblige."

"We're asking for nothing fancy," Boden said. "Just

simple, serviceable garments to see us to our journey's end.''

"Might I ask what happened to your clothing?''

"The goat ate them.''

The widow raised her brows, but that was the extent of her commentary. Apparently there was little else that needed to be said.

"Well . . .'' She blinked. "Let us begin then.'' Stepping forward, she slipped the cape from Sara's shoulders and blinked at the man's tunic beneath. Removing the ever-present pouch, she seized the tunic and pulled it tight against Sara's waist.

Boden held his breath, for though the fabric was coarse and the pattern unflattering, he could well imagine the womanly curves beneath his garment.

Their gazes met and locked over Fran's frizzy head. Sara's cheeks were pink, her eyes dilated wide, an open window to her soul, her desire.

"I'll gather our other needs,'' he said, and turned numbly toward the door.

"But what of your tunic?'' asked Fran.

Boden hesitated a moment. "The lady can decide.''

"And something for your babe, mayhap?''

There was silence as deep as a well. Boden found Sara's face, suddenly pale now, her eyes bright orbs of thought.

"He is not mine.'' For the first time in his life, he felt regret for not having heired a child. What would it be like if Thomas was his? His and Sara's.

"Nay?''

"Nay. I am but escorting the lady and the babe to their lord,'' he said. And with that harsh reminder, he made his escape.

"Oh.'' Twas a simple statement, but it seemed to speak volumes as the widow turned back to Sara with a blink of her pale eyes. "So he's not yours. What a pity. And he's got such a nice . . . voice.''

Sara blinked back and wished for all the world that she could disappear into the ground.

Boden returned some time later, little relaxed or recovered from his last moments with Sara. The sun felt warm against his back as he dismounted. The cottage loomed like a temple of temptations. But the worst was yet to come, for at precisely that moment, Sara stepped from the hut.

For one sparkling moment all the world was forgotten, and she was his. Not a duke's mistress or a dead man's widow, but his to hold, to have, to cherish.

"Are you content with my work?" asked Fran.

Dear God, she was beautiful. True, she was not attired as richly as she should be. No gold-edged coif adorned her head. But her hair had been plaited with ribbon and wound about her skull like gossamer strands of precious metal.

No fine, rich velvets draped her form, but her skin above the square neckline looked as smooth and as rich as pale, warm cream.

She wore no stomacher or girdle to cinch her middle, and yet her waist looked no bigger than his thigh.

The pale pink brocade set her skin aglow. Or was it the light? Or was it simply her?

The seamstress cleared her throat. "I will assume you are content," she said.

Boden wrenched himself from his reverie with a scowl. "Your pardon?"

Just the crack of a grin nudged the widow's lips. "I was lucky to have the gown nearly finished. Twas an order from the mason's wife. But . . ." Her voice seemed to fade to nothing.

Sara's hands were so delicate, her eyes so wide. She should be no man's mistress, but a wife. *His* wife.

"It fits her well, does it not?"

Too well. Far too well.

"Tis laced up the back."

Good Lord! Why would he need to know that? Even his knees were beginning to sweat.

"Tis what makes the marvelous fit."

Nay. Twas the woman within that gave the dress form.

Fran chuckled again, but he barely heard her until she reached for a pile of fabric and approached him. Lifting the first, folded article, she said, "The old tunic. Yours, I suspect."

Boden shifted his gaze to the widow and in that moment, the truth was perfectly clear; he was an idiot if he thought he could pretend disinterest in this woman. Even this seamstress, whom he had never seen before, knew his feelings for Sara. And if she knew, how much more would Haldane know?

"Aye." His voice sounded horribly guilty as if reciting heinous sins to his confessor. And why? He had done nothing. He had done *almost* nothing—but he had wished to do much. "Tis mine," he said, taking the tunic.

"And the new one," Fran said, holding up the new tunic by the shoulders.

Twas a leather garment. He raised his brows in surprise. "You're a tanner as well?"

Fran chuckled. "I but took it in trade. I thought it would suit you."

"It will suit me well. What do I owe you, mistress?"

She stated her price, and he paid the due. Finally, donning the simple shirt, he escorted Sara and the babe from the house.

Outside, the sun was bright and hot. Tilly lay close to Mettle's huge feet, chewing her cud.

Entwining his fingers, Boden helped Sara mount, then steadied her as she settled into the deep-seated saddle. Through the soft cloth, her thigh felt warm and alive, and for a moment he could remember nothing but her standing on the moon-colored sand, watching him.

"We'd best be on our way," she said.

"Aye." He managed to lift his hand from her leg, and in a moment had settled himself behind her.

The tension between them was as thick as fog. Though she tried not to, Sara could feel his chest against her back. She had hoped the tunic would somehow shield her from him, guard her from his allure, but twas a foolish hope, she knew now, for a full suit of armor and a wooden barricade would do little to lessen his effect on her.

She had to quit thinking, is what she had to do. She had to concentrate on the duties at hand. She had to *escape*. Now! Today! Before she could not bear to do so, not for the sake of the child, or even her own life.

"Is there ought you wish to purchase before we journey on?" he asked. The feel of his voice whispered down the nape of her neck. She should have kept her hair down, as an insulation against him. But what foolishness! It would do no good. She had to get away—before they left the village. For he said any beast could track in the woods, surely that meant he would find her there.

"The gourd will not last much longer," she said, thinking fast. "Mayhap I could obtain a bladder for milk."

"Had I the time I would make you one," he said. The words shivered over her skin again, causing the small hairs to raise on the back of her neck and creating an unwelcome image in her mind. She could see his sunbronzed hands, tapered fingers working, suppling, preparing a skin for wee Thomas.

"Ye have skill with leather?" she asked, trying to find words to keep between them.

"A bit."

He would fill the bladder with milk, then take the babe in his arms, settling the child against the heaped muscles of his bare chest. His nipples were dusky and peaked, his stomach flat, and just below his navel was a thin line of dark hair.

Quit thinking!

"Look!" she said, startling even herself with her desperate need for a diversion. "There is a crowd gathering near that platform."

She felt his gaze slip from her face and over her head. "Aye. Tis."

"Mayhap someone there could direct us to a leather shop," she said, and against every bit of sense she possessed, she turned in the saddle. Her thigh burned against his.

He leaned closer, as if pulled by invisible strings.

"Look!" She jerked away from him, her heart racing like a wild steed's. Please God, give her strength. "Tis a show about to begin," she continued desperately, but suddenly a man stepped onto the stage in front of the crowd, and her jaw dropped as she recognized him.

Chapter 10

The balls swirled in front of Liam's eyes, making a blur of vivid colors. He had no need to watch them, for his hands knew the routine, leaving his head to concentrate on more important things. Such as the bonny brunette at the front of the crowd. And the redhead. But no, not a redhead for him. For she would remind him of another who did nothing but drive him to distraction.

His gaze skimmed the throng. Twas a fair-sized gathering for a small village, with the average type of fare: farmers come to town with their pigs, maids with milk buckets.

"Watch the balls, my good people. Watch the balls," he called. "Nay, ladies," he cried, sounding affronted, "not *those* balls."

There were snickers and a few outright laughs.

"Well, all right then, ladies, if ya cannot help yourself. But ya may miss the grand finale if your attention is diverted even for a fraction of an instant. Before your very eyes I will make these balls disappear. Disappear completely . . ." He paused, drew a deep breath and grinned, flashing that self-effacing smile that always helped win a crowd, perhaps a meal, and if he were really lucky, a night in some willing woman's arms. "Hush now, hush," he warned. "This takes the utmost concentration." But his concentration was elsewhere again.

Ahh—there was a likely lass, not so young that he would feel the cad, yet comely in an earthy way with pretty eyes and a gown cut low enough to suggest she knew her way into a man's . . .

God's nuts! Liam's mind spun as his gaze caught on the woman on the gray charger. Twas Sara! *His* Sara!

For a moment Liam's hands forgot the pattern, and the balls nearly crashed onto his head, but he found the rhythm just in time and spun the orbs off into space again as he stared at her.

Sara looked down as Boden dismounted. Her heart thumped wildly in her chest. This was her chance to escape. Liam had noticed her. She was certain of that. Their gazes had met, and in that moment the bond that had formed long ago had welded again. He had seen her and he would help her. She had but to slip into the crowd and hide long enough for Liam to find her. For he surely would.

Boden glanced up at her, his face half-shadowed by the nearby oak tree. Sara looked quickly away, scanning the crowd and hoping she appeared casual.

She felt Boden's gaze slip away as Liam's voice grew louder. Just one more moment. Just one . . .

"Pay close attention," Liam called.

Boden took a step forward, gazing over the crowd to the stage, and Sara acted.

Quick as light, she slipped from the saddle. Without looking back, she jolted away. One stride. Two, her heart pounding in her chest.

"Where are you going?"

Sara jerked about as Boden's hand closed over her arm.

"Let me go." She felt as desperate to get away, and desperate to stay with him.

He scowled, his brows lowering over his dark eyes. "What are you doing?" he asked, pulling her closer.

"I was just . . . trying to find a better vantage point to watch the show."

"You were on Mettle, well above the crowd."

"But I was behind a tree. I couldna see the stage."

He stared at her as if he didn't believe her, but finally pulled her closer to his stallion. "Get on. I'll make certain your view is unimpeded," he said, and pushed her aboard Mettle.

Sara settled stiffly into the saddle and glanced toward Liam. Their gazes caught for an instant, then shifted away.

What the devil was Sara doing here? Liam wondered. He had seen her off to London himself. Had prayed for her happiness, had placed Dragonheart about her neck with his own fingers. Why she was here he could not say, but he had seen the warrior snatch her back to his side. Liam was certain of one thing: Sara was being held against her will, with a babe in her arms and fear in her eyes.

She needed him! He knew it as well as he knew his own name. His wee little lass needed him, and that was all he needed to know. But first he must distract the crowd completely.

"Watch the balls now. All eyes up here, for as sure as you live and breathe, they're about to disappear," he called, still juggling madly. "In fact I'll give a silver groat to any person who can lay his hands on a single ball."

"A silver groat!" The words were murmured through the crowd, but Liam's attention was elsewhere.

God's nuts, who the hell was the man who guarded Sara? He was big as a damn castle, built like a destrier, and about as cheerful as a lonely bull. Leave it to his Sara to be abducted by such a man. Couldn't she have found less of a challenge for him? Someone old and decrepit. Maybe a little lame, blind in one eye? But she needed him now, and he would not fail her again.

"Watch now. Watch closely," he called, and making certain the mountainous warlord was looking directly at him, he performed his finale. Tossing the balls high into the air, he yanked the string at his waist. Black powder poured from the tiny bag stashed in his hose. With one quick movement, he struck a spark with the flint on the bottom of his shoe, tripped a hidden lever, and dropped through the trap door to the ground beneath. The powder exploded—a bit early, almost singeing his hair on the way down. But twas no time to worry about that. Smoke sprouted up above him. The balls hit the replaced trap door with a wooden clack. But already Liam was running, grabbing his cloak from the top of a box as he flew past. Twas a simple disguise, but one that would gain him a few precious seconds. He dashed behind the wooden fence, stepped into the crowd, spotted his prey, and voila! She was in his arms.

Boden jumped at the sound of the explosion. He gripped Mettle's reins tighter and stepped close to the horse's head. Still he kept his attention on the stage where smoke rose in roiling waves. The juggler! He was gone. But where? The balls clattered to the wooden floor. The audience swayed back with astonishment, before gathering its courage and rushing onto the stage. They scrambled to reach the closest ball, shoving others aside, warring for the promised silver coin like dogs for a bone. But that was not the reason for Boden's interest. Hardly that. Why had Sara seemed so stunned when she saw the magician? Why was she so interested? Did she know this man? If so, how? What did he mean to her? And where the hell had he gone?

Boden turned, and lifting his gaze, prepared to ask Sara those very questions. But in that instant his stomach knotted and his mouth fell open. St. Thomas's sacred teeth! She was gone!

Their passage through the crowd was frantic, their journey down the side alley, quick and furtive. In a matter of minutes, Liam pressed Sara through the door of a simple cottage and stepped in after.

An elderly woman rose with a start from behind a battered table, but for a moment Liam ignored her as he dissected his own thoughts. If he was any judge of people, and he was, the warlord would be about thirty seconds behind them. And in that time, Liam was willing to bet, the man would have worked up a pretty good rage. Best to get completely out of sight at least for a few minutes, until the warrior decided they had already left the village.

"I hear you make a hearty stew and England's finest pudding," Liam said, desperately trying to find a reason for their presence in the cottage and smiling at the old woman who stood speechless behind her table.

Dropping her paring knife with the potato she'd been peeling, she gasped, "Who are you?"

Liam scanned the hut quickly. Twas small. One room. Soot-darkened beams overhead. One tiny window—too little to fit through. Details flooded in, assuring him they were safe for the moment. But Sara was nervous. He could feel her emotions through the small of her back. If that bastard had hurt her, Liam would kill him with his bare hands. The man *was* rather large, though.

"We be but hungry travelers. Is the meal nearly ready?" he continued, not missing a beat as he scanned the cottage. There was a place set for one on the crude table—a wooden board, a single knife and a clay mug, stamped with, if he wasn't mistaken, a red dragon with a raised paw. The symbol of the Welsh.

"Nearly ready?" The gray-haired lady reared back in surprise. "I've not seen you before in my life."

Liam laughed, showing a good deal of teeth, but not too much, he hoped, because judging by the humble surroundings, the woman was a widow and therefore more vulnerable than most. Time to put her at ease, he thought, and added just a hint of a Welsh accent to his next words. "Of course you haven't seen us. Tis that not the way with passers-by? But my apologies for not introducing myself earlier. My name is Roger and this be my lovely bride, Mavis.''

The old woman's face crinkled thoughtfully as she glanced at the babe strapped to Sara's chest. ''Bride?''

''Aye, well . . .'' Liam laughed again. ''Even *I* was not man enough to wait for the wedding. But I *was* man enough to convince her to marry me. Aye, my love?''

Sara's eyes were blue and wide. For a moment he thought she would falter, but she didn't.

''Aye,'' she said, and somehow, to Liam's surprise, she was able to produce a fine blush as if to attest to his manly attributes. ''Ye are the only one for me,'' she murmured, touching his arm. ''I knew it always.''

For an instant Liam was lost in those confusing feelings she had engendered in him ever since their adolescence. She was his wee Sara, like a small, angel sister, but more, always more. Even as a child she had possessed an indefinable something, a sparkle, a promise. Now that promise had been fulfilled. She was complete— a woman, with a woman's allure, and a woman's wit. Sometime during their separation, his Sara had grown up and could keep pace with him without a moment's hesitation.

She nudged his arm slightly, prodding him back to the present.

''Aye,'' he said, remembering the Welsh accent as he placed a hand over Sara's and glanced toward the widow. ''We've been traveling a goodly ways, mistress, and her father be close behind us.''

''So your sire does not approve of you marrying a Welshman?'' the old woman asked Sara.

Liam acted surprised for a moment, then chuckled. ''Is my heritage that obvious then?''

''If one has Welsh blood herself, it is,'' said the old lady.

''Nay. You too?'' he asked.

''My mother's family.''

"Ahh. I should have known by the bloom in your cheek, lass."

The old widow waved away his words with a girlish giggle. "You've got the Welshman's way about you, that you have. But I fear you've been mispoke to. I do not cook for the public."

"Nay?"

"I told you, my love," Sara murmured. "Twas not the third cottage down at all. Twas the thirteenth."

"And it looks as if you were right again, my—"

There was a clatter outside the door. "I asked if you have seen a lady!" a gruff voice demanded.

Sara tensed. Liam scowled, then pulled a dirk from his boot.

"Nay!" she rasped, pushing the knife down in terror.

"Her father?" whispered the old woman.

"Aye. The bastard!" Liam growled.

"Put away the blade," ordered the widow. "What would your lady think if you spilled her sire's blood?"

Sara's celestial eyes bored into his. He slid the knife back into his boot.

"I'll hide you," said the widow.

Liam glanced about, but Sara was already tugging him toward the door. He scowled. She motioned toward the beams near the ceiling.

He nodded once, hoisted her up the wall, baby and all, and was soon perched there beside her.

In less than a heartbeat, the house reverberated with the warlord's pounding.

The widow glanced once at them, pressed a gnarled finger to her lips and limped toward the door. It creaked open just a few inches beneath their feet.

"Have you seen a lady?" asked the warrior.

From above, Liam could see little more than a head of dark hair and a hand wrapped hard and fast about the hilt of a black sword. He didn't look any smaller from up above. But surely if Liam catapulted down on his head, Liam would have the advantage. Maybe. However, one glance at Sara's wide, worried eyes kept him in his place.

"A lady?" the widow asked.

"Aye." The single word was gruff. "Aye. She has a babe with her." He paused for a moment. His fingers loosened, then tightened on his sword.

"There are many with babes in—" began the old woman, but the warrior stopped her.

"You'd notice her if you saw her," he interrupted, then shuffled his feet as if loath to go on. "She's like the sunrise. You cannot miss her."

Poetry from a *warlord*? Liam glanced at Sara, saw her expression soften, her lips part. Raising his finger to his own mouth, he motioned her to silence.

"Nay. I've seen no such lady," said the widow. "Mayhap she is visiting the dressmaker. She lives not far away."

Liam watched the soldier peer into the hut, but there was little to see.

"My thanks," he said.

The door closed behind him, and Sara's heavenly eyes went flat.

Their flight from the village had been quick and silent.

The firelight seemed unearthly bright set against the night. The woods around them were quiet. Sara sat very still, watching the flames. Thomas slept in the sling that remained about her neck but rested on her lap.

"How did you manage to get Tilly?" she inquired.

"The goat?" Liam asked. She could feel his gaze on her face. "'Twas simple enough. After I hid you away, I went back to the village. It only made sense that the warlord would not be dragging the nanny about behind his charger."

She looked up quickly to find Liam's eyes. They were even brighter than usual by the firelight's glow. "I thank ye," she said.

"What happened to Caroline, Sara?"

"She died." Her words seemed far away.

"The warlord?" he asked, rising quickly.

"Nay!" The shock of his question nearly brought her to her feet. But Thomas had fallen asleep and she had no wish to wake him. "Nay. Twas not Boden. He saved both me and the babe. Were it not for him we would surely be dead."

"Boden?" Liam said the name stiffly.

"*Sir* Boden," she corrected softly. "Twas brigands that attacked us. But not for the first time." She scowled into the dancing flames. Memories loomed, too dark to be borne alone. Where was Boden now? "Liam?"

"Aye?" He still watched her.

"I think they are after Thomas."

"What?"

"Tis all I can figure. While we were yet in London, brigands broke into Holly House. They took nothing, but went straight away to the nursery." She squeezed the babe to her chest, remembering.

"And?"

"I screamed. One of them grabbed me." Her voice shook. "I got away. Caroline kept guards. They were large and well armed. The brigands ran off."

"No one was harmed?"

"Nay. But we were badly frightened. Caroline wished to return to Haldane. But I . . ." She drew a steadying breath. "I didna think it wise."

"Why?"

"I have dreams, Liam," she murmured. "Ever since I left my homeland."

"Dreams?" His tone was suddenly sharp, his gaze intense. "What kind of dreams?"

"All sorts," she said, feeling silly now that she'd said the words, as if her dreams might have some mystical significance. As if she were still the shy child who believed every fanciful tale Liam told her.

"Tell me about them," Liam said.

She turned away. "I canna remember them just now."

"Sara." He shook his head, causing his dark mane to

brush the bright red fabric of his doublet. "You've never been afraid to talk to me, lass."

"I fear my own mind," she whispered. "Mayhap I am going mad."

He stepped past the fire, and kneeling before her, took her hand in his own. "Madness is not so bad, my love." He grinned. "Trust me. I would know."

She smiled and turned back toward the fire. "I fear tis not a joke, Liam. I have dreams that seem to—to tell me things. Or that *try* to tell me things, if I can but interpret them."

"And what are they trying to tell ya?"

She faced him suddenly, finally acknowledging her fear as she clasped Dragonheart in tight fingers. "Not to trust . . . anyone."

"Anyone?"

She sighed. "The dreams, they're confusing. I see . . . things."

"What things?"

"Swords. Blood!" She closed her eyes and dropped her voice to a whisper.

"Who spills the blood? The warlord?"

"Nay." She paused. "Aye. Maybe. I dunna know. But I know . . . I *feel* that Lord Haldane is somehow involved."

"Haldane? The boy's sire?"

"I know it sounds mad. And yet . . . I no longer trust him."

"Why?"

"There are many reasons. The attacks. The snakes."

"Explain."

"Near Caroline I found a black metal snake."

Liam was silent for a moment, then, "Ya said *swords.*"

"The black adder is in Haldane's coat of arms, as well as on the hilt of his sword. Boden's sword is the same."

"Are ya certain?"

"Aye."

"So ya think that Haldane may have sent whoever killed Caroline, as well as having sent the warlord I took ya from?" He paused a moment, thinking. "Tis not that I wish to trust the warlord, Sara, but if he planned to kill the babe, would he not have done so by now?"

"Unless Haldane told him to bring Thomas to him unharmed."

"And then planned some evil?"

She nodded.

"Why would he do that?"

"I dunna know."

"And ya dunna trust Haldane."

"Nay."

"But ya used to," he said softly. "Ya used to trust him and care for him."

She turned away.

"Don't." He squeezed her hand, drawing her gaze back. "Please, Sara. I've no wish to fail ya again."

"Ye've never failed me."

"Aye. I did not know about your husband's cruelty until too late." A muscle clenched in his jaw. "Now that I do, there is not a day goes by that I don't regret not killing him."

"Liam—"

"He hurt you," he said, his tone flat. "And therefore he should have died by my hand."

"You are not my kinsman to avenge me."

"Nay," he said, "I am your friend, vowed to come to your aid when you are in need. Do ya not remember?"

"Ye never vowed."

"Nay!" he agreed. "I did not. Rachel did. Long ago when she invoked the spell on the dragon amulet."

She reared back in surprise. "How do you know about that?"

He grinned. "Might you remember the noise made by the mice in the corner that night of the terrible storm?"

She stared at him.

"I was the mice."

"Ye were there?"

"Aye."

"But still . . ."

"Rachel said that everyone in that room must protect the others."

"But . . ." She laughed. "Twas just a silly game."

He smiled. "Tis good to hear you laugh. And aye, was a silly game, but what of the years since? Do you forget how you defended me when Simon accused me of stealing his dagger?"

"Nay. I dunna forget. I knew ye were not capable of such a thing."

Liam let the silence lie for a moment. "But I did steal the blade, lass. Only, when ya trusted me so, when I heard ya defend me, there was naught I could do but return it to him. There was naught I could do but try to live up to the good ya saw in me."

"Ye are good, Liam," she said. "Ye always were. And glad I was to see ye this day. Tis lucky I am that ye appeared when ye did."

"Aye," he said, but for a moment his gaze rested on the amulet that winked above the neckline of her gown. "Lucky."

"Why *were* ye there?"

He shifted his gaze back to hers. "It seems as likely a village as the next. But tell me about you, Sara. What are *you* doing here?"

She hesitated a moment. "I told Caroline we would be safe in the Highlands." She drew a deep breath. It wasn't her fault Caroline had died. She'd not wished for such a thing to happen. She hadn't, though she'd loved Thomas from the first. Guilt twisted her gut. "Twas night when the brigands attacked. I was dreaming, and suddenly I awoke. The terror felt bitter in my mouth. Caroline was nowhere to be seen. So I grabbed the babe and fled the tent. I was going to find his mother. Truly I was, but . . ." She shook her head, not wanting to remember, yet having no choice. "The brigands, they came out of nowhere.

The screams! Like animal sounds, they were." She shuddered.

"Tis not your fault, Sara," Liam murmured, pulling her into his arms.

"Aye it is. I failed her."

"Ya couldna have known."

"I failed her," Sara repeated. "But I willna fail her child."

"Ya give too much, lass. Ya always have."

It wasn't true. She was far too selfish, and now she had what she had wanted—a babe of her own. But at what cost?

Liam squeezed her hand. "How did you get away?"

"I ran and I lived, but she died." Sara winced when she said the words. "She was so pretty, Liam. So young and full of life."

"Tis not your fault. It is not shameful that ya survived when she did not. Perhaps twas your concern for the child that made it possible."

"I wandered for days," she said, "hiding like a ferret in any hole I could find. Then Boden appeared." She shook her head, feeling weak from the expenditure of emotion. "He said Lord Haldane had sent him to see us safely to Cinderhall."

"But *you* dunna need to go, Sara. Why does he not simply take the babe?"

"Thomas?" She hugged the baby to her. "Twould not be right to take him from me."

"Sara, tis no proof that you cannot bear children of your own. Just because your husband the pig did not get you with child."

"He had other children."

"Were they human?"

"Liam," she said, but his levity lightened her own mood. She loosened her grip on the baby. "Thomas is . . . Well, it *seems* as if he is mine."

"And what about his sire?"

"I will not return him to his sire. I dare not."

"Tell me you jest."

"I do not."

"God's balls." He stood up quickly, dropping her hand. "What will Haldane do?"

"If he finds me?"

"*When* he finds you," Liam corrected.

She shrugged, feeling weak. "Kill me?"

"Is he capable of that?"

She let out an unsteady breath. "I would not have thought so. During my marriage to Stephen he was very kind to me. Always considerate. They were friends. But then they went hunting together and Stephen died."

"Are ya saying Haldane killed—"

"So, Liam," said a voice from the darkness.

Liam spun about. Sara rose with a start, searching the shadows, and then, suddenly, soundlessly, an old man stepped out of the night. His dark cloak swirled around him.

"We meet again." The voice was soft and came from the midst of the old man's shadowing cowl.

"Warwick." Panic welled up in Liam.

Why was the dark wizard after Sara? And how many men did he have with him? In the darkness it was impossible to tell.

"So we have come for the same thing." The old man's words were whispered, meant for Liam's ears alone.

Liam shrugged, his mind racing as he took a casual step forward onto a low, flat rock. "Have we?" he asked.

The old man laughed, but the sound was humorless. "There is little reason to act the fool with me, and less reason to lie. Do you have it on you?"

"Do I have what?"

The old man laughed. "So you have finally learned its worth, and have no wish to discuss it anymore. I knew you would eventually." He stepped forward. "Show it to me. We shall work together, and then all men beware."

Liam shook his head, stalling. Whatever Warwick was

after, Liam didn't have it. But the ancient wizard had already made up his mind to the contrary. The best Liam could hope for was to escape and draw the brigands after him, leaving Sara unmolested. ''I don't have it. The woman does.''

For a moment the woods were silent, and then the old man laughed. ''So you are more like me than I knew—ready to sacrifice another at any time. I feared you may have been ruined. But you lie well. Thus I know the woman is of no consequence to me now.''

''But I am?''

''Oh yes. You are. Long I have wanted our talents to be united. Join me now.''

''Is this a request?''

''You can consider it that if you like.''

''Then I must decline.''

For a moment Liam sensed Warwick's frustration. But finally the old man nodded toward him. Dark shadows of men moved forward.

Liam remained relaxed even as the brigands closed in. He contained his panic as long as he could, and then he pulled the string that loosed the black powder.

He struck a spark with his shoe on the rock, and the powder exploded.

Men screamed. Smoke billowed up.

''Run!'' Liam yelled.

Chapter 11

~~~⌒⌒⌒⌒~~~

Sara bolted for the woods as terror fanned through her like wild flame.

"Get them!" shrieked Warwick.

Evil surrounded her, pursued her. She felt it like a tangible force.

Behind her, men yelled and steel clashed.

"Liam!" She screamed his name, but she dared not stop. Above the sound of Thomas wailing in his sling, she heard the crashing of brush as men followed her.

It was dark. She knew she must hide, but the terror was overwhelming. Even as she ran, she quaked. It was hopeless. She could not outrun them, could not hide. Death clawed at her back.

Her lungs ached and her legs shook. It was no use. They would kill her and the babe. She stumbled to a halt and turned, knowing she would die.

In her mind's eye, as clear as daybreak, she saw herself covered in blood, dead. No. Not dead, for she could see now that she was crawling, trying to crawl, to drag herself forward, her hands formed to bony, bloody claws. Someone laughed. She lifted her face, and she saw now that her eyes were gone!

A scream ripped up her throat. But suddenly a hand covered her mouth, muffling the sound as she was yanked backward. She screamed again, thrashing wildly as the horrible images burned through her mind. She was suffocating, dying. Her hands were caught. She ripped one free and swung wildly around to face her attacker.

Moonlight glistened in his cruel, dark eyes. She tried desperately to pull free as fear burned in her. She swung with her free hand, wildly aiming for the brigand's face. But again her blow was deflected and bumped off Thomas's head.

"Cease!"

She swung again, but this time her arm was captured.

"Cease!" growled the man. "Sara, tis me."

She fought him with desperation, terror overriding all her senses.

"Sara! Quit, before you harm the child." The words were husky, growled from between clenched teeth.

Her thrashing slowed. "Boden?" Her voice quivered as she said the name.

"Tis me, lass."

"My eyes!" she whispered, her mind still blurred by the evil that had invaded the woods. "My eyes are gone."

"Sara!" Boden shook her with some force. "The babe's life is at risk! Cease this!"

Reality streamed back in white waves. She was neither blind nor doomed. Boden was with her. She drew Thomas to her shoulder. Her hands shook as she crooned to him.

But regardless of her own panic, Thomas calmed.

"What happened?" Boden asked, his voice deep as the night that surrounded them.

"Evil." Twas the only word that seemed right. But she could not dwell on her own fear, she had to concentrate on surviving. Readjusting the sling, she settled Thomas against her back. "The old man brought evil. I felt it in my soul."

She knew she made no sense, and yet he didn't question it, as if he felt it too.

"You were followed?" He turned, peering through the darkness, his legs apart, braced, ready.

"I thought they were right behind me. It was as if . . ."

"What?" he whispered.

"It was as if they controlled my mind. Liam knew. Liam!" His memory returned with a jolt. Guilt washed over her. She had left him to die! She bolted suddenly back toward the campsite.

Boden caught her by the hand, but she fought him, trying to break free. He wrapped his arms about her, stifling her struggling, quieting her words.

"Sara." He crooned her name against her hair. "You can't go back."

"I must. Else he will surely die. They will kill him."

"How many were there?"

"Many. An army."

"How many did you see?"

Her mind was foggy, uncertain. She fought to clear it. "I dunna. Tis all unclear. They were coming. We must find Liam."

It seemed as if Boden's whistle came from a great distance away. But suddenly Mettle was there, nosing them.

"Get on my horse."

"Nay."

"Sara." He held her face between his hands, forcing her to look at him. "I will save the juggler. But only if you vow to flee at the first sign of trouble."

She shook her head.

"You must promise to ride away if trouble approaches."

"Nay."

"Sara." He shook her again. "If you are caught, they will take the baby. They will hurt him. They will kill him if you don't escape."

"Tis not fair to sacrifice Liam for Thomas. Tis not fair that you ask me to."

"But I ask it nevertheless. Only if I know you are safe will I save your friend. Do you agree?"

She nodded, and in a moment she was astride. For an instant his hand rested on her thigh, and then, like a phantom, he was gone, blended into the night shadows.

Minutes ticked by. Silence surrounded her. A twig snapped. Sara jerked Mettle about, but it was only a small animal, scurrying for cover. Her heart raced in her chest as frayed images of death and torture gnawed at her. She shoved them back.

She was safe now that Boden was near. Mettle fidgeted, mouthing his bit, his ears pricked forward. But still no sound more evil than the night woods disturbed the silence.

Where was Boden and what had happened to Liam? Perhaps even now they were lying wounded. She must find them, but what of Thomas?

Minutes slipped into the darkness. Mind-numbing fear grated on her nerves, severing her confidence.

But finally she could wait no longer. Her first loyalty was to the babe, true, but she could not teach him loyalty and courage if she had none herself.

Her hands shook as she nudged Mettle into motion. His huge body was taut with tension as he lifted his legs in mincing steps high above the bracken. Remembering the sword Boden had claimed for her, Sara drew the blade from its scabbard near the cantle. It tinged quietly as she pulled it out. Nearby, an owl called. The sound paralyzed her, and for a moment she was tempted almost beyond control to turn back. But she squeezed her legs, urging Mettle on.

He pranced cautiously forward.

Suddenly, a monster loomed over her. It was huge and horned like a giant Minotaur. Sara swung the sword with desperate strength, but the ogre caught her hand in a deadly grip. She jerked away and swung again.

"Sara. Tis me."

She cried out as she stopped the sword in mid arc.

"Boden?" she gasped, and suddenly the monster bent to drop Tilly from his shoulders and straighten to his usual height.

"You're safe." She slipped off the horse and into his arms. "I was so afraid."

"Shh." She was the essence of heaven, and for a fractured moment, he allowed himself to close his eyes and let the emotions seep into his soul. She was alive. She was well, and for this moment in time, she was his. "All is well." He breathed the words into her hair. "All is well."

"I was a coward."

"Nay, not you, lady," he whispered and drawing her closer still, he kissed her hair. "You are all bravery."

"I feared you were dead and it was my fault."

"Nay, lady, I will not die." Reaching out, he smoothed his thumb over her lips and his hand over her cheek. "I will not leave you unprotected." Her eyes were as wide as forever, as bright as hope, and he could not help but kiss her. Needs as sharp as a blade slashed through him, but he fought them back. "The brigands are gone," he said. "But they may yet return. We must go."

She opened her eyes slowly and nodded as she focused on reality. "What of Liam?"

"There's no time for questions," he said brusquely and turned away.

Tilly allowed herself to be tethered to Mettle while Sara settled the babe against her chest. Her body felt stiff as Boden hoisted her onto the charger's back. In a moment he was seated behind her. Mettle stepped off, his forelegs lifting high. The rhythm rocked them together. Darkness slipped by, carrying them from the evil. Minutes ran along.

Unable to resist, Boden wrapped an arm about Sara's waist. Peace settled slowly into his soul. But it did not last long. A warm drop slashed against Boden's hand. He glanced upward, but the sky was clear. Another drop. The truth dawned on him. Sara was crying.

"Sara?" he whispered, trying to see her face. "Are you hurt?"

She shook her head, but refused to speak.

Desperation ripped at his soul. "What's wrong?" he crooned.

"Tis Liam," she whispered. "He is dead, isn't he?"

Emotion smote Boden like a mace to his heart.

"He is dead," she surmised, barely forcing out the words. "And tis mine own fault. I should not have left him. He risked his life to save mine."

"Is that how you see it, lady? That your life was at risk while you were with me? Am I such an ogre that he must save you from me? Is that why you left me?"

"There are things you dunna understand."

"But the juggler does?"

"Long we have been friends."

"A friend would not have abandoned you."

"Abandoned me!" She turned quickly toward him. "He risked his life when he knew I was troubled." She closed her eyes and faced forward again. "Liam is not a warrior. Yet he stayed to fight so that I might escape."

"Then where is he?" The words seemed to rumble up from Boden's chest.

"Ye didna find him?" She twisted quickly back to face him, and he saw that her eyes were alight with hope. "He was not dead?"

Boden was not a stranger to his own faults, but jealousy was not generally amongst them. And yet, when he watched her eyes, so hopeful, so soulful, he could not help but wish she felt such emotion for him.

"I could find no trace of him," he said, keeping his tone even.

"He was gone?"

"Aye."

"And the others? The brigands? The old man?"

"Nothing," he said, but that was not quite true. In the

darkness, he thought he had seen a black ring on the earth. As if the area had somehow been scorched. The juggler had scrambled north from that point, and every brigand had followed him.

So why had Sara thought they had followed her?

The night wore on. Morning dawned. They found a place deep in the woods where the world could not find them. Fatigue weighed like a sack of meal on Sara's shoulders, and yet, even after Thomas was fed and settled onto a soft bed of pine needles, she couldn't sleep. Thoughts raced through her head like hounds chasing their tails, faster and faster, circling, never ending.

Leaving Mettle to forage on his own, Boden approached. She felt his eyes bore into her, and when she turned, his face was impassive, chiseled, solemn. "I have never harmed you," he said, his voice low. "You were safe with me. Why did you leave?"

For a moment she wondered if there was hurt in his tone, but that couldn't be. He was angry, frustrated maybe. After all, he had vowed to return her to Haldane, and he would not take kindly to her interference with that promise. "I had no wish to make your task more difficult."

"Difficult!" he growled and strode toward her.

She stumbled to her feet, but suddenly she was wrapped in his arms.

Sara closed her eyes against the crush of feelings. Her mind told her that she should have tried harder to escape him. But her traitorous heart was glad she had not.

She pressed her face against his chest and felt the granite strength of his arms tremble. But why?

"Were ye scared for me, sir?" she asked, and though she knew she was a fool, she hoped he might care for her as she did for him.

"Scared?" The word was muffled against her hair. "I am a knight!"

She smiled just a little against his chest. "Were ye scared?"

"I thought I had lost you for all time." He whispered the words.

"That will never happen," she murmured, for in that moment, she knew that none other would ever win her heart.

"What?" He eased her out to arm's length and stared into her eyes. "What did you say?"

She shouldn't have spoken, shouldn't have even hinted at her feelings for him. "I said, we must not let this happen." His loyalties lay with Lord Haldane. Twas his duty to take her and Thomas to the duke. Twas hers to make certain that did not happen. And how could she do that if she allowed herself to love this man?

"We must think of Lord Haldane."

The reminder seemed to pull his arms from her. He stood back. "Do you love him, Sara?"

There was pain in his eyes. More than anything in the world, she wanted to erase that pain, to tell him the truth. But what would happen then? His future, his fortune, lay with the duke. She would not rob him of that.

"I am but his knight, pledged to him," Boden said. "But you . . . You are a lady, nobly born, gently reared. What hold has he on you?"

She searched for an answer. "I owe him much."

"For what? What favor would be worthy of the prize of your body?" he murmured. "Did he save you from Stephen? Did he buy your loyalty by killing your husband?"

"Nay! Lord Haldane did not kill Stephen. He was killed by a deer."

"Are you certain?"

Could Haldane have planned Stephen's death? The duke had made no pretense about his feelings for her. But he was a kind man, far above murder. Wasn't he? But if he was kind, why did she hope to keep his son from him?

"If the truth be known, I would think no less of Haldane if I knew he had killed your husband. I but regret I did not do the deed—''

''He didn't kill Stephen.''

''Then why are you loyal to him?'' Boden asked. ''Do you love him?''

Nay, she did not love the duke. But would it not be far safer if Boden believed otherwise? If he knew she did not plan to return to Knolltop, surely he would watch her more closely and she would have no chance to escape into the safe folds of the Highlands. But if he thought her devoted to Haldane, wouldn't the feelings that sparked between them be easier to douse?

''I love him,'' she lied.

The muscles clenched in Boden's jaw. ''Then why did you leave me? Surely I am your quickest means of reaching Knolltop. Is my company so heinous?''

''Nay,'' she murmured. ''Your company is so tempting.'' Dear God, she should never have admitted the truth.

''Tempting?'' he asked, his tone cautious.

She could not admit her feelings for him. She could not!

''Well!'' She laughed. The sound was harsh. ''The duke may be rich and powerful, but he will never match your physical allure. Thus far I have been true to my lord. Indeed, I tried to leave you rather than betray his trust.''

''So you see me as a stud to be mounted and nothing more.''

''Nay,'' she said, and though her face flushed, she forced herself to go on. ''Not nothing more. But I fear once I've ridden, I may never be content to walk again.''

Boden stared at her in silence, then, turning on his heel, he strode into the woods.

Chapter 12

It seemed as if they rode forever. Rarely did Boden speak. Sara could do nothing but go along, and try to pretend she didn't care. But always it seemed that she could feel Boden's gaze on her, watching, assessing.

Twas on the third evening when he finally spoke.

"When I found you in the woods, you were terrified," he said. "Why?"

She rose to her feet, feeling terrified now, afraid that for as long as she lived she would never find another that would make her heart pound like he did, never long to look into a man's face as she did his. She pushed the thoughts aside, needing to think of something else—anything.

"I canna explain it," she said. "I was there with Liam and Thomas. Just the three of us, and suddenly it came." She shuddered with the memory, for even now terror struck her heart.

"What came?" he urged.

"I canna explain it."

"Try."

Since she had told him she loved Haldane, his tone had never changed from that which he used right now. Cool, remote, as though he spoke to a complete stranger. As if their lives had not been entwined, as if she had no reason to love him. She shut the thought from her mind.

"Evil came. Ye canna understand the fear," she murmured.

"Tis true," he said, his tone caustic. "I cannot understand fear. After all, I am a—"

"A knight!" she finished for him, anger exploding within her. She clenched her fists at her sides. "Aye. You are a knight, trained, nay, *born* for battle."

"Or born to tan hides."

"What?"

"Tis nothing," he said, turning away.

"What did ye say?"

He swung back, his body rigid, his eyes ablaze. "I was born to a drunken tanner and a mother who would sooner run off with a peddler than be near me."

"But ye are a knight," she said, breathless with surprise. "Surely, ye must be of noble birth."

He shrugged. The anger dulled a bit in his eyes. "Tis sorry I am you could not have been rescued by someone more prominent."

She stared at him in amazement. Sir Boden Blackblade was the epitome of knighthood.

"Part of what I told you was true regarding Lord Haldane's scalp. Although the duke has no birthmark there. I only said that to force you to admit that the child was his. Tis what the common man does," he said, and shrugged. "He lies. But twas the truth about the head wound. Haldane was injured in battle. In fact I was there when it happened."

"Ye saved his life," she said, certain somehow that she was right.

"Twas not intentional, I assure you."

Silence dwelled between them for a moment.

"I myself have a tendency to accidentally save the lives of dukes," she said.

"You think I lie?"

"Aye."

He cocked a dark brow at her. "Nearly five and ten I was when I became a soldier for the duke. They give you very little training you know, but it didn't matter. I had a spear. Surely that was enough, I thought. I had reached nearly my full height, and it made me feel like a man.

"The duke was a powerful presence. Few people thought it wise to anger him. But when they did, the problems could generally be resolved with nothing more than a skirmish. When you have a host of mounted knights behind you, you gain a good deal of respect.

"I had been in Haldane's employ for over a year when the trouble started. Twas at harvest time when rents are due. The Welsh are not ones to give up their goods without a grumble. Haldane owns a fair-sized estate near the coast. It seems the villeins took offense to paying an Englishman's taxes. Normally, a lord would simply send his army to take care of the problem, but Haldane was healthier in those days and very lordly; twas not uncommon that his mere presence would settle a dispute.

"The Welsh though . . ." He shook his head, remembering. "We were a small garrison of men. Haldane was safely surrounded by a handful of knights. The villains . . ." He chuckled without humor. "They were farmers, really, armed with nothing but their harvesting tools. But still I thought myself a fine soldier when they were on the run. We followed them between the bundles of hay they had stacked together, running, yelling our battle cries, blood lust pumping through our veins. The mounted knights followed, too. They had just passed me when, from behind each stack of hay, a host of Welshmen sprung from hiding. The farmers turned to fight. Our men were well mounted and well armed, but the Welshmen had rage on their side and now our knights fell like ripe apples in a storm. I saw them go down. God's mercy!" he whispered. "Blood was everywhere. The screams of the dying! I could barely breathe for the smell of death. Never had I seen ought like that. My stomach curdled. I couldn't think. Fear turned my muscles to pudding and my mind to straw. I wanted nothing but to be gone from the killing or to die trying. I think for a time

I was insane. I didn't realize the duke had been thrown from his horse and cut his head, nor that his retinue of guards was gone. Neither did I care. In my haste I stumbled over Haldane. By the time I'd righted myself, the Welsh had surrounded me. Twas nothing to do but kill or be killed.'' He drew a deep breath. "Tis a strange thing what muscles of pudding and a mind of straw can do when one is cornered.'' He shrugged. "When the haze cleared from my eyes we were surrounded by dead Welshmen and Lord Haldane was dubbing me a knight.''

"Bravery comes sometimes when one least expects it,'' she said quietly.

"Aye, bravery,'' he scoffed. "I lost my breakfast moments later.''

She took a single step forward. "Ye were but a lad,'' she said. "Surely ye dunna blame yourself for your fear.''

She watched him tighten one hand into a fist. "Nay. Certainly not. I am a knight now. We are without fear, you know. Tis not allowed to hurl before a battle.''

This was a side of him she had not seen—had not been allowed to see. Was this the real Boden? she wondered, the man who abhorred killing and feared death. Or was the invincible knight the true man?

"Would a tanner's life have been so bad?'' she asked, trying to place him.

"Tis a strange thing about me,'' Boden said. "I like to eat, and Father and I did not see eye to eye. Twas not me who was his apprentice.''

Again she saw the boy with the dark moppet of unruly hair. How could a father disregard such a gentle, lovable lad, leaving him with no options but to kill for a living? "Not every gentle man is gently borne,'' she murmured.

He laughed at her implication. "And not every gentle woman wishes to see the truth,'' he said.

"And what is the truth, Sir Knight?''

For a moment, she thought he might speak, might tell

her who he truly was, might open up like an eagle on the wind.

But suddenly the curtain to his thoughts closed. "I have been sent by Lord Haldane to bring you safely to his side," he said. "I cannot do that if I do not know what I am up against. Who is after you?"

"Evil!" She breathed the word.

"What does that mean?"

"I dunna know," she said, frustration and fear spurring her emotions, fatigue weighing her mind. "I am not a knight, trained to battle. I but know what I felt. And I felt evil. Tis sorry I am if that seems strange."

"This juggler of yours, who is he?"

She raised her brows at his choice of words. "A friend. From Ireland, he is."

"A witch?"

"Nay! Hardly that! Why would ye slander him?"

"And why would you defend him?" he shot back. "Why did he take you? How did he take you?"

"He is clever and he is quick," she said, then lowered her gaze and steadied her breathing. Boden's closeness did dangerous things to her equilibrium. "And he thought I needed saving."

"Why? From what?"

"I canna say what was in Liam's mind," she said.

"If you did not know what was in his mind, why did you go with him?"

"I told ye, he is a friend."

"And what am I?"

What indeed? "He must have thought you meant to harm me. Perhaps, seeing Thomas in my arms, Liam reasoned that Caroline was dead and that I was, therefore, in danger."

"And you think him better able to protect you than I?"

Certainly. For how could Boden protect her heart when he was the very man who threatened to steal it. When he was the man who made her heart run wild and her mind turn to oatmeal. When his smile made her melt and the touch of his hand made her giddy. Dear Lord, what was wrong with her? Twas not like her to swoon at the sight of a brawny muscle, not at the best of times, and certainly not now, when her very life demanded that she keep her wits.

"I had best get some sleep," she said, and though she took a step backward, she found she could not wrest her gaze from his face.

He stepped forward with her. "The evil you felt, mayhap it was from the Irishman?"

"Liam? Nay. Twas from the old man." She shuddered, though she wasn't cold. "Warwick."

"Warwick?" Sir Boden shook his head. "Who is he? You've not mentioned him before."

"I dunna know." Confusion set her mind atremble. "I must have heard Liam say his name. Tis all I can remember."

"Why would the old man wish you harm if you don't even know him? You thought he followed you, but all the tracks followed the juggler."

"Ye think I am insane," she murmured.

"I but need the answers if I am to keep you safe."

"Well, I have no answers." She turned away, but he caught her arm.

"The juggler," he said, his tone low. "Did he take you by force?"

"Take me?" she asked, narrowing her eyes and canting her head at the possible double meaning.

She watched his face darken. A muscle tightened in his jaw, flexing the scar that lifted his lips into the parody of a smile.

"Did you go with him of your own will?" he asked finally.

Is that what he had meant or was he implying something more base? "I went willingly," she said, lifting her chin slightly.

"Why?" he snapped.

"Have I not told you already?"

"Oh, aye!" He laughed. "I am so alluring you could no longer hold yourself from me."

The night fell silent.

"Is that so hard to believe?"

"Aye. It is."

"Not for me," she whispered.

"Why did you go with him?" he repeated, his tone level now.

"I have no reason to trust ye," she murmured.

"What has happened to the good old days when saving a damsel's life meant something?"

She snorted. "Aye. Ye saved me life. But why?

"Beside Caroline's dying body I found a piece of a black, metal snake. A snake identical to the one on your sword."

"Nay!" he said.

"Aye. Explain that, Sir Knight. Explain anything. I am being followed. Why? My life is threatened. I dunna know why. Ye think that makes me trusting?"

He opened his mouth to speak, but she raised her hand and hurried on.

"I have watched my friends die. I have fought the brigands myself, and still I know not why. What are they after?" She felt desperation rising. "I have not riches for them to gain at my expense. I have not power. Why do they follow me?"

A moment of silence stood between them, and then he reached out, seemingly against his will to touch her face. "What man would not die to possess you?" he asked softly.

She closed her eyes to his touch. "I am no great beauty, neither refined nor regal."

"You are like sunshine," he said. "Like balm to an open wound."

"Sir—" she said, trying to catch her wits.

"What man would not give his life to have you for his own, if only for a minute?"

His fingertips grazed her cheek. She shivered at the touch. Against her will, her eyes fell closed.

"Your skin is like velvet," he whispered. "Rich and soft. Your hair . . ." His fingers slipped into her loose tresses, skimming beneath it to smooth across her scalp with splayed fingers. "Tis like moonlight spun in strands of gold. Who would not gladly die to touch you? Who would not give his soul to kiss you?" he asked, and suddenly his lips met hers.

Desire seared through her body. Sweetness flooded her soul. Her arms wrapped around him of their own accord. She tilted her face up to his and now he was kissing her cheek, her brow, her eyelids. Feelings as bright as rainbows arched through her. She knew she should pull away, retreat. She opened her mouth to speak, but suddenly he was kissing her again and she could do naught but kiss him back.

Time ceased. Their heartbeats melded. He slid his fingers down her throat, shooting sparks from the contact until they lay against Dragonheart. Suddenly their thoughts entwined, and for one wild moment truth arced between them like lightning.

"Lady." He breathed the word against her face. "You lie. You don't love Haldane. Do you?"

Reality snapped her back with the force of impending death. She jerked away, breathing hard. "I am sorry." She touched her lips, feeling the bruise, the fire. "I did not mean to do that. There is something wrong with me. I shouldn't have."

He took a slow step forward, his eyes alight. "There is naught wrong with you. But that you lied."

"Nay. I did not." Panic was rising. She could not love this man. He was Lord Haldane's knight, pledged to protect and serve. What would happen to him if he reneged? "I am loyal to my lord."

"Aye, you are loyal. But do you love him? You must not," he said, answering his own query. "You must not or you would not have kissed me as you did," he said and stepped closer still.

Her back bumped up against a tree. She lifted a hand as if she might fend him off, but he pressed his chest up against it, daring her to touch him.

"I dunna deny that ye move me," she whispered. "For ye are bold and ye are beautiful, but that doesna mean—"

"What? That you cannot love another and still desire me?"

Beneath her hand, she could feel the heat of his flesh, but she managed to nod.

"So again you try to convince me that you are the kind of woman to cherish one man and desire another?" he asked, his eyes aflame with emotion.

"Aye."

"You must think me a terrible fool," he said and leaning forward, he kissed her again.

Lightning seared her lips. Desire flashed like flame across her mind. Dear lord, she could not resist. But she must.

"Nay!" She squirmed out of his arms, breathing hard and backing away. "Nay. I canna do this."

Boden watched her. He was a man fully gown, a score and six years of age, and never in all that time had he felt what he was feeling now. Oh yes, women had always drawn him. Everything about them intrigued him, every small difference between him and them fascinated him, the softness of their skin, the silky length of their hair, how their hips flared and their lips pouted. Their clothing, their voices, their scents. And the more noble the woman, the further above him they seemed, the more he was impressed. But Sara was not regal and elegant like the women of court. Nay. She was like the earth, giving and wholesome. Like the sun, bright and warm. Like no one but herself, and never had he been willing to give up everything for another's touch. "You don't love him, lady. Say it."

"Nay!"

Frustration consumed him. "Say it!" he demanded, stepping forward.

"Nay!" she cried and pivoting on her heel, raced into the woods.

He lunged after her, but in a moment he stopped. Jesus! What had he done? He had no right to take her as his own. He had no wish to incur Lord Haldane's wrath.

He must think. Running his hand through his hair, he tried to do just that, to forget the bright color of her eyes, the velvet softness of her skin. She was not a panacea that would cure all his ills. She was but a woman, tender, soft, pleasurable, true. But just a woman, once touched and soon forgotten. But in his mind he knew twas not true. He would not forget her. She was not the kind of woman a man used and abandoned. She was the kind of woman to save a man's soul. The kind a man married. But surely Haldane was not planning marriage, for he had already taken a wife.

Then why could Boden not have her for himself? Because he was naught but Haldane's servant, with nothing to show for his service. Nothing, unless he returned Sara and the babe to the duke's household. But she did not belong there, like a whore to spread herself beneath him. She did not love him. That he knew—felt it in his heart. He was certain . . .

Suddenly, her scream shattered the night.

Boden ripped Adder from its sheath and spun about. Dear God, what had he done?

Chapter 13

~~~❧~~~

"You have not changed your mind about returning the babe to his father?" Liam asked. He had propped one foot casually upon a rock as he absently sharpened two knives, one against the other. Their razor sharp blades gleamed in the light of the nearby fire as Sara watched him.

The day had come and gone, passed in a fog of emotion and fatigue. How the Irishman had found her, Sara couldn't say. But he had, and with his usual aplomb he had taken her again. The scream she'd heard had been his, and yet, somehow, he'd made it sound more like hers than her own. It had scared the wits from her, but in a moment she had heard Boden crashing off in that direction. A heartbeat later, Liam had whisked her away.

The babe! She had to get the babe! she had cried, but Liam shushed her protests and in a moment she saw that Thomas was already sound asleep in Liam's narrow wagon. Tilly was tied in a corner munching on God-knew-what, and though Sara protested, Liam tethered Mettle to the tailgate, saying twould surely slow down the warlord to make him go afoot.

Sara couldn't argue with that logic, and after Liam promised to make certain the charger was eventually returned to his owner, Sara fell silent.

A mismatched pair of geldings pulled the wagon.

168

Shaggy steeds they were and none too tall, but beneath their hirsute hides pumped blood as blue as royalty. They had run like the wind, swift and sure in the darkness, until Sir Boden was left far behind.

Twas good, of course. Twas as it had to be.

Sara stared into the fire, feeling as though her heart had been ripped from her chest.

"Nay, dear Liam, I have not changed my mind," Liam said, mimicking her higher tone. "And have I thanked ye for saving me from the dread warlord?

"Well, nay, wee lass, you have not.

"Then let me do so now, sweet Liam. Let me tell you how clever you are. Never have I known a man half so clever. You are surely the cleverest—"

"Were ye saying something?" Sara asked, drawing her attention from the flames with a start.

Overhead, thunder rumbled, threatening rain.

Liam's gaze was steady on her face, his expression soft. "You still plan to keep the child from Haldane?"

"I have no choice," Sara said. "I made a vow to keep him safe."

"And yer certain he would not be safe with his sire?"

She stood quickly. She'd fallen asleep in the wagon and now felt fidgety and restless. "I wish to God I knew, Liam. But I dunna and I dare not take a chance. Not when the nightmares plague me so." She paced, wishing she could sleep again, wishing she could lie down and wake to find that it was all no more than a horrible dream. "What am I to do?"

Their gazes met. A slash of lightning scarred the sky and faded.

"About the babe?" he asked.

She closed her eyes. "I must take him to the Highlands. And there, somehow, I will find a way to keep him safe."

"And will his father not come after him?"

"He sent the mother away," she said, wringing her

hands. "He did not want her. Does he, then, deserve the child?"

"Mayhap the question is not whether he deserves him, but whether he will take him, sweet Sara."

"He does not need the babe. He does not *want* him!" she said, her tone desperate.

"Not as much as you do?" he asked softly.

"Aye." She faced him in the darkness. "Not as much as I do."

"Will ya hide him away and raise him to manhood in secret then?" Liam asked. "Will ya deny him his birthright?"

She paused, letting the silence settle in. "I made a vow."

"And what of the warlord? He doesn't seem the kind to give up with a shrug and trot home."

Sara's heart pinched painfully. "Aye. What indeed shall I do about Boden?"

Liam's gaze was as steady as the sea. Without looking up he tossed a blade into the air. Fire flashed along its edge. Seemingly without thought, he caught it by the handle. "I could kill him for you."

"Nay!" Sara gasped, jerking toward Liam. "Nay! Ye would not!"

"That depends." He straightened, glaring into her eyes. "Did he harm ya, lass?"

"Nay!" she breathed, calming herself. "Never."

"Did he . . ." Liam paused and for a moment he gritted his teeth as though unable to go on. "Did he dishonor ya?"

"Nay, he did not." She turned toward the fire again. "But I nearly dishonored myself."

"So you love him," Liam said.

"No!" Terror spurred through her heart.

"Then let me kill him."

"He's done naught to deserve death."

"He's a knight, lass, trained to kill, surely there's something in his past that deserves death."

"Liam!" She grabbed his arm, feeling panic wash her like a cold wave, feeling her hands shake as she took hold. "I beg of you! Please! Dunna harm him."

"He will follow ya, Sara. He will try to take ya back."

"Ye took his horse," she reminded.

"But he'll come. He will take the babe."

Her fingers tightened in his sleeve. "Promise me, Liam. Promise ye will not harm him."

"Even for the babe's sake?"

"Promise me!"

Liam was silent for a moment, then, "He's a lucky man," he said softly, "to *not* be loved by ya."

"Please promise," she whispered.

Liam shook his head and chuckled softly as he dropped his foot from the rock and grinned at her. "I'm flattered by your faith in me, lass. But think on it," he said, covering her hand with his own. "How would I kill him? He's as big as a tree and solid as a rock. I'm a magician, not an executioner."

She relaxed her grip and tried to draw in a steady breath. "Then I have your word?"

"What have I ever done to make you think I would do ought against your wishes?"

Sara forced herself to relax and turn their attention from the knight that haunted her thoughts. "Do I disremember or did ye not once fill my bed with toads?"

Liam grinned, lifting that smile that, once upon a time, had made two wee cousins swear each would be the one to marry him. Strangely enough, it had made the third swear to see him hanged.

"I thought twas *Rachel's* pallet," he said.

"Never will I understand your dislike for each other."

His expression sobered and he turned away. "I did not say I disliked her," he said softly.

"Nay. I believe *detest* was the word ye used."

"Well, aye, *detest*, but not dislike."

"I do not understand ye, Liam," she said.

He turned back, his green eyes steady. "Aye. And you don't love the warlord."

"What do ye mean by that?"

"Nothing."

"Do ye mean to say ye have feelings for Rachel?"

"Shh," Liam said, and suddenly he was crouching, staring into the shadows as if the very devil was there, watching from the darkness.

Sara froze. Fear streaked up her spine, freezing her muscles.

Liam turned, quick and quiet as a snake. She watched him. He turned again, listening for a long while. But finally he straightened slightly.

Sara dared a careful breath. "What?" She breathed the word.

He lifted the two knives to his lips in a signal for silence, then vanished into the woods.

Sara finally took a step toward Thomas. He was sound asleep. Bending, she tucked a blanket more closely about him, then pulled her small dagger from its sheath at her side. But never did her gaze leave the woods.

What had Liam heard? And where was he? Eternity passed on grinding wheels. How long had he been gone?

Lightning crashed behind her, and suddenly a man's shadow towered dark and high above her. She pivoted with a scream in her throat.

"Don't scream," Liam warned, shrinking back to his normal size as the light abated. "Even with the thunder it might be heard."

She drew in breaths like a winded steed, trying to calm her heart. "By whom?"

Liam grinned. "Who knows? Mayhap your warlord be a hell of a runner."

"Is it Warwick ye fear?"

His hand covered her mouth in less than an instant. "Don't say that name."

She stared at him, her heart still pounding in her chest, her mind boggled. His hand slipped away.

"My apologies, lass," he murmured, and chuckled, but the tone was strained. "Tis a bit jumpy I am."

But Liam was never jumpy. Conniving, yes. Twas always true. But not jumpy.

"Who is he?" Sara whispered.

"Tis someone to be avoided."

"Liam, dunna treat me like a child. Who is he? Why did I feel . . ." She paused, searching for words.

"Terror?" he asked. "Despair?"

She nodded.

"Tis because he deals in terror," Liam whispered. "He *is* despair."

Prickly fingers of fear crept up Sara's spine. She turned her head slowly to peer into the shadows behind her, but there was no one there.

"Ye are making no sense, Liam. Surely he is naught but an old man. But what is he after?"

"In all honesty, I dunna know, lass." Thunder grumbled. "Mayhap ya would have been safer with the warlord." Lightning slashed overhead again. Liam lifted his hand, and suddenly, as if by magic, the amulet fell from her neck and into his palm. "Tell me, have you worn Dragonheart every day since I gave him to ya?"

"Why?" she asked, feeling the hair stand upright on the back of her neck. It prickled against her collar. "What has that to do with Warwick?"

"Hush," he breathed. "I warned you not to speak his name."

"Liam!"

"I'm sorry." He turned away, curling his fist about Dragonheart. "I don't mean to frighten ya, lass, but there are some things I must know."

She nodded.

"Have you been wearing the amulet faithfully?"

"Aye. Every day since ye gave it to me, just before I left for London."

"And have you been safe?"

"Liam, whatever are ye—"

"Please, lass!" His knives had disappeared and now he grasped her hand in his. "Answer me."

"Since leaving Scotland the world has gone insane, Liam."

He scowled. "But *you*, you have been safe?"

"Aye," she said slowly. "I have not been harmed. Why?"

"Even when the brigands attacked?"

"Nay."

"And *he* . . ." Liam said softly. "*He* has not appeared?"

"Ye mean—"

"Don't say his name. He is a sorcerer, Sara. Some call him the dark wizard. Don't let his age nor his seeming frailty fool ya. Tis said the king himself ordered him to be blinded and burned for his witchcraft. But somehow he escaped, and now he is more powerful and more evil than ever."

She laughed nervously, wondering if he was merely telling her another story to frighten her as he was wont to do when they were children.

"There's much we do not know, Sara. Much we take for granted. He is a sorcerer. Take that to mean what you will. But don't doubt that he is dangerous."

"Liam, ye canna be serious."

"I am as serious as death, lass. More serious. For he can do more than take your life."

"Was it he who sent the first brigands?"

"I dunna know."

"What did they want? Why me?"

Liam shook his head in uncertainty. "He hungers for power as a starving man hungers for bread. He will do anything, work for anyone so long as it feeds his appetite." He opened his palm to gaze into the dragon's ruby eye. "Tis said the old man has made kingdoms fall and princes rise from nothingness."

"But I have no kingdom," she whispered. "No power. What is he after?"

"Has anyone asked you about Dragonheart, Sara?"

"Nay. None but Boden."

Liam's gaze snapped to her. "And the warlord," he said softly, "did he try to take it?"

"Nay. Of course not. Liam, what are ye talking about? Why these questions?"

"Will you do me a favor, Sara?" he asked. "For me, for the past we have shared?"

She caught her breath. "Liam, if ye want the amulet, just take it. Tis yours."

"Nay!" He pressed it quickly toward her. "Nay, I don't want it. I would ask that you wear it always. But keep it hidden, perhaps against your back."

"Hidden?" she asked, taking it from him.

"Don't tell anyone about it. Wear it against the heat of your skin."

"Ye make no sense. Please. Tell me what this has to do with Warwick!"

But the last word was lost in a crash of thunder. Lightning scoured the sky to white-hot intensity.

Something screamed! And there against the white sky stood a black-cloaked man.

"Nay!" Liam shrieked. His knives sang toward the monster.

There was a roar of pain from their attacker, and suddenly he swept toward them.

Lightning flashed, illuminating everything.

There was a bang, a puff of smoke, and then Liam was gone.

Chapter 14

⌒⌒◯◯⌒⌒

The monster careened to a halt.

Sara was too terrified to move, too shocked to think. But suddenly the lightning retreated, reducing the villain to his normal size and shape as Boden's cape settled back around him.

"Boden?"

He held his sword ready as he turned in a crouched position. "Where is he?" he growled.

"How did you find me?"

"Where is he?" he snarled.

"Liam? He is gone!" she said. But where? She shifted her gaze toward the woods, seeing the blood lust in the knight's eyes and hoping the Irishman would stay gone.

"He abandoned you?" Boden's voice was very low, little more than a growl. "He left you again?"

It sure looked like it. She glanced about, making certain they were alone.

"Liam wounded ye by accident. He thought ye were the wizard. Please, let me tend ye," she said, touching his arm.

He pressed her hand to his flesh. "Do you love him?" he whispered.

"How did ye find me? We took Mettle."

His eyes blazed in the light of the fire. "Do you love him?"

Her heart ached. The world stopped turning. There was nothing to see but his eyes. Nothing to think about but that he had come for her. But she could not tell him that, for if the truth were spoken what chance would she have to fight it? She lowered her gaze, trying to hide the truth.

"Get the babe and get on the horse," he said, his voice very low.

"Nay." She whispered the word. "I canna. I must stay with Liam."

"He abandoned you. Left you to me, not knowing . . ." His words careened to a halt. His eyes blazed in the firelight. "I am not a noble man, lady. You will come with me, or I swear I will kill him."

Sara felt the air press from her lungs. There was nothing to do, nothing, but go with him.

The rain came down in curtains of hard, cold gray. Night gave way to grim daybreak, and still they rode on, stopping for nothing.

Under Sara's cape, inside his pouch, Thomas slept on. Tilly followed along behind. Sara sat miserably crouched atop Mettle who flinched with each crack of lightning. Boden was silent, saying nothing, barely moving.

He would have killed Liam. Killed him! she reminded herself. She didn't know this man. And yet she was bound to him, as was Thomas. What was she to do? She must escape before they reached Lord Haldane, but what chance did she have against this warrior? Even without his steed he had found her. Something swelled in her heart, but she refused to acknowledge it. He had not followed out of love, but out of duty, she reminded herself. Yet even now she could feel the well-honed muscles of his chest as he pressed into her, the indomitable strength of his arms as they surrounded her.

He leaned harder, and then she felt him tremble. It was difficult to turn, for he was pressing her forward, but she did so, and found that his eyes were closed.

"Boden."

He awoke with a jolt and a grumble.

"Ye were asleep. Are ye well?"

"Aye," he said.

Rain streamed down his face. Who could sleep in the rain?

"Are ye certain?"

"Aye," he repeated, but now she felt him shiver.

She pressed the back of her hand to his brow. Heat seared her fingers and she gasped. "You're fevered."

"Nay." He shook off her hand. "Just tired."

"Ye are sick," she repeated. Fear made her voice taut. "We must get ye out of the rain."

His eyes dropped closed again. "Mayhap ye brought your father's castle, that we might rest there," he said.

She couldn't tell if he was delirious or just sarcastic.

"Are you all right?"

"Aye. I try to slice myself up twice a week at the least. Truth be known . . ." His head lolled back slightly. "Your lover did me a favor. Now I won't have to go to the trouble."

"Boden!" she said, catching him as he listed to the right. "Wake up."

"I'm awake!" he said, righting himself. He narrowed his eyes, then lowered them to gaze at her. "St. Aidan's arse, you're beautiful."

"And you're delirious," she said.

One corner of his mouth lifted in unison to his hand. His palm felt hot against her cheek. "Strange that you don't believe me."

Fear was rising in her. She couldn't be responsible for this man. But neither could she turn her back on him. Panic welled up.

"Why do you not believe me, lady?" he whispered, his eyes falling closed again. "With all the men that desire you? But mayhap I am the only one who will die for you."

"Dunna say that!"

His eyes snapped open in surprise. "*Would*. I meant I

am the only man who *would* die for you. Lord Haldane . . ." He gazed over her head and fell silent. "I wonder, how could he bear to send you from his side. How could he bear it, even for his wife?" He lowered his gaze to hers. "Though she is young and comely. There are those who call her a saint."

"And there are those who call her a witch," Sara said, remembering Caroline's words, but immediately feeling guilty for repeating them. She was not usually prone to jealousy. "Which one are ye, Sir Knight?" she asked.

His gaze didn't shift, but his tone was slurred. "She looked like a dark angel when she came to me. But not . . ." He shook his head, remembering. "Not like you. Her eyes . . ." His voice trailed off. "They didn't speak of heaven. Still, she was lovely. But I have been loyal to Lord Haldane," he said. "Always loyal. Despite everything. Twas the one thing I have been."

What was he talking about? She tried to form a question, but he spoke again.

"The juggler left you, lady."

"Is it me or are ye obsessed with that fact, Boden?"

"I am obsessed," he murmured, his gaze unwavering.

"Does it seem so strange to ye that he would choose to save his life?"

He chuckled. The sound seemed hollow. "Nay. Not strange atall. Tis a coward's way to think of his own safety first. You can trust me to know this."

Beneath her hand, she felt his muscles tense as he struggled to straighten in the saddle.

"He thought ye were Warwick," she said softly. "Mayhap when he saw it was ye, he decided I was safer at your side than his."

"Then mayhap he is a fool," he whispered, and slipped sideways.

Sara shrieked, trying to hold him upright, but finally abandoned him lest she be pulled off and land atop him.

Boden crumpled like an autumn leaf, then slid to the earth beneath Mettle's huge hooves.

"Boden! Dear God! Boden!" she cried, jumping to the ground.

He lay unconscious, his head cocked at an odd angle, one leg bent beneath him. And suddenly she realized that the lower half of his cloak was soaked in watery blood.

She tore her gaze away. "Please, Boden." She touched his face. Raindrops splattered on his closed lids. "Wake up."

"You do not love Lord Haldane." He opened his eyes and grumbled the words, as if that were the only thought that was clear in his blurry mind.

"Ye must get up, Boden. I will find somewhere warm for ye to rest and mend."

"Tell me," he whispered. "Tell me the truth."

"Mettle waits and worries. He does not seem to like the rain. Please get up."

"Never have I met a woman like you. Never have I thought I would want to. Tell me the truth, lady. I need to know."

Sara glanced at Mettle. He stood with drooping head, his eyes showing their white rims through the holes of his armor. "Mount your steed and I will answer ye."

"You swear it, lady. You'll tell me the truth?"

"When have I ever lied to ye?"

He snorted. "Just after you tried to kill me."

"Get on the horse."

"This isn't some pathetic attempt to keep me alive is it?"

She laughed. The sound was very close to a sob. "Nay!"

"Twould be a kindness to leave me to die, you know."

"Dunna say such a thing. Please. Get up."

"All right then." He moved his limbs, failed to sit, but managed to straighten his head and glance crookedly at Mettle. "God's bones, that horse is big."

"He hasn't grown," she promised, taking his hale arm and trying to pull him to his feet. "I swear it."

"You never know." He sucked air through his teeth as he sat up. "He eats like a horse."

"He is a horse," she blathered, trying to keep him distracted.

Twas the devil's own battle getting him on his feet, but she managed. He braced his legs and held himself up with the fingers of his right hand tangled in Mettle's mane.

"Up now," she urged after a breather.

He leaned against the steed's side. "You're a very cruel woman. Have I mentioned that?"

"Last time ye were wounded."

"Which was because of you, as I recall."

"Up now," she said again, and miraculously, he mounted, though his face went gray with the effort.

"Tell me now. Do you love Haldane?"

Worry left no room for lies. "I owe him me gratitude," she said. "Mayhap, I owe him me very life. But I dunna love him."

He stared at her for an eternity, then let his eyes fall closed. "Maybe I'll decide to live a bit longer."

The rain continued forever. Several hours after noon they came to a road. Sara pulled Mettle to a halt. Thomas slept in his sling against the aching middle of her back. Mud was splattered halfway up the skirt of her gown. It hung heavy and scratchy, but she had no time to think about that. Boden sat hunched in the saddle, bent like a weary old man over the pommel. He needed attention. He needed rest, and he needed it soon. But where could she go? Would they be safe on the open road?

She had no answers, only questions and nagging worries. So she closed her eyes for a moment and prayed with deep ferocity. Finally, needing to do *something*, and feeling no particular divine direction, she turned Mettle to the left and trudged down the muddy trail.

It was nearly dusk when she saw the pale peak of a

church rise from the green hills ahead. Just before night-fall she came to the village.

"Who goes there?" someone called from the far side as she approached the gate.

Fatigue weighed on her like a millstone. "I am called Bernadette. Please let us in." It seemed all she could manage to say.

"Who is with you?"

"He is a knight," she said, steadying him with a hand to his thigh. "Badly wounded and in great need."

There was a buzz of voices, but in a moment the gate creaked open.

"Thank ye," she said, leading Mettle through.

"You've no need to thank me," said the gatekeeper. "We've no psychic here in Cheswick, and your husband looks unwell."

"Is there an inn?" she asked. "Somewhere out of the rain?"

They directed her down the muddy, rutted street. Met-tle stopped finally and let his head droop. Steadying Boden again, Sara rushed to the door. "Sir Boden is badly wounded," she said. "Please, have ye a room to let?" she asked the man that appeared there.

He was a big man, stooped, graying. His gaze skimmed her. "Not for the likes of a bloody Scot," he said, and moved to close the door.

Rage roared to life in Sara's breast, and suddenly she had a foot in the door and one hand clutched the man's tunic. Her other reached for her dagger. It slid from its sheath and in a moment it pricked his neck.

His gasp rattled up his throat as he tilted his head back. A dark droplet of blood seeped away from the pinpoint blade.

"In the past fortnight I have been thrice attacked by brigands," she said. "They are dead. I am not. Ye know us bloody Scots. We're a vindictive lot."

The innkeeper swallowed.

"The knight is badly wounded. Have ye a room to let?"

"Aye." The single word squeaked out. "Aye, one room for the good knight and his lovely lady."

Not for an instant did Sara consider trying to explain their circumstances. "Then we will take it."

"Good. Good." His head was still cocked back, his eyes very wide as he tried to see the point of the blade. "Can I help you get my lord to his room?"

"Aye." She drew the dagger slowly away and stepped back. "That would be appreciated."

Between herself and the innkeeper, they dragged Boden upstairs to a room. He groaned as they eased him onto the bed.

The innkeeper backed away. "Is there ought else you need, m'lady?"

"Aye." Still sitting on the bed, she turned to him, vaguely realizing that she must look like Satan incarnate, for she certainly felt like it. "We need spirits to help him warm up, and we need them immediately. We need a bathing tub, hot water, and a warm meal." She struggled to her feet and eased Thomas's pack from around her neck. After one quick glance inside, she laid him carefully on the bed. "We need extra blankets, bandages, and a kettle."

"Aye, m'lady." He bobbed again, still sweating. "Anything else?"

"Someone to take care of the animals."

The innkeeper shifted his gaze sideways. "I'd be happy to see to such a proud beast," he said, and turned away.

Sara scowled. "And innkeeper," she said, straightening her back. "They call me husband The Blade and he is very fond of his horse."

The man nodded, birdlike, and hurried out.

"What happened to the sweet woman with the soft voice?"

Sara turned to Boden. He lay flat on his back with his

right leg bent and his left limp. His cape still covered the wounds. "She got wet."

A corner of his dusky mouth lifted. "You must be the very devil in the spring," he said.

She nodded, but her attention lay on the wound she had yet to see. "We must get ye out of those clothes," she said.

He closed his eyes and let his face slump closer to the mattress. "I like this wet lady."

She approached him slowly, then reached for his cape and paused. "I am scared."

"Not you," he said and lifted a hand to her cheek. "Never you."

"I am not a healer and I fear ye are badly wounded."

He nodded shallowly. "My apologies lady."

"Apologies?" Her eyes filled with tears. "Why?"

"I always talk gibberish when I'm wounded. Tis the coward in me."

"Nay, Boden," she whispered. "Ye are brave beyond words. Beyond imagination."

He opened his eyes slowly. "Do you ever see the bad, sweet Sara?"

"Not in ye."

His eyes looked moist. "I will heal, lady, for you."

"I will see to your wound."

"Nay!" He said the word quickly, then drew a deep breath and chuckled at his own fear. "There is no need."

"Aye, there is."

A knock sounded at the door. Sara answered it and took the bottle from the boy in the hall.

Boden's gaze found her immediately. "You need rest, lady. Sleep."

"Not until I've seen to ye, surely."

"Please?" The plea sounded pathetic to his own ears. "I will mend if I rest."

Taking her ever-present pouch from her belt, she opened it, drew out a small leather bag and tossed a pinch of powder into the bottle. "Here. Drink this first."

"Then I can sleep?"

"I should tend your leg."

"Nay! Truly, tis fine."

There was sorrow in her eyes, and worry. "Are ye certain?"

His leg was going to burn off and in a minute he was probably going to start bawling like a baby. But he was terribly, incredibly tired. Perhaps there was a chance he could fall asleep and wake up healed. Twas said that miracles could happen.

"Aye, I'm . . . certain," he said, taking a quick swig. Grimacing, he stared at the bottle, then at her. She touched her finger to the glass, tilting it back to his lips. It tasted no better the second time. Or the third. But he'd drink tiger piss if she'd promise to leave his leg alone. "There is room beside me." He patted the mattress on the far side of him, finding it ridiculously difficult to make that simple movement. "Here." He tried to turn his head toward the indicated spot, but it didn't work. "Lie . . . down. Rest." Darkness was coming for him. "Sweet . . . Sara."

"As ye wish, sir," she whispered, leaning close. Her voice was like a warm breeze singing softly through gossamer leaves. "Sleep then. I'll not bother ye."

"Saint," he whispered. "Saint Sara."

"Holy, fucking hell!" Boden roared. Pain ripped through his leg. He grappled to rise.

"Hold him down!" cried Sara. "Hold him!"

The smell of burning flesh stung his nostrils. Jesus, God! It was *his* flesh! He gasped a deep breath, recoiling for another effort, and in that moment hell was revisited.

He roared in agony, bucking against the mattress.

"Tis done! Tis done!" cried Sara, dropping to her knees beside him.

He roared again, trying to break his arms free. But it was no use. He rolled his head to the side. Her face was as pale as winter, accented by eyes wide with terror.

Damn her to hell. She *should* be scared, for in her lily white hand she still held the instrument of torture—his own damned knife, still smoking from the fire. And he would make her pay.

"Couldn't you let me sleep in peace? Not for a moment?"

"You've been sleeping," she said. "I could wait no more. I had to cauterize the wound. It is not so long. Just a couple of inches. But I worried. Twas my fault. Liam mistook ye for the enemy and threw his knives. He did not mean to harm you. I'm sorry."

"Sorry!" He managed the word through gritted teeth. "You *will* be sorry. As will you!" he yelled, turning his head to roar at the others who stood nearly out of his line of vision.

Three men scrambled toward the door. Boden tried to reach them, but his arms were still bound to the bed.

The innkeeper stopped in the doorway. "If . . . if that's all you'll be needing, my lady . . ."

"Aye." She rose slowly to her feet.

Her voice sounded weak. Good! He hoped she fainted dead away. Who knew what evil things he could think to do to her before she awoke. If she'd just take the damned ropes off his arms. St. Silvester! His leg burned like the fires of hell! He jerked at the ropes again, but they didn't budge.

"That will be all," she said. "Ye . . . ye have me thanks. And Sir Blade's."

Boden growled. The innkeeper scrambled after his friends.

Boden turned to look into her face again. She was just as pale as before.

"You are a conniving little liar!" he accused.

"I thought twould be better for ye if ye were asleep."

"You burnt my damned leg!" he roared. "You thought I would sleep through it?"

Her eyes got wider still, and he saw now that her hand that held his knife was shaking. Good. She deserved it.

Even though she looked like she hadn't slept for a month. She'd walked while he rode—carrying the baby—in the rain. He remembered it all now. Still, she had no right to lie to him. After all, he was a knight, trained, true, tested. It wasn't as if he couldn't have borne a little pain while awake.

God, his leg hurt.

"Sit the hell down," he growled. "Before you fall over."

"I do feel a wee bit faint," she said, wobbling a little on her feet.

"No you don't. No you don't!" he said, jerking at his bonds. "Cut me loose before you pass out."

She stumbled toward him, then sawed weakly at the rope that held his left arm. An eternity later, it frayed loose.

She stood, wobbled, then weaved around to the far side of the bed. Again the blade was set to the rope, but the strokes were weaker yet.

"Sit down!" he ordered, and taking the knife from her, sliced through the hemp. "Sit down!" he said again when he realized she hadn't obeyed.

She did so now, plopping down on the bed beside him.

He sat up with a considerable effort, then. "Tell me, lady," he said, gazing down at himself. "Wasn't it humiliating enough to tie me to the bed and mutilate me while I slept? Did I have to be naked as well?"

"You were covered with a blanket."

"The blanket seems to have abandoned its post," he said, glancing at the woolen on the floor.

"I thought . . ." She didn't sound so good. "I thought ye might have sustained other wounds."

"Where?"

"Under . . . Ye know."

"If you thought I'd been cut there you might at least have been kind enough to just slit my throat instead of frying my poor, tattered, bloody—"

She made a strange noise. He turned toward her. She

gagged again, and his hand shot out just in time to grab the nearby kettle and jam it under her head before she expelled the contents of her stomach.

A tortured minute later, she straightened.

"Are you all right?" he asked, setting the stinking kettle aside.

"I dunna feel so well."

"Good!" he said, but in a moment he reconsidered and slammed the kettle back under her nose.

She gagged into it, then finally straightened. "Sorry."

She looked like a small, bedraggled kitten, wet, skinny, lost.

"You should be. Feeling better?"

"I think so," she said, and shivered.

He glanced down at her. She was wet from her head to her shoes and dirty, though not quite so dirty as he remembered her being.

"We're going to have to get you out of those clothes."

Her head came up with a snap. Twas a wonder, he thought, that her eyes didn't pop out of her head.

"What's good for the goose . . ."

"You're a knight," she said, "bound by ancient codes of honor."

"You lied to me," he said. "All vows are off if the lady lies."

"Boden . . ."

"Oh shut up!" he said, and wincing, turned her away to loosen the ties at the back of her gown.

They were soggy and twisted and tied in tight knots. He considered cutting them loose, but thought better of it. In a moment they came free.

"There now." The fabric slipped from her shoulders. They were pretty shoulders, very white, soft, smooth. He swallowed. "Take it off."

"I can't."

"Look at me."

She turned, but her gaze didn't quite manage to reach his eyes.

"Do I seem to have any clothes on?" he asked. "Even a stitch?"

"Nay." She didn't raise her eyes to his.

"St. Peter's peter!" he said. "Tis too late to act the modest maid now. Tis far too late after . . ." He waved his hand up and down through the air, indicating his own nudity.

"I had no wish to hurt you."

"But you wished to undress me."

He thought he saw the corner of her lips twitch. "Aye."

Dear Lord, she was beautiful. He slid to the edge of the bed and rose to his feet. For a moment, he considered fainting. But it didn't seem like much fun.

"Hand me that blanket."

She did so, managing it without looking at him.

With a twist and a tuck he wrapped it around his waist.

"All right then, get up here," he said and pulled her to her feet.

Still, she did nothing to undress and her skin felt cold as death beneath his hands. Cold and smooth and oh so soft. He slipped the bodice lower. Her breasts came free and he forgot to breathe.

Instead, he stood like a great, beached whale, staring, longing, fantasizing.

"Sara . . ." He breathed her name.

She lifted her gaze, and her cheeks were no longer pale, but flushed bright with life and beauty. "Aye?" she whispered.

He watched her lips move, then against his will, he smoothed his thumb over them and felt her shiver like a frail leaf in the winds of a storm. But she was not frail. She was a woman, strong and hale, and beautiful beyond hope.

And she was not his. She was *not* his. And if he wished to live out the year he would remember that.

"I . . ." He was breathing hard now, trying to think, to remember that he wanted to live. Even without her, he wanted to live—didn't he? "I need . . ." He touched her lips again, but suddenly Lord Haldane's memory reared its ugly head.

"Aye?"

"The pain is terrible," he said hoarsely, and managed, just barely, to turn away.

"Oh." He heard her breathe the word behind him, and it seemed he could *feel* her pull her gown back into place. He nearly cried when he knew she covered herself. "'Tis sorry I am. I should have realized you'd need something to dull the ache."

God yes!

She hurried past him, picked up the disgraced kettle, and dispatched it to the hall. Then, retrieving the bottle he'd tested before, she brought it to him.

He glanced at it with a scowl. "Did this stuff knock me unconscious, or was it the effort to find you that exhausted me?" he asked.

"It was finding me," she said, looking guilty. "Besides, that was a different bottle."

"Where is the other one?"

"The innkeeper took it."

"When?"

"After you passed out."

"Passed out?" he said narrowing his eyes at her. "How long did I sleep?"

She bit her lip. "A day and a night."

"A day and a—!" He nearly screamed the words.

"Fiona didn't tell me it would make you sleep. I didn't mean to trick you. I fell asleep, too, but you were sleeping so long and—"

"You got bored?"

"I was worried."

"So you thought you'd wake me up with a hot knife."

"I'm sorry," she murmured, sounding just a little miffed. "But your fever is down. And I've had time to search for new herbs."

"So that's how you got wet?" he asked. "Dashing

around in the rain for medicines to cure me while I slept like a . . . like an overgrown turnip?'' He glowered at her.

She almost smiled, but seemed to think better of it. ''Drink the wine,'' she said.

If she got sick it would be his fault. But of course she wouldn't. He was the weak one. Adversity only seemed to make her stronger, brighter, more beautiful.

''Drink,'' she repeated.

Yes! he thought. He'd get drunk. Twas a fine idea. Twas a great idea. Twas a—No. He couldn't get drunk. If he got drunk he would . . . He looked at her. God, even wet, even freezing, even exhausted, even really, really aggravating, she was alluring beyond words.

He couldn't get drunk. Pain had a tendency to lower his inhibitions. But spirits killed them.

''Drink,'' she said, and he did.

Chapter 15

Boden drank again, then, looking at Sara, saw that she shivered and handed her the bottle.

"Drink," he said.

She did, then trembled, and drank again. He watched her throat move, then lowered his gaze. Although she had replaced her bodice, she hadn't taken the time to pull the ties tight. The neckline sagged slightly. That alone was enough to cause him heart palpitations. Under that gown she was naked. It was a strange thought. And odder still how it affected him. He remembered her breasts, small and firm, and unearthly soft. In fact, he remembered them so clearly that they might as well have been bared. But they weren't. He took the bottle back and drank.

"You'd best take off your clothes, lady," he said.

Her eyes widened. How was it that she seemed so young sometimes, so untouched, and then at others she could hold the whole world at bay for the sake of an unprotected infant that was not hers?

"Take them off." He wished he was drunk now, beyond caring, but his tone sounded disturbingly sober. "I'll try not to look."

"Try?"

"I mean, I *won't* look."

For one crazed moment, he thought he saw the pink bow of her mouth lift into the whisper of a smile. He stared, trying to make sure, trying to decipher her moods, her thoughts, but she was forever an enigma to him. How, he wondered, could she be so alluring even under these circumstances? Wet, cold, bedraggled, with her hair hanging down around her face, she still made his brain stop and his heart pump blood to all the wrong places. He drew a deep breath and tried to look away. He should be accustomed to failing miserably. "The bathing tub. It looks ready to use."

"Aye." Her voice was as soft as a dream. "They sent it up the first night, but ye slept for so long, so we waited to fill it. This day I had them bring water and a meal for I was fairly certain ye would wake up when I . . ." She motioned to his leg and winced, then cleared her throat. "Tortured ye."

He almost laughed at her choice of words. "Aye, well . . ." Scowling down into her pale face, he realized what it had taken for her to cauterize his wound. It had been a difficult task. Though it was not a large wound, he knew how they could fester. Twas possible she had saved his life after Liam, the bastard, had cut him. But surely Boden didn't have to thank her. Did he? After all, she'd lied to him—said she was going to sleep beside him and all the while she'd been planning wicked things. He shuddered at the thought. His leg hurt like hell.

"You'd best bathe afore the water cools," he said.

"I'll see to your leg first," she countered.

He felt himself pale. "Nay." His voice was hoarse. "You've done quite enough." And more.

"Twill not hurt," she vowed.

"Ha!" He barked a laugh. The wine sloshed messily in the bottle.

Her eyes were wide and solemn. "I should have said, it will not hurt when I am finished. Come now, Boden. I only did what I thought was right. Twas not any evil intent on my part. Please. Let me tend ye."

Tend ye! How was it that she made that sound appealing? He knew she was planning to do evil things to a part of his anatomy that was horribly close to another part he was very fond of.

"Nay," he said. "It will heal well on its own now, I'm certain."

She stared at him with obvious skepticism.

"You have mended it for good and always. See," he said, managing with a sweating brow to bend the leg back and forth beneath the blanket. He was quite proud that he didn't swoon to the floor like a lady in waiting. "It hardly hurts at all. The pain is gone. How clever you are. I don't know how you managed it."

Her lips turned up ever so slightly. "Have ye ever considered a career on the stage? Ye're quite an actor."

"And you're not going to touch my leg."

She laughed. Actually laughed. What a mean-spirited little thing she could be sometimes. But the sound of her humor softened something in him, making him want to hear that sound again and again.

"I promise I will not hurt ye," she murmured.

There was that sweet tone again. Damn her! But he knew now what she was really like. She was like a wild-cat. Soft and deadly.

"I'm not scared if that's what you're thinking," he said.

"Nay." She blinked, all innocence. "Of course not. Lie back on the bed."

No! God no! Please! he wanted to whimper. But instead he swallowed, lowered his brows, and tried his frantic best to think of a way out of this predicament with a shred of dignity intact.

"Take off your clothes and I'll do as you ask," he said.

Her face went white as hoarfrost. Merciful God! He'd found a way out.

"That's unfair, Sir Boden."

"Unfair." He laughed. "You burnt my leg. All's fair. But believe me, I have only your best interests in mind. Twill be good for you to get out of those clothes." He

allowed himself a grin and another swig from the bottle.
"And it will do me no harm either."

"I thought ye were a gentle man."

"Well, Lady Sara, you thought wrong. Take off your
wet clothes and I'll allow you tend my leg."

"I have no other clothes."

"And you imagined I didn't realize that? I'm
wounded, not dead!"

Her face was bright with embarrassment.

"What if Lord Haldane learns of this?" she asked.

"Surely your life is worth more than the slim risk of
a scandal," he said.

"I was thinking of you."

"Me?"

"Ye are his trusted knight, sir. What will he think of
you if he learns of these circumstances?"

Peter's pecker! He hated it when she was selfless, and
she was being selfless now, while he was being . . . Well,
the word randy came to mind—and with a leg wound,
too! There were probably all kinds of unwritten physio-
logical laws against that.

"My Lord Haldane will hear naught of this night,
Sara," he vowed. "These simple village people have no
interest in our lives. And they think us man and wife.
There will be no gossip."

She watched him in silence, but he saw her shiver
again.

"Remove your clothing," he said. "Wrap in a blanket."

Still she was silent.

"I'm a knight, vowed to protect the fairer—"

"Do ye think I believe I canna trust ye?" she whispered. Then, "Tis not the case, sir, for I know I can."

Her voice was breathy and went straight to his heart.
She trusted him, she said. But why? Didn't she know
what she did to him?

Against his better judgment, he touched her face,
smoothing his palm across her satin cheek. She closed

her eyes and leaned ever so slightly against his hand.

"Tis myself I dunna trust," she murmured.

It was beyond, far beyond time to get drunk. She smiled a little, a sad sort of expression.

"Turn around," she said softly.

He did so in something of a fog. Time ceased to have meaning as he tried not to think of her getting undressed behind him. He attempted to pretend she was just another woman, no more appealing than many of the fairer sex. But there were her eyes, and her laughter, and the sound of her voice. And that wasn't even considering all those soft attributes below her neck.

He had to quit thinking, or soon he was going to fall on her like a hound on a chair leg. Now there was a charming thought. And if that wasn't enough, there was the memory of Lord Haldane. If he touched her, the duke's anger would make her medical attention seem like a fine walk in the park.

"I am finished." Her voice was soft, as soft as the underside of her breasts would be. As soft as the curve of her firm waist, the swell of her buttocks, the . . .

"Sir?"

"Aye." He started from his reverie. God, he needed help.

"Lie down on the bed."

"If you insist," he said, but reality sprang at him suddenly, tightening his muscles. Regardless of the soft shiver her tone caused to spurt up his back, she probably didn't have in mind what *he* had in mind. Was he drunk yet? And didn't she need to undress some more?

"Lie down," she ordered again, but like an angel.

There was no point in arguing. She would win.

The mattress ropes groaned under his weight. Every inch of him ached with the thought of the pain she could cause him, with the thought of the pleasure she could give him. "The baby!" He jerked upright suddenly, certain he'd found an escape. "Where's the babe?"

"The innkeeper's wife took him." She looked quite complacent. Damn.

"Surely you cannot trust her with the child." He rose to his feet with an effort. She pressed him back down with no trouble at all.

"Aye. I do trust her."

He settled back against the mattress with a scowl. "Why?"

She shrugged. "I just do."

"That's no reason. He may be hungry."

"She'll feed him."

"But . . . he's probably scared. Surely he misses you—your gentle touch, your sweet voice—"

"Sir Knight," she said in that ethereal voice. "You're blathering."

"I never blather."

"'Tis sorry I am that I've hurt ye," she said. "But I'll not do so again."

"Promise?" His voice distinctly lacked that harsh, arrogant tone he had worked so long to hone. But it seemed like such a waste of effort suddenly.

"Ye've me word as a Scot."

He snorted, but when she smiled the room lit up like a basilica at Michaelmas. He could no longer speak. Indeed, a bit of pain hardly seemed to matter when she looked at him like that. Hardly.

"You must push up the blanket," she said.

He eyed hers breathlessly. "Really?"

"I mean *your* blanket."

"Oh." The disappointment was bitter, but he did as she requested, easing up the woolen an inch at a time. Even that pressure against the wound sent waves of pain shooting up his leg, but it was time to act like a man.

Or not. Maybe he could pass out again instead.

She had turned away. He watched her bend to take a kettle from the fire and wondered how and if she managed to keep the blanket in place as she did so. But soon she was back. She rummaged in a pouch for a few moments, then dumped a handful of herbs into the steaming pot. A fresh, minty aroma filled the air.

Sir Boden took a deep breath, and against his will, felt himself relax. From a leather bag, she took a dab of dusty-looking powder, which she placed in a wooden bowl. Then, adding some of the liquid from the pot, she stirred it with a spoon.

Boden eyed it dubiously. It looked rather like someone had hurled into the bowl. "Is that the same stuff you put in the wine?"

"Aye."

He scowled. "What are your plans for that concoction?"

"I will smear it on the wound."

He stifled a shiver. "Do you hate me so?"

"It may sting a bit at first."

"Before it burns a hole through my thigh?"

Her eyes were laughing when she lifted them to him. "Are ye certain you're a knight?"

"Have I not told you I am——"

He sucked air between his teeth as white-hot pain seared his leg. Agony sizzled through his senses. Darkness rushed in. Boden grasped the bed sheets and dropped his head back, grappling for lucidness. But in a few moments the torture had lessened to a dull throb, then eased even more.

He raised his head weakly and scowled down at his wound. "What did you do?"

"Tis Fiona's secret," she said and, slipping a shaky hand under his knee, bent it upward. "She said to use it wisely. If inhaled it may boggle the mind, but it will also ease one's aches. And if applied directly to a wound, tis little short of magic."

"You mean to say, you could have used it for my arm?"

"Fiona cautioned me to use it on only the most grievous of wounds."

"My arm was grievously wounded," he said.

"Do not forget, there was a reason I stabbed ye.
Twould have made little sense to immediately try to heal
ye."

He snorted.

"I must bandage ye now."

His leg felt somewhat numb, heavy, oddly content.

"You could have used it for my arm later."

"Does it still hurt?"

"Aye." He looked at her through dark-lidded lashes,
and for a moment she was tempted almost beyond control
to touch his face, to still her trembling against the warmth
of his skin. But she could not risk that. Far too much
was at stake, not least of all, Boden's own life. So she
smeared the tiny remainder of ointment from the bowl
with her fingers and smoothed it gently across the healing
scar on his biceps.

Then, because she could not resist, she slipped her
hand down the strength of his arm and back to the ointment.

He dropped his head back slightly. His throat was thick
with muscle and very dark, but for the quickly healing
wound he had sustained at her own hand.

"Do ye feel better?" Her voice sounded strange to her
own ears—far away and husky.

"Aye." His was throaty and deep.

"Anywhere else that I can touch? I mean . . ." she
corrected quickly. "Is there anything else that needs my
ministrations?"

The scar at the side of his lips danced, and then his
hand moved, slowly, to point at an old scar on his pectoral. Dipping her fingers into the bowl, she smeared
them against the oily side, then drew them out to smooth
them gently over the scar.

His eyes fell closed. A feeling, hot as hell, spurred
down her throat to her belly, and when she spoke, her
voice was just above a whisper.

"Anywhere else?"

His fingers moved again, ever so slowly to the next

scar. His torso was crisscrossed with them. And yet it seemed like heaven to touch each one, to smooth her fingers over the aged wounds, to skim her hands over the curve of his biceps, the cap of his shoulder, the bulge of his chest, and then lower.

The rippled muscle of his abdomen danced when she touched it. She felt the sharp intake of his breath in her very soul. The warmth of his skin seeped through her fingertips, intoxicating her, and suddenly her head felt light and her limbs heavy. It seemed she could hear the very beat of his heart, could feel the hot blood pumping through his veins.

"Sara." His voice was as deep as forever. She opened her eyes, and realized rather foggily that she was caressing his belly with a slow, steady rhythm that matched the pace of her heart.

"You are beautiful beyond words."

But suddenly she didn't know if the words had come from him or her. Her blanket had fallen away, that much she knew, for she could feel the cool air caress her shoulders. Perhaps she should be cold, but she was not. Still, she forced herself to pull the blanket up and wrap it casually about her torso, tucking it beneath her arms.

"I must tend yer leg," she said, and picking up a long strip of cloth, she wrapped it about his thigh. It was a big thigh, heavy with muscle, dark skinned, dark haired, long. She covered the wound and tied off thé cloth but her hands didn't leave his leg.

The blanket lay bunched about his waist, and beneath that heavy woolen . . . She shivered. The tremble felt delicately delicious, like a forbidden drink.

And suddenly she realized his fingers had touched her face and were slipping with languid slowness down her throat. She shivered again, but remembered her duty. Taking his hand, she helped him rise to his feet. He did so slowly until he stood over her like a towering elm, silent, venerable.

It took all her control to turn away, to lift the herbed

kettle from the floor. She drew a deep waft of the hot air
into her lungs, then poured the water into the tub. Curls
of sweet steam filled the air. She heard Boden inhale it.

The tub was more than half full. Tugging at his hand,
she urged him to step inside. He moved closer, and then
his hand lowered, and with the slightest movement, the
blanket fell from him. The hard thrust of his manhood
loomed into sight. She nearly reached out. Nearly
touched it. But even now, in her strangely disembodied
state, she did not. Instead, she urged him toward the tub.
He stepped inside.

"Again you have me at a disadvantage," he murmured. "Watching me bathe and without even the darkness to cover me."

Her gaze skimmed down his hard-muscled body.
"There is a God," she whispered, and raising on her
tiptoes, kissed his lips.

He tried to pull her to him, but she pulled away, urging
him into the water. It washed over him, and there seemed
nothing she could do but watch him. Dear God, he was
beautiful, even wounded and scarred, he was beautiful.
Or did those imperfections only make him more appealing?

Somehow the questions were too heavy to ponder. It
took a moment for her to realize he still held her hand.
They stared in unison at the bond between them. Finally
she tugged on her fingers and he relented. But she didn't
move far, indeed, not out of reach, for it seemed impossible suddenly to keep from touching him.

Instead, she lifted a sponge from the water and draped
it over his shoulder. Water ran in silver rivulets across
his chest, down his back, over the healing scar on his
arm. She watched it flow, mesmerized by its path, by the
loving way it caressed his flesh. She dunked the sponge
again, and draped it over the other shoulder. The water's
course was much the same, and yet it fascinated her no
less, and with every drop of water she watched, she felt
the heat in her body building.

His face was slightly turned toward her. She could see his hard, chiseled profile, the jut of his jaw, the hollow of his cheek. His brows were dark, low, his eyes hidden beneath closed lids.

Her hand fell automatically, then lifted again to douse his hair. His head dropped back a fraction of an inch. She watched the tendons in his throat tighten, and in a moment she found that her hand had gone there, touching the cords that stood out in sharp relief against his dark throat. His skin felt like sun-warmed velvet, and when she touched his arm, it seemed that the strength of a stallion had been imbued in this sculpture of a man. She washed the sponge down his arm, leaving behind a fine sheen of oiled water until she reached his fingers. She washed each one, then slid her hand sideways onto his hip. Her hand curved out of sight.

His eyes opened slowly. There was light in them, a light so bright and fierce that for a moment she couldn't breath. She realized foggily that her blanket had left her completely.

"It seems my blanket has abandoned its post," she whispered.

"There is a God." He repeated her words, then reached for her.

She told herself it was not too late to retreat, but the air was heavy with anticipation, and deep inside she ached with a desire that would no longer be ignored.

It didn't feel as if she stepped into the tub, instead, it seemed that the water rose to meet her, flooded the edges of life, sliding up her calves, her knees, her thighs as she slipped down beside him.

Warmth and peace wrapped them together. It seemed as natural as breathing that he kiss her face, her hair, the swift pulse in her throat.

Her fingers still held the sponge. She ran it up his arm, onto his shoulder, and higher. Warm water rinsed his midnight hair. He dropped his head back and with that movement, his chest pressed against hers. She closed her eyes at the impact. They shivered in unison, and when she looked at his face again, his hair was washed back, black as ebon, to show his every feature as if it were etched in granite.

Leaning back slightly, she lifted the sponge to press it against his chest. Rivulets streamed around his left nipple, leaving the dusky summit dry in their wake. And suddenly it seemed there was nothing she could do but kiss it.

She did so, then drew back to watch it pucker. Leaning forward again, she sucked it into her mouth. His hiss of breath sounded like agony. Her arms slid about his waist. Her breasts slipped wet and hot against his belly. It felt strangely perfect. But there were sights to see. She moved lower, kissing his ribs, his abdomen, feeling his muscles tense and relax beneath her hands and lips.

His cock was as hard as sin, long and smooth. She touched it gently, feeling strangely unembarrassed. It felt wild, as if it contained a life of its own, smooth as satin against her lips. It danced beneath her kiss. She trickled her fingers over the tip and moved on. His scrotum felt hot, his thighs tense as she slipped her hand between them.

Her wrist smoothed against his thighs, her arm against his testicles. He moaned at the touch, distracting her. Her head felt heavy when she lifted it. Still, there was naught she could do but slip up the endless length of his body to kiss his lips again.

His moan turned to a growl in her mouth. His arms encircled her, drawing her against him like hungry bands of steel.

His chest was hard and hot against her breasts. The muscles of his abdomen danced against her belly. Below that, she felt the hard evidence of his desire press between her thighs.

And now his hands were everywhere, cupping her buttocks, sweeping across her back, encompassing her waist. Need melded with desire, right with wrong. There were no feelings but those evoked by his hands. His voice felt hot, his hands spoke of magic, and between their bodies, Dragonheart gleamed. Boden's lips brushed it aside as he kissed her throat, her chest, the aching tip of one breast.

The gasp must have been hers, but she knew not when it escaped. All the while his hands were working their sorcery, slipping over her hot skin, pulling her closer and closer, gripping her thighs and lifting them around his hips, drawing her irrevocably against him until it seemed like they were one—until they *were* one.

The world ground to a halt. Sara stopped, poised above him, her head thrust backward, her spine arched.

Twas the final chance to retreat, she knew, and yet it was but a fleeting thought before she slowly pressed him into her.

Heaven's gate closed around him. Boden sucked breath between his teeth. She gripped him hot and hard, soft as a velvet sheath, strong as a leather gauntlet, pulling him inside. He should retreat, he should retreat, but, oh God, he would not, not when she seemed as eager for this union as he, not when all his life seemed to be poised in this moment, waiting for the fulfillment of his worth. He pressed into her. Her head dropped back farther still. Her breasts, white as lily blossoms capped in pink, pressed closer to him. He pushed in harder and heard her gasp.

Had he hurt her? The thought made him freeze. It took a moment for her eyes to open. They were as blue as a dream, but smoky somehow, and in their depths he saw her worry.

"Sir . . . Boden." Her breathing had resumed, but it was harsh. "Do ye hate me so?" Her body rocked gently against his.

"Nay," he whispered. "Nay, I do not."

"Then please. Dunna. Stop."

Twas a soft plea, and disjointed, but Boden knew that she begged him to stop. Something ripped in his heart. So now was the true test. All those past trials that he thought had been difficult, all those battles, all the fear, they were as naught compared to the discipline required now. But he wasn't disciplined. He wasn't a gentleman. He was a cad, a fake, a rogue. And her eyes were so damned blue.

She was an angel, and for the angel, he would cease. With every bit of power in him, he forced himself to draw away.

"Please." There seemed to be panic in her voice now. It was husky, low, begging, as her thighs wrapped more tightly about him and her breasts dipped toward his chest. "Please dunna stop."

For a moment Boden couldn't believe his ears. But her heavenly rhythm against him had become more powerful.

She was right; there was a God! And He even watched over cads like himself.

Gratitude flowed through Boden, making his movements slow but sure. He pushed into her with careful patience now, watched her head fall back, heard her shallow breathing, felt her encompass him completely.

Water sloshed over his belly, between his legs, slapping against her buttocks, caressing his balls. Tension soared through him and the pace increased. He pushed in deeper still, faster, and she rode like the queen of the eve, her wild hair wet, her face shining, her thighs lean and strong.

They rocked together, reaching, panting, pleading for release, until finally in a raw explosion of feeling, Sara's hands clawed his chest. Her gasp filled the room and with that wild emotion, he exploded inside her.

He felt her go limp. Her head dropped forward, and her breasts, when they touched his chest, were as soft as thistledown.

He opened his eyes and breathed in heaven. The world was a masterpiece. The water was soft. Her scent was delicious. Even the weight of her body against his own wounded one seemed perfect.

He found her lips with his own. Their kiss, too, was

perfect, gentle, yielding. Where her body had been tense and driven, it was now relaxed and supple, like a fine piece of gold silk draped against him.

He kissed her shoulder, her arm, the bend of her elbow, her fingers. She didn't open her eyes, but shivered against his touch, making him need to explore further, to nibble on her pinky, lick the shallow cave of her palm.

"You *are* kind," he whispered, and slipping up beside her, kissed her lips.

She smiled sleepily. "I told ye that at our first meeting."

He kissed her ear. "Mayhap your stabbing me in the arm confused me. But I would gladly be stabbed again ..." Bending, he smoothed his lips across her breast. "For this."

She shivered at his touch. "Tell me, Sir Knight, do ye think I did this out of kindness?"

"Why else?"

Her hand felt wet and warm as it slipped over his chest to his abdomen.

"Because I couldna resist," she whispered. "Because every moment I was with ye I thought of this."

"Then our dreams have truly meshed," he said.

She sighed. The sound caressed his ears. He pulled her nearer, draping her arm about him until she was pulled close. Then he laid her back in the water. Her hair floated on the surface, molten gold, soft as kitten fur. He tangled his fingers in it, glorying in the feel, in the smooth length of her body stretched beside him.

The sponge floated nearby. He reached for it like one in a dream and smoothed it across her shoulder, over her breast, down her abdomen. Again she shivered. Water sloshed over her. A bar of scented soap lay on the nearby commode. He picked it up and slipped his fingers into her hair again, massaging her scalp, running his hands through the silky strands, then wrapping the great length around her arm, spreading it over her breasts, and then, because he could not help himself, kissing the nipple that shone through the gossamer strands.

She reached for him, pulling him down, and now they lay side by side, embraced by the scented water and each other. Their lips met. Their limbs entwined. Hair swirled about them in gold and black, tangling, mating. And so they lay like water nymphs, wrapped in ecstasy, until Boden felt Sara's head droop against his arm.

He roused himself with difficulty and realized in a moment of panic that she had fallen asleep.

She felt light and soft as he lifted her from the water. No pain accompanied his journey to the bed. In fact, ecstasy would have well described every element of his life at that moment.

She moaned as he laid her on the mattress, and it was all he could do to abandon her long enough to retrieve a blanket and the board of food. He fed her with his own fingers, until finally sated, and weary, they fell asleep wrapped in a cocoon of warmth, pressed against each other.

Dreams of her filled his head, his heart, and in the middle of the night he reached for her again, pulling her against him, nuzzling her breast until she arched against him.

It seemed utterly right that he slip inside her, almost ordained that she wrap her legs about him, natural as the sky that she urged him farther in, rasping his name until she went limp and he exploded once more.

Sleep found them again, that soft warm friend, caressing them in the darkness, bringing them closer still until Boden awoke. Only minutes had passed, he was sure, and yet he was hard again, eager, nay, desperate, for her to hold him inside her, to fill her, to love her. Already it seemed that they were rocking together on the border of ecstasy. He opened his eyes slowly. She was there, her lips slightly parted, her hair a wild hurricane of gold.

A faint glimmer of pink light seemed to glow in the room, but he was not surprised, for had not his world taken on a new light? She shone. Twas the only explanation. Night had just begun. She was his, body and soul, for now and ever. Dreams still rocked him. The sweet essence of her medicine still soothed him.

He kissed the corner of her mouth. She moaned softly and turned toward him. Her eyes did not open, but her legs did, wrapping around him, pulling him in. And he did not resist. Twas all so right, so simple, so obvious. They were meant to be together, bonded for life. Anyone would know that. Twas not a doubt. He arched into her. She pushed back.

The world opened its happy arms.

"Madam!" A voice, harsh as reality, broke into the world. "The baby is crying!"

Boden felt Sara's body go stiff, felt his world snap back into place, and then her eyes popped open.

"Dear God!" she gasped and like a charger at full tilt, tumbled him onto the floor.

Chapter 16

"**W**hat are ye doing?" she gasped, scrambling to her feet in the middle of the bed.

But Boden couldn't answer, for hot pain sliced through him like a nail through an iron shoe. "Jesus!" The word barely hissed between his teeth.

"Madam?" called the woman again, and now they heard the baby's cry. "Tis sorry I am to disturb you, but I must be starting my morning chores."

From the agony of the floor, Boden heard the sharp gasp of Sara's breath and looked up just in time to see her stare down in shocked speechlessness at her own nudity.

"I'm naked!"

"Aye." It was the only word he could manage. For a moment the pain left his body, for even now, with the cold light of reality gripping his world in its cruel hand, she was stunning. She, however, did not seem to find anything wonderful about her state. In fact, she snatched a blanket from the bed and whipped it about her body with the speed of an executioner's hand.

The sun dimmed in Boden's befuddled mind. "Sara," he breathed, reaching for her.

She lunged from the bed, her bare legs visible past the knee where the blanket kindly parted.

"Madam?"

She jerked toward the door. Sheer panic showed on her face, and the hand that held her blanket in place seemed to tremble. "I am . . . coming," she said, but her tone made it sound like a question.

Hard reality turned to pain once more, and Boden, under Sara's wild stare, picked himself up from the floor. Then she was rushing to the door. It opened beneath her shaky hand.

"Madam," said the innkeeper's wife. "'Tis sorry I am to wake you."

"Nay. Nay," Sara breathed. Dear God! What had she done? "I was . . . I was awake."

"Oh," said the woman, but her brows had risen into her gray wimple and Sara realized suddenly that the woman could see past her own body.

She turned with a snap and saw Boden standing beside the bed, his lower body hastily wrapped in a blanket, his torso bare and gleaming with oil and hard muscle.

"Well . . ." The woman giggled like an untried maid. "I guess I can understand the cause. But even with a leg wound?" She giggled again. "You're a lucky lass indeed. Oh, here," she said, handing over a pair of black hose. "To replace that ones what was ruined. And here . . ." She handed Thomas to her much more regretfully.

Dear God, how could she have neglected the child so? Sara wondered. What kind of woman was she? She reached out, took the babe from the woman's arms and cuddled him against her chest. "I am in your debt," she breathed, but the woman hushed her with a wave of her plump hand.

"'Twas no trouble atall. Has been many a year since my own babes were so tiny. He was a saint. Slept like a lambkin all night. But he just awoke and I've had no time to feed him. A pleasure it was, really. And I hope . . ." She glanced past Sara again with a sparkle in her eye. "I suspect it was just as big a pleasure for you."

She bustled away. Sara stood speechless and immobile.

Thomas whimpered and sucked on his fist. What had she done? Against her chest, Dragonheart glowed warm and heavy.

She closed the door like one in a dream and turned back toward the room, refusing to lift her gaze. The air struck her like a broom to the midsection. The scent here was heavy and sweet in comparison to the draft from the hall.

Fiona's medicine! she thought, and suddenly she remembered her aunt's words. *Tis the strongest potion at my disposal, but there are risks with it, for though it relaxes and eases pain it can boggle the mind if the steam is inhaled.*

Slowly, irrevocably, Sara lifted her gaze to Boden's. He stood like a frozen statue, his great chest bare and just as beautiful as it appeared in her hazy memories. "Dear God!"

"What?" His voice was no more than a rumble.

She hadn't meant to say the words aloud, but he was watching her now like a hawk on a mouse. "What have we done?" she whispered.

"Nearly everything." Boden's voice was deep as he stepped toward her. "And not nearly enough. Sara . . ."

"Nay. Dunna say it." Her voice shook, as did the hand she stretched toward him. "Dear Lord. I am sorry."

"Sorry? If the truth be told, lass, sorry is a far distance from where I am."

"I didn't mean to do it."

"That didn't seem to be the case some hours past."

She shook her head, looking frantic. "I drugged ye."

"Drugged—"

"I drugged *me*," she rasped, realizing suddenly that it was true.

"Sara—"

"Nay! Please. Ye . . ." He what? He was beautiful? He was glorious? He felt like heaven when she rode him astride? And she was a slut.

"Nay!" His response was growled, and though she

hadn't spoken aloud, he heard her thoughts. "Don't say that!" he said, stepping forward.

"I said nothing."

"And yet it no longer matters," he said. "For I can see your thoughts."

"Then ye know I am sorry."

"Sweet Sara," he murmured, touching her cheek.

She covered his hand with hers, then backed away. "I have no right to compromise your place with your lord because of my own needs."

"*Your* needs?" He almost laughed. "Aye, twas a selfless thing I just did. And an onerous task. But I'm willing to sacrifice myself again if needs be." He stepped eagerly forward.

She retreated just as quickly. "Please dunna be charming, Boden. Not now."

"And if I cannot help myself?"

"Please."

He sighed. "Then I will see to Mettle and the goat." He turned to find his clothes. There was a moment of silence.

"Ye will not," she said.

Her words stopped him in his tracks. "What?"

"Ye will not see to the animals," she explained.

"And may I ask why, Mistress Sara?"

She jostled the babe lightly. In the pink light of dawn her face looked as bright as a spring rose. "I have done everything I know to heal ye. I will not let ye break open your wounds now."

He considered reminding her that it had not been long ago that she was not the least bit worried about his wounds. But such words would be foolhardy, for the woman who had reveled in his lovemaking was gone, slipped into the perfection of the night.

"Get back in bed," she ordered.

He lifted one brow at her. Frustration was building like a storm within him. It had been a long while since he'd taken orders from a woman. He didn't plan to begin again now. Crossing his arms against his chest, he glowered down at her, employing his darkest tone and expression. "Lest you forget, I am a knight, lady, fully grown, much exalted, and well dubbed. You will not be the one to send me hither and yon."

She stepped back a pace, seeming to shrink before his reprimand. She was, after all, not a large woman, but small, finely shaped, and very feminine. Perhaps he should not have been so harsh.

"Lest *you* forget, I have yer clothes?" she said, lifting the hose she had just received. "Or rather . . ." She stepped toward the window, and suddenly the garment was gone, dropped from sight. "I *did*."

He raised his brows. "Why?" was the only word he managed.

"I have told ye. Ye will not open the wound. Not while I can prevent it."

"So I am to be held hostage in this room?"

"I will not have yer death on my hands, Sir Knight."

He stepped forward, unable to help himself. "And what would you have your hands on, Sara?"

She stepped away. "Ye are no gentleman."

He stepped closer still. "Tis no surprise to me."

"I must fetch milk!" she stammered, and shoving Thomas into Boden's arms, darted for the door.

"Sara!"

Her hand was on the door latch, and for a moment he thought she would flee. But she turned, her face ashen, her hand still gripping the door latch behind her. "I must leave before I am overly tempted again Boden. Twas wrong of us to do it once. Twould be doubly wrong to do it again."

"Maybe you're right," he said, holding the babe at arm's length. "But if you must rush off like this I would ask that you take some sort of weapon with you."

He watched her try to puzzle out his words.

"I would suggest taking Black Adder," he said, staring at her bared shoulders. "But if you insist on going out like that it's doubtful an entire regiment of soldiers could protect you from your admirers.''

She glanced down at her pale shoulders, her draped body, her half bare legs. He watched her mouth form a silent "oh" before her bewildered gaze floated back to his face.

"Well, lass, which will it be?" he asked. And what the hell was he going to do with the baby while she was gone? "The gown or the sword?"

She blinked. Strange it was, to think she was the same woman with whom he had shared a bed only minutes before. Had she, or had she not scraped grooves into his chest while in the throes of passion?

"Ye must turn yer back," she said finally, but the words were very small.

He didn't smile, and was quite proud of that fact. Instead, he cocked his head to stare at her. "It seems that would be the gentlemanly thing to do," he said. "So I must refrain . . . since you said yourself that I am not of that exalted class."

"Surely we have sinned enough."

Had they? He watched her carefully. She was lovely beyond words. "In truth, lass," he murmured, "I have sinned a great deal in my life. Never did it feel like the night just past."

"Sir . . ."

"Boden," he corrected.

"Sir Boden." It was interesting to watch her draw herself up, as if gathering her dignity like a hen might gather her chicks. "Ye must look away while I dress."

"I cannot," he said, and turning slightly, he seated himself on the bed, only wincing a little, though the pain was sufficient. Thomas was heavier than Boden would have thought and it was quite tiring holding him upright under his arms. Besides which, the babe didn't look all that happy. So he turned Thomas about and settled him onto his hale thigh so that they could both watch Sara.

"I am completely undisciplined in this regard, for I cannot turn away."

Her lips moved for an instant before she found any words. "Well, try."

He laughed. "If you had left me my clothes I would milk the goat myself. But . . ." He shrugged, enjoying himself. "As it stands, I have nothing to do but sit here and watch you."

Her color had changed from the hue of a rosy sunrise to that of a ripened apple. How low, exactly, would that color reach?

"Please, sir," she murmured.

He felt himself weaken. But damn it—she'd stabbed him, lied to him, burned his thigh, then seduced him; she owed him this. It was shaky logic at best, but he was sticking with it. "Oh!" he said, suddenly remembering another of her sins against him. "And you insisted that I couldn't see you bathe, and then you watched me. When I was bathing in the river you watched me."

She remained very still. Her face couldn't get any redder. Even her ears were bright. How charming. "I did not say I was strong. Indeed, I am weak."

"Weak!" he scoffed. "You tied me to the bed, woman. You burned my leg!"

"'Twas for yer own good."

He smiled. "And this is for my own good too."

Thomas giggled, seeming to applaud his outstanding male logic. Sara scowled at them, first at Boden then at the babe.

"Tis my due," Boden said. "Look on it as a debt owed."

"I cannot."

Thomas whimpered.

"The babe is hungry," Boden said.

She glanced at Thomas, at Boden, at the baby, and then, to his utter surprise, she dropped the blanket from her body.

Air whipped from Boden's lungs. True, he had seen

her naked, but his mind had been dulled with drugs. Indeed, mayhap it still was, for surely nothing could be so lovely as she seemed. Nothing could be so alluring, he thought, but in a moment, she had grabbed her gown from the floor and snatched it over her head.

The sun dimmed. Thomas cried. Boden sighed as she slipped into her shoes and retrieved the kettle. "If you insist on going," he began, then cleared his throat and paused.

She turned at the door.

"Could you take the beast a bit of a treat? He'll sulk if you don't."

She raised her brows at him.

"Mettle," he explained, feeling foolish and refusing to meet her gaze. "He likes bread."

The air was still heavy with rain, and dark clouds hung low over the green hills that surrounded Cheswick. A young boy pulled a cart piled high with soiled straw. The pungent smell of cow manure wafted up. Across the rutted, muddy street, a soldier flirted with a weaver.

Sara hurried on toward the stable at the back of the inn. The door creaked open beneath her hand. Mettle whickered from his stall, the noise low and homey. He thrust his Roman nose over the Dutch door, his long ears pricked forward, his black eyes greedy.

Hurrying down the dirt aisle, Sara offered him the bread, then stepped inside the box while he munched.

"Lonely?" she asked him. "Your master wanted to come." The huge horse stared at her balefully as if doubting her words, then nudged her arm, begging for more. Opening her hand, Sara showed him her empty palm, but he nudged her again, so she reached up to scratch his ear. Mettle sighed heavily, cocked a gigantic hip, and closed his eyes.

Sara smiled. To a stranger he may well look like the ultimate war horse, invincible and independent. But if you knew him well he was much like his master. Mettle dropped his head even lower as his prickly upper wiggled in time with the movement of her hand.

" 'E likes attention."

Sara jumped at the words.

"Sorry t' scare y'," said the speaker, taking a scant step back from the stall door. He was a skinny lad with straw-colored hair, a pimpled complexion, and one hand tucked into the belt of his tunic.

"Nay. I am but fidgety," Sara said. "Mettle is doing well?"

"Is that his name?"

"Aye."

The lad bobbed a nod and stepped closer to the stall again. "He eats good and . . . well bless me," he said, gazing into the box. "Where'd the goat come from?"

For the first time, Sara noticed Tilly, happily munching Mettle's tail in the dark recesses of the stall. She winced. "We'd best get her out of there."

The lad opened the door, stepped inside, and after a moment of chasing Tilly about in circles, dragged her out by the frayed end of the rope still tied around her neck. "I had her tethered down the way. I swear I did."

Sara eyed Mettle's tail and sighed. "I dunna doubt it atall. Might ye hold her while I milk her?" she asked.

The boy had seen perhaps ten and six years and seemed eager enough to spend his time in her company.

Tilly, however, was not at all content to be parted from Mettle, so in the end, they put her back in the charger's stall and milked her there. Once finished, the lad insisted on carrying the bucket back to the inn for Sara.

He stood at the door looking nervous and eager. "Will y' be staying long in Cheswick?" he asked.

Had she ever been so young? Sara wondered. "Nay, we shall be moving on as soon as my . . . husband is mended," she said.

"Oh." His expression proved his disappointment at her marital state, but in a moment he brightened. "Mayhap I will see you in the stable this eveningtide."

"Aye," she said and turned away. Her husband! She felt her face burn with the necessary lie and the memory of the night before. How could she have been so wanton? she wondered as she ascended the stairs of the inn. Had she no morals at all? She was supposed to be a lady. Twas her identity for as long as she could recall. And he . . . he was a knight of the very man whose child she guarded. How had she let herself be so carried away? Never had she been so tempted by a masculine form. She was no great beauty, she was no silly lass. She was Sara of the Forbes, and long ago she had learned her place in life, nurturer, friend, confidante.

Remembering Boden's hose that she had tossed from the window, Sara turned and hurried back down the stairs to retrieve them. Finally, she reached the door to her shared room and stopped, drawing a deep breath and trying to calm her breathing and steady her mind.

Twas not like her to abandon herself merely for the wild, lecherous pleasures of sex. Therefore, it must have been Fiona's drug. True, he had affected her strongly before, for he was beautiful. Her heart twisted. Longing lodged there. But she would not think of him. She would not be tempted again, just because his chest was like granite and his arms like heaven. Just because the night past was, without a doubt, the most beautiful of her life.

She drew another careful breath and found that the milk was sloshing gently with her emotions. Dear Lord, she had to get a grip on herself. So every time she touched him her stomach did flips and her heart tried to leap from her chest. Twas only physical attraction. Nothing more.

Convinced, her hands nearly steady, she opened the door.

Sir Boden Blackblade lay on the bed with nothing but a blanket wrapped about his waist. His lips were slightly parted as he slept, and his chest, that great, muscled expanse of flesh, was bare, rising and falling. And snuggled against it, like a tiny, helpless kitten, slept Thomas with his fingers wrapped tight in a blue-black band of Boden's hair.

Raw emotion swamped Sara. For a moment it all seemed real. *Her* baby, *her* husband! Everything . . . nay, perhaps even *more* than she had ever wanted.

Moments ticked by. Reality trickled in. Pain, sweet with longing, filled her. She could not have them both. Indeed, she would be truly lucky if she were not left entirely alone. But she had made a vow, and she would do everything in her power to keep the baby safe. She must be wise and strong. And she must leave Boden at the first possible opportunity before it was too late.

Chapter 17

Forcing herself across the room, Sara retrieved her feeding gourd and poured milk into its battered bowl. Then, with her heart in her throat, she bent to lift Thomas from the bed.

Boden immediately opened his eyes. Their gazes met.

"You've returned." His voice was husky, deep.

"Aye." She settled Thomas absently into her arms, then tried and failed to concentrate on the child.

Boden sat up, his knees bent, his bare feet flat on the mattress. She saw him wince at the pain in his thigh and felt her heart lurch.

"Ye should lie down," she murmured.

Thomas awoke with a whimper. She pressed the gourd gently to his lips and he fell to feeding.

"I dreamt." It was all Boden said for a moment, but his gaze didn't leave hers. "I dreamt that you were mine."

Her heart pounded like running hooves in her chest, but she dare not show it. How did their thoughts meld as they did? Twas too frightening. "But I am not," she whispered.

"Twas night and you lay in my arms." He continued as if he hadn't heard her. "We wore nothing but the warmth of your hair. And your—"

"Boden!" Her voice sounded panicked to her own

ears. "I have sinned. I am sorry. I should not have done what I did. Twas the herbs," she whispered.

He raised his brows at her. The scar beside his lips twitched. "And we didn't realize what we were doing?"

"Aye, tis so."

"Tis a lucky thing I was not here with the goat, then," he said.

She couldn't help but laugh. "Tis not a laughing matter."

"And I'm not laughing," he said, still watching her. "Don't go out alone again."

The change of subject confused her. "What?"

"Twas not the herbs that caused my weakness, lady. Twas you and you alone. I was a fool to let you go alone, unguarded."

"I took yer clothes," she reminded.

His gaze didn't drop from hers. "Better naked by your side, than clothed like a king alone. Tis not safe."

"Do you think we are still followed?"

"Aye. We are followed. At least by the juggler, unless he is a fool."

She scowled.

He was silent for a moment, and when he spoke his voice was very soft. "What kind of man would let you go?"

"Liam is naught but a friend, Boden."

"Do your friends always attack your protectors?" he asked.

"I am sorry. He thought ye were the sorcerer. Then when he learned twas ye, he feared for his life, and thought me safer with ye than with him. I am certain of it. He meant ye no harm."

"You are wrong, lady," he murmured. "He meant to take you from me."

His meaning was perfectly clear. But she could not afford to dwell on it, for if she believed he cared for her as she did him, she might never find the courage to leave.

"We must leave," he interrupted. "Before we are found again."

"But ye cannot. Ye must rest."

"I will not risk you."

"Please." Thomas abandoned the gourd and cried. Sara put him to her shoulder and reached past him to touch Boden's arm. "Please. I beg ye to rest. Just for a short while. A few days."

He shook his head, but she could not give up.

"And what if yer leg does not heal?" she whispered. "What then? What if ye die?" Fear tore a ragged hole in her heart. "Do ye think I could survive without ye?"

Emotion smoked between them.

"I will rest then," he said, "but only so long as you stay in this chamber with me."

Sara nodded. Thomas cried again, and she rose to pace the floor and pat his back.

It took nearly an hour for Thomas to become content again. Sara crooned softly to him as she walked. He was finally asleep and felt soft and heavy against her shoulder. She should put him down to sleep, she knew, for she was tired, exhausted really. But once her hands were empty—what then? There was nothing to do but lie down, and there was only one place to do that.

"So you think you can't trust me enough to share a bed?" Boden asked.

Surprised that he was awake, Sara turned quickly toward him. "'Tis myself I dunna trust," she reminded him.

"Good," he said and showed that hint of a smile that made her heart trip. "Come. Lie down. Rest."

There was no way to argue, and very little point. Finally, she placed Thomas carefully on the bed and lay down with the child between them.

She was tense for a while, but when she looked over at Boden, she saw that his eyes had fallen closed. She lay in silence, watching him, feeling the dull, melancholy ache of love in her heart until sleep took her.

*   *   *

Sometime in mid-afternoon, they ate. Then, content and fatigued, they slept again. Dreams as sweet as clover honey filled her sleep. There were images of herself playing in the water with a young boy who giggled as he splashed. On the shore, Boden chuckled as he watched. A family. Her family.

She opened her eyes, and found Boden watching her, his expression solemn, his dark eyes steady in the encroaching darkness.

"The child is lucky to have you."

It took a moment to realize he was speaking of reality and not of her dreams. Wasn't he?

"I am luckier to have him," she answered softly. Dragonheart felt warm against her skin. And suddenly she was no longer surprised that Boden could step into her dreams, read her thoughts.

"Nay." He shifted one hand under his cheek. His fingers were sun-browned and battle-toughened. "You will forever have babes to love. Tis in your nature."

She lowered her gaze to Thomas. His lips had opened and he breathed softly through his mouth.

"What do ye know of my nature, Sir Knight?"

"A good deal."

"Such as?"

"You were meant to be loved."

"Everyone is meant to be loved," she whispered.

"Are they?" For a moment his eyes looked haunted, but he shut the expression quickly away. "You will make an extraordinary mother."

"Nay." The word was very soft. "I willna."

"How little you know of yourself."

"I canna bear children," she said.

"Tis not true."

"Aye." Her woman's time had never been normal or predictable. Though Fiona had prayed Sara would be fertile, it had been plain she had had her doubts. But the truth was obvious now. She was not meant to bear children of her own. Bravery had never been her hallmark, but she tried to keep her expression stoic. Such facts of life were not to be changed and it did little good to cry over them. Especially now, when the slightest splash of emotion could send her into Boden's waiting arms. "Tis true."

"You cannot know that," he denied, his tone husky.

"Stephen had children by other women," she explained.

A muscle jumped in Boden's stubbled jaw as if he tried to hold his tongue, but finally he spoke, his body tense. "I expect you wished to bear his children."

This was not a simple question, and though, perhaps she would be wise to give him a simple answer, she found she could not. "I wished very much to have *a* child," she said. "Someone to love. And mayhap I thought if I could deliver a babe, he would not hate me so. Twas a selfish reason."

"Hate you! He couldn't hate you." His words were absolute, without question.

"He beat me."

"Jesus!" He raised himself to his elbow.

She sat up, wishing she hadn't spoken of her shame. "I should milk Tilly before Thomas awakes," she said, but Boden reached across the babe to grasp her arm.

"Sara, I am sorry."

"Dunna be." Though she tried to sound flippant, the words came out flat. "For some time I tried to figure out why he hated me so. Now I know he was simply cruel. I should have . . . In truth, I still do not know what I should have done. I fear I lack the spirit of my ancestors."

"No spirit?" His grip tightened on her arm. "I have seen you challenge a dozen armed brigands with little more than a twig to protect you," he rasped, his eyes deadly level. "And you tell me you have no spirit?"

"But Thomas's life was at risk then."

For a moment all was silent. "So the babe is worth the battle," he murmured. "But you are not?"

There it was. The truth laid bare.

"I was yet young when my mother died. It became my job to care for Da and all the people of Nettlemore. Twas a good deal of work, but in truth, I reveled in it, for it gave me worth. Tis what I do. Tis what I am, and I thought Stephen would appreciate my skills. But what good is a woman who cannot produce an heir?"

"Tell me the name of the man who said that and I'll give you his head on a platter."

Such horrid violence. She smiled. "I fear he is already dead."

Boden stared at her, but finally his grip relaxed and he released a heavy sigh. "There seems little good to this foolish knighthood if I can't even kill who I wish to."

Surely that was nothing to laugh at. But she couldn't help herself, for his anger on her behalf took the sting from her own words. "Thank you," she murmured finally.

"For being a lousy knight?"

She smiled again. Twas like having a tamed wolf in one's bedroom. Twas a comforting feeling so long as he licked your hand. "You will make a fine father."

"Me?" There was honest surprise in his tone. "Tis highly doubtful."

"Nay."

"Aye," he disagreed. "My father was . . ." He sighed. "Not to speak poorly of the dead, but he was a bastard, and I mean that in the worst possible way. And my mother—"

It was her turn to reach across the babe. She laid a gentle finger to his lips. "Ye will make a fine father," she repeated. "I know it." Indeed, she had seen it in her dreams. But her dreams always became muddled, and for a few moments of bliss she had believed she would be the one to bear his wee ones.

He lifted her hand gently and kissed her knuckles. "The truth is, Sara sweet, I am a score and six years of age. I have been soldiering for nearly half my life and I have naught to show for it but an opinionated steed and a much-scarred sword. I have nothing to offer a wife.''

''How little you know of yourself, Sir Knight,'' she said, smiling. ''Ye have much to offer.''

Agony smote his heart. God, he could not live without her. He could not, yet he must. He must keep quiet, take her back to Haldane, be content. But he could not stop the words. ''Lady—''

She pulled her fingers from his hand to cover his mouth again. ''Dunna say it! Ye know it canna be. Yet even so, ye make me feel...'' Beautiful. Loved. ''Whole,'' she said softly.

Agony again. He let it come, let it take his soul, let it sweep over him, then seep its ache into every corner of his being. He nodded, forced himself to roll away, and stood up. He barely noticed the pain in his leg, though it seemed little equipped to bear his weight.

''I'll see to the beasts.''

''Nay.'' She sat up quickly. ''Nay. Please. Stay. You will open your wound.''

He stared at her. Such beauty—never to be his. ''It's already been opened,'' he said, and lifting the bottle of ale from the floor, turned away.

Inside the stable, Boden held the bottle in one hand as he rubbed Mettle down with a twist of straw. It was dark now but he had lit no lantern, for the blackness matched his mood.

Behind Mettle, Tilly munched on something unseen, but Boden's thoughts were far away. The pain in his thigh had progressed to a wild throb, making the sword strapped to his side seem a comical thing. For indeed, if he were attacked, there was little he could do other than fall on the foe and hope to crush him beneath his weight. Walking was painful enough.

Which made Sara more vulnerable than ever. He scowled into the darkness and took another swig from the bottle. She would never be his. Never. He knew that.

Had known it all along. And yet he could not stop the dreams.

He had to stop dreaming and start thinking! What the devil were they doing here? Anyone could find them here. Anyone.

They had to leave. The realization hit him suddenly in a sharp spark of fear, like a pain in his heart. She had asked him to stay and he had obliged. But now, when he could not see her pleading eyes, he could think more clearly. He was only one knight, and not a very good knight at that. He was an idiot! Someone was following her. Someone wished her ill. That much he knew. His only hope of keeping her safe was secrecy and flight, for they were up against a force he did not understand.

Slamming the cork into place, Boden stalked from the stall, stashed the bottle in his pack and picked up his saddle. Reentering the box, he began tacking up. The stallion grunted as Boden pulled up the girth. Tilly trotted forward, easily seen even in the darkness.

Turning stiffly about, Boden searched for his bridle.

"Where is it?" He almost yelled the words. Fear had turned to sudden, bitter panic.

"Sir?" A youth stumbled toward him, apparently just awakened from slumber in the nearby chaff. "Did you call?"

"My bridle!" He was being ridiculous, like a panicked child, and yet he was sure there was no time to delay. She was in danger.

"Tis here, sir," said the youth, handing over the headstall still attached to the chamfrein. "Are you leaving?"

"Aye."

"Now?"

"Aye." He tore the pouch from his belt and tossed it over. "Take two coins. Give them to the innkeepers."

"As you wish."

"Are the gates of Cheswick locked at night?" Boden asked, rapidly slipping the bit between Mettle's teeth.

"Aye. Every night at dusk."

''Is there any way a . . .'' He paused. Terror, unreasonable in its flaring intensity, burned through him. Sara was afraid. He did not know how he knew it, but he did. ''Is there any way brigands could get in?''

''Brigands? Nay. The gate is well fortified and Simon guards it.''

Pain slashed through Boden. Evil had come. He felt her thoughts and screamed her name as he dragged himself onto Mettle's back.

The youth jumped aside. Mettle whirled and thundered outside.

Sara! Boden saw her in his mind, cowering. He spurred Mettle toward the inn, but she was not there. Somehow he knew it.

Where was she? A cross! She was near a wooden cross.

He wheeled Mettle about and thundered toward the cathedral. Terror rode with him. Evil loomed before him, rising with the church's spire. It struck him like a weighted mace. Go back! He must go back! He felt the words in his soul, and suddenly he realized that he had reined Mettle to a halt before the church doors.

Sara's scream ripped through the night, through his mental blindness, tearing away his immobility.

He roared his battle cry. Mettle reared, striking the wooden doors with immense forefeet. They burst open in splintering rage, and Mettle lunged inside.

Sparks flew from the gray's iron-shod hooves as Boden spun him in a circle, searching wildly. Then he saw her. She lay on her side with Thomas on her back and a dark form leaning over her.

''Leave her!'' Boden roared.

The dark-robed figure turned slowly toward him.

''So you have come, Sir Knight.''

Mettle shuddered to a halt. The air left Boden's lungs in a rush, as if he'd been struck hard across the chest. Terror welled up anew, like a woolen blanket come to smother him.

"Aye." He could barely force out the word. For suddenly it seemed there was nothing in the world but this man before him, this man who held the power of the universe in his hands.

"But why have you come?" asked the sorcerer, his voice slow and steady. "To watch the woman die?"

Yes. To watch her die.

The old man laughed. The sound echoed against the stone walls. "You are not a knight!" he shrieked, raising a clawed hand. "You are nothing!"

He had to leave, escape! Before it was too late!

"Yes! Go! Leave now and your life will be spared."

Boden whirled Mettle about. Behind him, he could feel the old man turning.

"No!" Sara cried.

Boden's hands were shaking as he pivoted Mettle back around. "Leave her!" His voice was barely a rusty gasp. "Leave her be."

The old man turned back, and suddenly Boden realized his eyes were as white as winter, and yet it mattered little, for here lay a power far beyond sight.

"You, a leather-wright's son, dare to challenge me?" asked the sorcerer.

No. He was nothing, insignificant, terrified.

"You dare?" roared the old man.

Boden ripped the fear aside. "Aye!" he screamed back, and spurred Mettle toward the wizard. Boden swept out his sword, raised it, swung, and . . .

The blade snapped in two.

Chapter 18

A whimpering cry fell from Boden's lips. The wizard reached for him. But in that instant, Sara's face flashed in Boden's mind.

"Nay!" he roared, and wheeled Mettle into the sorcerer.

The old man was slammed against Boden's leg, then fell with a hiss of anger. Pain shot through Boden's body like a thousand deadly spears. But Sara was there, on her feet, so near.

Mettle lunged toward her. She lifted her arms, reaching for Boden. Their hands met and clasped. Momentum and desperation swung her and Thomas up behind him.

"Kill him!" the old man shrieked.

Mettle wheeled about.

Men loomed in the doorway, swords drawn. The exit was blocked, and terror reigned anew.

Boden spun Mettle about, spurring the steed toward the window.

He heard the old man scream for them to stop, but already they were flying through the air in a moment of breathless anticipation. Then Mettle's armor struck the window. Glass shattered, spraying shards in every direction. Men screamed. The earth lurched toward them. Mettle stumbled and dropped to his knees, then scrambled in the mud, trying to regain his feet.

Sara's hiss of fear was loud in Boden's ear. Already the old man was behind them, like a wraith, his black cape swept wide, his cackle loud.

But Mettle righted himself. And they were off, flying down the rutted street, fear streaming after them. Hoofbeats sounded from behind. Terror rode them hard to the city entrance just ahead. They had to get through.

"Open up!" Boden yelled, though the gates were already spread wide. Two bodies lay crumpled in death across the road as onlookers stared in horror.

"Their eyes!" He heard the hushed words. "Their eyes are gone."

The moon was nearly full, showing the cart trail that led from the village. But it would also show their exodus. Boden urged Mettle to greater speed. Behind them, the hoofbeats drew closer, for Mettle was slowed by a double load.

Ahead, a river flowed silver gild beneath the moon. A bridge yawned across it. They thundered over the wooden planks with the noise of their crossing echoing around them. Thomas shrieked nearly as loud. Black forest stretched just ahead of them. They leapt across the final expanse of bridge, then at the last second, Boden wheeled Mettle about. They careened downhill well aware that the riders were nearly upon them. He could hear the pounding hoofbeats of their galloping horses. There was no time to turn back. No time to change course. Water rushed against Mettle's legs. He tripped on an unseen rock and nearly went down. But in a moment, they were beneath the bridge.

Hoofbeats boomed like heavy artillery above their heads.

Boden sat immobile, knowing he could not fight, yet prepared to do just that. But in an eternity, the hoofbeats dimmed into the distance and the night became still.

"Sara." He breathed her name as he turned in the saddle.

"I am well. I am fine," she said.

"And the babe?" He noticed now that she had somehow wrestled the child from her back and had managed to quiet him.

"I thought I had smothered him with my hand—quieting him. But he is fine."

He touched her hand and felt his heart fill with that one simple gesture. They were safe. For now. "You've the heart of a lion, lady."

"Me!" Her laughter sounded on the verge of hysteria. "Nay. Tis ye that saved us. Ye to whom I owe me life again."

Their gazes fused. If he had any balls at all he would ride north and keep riding and damn the consequences. She was his, and Haldane could rot in hell. But he would not do that, for without his damned knighthood, he had nothing.

Turning Mettle downstream, they stumbled into the darkness.

Some hours later they stopped in the midst of the dark, dank woods. Except for a few cuts sustained from their flight through the window, they were all unhurt. Fatigue was a heavy load and yet, after the terror-seeped events, the idea of sleep was ludicrous. Thus, they sat in the darkness, trying to pretend they were not afraid.

Thomas, however, had the very young's innate ability to sleep, and did so now, snuggled deep in his handmade sling.

"How did you find me?" Sara asked, fear making her voice tremble.

"I don't know." His words were slow and deep.

"I prayed ye would. I prayed you'd come!" Her voice broke. She could feel his gaze on her face.

"Why did you leave the inn?"

She rose stiffly to her feet, unable to remain immobile any longer. "I could feel the evil." Her hands were shaking again. She clasped them together and stared into the darkness, certain she saw eyes watching her. For an instant she couldn't breathe. But finally she realized the image was nothing more than the reflection of the moon shining off a wet rock. "I was so afraid," she whispered. Even now she could sense the evil, though it did not seem so close. "I could feel it coming." Sometime long ago she had heard it was helpful to talk about one's fears. What a crock! With every word, the terror seemed to creep in anew. "I could feel it like a hand on my throat," she whispered. "All I could think was that I had to find ye. I grabbed my pouch and Thomas and I ran. We hid but . . . I forgot his feeding gourd." Her voice broke.

"Sara."

"I forgot his blanket."

"Sara, come here."

A noise startled her. She jumped, turning to find it was only Mettle, wandering close to stare at them from the woods. And yet her heart hammered in panic.

It was Boden's hiss of pain that drew her attention back to him.

"What's wrong?" she asked.

He winced, spreading his fingers over his right thigh as if he tried to hold back the pain. "Nothing. I'm fine."

"Nay, you're not."

"Aye," he said. "I am well." He bent his leg and grimaced. "Don't trouble yourself."

But she hurried over and knelt down beside him. She had been a selfish fool, worrying about herself when he was the one wounded. "Is there ought I can do to make ye more comfortable."

"Nay. Just rest, lass," he said, forcing a brave smile.

"Please," she whispered. "Ye've saved my life, and Thomas's. Let me help ye."

"Well, I . . ." He shrugged. "I could use something to support my leg."

She was on her feet in an instant, hurrying into the darkness. In a moment she found a stout log, as tall as herself and nearly as big around. It took some effort to move it, but she did so, wrestling along with it between her legs.

"Here," she said, falling to her knees to push it closer to his thigh. "If ye can bend your leg, I will shove it under."

For a moment she almost thought she saw the hint of a smile.

"Boden?" she said, thinking it must have been a grimace of pain. "Are ye well? Do ye need help bending it?"

"Aye," he said. "A bit of help would be appreciated."

She hurried to do as requested, grasping his leg near the knee and gently lifting upward. Then, straddling the log again, she tugged it underneath.

"Better?"

"Much." He sighed. "Much better."

"What else can I do?"

"Nothing. You've done more than enough."

"But there must be something." She glanced around. Thomas was content and sound asleep.

"Well, my arm does hurt a bit."

"What can I do?"

"It feels better propped up. Perhaps, if it's not too much trouble, you might . . . sit here beside me?"

She was there in an instant. He slid over an inch, allowing her back room against the rough bark of the buckthorn. Very gently, she took his arm and raised it about her shoulders.

"Better?"

"Could you scrunch down? Just a mite?"

She did so slowly, careful not to jostle him as she slid down so that her hip was cocked against the earth and her head rested on his chest. She blinked up at him. "Like so?"

"Just so," he said.

"Are ye certain this helps ye?" she asked. It seemed a ridiculously comfortable position for her to be in when she was intent on helping him.

"Absolutely."

They both fell silent. Far away a nightjar sang. The darkness stretched away. Sleepiness stole over her.

"Boden?" She could barely keep her eyes open, for through his tunic, she could hear the strong, rhythmic beat of his heart. "Were ye scared?"

He tightened his arm around her and closed his eyes. "I'm a knight," he rumbled as if that answered everything, and she fell asleep with a smile.

They were coming! She could feel the evil! But she couldn't run! She was tied down! Couldn't breathe! Her eyes! No!

Sara awoke with a smothered shriek. Boden jerked up from beside her, his hand already tight about the hilt of his sword.

Tilly bleated again and trotted out of the trees toward them.

"Addai's arse!" For a moment, Boden was certain he would faint, so great was his relief.

"Tilly!" Sara scrambled to her feet. "Tilly! How did ye find us?"

Boden just stopped himself from putting his hand to his heart to make certain it hadn't leaped from his chest.

Sara's sharp gasp brought him back to the present.

"I'm fine," he said, certain she could see the terror in his expression, but she was staring at his hand instead of his face.

"Yer sword!"

He glanced at the blade. It was broken off less than a hand's breadth from the hilt.

"Damnation!"

"How——" she began, but then memory flooded back and her face went pale.

"Damnation," he said again.

"Do ye still have the other blade?"

"Nay. Twas left behind."

He frowned, then glanced at Mettle. The horse stood

not far away, his ears laid back irritably as Tilly tried to nuzzle his nose. Behind his saddle was the crossbow but it would do little good in hand-to-hand combat. Damnation.

"We must get ye another sword," she said.

Boden almost smiled, for she made it sound like she spoke of purchasing a wooden doll for a child.

"Where might you suggest?" he asked, sheathing the truncated blade. "I'm in no great hurry to venture into another village."

"But I fear we must," she said. "For I've no way of feeding Thomas."

It was the problem of the hour. Although Tilly was happy enough to be relieved of her milk, the feeding gourd was lost. Finally, they dipped a bit of cloth into the still-warm liquid and let the babe suck on the tip. But it was unsatisfying and messy.

By noon they were traveling again, skirting the road and heading north. They kept their minds open and their eyes sharp, trying to think of a new way of dispensing the milk. But it was no use.

Thrice more that day, they milked Tilly and repeated the entire procedure, but it was clear they could not continue like this. The process was slow and frustrating, for the child as well as the adults.

They spent a cold and hungry night with a fussy baby and a light drizzle. By morning they were moving again. The day was just as miserable. Towards dark, Boden shot a buck. Hunger drove them to chance a fire, and that night they feasted.

"If I'm not mistaken, there's a village some leagues ahead," Boden said.

Immediately, he could feel Sara's tension. And when he glanced at her across the fire, he could see that her face was pale.

"I'll go in alone," he said.

"Nay. I will go with ye."

"Twould be foolish to endanger us all."

"Then I am foolish," she said, and by her expression, he could see there was nothing he could say that would dissuade her.

Morning had passed by the time they reached the village Boden remembered. It was more a shamble of gray stone hovels than a town. Though enclosed by a wooden palisade, the gates were open and gave the impression that they had not been closed for a long while.

Two small boys played in the mud, their feet nearly as black as the soil in which they sat. A woman turned from the well, her face marred by the scars of a plague long past.

There was an oppressive feeling about the place.

Some way down the littered road was a long flat building constructed of the same gray stones as the rest as the town. Above its warped, arched door hung a sign slightly askew that showed a picture of a mug and a loaf.

Sara dismounted first. Boden followed, trying to ignore the ache in his leg as he scanned the street behind him. But if the dark wizard was there, they neither saw nor sensed any sign of him.

Inside the public house it was dark and smelled rancid. A woman cackled and a man swore. Boden glanced at Sara, sorry now he hadn't tried harder to dissuade her from coming with him; but leaving her alone was unthinkable.

"And what might you be wanting?" The woman straightened away from the three men by the fire. They were a beefy trio, burly, bearded, intoxicated. The smallest of the three had buck teeth with hair the color of chaff showing beneath the cap that was tied below his chin. The other two might have been twins, matched almost identically in size and girth, though one was nearly bald while the other was thatched with dark, greasy hair. Who were they? Mercenaries? Brigands? Either way, the scenario was not good, Boden decided, for he was wounded and they were . . . alive.

"We wish for a meal," he said, turning his attention to the woman. She canted her head at him and chuckled. The sound was low and strangely suggestive.

"And is that all?"

"My steed would benefit from a bit of barley and a stable."

She laughed. "Birney!" she screamed again and after a bit a man staggered out of the nearby side door, hitching up his hose as he did so. "M' lord needs his horse seen t'."

"So long as yer not on your back, why don't you do it?"

She turned her head and glared at the man. Perhaps at one time she had been pretty, but years and ale had changed that. "Just because you can't get it up, don't mean the rest of us don't want it sometimes."

Birney raised his hand as if to strike her, but Boden caught the arm before he had time to consider his actions.

The man's evil expression turned to one of anger.

"My horse," Boden said softly. "He needs grain." He dropped the man's arm. Birney stumbled back, sloppy drunk, his eyes shifting. "And a gentle word. You will treat him gently, won't you?" Boden asked.

It took Birney a moment to realize it was a question, longer still to understand it was a threat.

"Aye. I . . . I will," he said and in a moment he was gone.

"Well, Leoma ain't never had me a champion," said the woman, pacing around Boden to study him from another angle. "You might just get yours for free."

Boden ignored her words, falling back on the stiff, knightly formality he had learned at Knolltop. "We'd be willing to barter some venison for a meal," he said.

From near the fire, the large, dark-haired man said, "She weren't offering no meal. She was offering a good f—"

"Shut yer trap, Will," she said, then chuckled. Her eyes were bloodshot and her hair tangled.

Dear God, this was no place for Sara, that was certain. But one glance at her eyes showed her fatigue. Surely twould be best to spend the night here, for he, too, felt the drain of the days past.

"So you want to trade venison for . . ." The woman called Leoma paused, eyeing him speculatively. "A meal?"

"Aye." He said. "And a bit of information."

"I can give you both." She glanced at Sara, then twisted up one side of her face into what might have been a smile. "And more. 'Ave a seat."

Boden ushered Sara to a plank table as far from the trio of drinking men as possible. She had taken Thomas from his pouch, and the babe fussed now, whimpering and squawking at intervals.

"Is he well?" Boden kept his voice low when he spoke to her, for surely the less attention he drew to them the better.

"Just hungry, I think," she said, but there was worry in her eyes.

It had been so simple to distract her with his own needs, simple to know she would soon forget her own cares in exchange of another's. And the solution had been so sweet, with her head pillowed against his chest and her breathing soft and quiet against the beat of his heart.

But right now he couldn't afford to be distracted by that memory, or by his worry for her. Perhaps they should have traveled on. Mayhap they should have taken more time to find an alternate way to feed the child. But he had no way of knowing how long a babe could last on a limited diet.

Leoma reappeared, carrying nothing but a bottle.

"The meal?" Boden inquired.

"You forever in such a rush?" she asked, bending close and leering at him. Her breath smelled foul, and her breasts, half freed from her failing bodice, nearly fell into his face.

"We are in something of a hurry," he said.

"A hurry, ay?" She straightened with a huff.

Thomas began crying.

"What's wrong with the brat?"

Sara looked up from the child. Boden could feel her increased tension and willed her not to speak. She may be unaware of her allure, but men, even dense, intoxicated men, would notice if she gave them any provocation.

"He's hungry." In the crude surroundings her voice seemed to ring with an unheard sweetness. "He needs milk."

The woman reared back with a snort. "So give him a tit."

"We need some way to feed him," Boden said quickly, not allowing himself to glance at Sara, and thinking perhaps he should have let Birney slap the wench. "Might you know of a way?"

"You mean them little titties of hers don't even give milk?" Leoma laughed out loud, throwing back her head so that her fat breasts jiggled. "You'll not find that problem with mine," she said, changing gears quickly, and leaning forward again. "I've nursed a babe, I have. Pampered her proper—for all the good it did—"

"Do you know where we can find a milk bladder?" Boden asked. Please God, don't let him think of her raising a child.

She scowled at him, not happy about the interruption. "Years back there was a sickly woman." She turned her gaze to Sara again, her expression derisive. "She couldn't feed no babe neither. Me, I offered to help her." She smiled, though the expression was evil. "But she was too good for the likes of me. The babe died." She laughed. "And I didn't shed no tears."

Boden felt Sara shiver beside him, and wished again that they had not come here.

"Where might we find the woman?" Boden asked.

"Tis not my task to—"

"I know where she is," said Birney, entering clumsily.

Boden shifted his gaze to him. "Where?"

"Hard to find," Birney said. "But I'll fetch her for you—for a shilling."

Everything in Boden made him want to slap the man up against the wall just for sport. But it probably wasn't honorable. "If she comes with a bladder, I'll give you half that."

"My time's worth more," Birney sputtered.

Boden stared at him in silence, then, "By morning you'll be sober," he said. "Think about it."

Birney narrowed his eyes, then glanced at Leoma and stumbled from the room.

Boden poured a tankard of whiskey and passed it to Sara as Leoma returned to the kitchen. Sara shook her head, but he nudged the drink toward her. "Twill do you good," he said.

She glanced toward the trio of men by the fire. "It doesn't seem to be doing them ought but harm."

Twas true, of course. The burly threesome was getting more obnoxious by the moment. The balding man had thumped the straw-haired man on the chest, knocking him clear out of his chair. Will was laughing uproariously, but the smaller one didn't seem to think it so amusing.

"Drink," Boden repeated. "I doubt if one drink will change you into the likes of them."

She smiled, but worry was in her eyes. Still, she drank. And finally, when their meal arrived, they ate, though the food was dubious at best, making their night of venison seem like an elaborate banquet.

A short time later, Birney wobbled in, followed by a woman. She was slightly bent and very thin, the leanness of her condition evidenced in her face, her hands, the birdlike bones of her wrists.

"I found her," said Birney, tugging the woman forward and giving Boden a much-needed excuse to break from his meal.

The woman bobbed them a quick curtsy, her eyes too large in her gaunt face, her bony hand clutched about a small hide. "You wished to see me, sir?"

"What's your name, mistress?"

"Garnet, sir."

"We've a need for a milk bladder, Garnet," he said, coming right to the point.

She lifted the small hide slightly, looking nervous as her gaze skimmed to the babe in Sara's arms. "I've . . ." She swallowed nervously and glanced toward Birney who stood behind her. "I've no need of it any longer."

"I am sorry." Sara's words were very soft.

Finding kindness in this place seemed to startle the woman. She turned toward Sara. The echo of a smile shown in her eyes, and she nodded her thanks.

"Tis no need to mourn," she said. "M' youngest is long past the need for milk."

"Oh."

Boden could feel Sara's relief.

"I don't have a great deal to offer," he said. "But I'll give you half a deer in trade for it."

Garnet smiled. "Your lady will need the meat to keep up her strength."

His lady!! The words wore a sweet, painful path to his heart. He glanced at Sara, feeling the path burn deeper.

"We wish to give you the meat," he said.

Garnet bobbed her thanks. "My babes will be grateful, and it will do m' heart good t' know the bladder is well used."

The decision made, Boden rose, and with a glance at Sara, stepped out to make the exchange. Birney, he decided, would carry the meat for Garnet. Once outside, he found a chance to slip her a coin, not simply for the bladder she had given them, but for her kindness as well.

When he stepped back inside the inn, the tension emanating from Sara was palpable. The men! he thought. But nay, they were still by the fire, and their attention was not directed toward Sara, but at a huddled scrap of a figure near the stairs. It was a child, thin and ragged.

"Ah, so there's little Princess Margaret," Leoma said. "Come on over 'ere, girl, so's the lady can see y'." Her voice was a strange croon.

The child shook her head. She had huge brown eyes that seemed to consume her face and a scar that sliced a diagonal path across her forehead.

Leoma's expression darkened. "Come over 'ere."

The girl cowered back.

Leoma gritted a smile at Sara, but her hands were clenched into fists when she turned back to the child. "What y' be doin' down 'ere?"

The tiny figure said nothing, only shifting her slight weight as if wishing to disappear into the floor.

"I asked what y' want!"

As the woman walked toward the child, the girl backed away, then bumped into the wall where she stood frozen for a moment before opening a palm and showing a crust of dark bread.

"Ahh." Leoma chuckled. "So y' want something to eat. And what for? That rat of yours?"

The child shook her head wildly.

"Y' know I don't like it when y' lie t' me!" Leoma said and snatched the child's arm. "Y' wanted ta be down 'ere so ya might as well come on out in the open," she ordered, dragging the child forward.

"So, Leoma, who's this?" asked the one called Will.

"This . . ." said the woman, pinching the girl's arm in a clawlike grasp. "This is my daughter. The princess," she said, but the word sounded ugly. "Birney's brat! Ain't that right Birn?"

The man snorted as he shambled past.

"Yours?" asked the blond man as he shifted his gaze swiftly from the mother to his friends. "Didn't know whores could 'ave children." He laughed rather like an ass with his tail caught in a door.

"Guess she ain't filled out so good like her mother," said the other man.

Leoma snorted and sneered a smile toward the speaker. "Y've always 'ad an eye for the women, 'aven't y', Danny," she said and shook the girl. "Aye, she's a skinny thing she is, and y' know why? She takes the food I sweat t' earn and she feeds it t' the rats! Ain't that right, girl?"

The child didn't answer, but scrunched away to the far end of her mother's reach.

"Ain't that right?" gritted Leoma, shaking her, but in that instant a furry something streaked out of the girl's sleeve and onto the mother's arm.

Leoma shrieked like one insane, shaking madly to rid herself of the vermin.

Panicked, the brown creature dropped to the floor and streaked beneath the men's table.

A hiss of pure horror escaped from the girl. A wild fear lit her eyes and she lunged after the animal. In a second, her hand was on it and it had disappeared inside her ragged clothing again, but just as quickly the smallest of the men had grabbed her by the arm.

He pulled her from under the table. " 'Ello girlie."

She leaned away like a cornered colt, all eyes and tangled hair.

"She's a witch!" Leoma shrieked, her face twisted. "A witch! Taking in vermin and doin' all manner of nasty things with 'em."

"Nasty things, huh?" chuckled Will. "I can think of a few nasty things myself."

Danny snorted, seeming to read his companion's mind. "The girl don't even have no titties yet."

"Nay," said Will. "But she will and till then . . . we can learn 'er some things. Sides, Lang likes 'er, don't y' Lang?"

The smallest man bobbed a quick nod and licked his lips. Will turned his gaze to Leoma. "Want me t' take 'er off your 'ands?"

The woman narrowed her eyes. "What would ya want 'er for?"

Will chuckled. Lang grinned, his eyes bright.

"Could be we'll think of something," Will said.

Leoma scowled. Boden could almost see the ragged thoughts lumbering through her mind. "Y' don't think you're gonna get her for nothing do y'?" she asked.

"Y' said yourself she's a skinny thing."

"Aye." Leoma set her hands on her hips and pushed out her generous chest. "But she'll grow."

Will chuckled. "If she lives so long. How much do y' want for 'er?"

"A sovereign."

"Yer daft," Will said. "I'll give y' a half angel."

Leoma laughed. "You'd be lucky if'n y' 'ad a farthing."

Will reached into a pouch. The girl jumped at the motion, but Lang held her tight and chuckled at her fear. Then, Will pulled out a gold piece and tossed it to Leoma. She caught it in one hand, then raised her brows at her good fortune.

"Nay!" Sara lurched to her feet. The lump in Boden's stomach turned over. "Nay," she said more softly. "Ye cannot sell her."

Leoma turned slowly toward her, her eyes deadly flat, her mouth sneering. "And why is that, mother earth?"

Sweat popped out on Boden's brow. His leg ached, and he'd be lucky to get the three of them out of this hellhole alive. "Sara." He kept his voice low and level. "Think of Thomas."

At some point, she had strapped the babe to her back. She stood now, her face pale as lily petals, her eyes as wide as the heavens. "I am," she said.

"I'm wounded," he reminded her, and cautiously shifted his attention to the three men.

Silence filled the place, and then she turned toward him. He could feel her gaze smite him, but refused to look up, refused to be drawn in by the weight of her emotions.

"Come 'ere, girl," growled Will.

"Please!" Sara's whisper filled Boden's head. In his mind he could see her eyes, wide and blue as God's heavens.

"I'll give you a sovereign," he said.

Chapter 19

~~~ ◦◦ ~~~

Big Will turned slowly toward Boden. In his eyes there was malice and in his oversized hands, the power to squash a small village. "She's ours." His tone was as flat as his eyes.

"I'll give you a sovereign," Boden repeated, not taking his gaze from Leoma.

"Deal's already been made," said Lang. "Tell 'im, Will."

"Don't rush me," said Leoma. "I ain't said for sure. M'lord 'ere says 'e'll give a sovereign. What will *you* gents give me?"

"We ain't got that much t'throw away on no scrawny brat!" hissed Will.

"She's mine," whined Lang.

"Then give me the coin," said the mother.

"She ain't worth no sovereign. What with Lang's 'ands on 'er and Danny's love of knives, she won't last out the week, skinny as she is. Now *you* . . ." He chuckled, slowing his words and turning his bloodshot gaze to Leoma's cleavage. "You'd do *me* fine, but I guess you ain't good enough for 'is lordship."

Leoma stiffened and glanced toward Boden.

Will smiled, showing teeth as rotten as his soul.

"Y' offered yourself t' 'im after all," he continued. "But 'e'd rather 'ave the whelp."

247

"Give me a sovereign for 'er and she's yers," insisted Leoma.

"We gave y' a angel," said Danny. "That was the deal."

"And y' know we'll be back, giving y' more business," added Will. "This gent . . ." He turned his eyes to Boden. " 'E can't barely wait t' be shut o' y', what with 'is fancy bitch on 'is arm."

Leoma turned toward Sara, her eyes mean.

"I got me a shilling," Lang said, digging into his pouch and drawing forth the coin.

"She's yers!" spat Leoma. "And good—"

"Please!" Sara stepped forward a pace, her fists clenched at her sides. "Please, for God's sake!" she whispered. "You're her mother!"

"You wanna come too?" asked Will. He rose to his feet, his gaze on Sara, his thoughts clear as death in his eyes.

Panic tasted bitter in Boden's mouth. "Sara, step back!"

"Maybe she be lookin' for a man what can satisfy 'er," suggested Will.

The panic settled slowly in the pit of Boden's stomach, like motes of fine dust on a forgotten road. "I recommend you keep your hands off her, friend," he said.

Will stepped forward. "Or what?"

Boden paused a moment for effect—and to wait for his trembling to cease. "Or you'll die where you stand." It was a good threat—stated flatly, level, with an almost flippant tone. His sword sang as he removed it from its sheath and swung it into the air.

There was a moment of silence and then, like a gust of ho. vind, Will threw back his head and laughed. "Fuck my ass! Tis a good thing y' didn't screw 'im, Leoma, 'cause his wick probably ain't no longer than 'is blade."

The other two men joined in the mirth, and in a moment Leoma too was laughing.

Boden stared at them, then turned his attention to his sword and swore. Dear God, he'd forgotten its pitiful state. He turned to Sara in horror. Her eyes were wide, but her expression said quite clearly, sword or no sword, there would be no backing down.

Wulfric's sainted wart, he was in trouble. "Let the child go," he said, hoping against hope that there was still a modicum of aggression in his tone.

"I don't think so, yer lordship."

There was no way out now, he knew, for if he didn't do something soon, Sara would take matters into her own hands, and the devil take the hindmost. "Let the child go," Boden repeated. "Or your next meal will be in hell." Not bad as hopeless, last ditch threats went, he thought, but just then, Will drew his sword.

"To hell yourself," he swore and lunged across the floor with a roar of rage.

Boden yelled back, though whether in fear or defiance, even he couldn't have said. Still, there was no time to delay, and in a moment of indecision, he flung his blunt sword at his opponent. It clanged against the other's, knocking it aside. Will sped on, and in the instant before he brought his weapon back to bear, Boden grabbed a dinner knife from the table and whipped it overhand.

It sunk into the soft hollow of Will's throat. The huge man staggered back a pace, dropping his sword. Grasping the knife in both hands, he yanked it from his throat and tossed it to the floor with a gurgled snarl of rage.

"Y' bastard!" shrieked Danny and launched himself forward. Boden glanced wildly about for a weapon. A ladle? A milk bladder?

Then, out of the corner of his eye, he saw Sara whip a hot kettle forward. The contents sprayed outward in a boiling arc.

Danny screamed as the blistering stew struck his face. Sara stood frozen in horror just as Leoma lunged forward, hands like claws.

Sara swung the kettle like a deadly mace once again.

It struck Leoma in the temple. She staggered to a halt, then crumpled like a broken doll.

Boden stared in fascination.

"No!" Sara screamed.

Boden snapped his attention forward. Will was barreling down on him, his gory throat frothing with blood.

"Mettle!" Boden yelled, and in an instant went down beneath Will's tremendous weight.

"Get 'im, Will! Get 'im!" Lang shrieked, forgetting the child in his excitement.

"Boden!" Sara screamed, but just then a movement caught her eye. The girl! Without another thought, Sara lunged after her, catching her by her rags and swinging her into her arms.

"Get Mettle!" Boden yelled again, grappling wildly with Will, and there was nothing Sara could do but run from the inn, the baby on her back, the child in her arms.

The stable was at the back of the inn. Sheer panic drove her until she reached Mettle. She tossed the child into the stallion's saddle. In the second stall, another horse was tied. Sara grabbed the animal's rope and yanked out the knot. In an instant, she was seated behind the girl, and dragging the smaller horse along behind.

They left the stable at a dead gallop and careened around the corner. Boden staggered out the door and threw himself at the trailing horse.

Sara tossed back the rope, and they were gone, thundering out of the village as if the hounds of hell were after them.

By midafternoon, Boden thought he would die from his myriad aches and pains. By evening, he hoped he would. Except for one stop, they kept moving at a steady trot, putting a good deal of distance between them and the hellhole they'd left behind.

Finally, unable to suffer in heroic silence, Boden slipped off the mare's bonny back and fell in a heap on the ground, quietly hoping to die before Sara discovered him there.

But luck seemed to have abandoned him completely.

"Boden!" She turned Mettle back. "Are you hurt?"

"Nay. Nay." He stayed where he lay. It was surprisingly pleasant there, beneath the nag's belly, half in the shade, half out, with his mind floating like umbrella seeds in the wind. "Never better, really."

Slipping from the saddle, she hurried to his side. "Where are ye hurt?"

"Me?" He shifted slightly, trying, without much success, to dislodge a stone that was pressed into the small of his back. "Tell me, Sara, why did you choose those men?"

"What?" She touched his brow, apparently feeling for fever.

"There are a lot of men in England, lady. Evil men, even. Why must you choose the largest of them?"

Her hand slipped from his forehead to cup his cheek. "Ye were very brave, Sir Knight."

Flattery. While it may soothe a scraped knee or a split lip, it would do little good for a leg that had been hacked in two, even when delivered in her melodious tones, with her expression showing a wealth of concern, and the softness of her hand reminding him of the unearthly smoothness of the skin of her breast, with her heart beating soft and strong and her hair like thistle down, and her eyes . . . He sighed.

"We could have been killed, tortured, mutilated. Did that ever occur to you?" he asked.

"I am sorry," she whispered. "But the child. You couldn't have left the child."

"I couldn't?"

"Nay," she said, and smiled. The expression warmed him like sunlight on his skin. "Ye are much too kind to leave her, Sir Knight."

"Kind?"

The mare shuffled away a few paces, careful not to

step on him, and thus assuring an improved opinion on Boden's part.

"Aye. And good," she whispered, and leaning forward, kissed his mouth.

Contentment shifted through him. "Good?" he asked.

"Aye, and . . ." She leaned forward again. He closed his eyes for her kiss, but instead, he heard her gasp of horror as she drew away.

He wrenched himself to his feet. "What is it?"

"Margaret!" Sara cried, and in that instant, he saw the tiny, ragged figure scrambling off into the woods.

"Jesus!" he ground out.

"She'll be lost," Sara moaned.

With a curse, Boden launched after her. It took a good fifty rods to run the child to ground, but he finally did, hauling her to a halt by the back of her scruffy gown.

She turned like a cornered wildcat, swinging at him. One small fist glanced off his thigh. He sucked air between his teeth and dropped her gown to grab her arm.

She sunk her teeth into his hand. He shrieked in pain and let her go and she was off like a race horse.

He lunged after her with a curse, caught her gown again and careened to the earth, dragging her beneath him. Pain shot out in lightning lances of agony as he tried to suck air into his lungs.

"Boden. Boden." Sara's voice finally reached him. "You're squashing her."

It was then, for the first time, that he realized he was lying on top of the child. He rolled off, wondering what body parts he would leave behind.

"Are ye well?" Sara asked.

"Well, my—" Boden began, but Sara interrupted him. "Are ye well, little one?"

The child lurched onto all fours and scrambled wildly forward. But in an instant, she twisted about with a small shriek of dismay and began digging frantically about in her clothes.

She stopped suddenly, and from her bodice, dragged

forth the sleek, limp body of her weasel. The girl stared at it for a frozen moment, then placing it to her heart, rocked slowly back and forth.

"Margaret," Sara said, staring at the marten's flaccid body. "I'm sorry. So sorry."

The tattered figure continued to rock in silence. Sara reached out, wanting, needing, to share her grief. But the child jerked back, and in that instant, Sara thought she saw the weasel move.

"Margaret." The child's eyes lit on hers, filled with a raw mixture of anguish, fear, and rage. "I think, mayhap, he is still alive."

It took a moment for the girl to grasp Sara's meaning. Air hissed between her teeth as she glanced down at the unconscious weasel.

"I have some knowledge of medicine," Sara said softly, flicking her gaze from the rodent to the girl. "If ye like, we could return to the horse. Behind his saddle I have my herbs."

The girl's hands shook, but after an agonizing eternity of silent debate, she pushed herself to her feet. Sara did the same, leading the way back to the horses.

"Don't concern yourself with me," Boden said, staring at the branches that leaned over him. "I'll be fine."

Digging into the packet behind Mettle's saddle, Sara silently admitted that she had no idea what she was doing, but she had to do something. She raised her gaze to the girl's. The child had not cried, only whimpered and hugged the rodent more fiercely to her chest, and that, somehow, seemed sadder than tears—beyond pain and into despair. So, to give herself time to think, Sara dragged out her armory of herbs. It was a pathetically small supply. Aunt Fiona would weep at the sight.

She turned and set her medicines on the ground. "May I tend him?"

Indecision crossed the child's face, but in a moment fear won out and she hugged the critter more fiercely to her chest. Not a spark of trust or hope shone in her eyes.

Sara sighed. Her shoulders ached from Thomas's weight and long hours in the saddle, so she slipped him off her back.

Margaret's eyes went wide as she watched Sara gently set the babe on a mossy spot on the ground. Only the top of his head was visible, and Sara wondered now what the child would think. Knowing something of her background, it seemed best to immediately assure her of the babe's well-being.

"This is Thomas," she said softly, and ever so gently, pushed the sling aside so that the girl could see his face. The babe didn't move and Margaret remained just as wide-eyed as ever.

"He is sleeping," Sara explained, wishing she knew what went through the child's mind. "Nothing worse. Just asleep." She was crouched beside the babe, looking up at the child. "Mayhap your wee friend is sleeping too."

Margaret turned her gaze to the limp animal in her hands.

"Mayhap, he but hit his head." Or maybe he was dead and far past her help. But it hardly seemed right that God would take the animal from her. For the marten was probably her only friend. So to fill the time and try to help the girl relax, Sara began to speak.

"Once upon a time there was a small boy whose name was Roman. He had a dog he called Dora. He loved her with a fierce loyalty," she said softly. "But one day when they were tending sheep, Dora was attacked by wolves. She was badly wounded. In truth, wee Roman thought she was dead, but he had heard of a healer, and he thought, mayhap, if the Lord willed it, she could mend his hound. So he carried his dog to her."

Margaret's gaze never flickered away and in their depths, Sara could see her question.

"Many years later, after a long and happy life, Dora had her last litter of pups. Five of them there are, and each of them looks just like her."

It seemed like an eternity before Margaret stepped forward. When she did her knees shook, and as she placed the weasel in Sara's outstretched hands, Sara could feel her fear like a tiny, tangible fist to her gut.

Their gazes met. Margaret pulled away as if struck by the other's attention. Sara lowered her eyes. Laying the animal down gently, she smoothed her fingers over its silky fur, and there, just behind its front leg, she could feel a pulse. She jerked her gaze to the girl's wide stare.

"He yet lives," she said, and with those words, Margaret clasped her hands together and held her breath.

Returning her attention to the marten, Sara felt along the tiny limbs. Though she was hardly an expert, she could find nothing amiss there. But on the top of its head she felt a slight bump. God only knew if that could cause this unconsciousness. And God wasn't telling.

"Here," said Sara. "Feel this bump."

But the girl stayed where she was, just out of reach.

"Did he have it before?"

No answer. But her eyes had gone wider still.

What to do for a bump on a weasel's head? Sara had no idea, but in that moment she had an image of Sir Boden in the bathing tub. He was surrounded by floating herbs, his dark skin slick and wet. Sweet mist filled the air. Pleasure filled her soul.

Margaret shuffled her feet, bringing Sara abruptly back to the present. Twas no time to think of that one night of perfection, and yet . . . the herbs! They seemed like a panacea, and thus, she retrieved a small bottle, filled it with water, and dropped a tiny pinch of herbs into it. She then dabbed a bit of the tonic onto the bump and legs. Then, prying the mouth open, she dripped a droplet onto its tongue.

When Sara glanced up, she saw that Margaret looked skeptical at best. And who would not be? There should be something more. And so, reaching under her gown, Sara tore off a bit of her kirtle to act as a bandage. The rodent had no wounds to bind up, and yet, if she wished to win the child's trust, it seemed wise to show some visible proof that she was trying.

So she wrapped the white linen about the creature's long, flaccid body and sat back on her heels.

"What—" began Boden, stepping into the clearing.

Margaret started, then lunged forward to snatch up the weasel and pull it to her narrow chest. Slowly, without moving her gaze from Boden, she backed away.

"What's the matter with her?" Boden asked, his voice deep, his brows cliffed over his eyes.

"She is afraid," Sara said.

"Of me?" he asked. The surprise in his voice almost made her want to laugh.

"Ye are, after all, a fierce knight," she reminded him.

He lowered his gaze to hers and for a moment she could think of nothing but touching him, for he was very close and the memories of a warm bath and a steam-filled room still filled her mind.

"Aye," he said quietly. "That I am. But surely she does not have to look at me as if—"

Something jumped from the woods. Sir Boden wheeled about, crouched low, legs braced, empty arms spread wide.

But it was only Tilly, sounding disgruntled as she looked about the clearing.

"Damn!" Boden stopped short of putting his hand to his chest to check the damage done to his heart. "That goat's truer than a hound."

Spotting Mettle beside the mare, Tilly trotted over and placed herself resolutely between the two.

Sara turned her gaze back to Margaret. The child was backing slowly away, ready to bolt into the underbrush.

"I'm not guaranteeing my ability to catch her again should she flee," Boden said softly.

"She's only a small child," Sara murmured.

"I've a hole in my leg," he grumbled. "And she's faster than she looks. Besides, she bites."

"But you're a knight, trained—"

"Hmmph," said Boden, then louder, "I suppose the weasel will require your medicine again soon, Lady Sara?"

It took Sara a moment to realize his ploy, but then she agreed. "Aye. He will need another dose by morning at the latest if he is to recover completely."

The girl stopped in her tracks, then, after a moment of deliberation, hunkered down half hidden behind a hazel bush. And as if she could will herself to be invisible, she became almost so.

"All right then," Boden said, turning away. "I'll make the fire and cook the venison."

"Nay." Sara turned toward him, aware that the child remained, silently debating whether to flee or stay. But either the talk of medicine or food kept her rooted to the spot. "Ye rest," she said. "Please. You're wounded."

"And the babe will soon wake. He'll be quite put out if you have no milk for him," Boden said. "'Tis debatable whether I'd rather lose my leg or listen to him squawk." As if by magic, Thomas squawked at that second.

Despite everything, the fear, the fatigue, the worry, Sara smiled. "'Twill only take me a short while to milk the goat. Ye rest."

He touched her face, his fingertips light against her cheek. "And of course ye are not tired, are ye, lady?"

"Not so very."

"And you lie poorly. Take care of the babes," he said and turned away.

Tilly was more recalcitrant than ever. But finally, after much fuss, she let down her milk, while Sara collected it in the usual kettle. After filling the bladder, nothing was heard from Thomas for some time as he nursed.

After a few tries, Boden managed to start a fire. He then cut up the venison and retrieved the bottle of ale he had taken from the inn. From the other pouch, he took a shallow wooden bowl into which he sloshed a good deal of the potent liquid. Striding back to the fire, he set it beside Sara.

"Drink it," he ordered, and turned back to the meat. Still Margaret crouched nearly out of sight as the sun disappeared behind the last treetop.

Finally, Thomas fell asleep, his peeked lips parting as his head drooped against Sara's chest. She lifted him gently and laid him on a blanket in a deep bed of green mosses.

The sweet aroma of cooking meat wafted up from the cookfire.

"She must be hungry." Boden's voice was low, and though he didn't raise his gaze from the venison he was cutting and placing on a rock near his feet, it was clear he was speaking of Margaret.

"Aye," Sara said, also not turning toward the girl. "But mayhap her fear of pain is greater than her fear of hunger."

There was silence for a moment, but for the crackle of fire.

Sara frowned into the flames. "When I think of what the child has endured I—"

"Don't," Boden said, interrupting her sharply. "Don't think about it. She's free from it now."

Sara raised her gaze to his, and wished with sudden intensity that she could wrap him in her arms.

He turned resolutely away. "I'll have to think of a new name for you. Saint Sara doesn't seem to apply any longer. Who taught you how to swing a kettle like that?" he asked, not looking at her.

In the firelight, his dark features gleamed. His hair was blue black and tied away from the strong, sharp angles of his face, his hands looked magical, and his eyes, deep as hope, entranced her. But she couldn't love him. There were repercussions. There were sins. Even if her actions didn't adversely affect her, she had to think of Boden and his life after she was gone. She closed her eyes for a moment and forced her mind away from her ravaging thoughts.

"Do ye think I killed her?" she whispered. "Margaret's mother?"

Boden flicked his gaze to the shadow that hid in the shadows. By the fire's fickle light she could see a muscle flex in his jaw. "I hope so," he said.

Their gazes caught again. "Will she ever forgive me?"

"'Tis impossible to know what damage has been done to the child, Sara. Don't hope for too much. Even you can't force her to trust."

Silence settled in. But after a while there was a rustle of sound, then a small hiss from the hazel bush. Sara glanced up, and in a second, a tiny, bandaged slice of fur darted through the grass and attacked a piece of venison.

Margaret was close behind. But, in a moment she skidded to a halt, her eyes wild, her hair a mass of tangles about her head.

Not a soul moved.

The weasel growled and gnawed noisily at the venison.

Boden lifted his gaze to the child's as he nodded to the cooked meat. "'Tis better hot."

She licked her lips, but dared not advance.

Boden turned his gaze to the snarling weasel that wrestled with his food. "You must have given him the same herbs you gave me, Lady Sara. I, too, was ravenous."

Despite Margaret's presence, Sara felt herself blush, for she well remembered Boden's appetite in the tub. Still, she wasn't such a fool as to misunderstand the reason for his words.

He was attempting to make the girl relax, and in time, mayhap, the child would realize they meant her no harm.

"The marten looks well," Boden continued as he slipped a piece of venison from the skewer. "'Tis too bad the girl doesn't eat." Waiting a moment, he tasted a bit of meat. "Soon she'll grow too weak to care for him."

This Sir Blackblade had a devious mind, Sara thought.

"Aye," she agreed. "The weasel needs his medicine again, and he'll trust none but her."

Though Boden's expression remained unchanged, there was a light in his eyes, and that light mesmerized her. She loved him. Beyond a doubt. She loved him, and the knowledge made her ache.

Lifting the spit from above the fire again, Boden slipped a browned piece of venison onto a small slab of board before handing it to Sara, who approached Margaret.

The girl backed away, but Sara only bent and placed the board on the ground.

"Your friend needs ye strong to administer his medicine in the morning," she said, and returned to the fire.

There Sara sat on a small log with her back to the child as she gazed into the blaze. "Did she take it?" she asked, keeping her voice soft.

"Not yet."

"Do ye think she will?"

For a moment, Boden didn't speak, then, "Hunger is a strong motivator," he said, bringing her another piece of meat.

"As is loneliness," she said, looking up.

Longing snapped between them. She ached to go to him, but she couldn't afford for him to know it, and so she turned her thoughts aside and lowered her gaze. "Do ye think she will try to return to her mother?"

"When *you* are near?" His gaze hadn't shifted from her face. She could feel his warm attention as he watched her. "She doesn't look daft to me."

"What—" she began, but the heat of his eyes stopped her words.

"Only a dolt would leave you by choice," he said.

Sara searched for an appropriate comment, but just then Tilly's entrance into the firelight gave her an excuse to look away. The nanny bleated as she turned her head from side to side, sniffing, walking with that strange jerky movement of the goat.

From behind her, Sara sensed more than heard Margaret snatch the meat and slip silently back into hiding.

"What shall we do now?" she asked.

Taking several more slabs of meat from the spit, Boden piled them on a board and handed them to Sara. "Eat," he said and turned to scowl into the woods. "But hold fast to your herbs lest she decide to treat the rodent herself. Then get some sleep."

"Do ye think tis safe?"

"Tis one thing I've learned for certain since meeting you," he said. "Nothing is safe."

Chapter 20

❧───⟨♦⟩───❧

Boden had left their small camp long ago. Firelight had a tendency to draw his eyes and his thoughts, and he needed to patrol the area. Though the woods were very dark, he felt reasonably certain the dark wizard was not nearby, for he could feel no evil. So he settled his back against the trunk of a stout tree. Not far away, he heard Mettle grazing. He'd removed the charger's bridle and head armor, but for emergency's sake, the saddle was still in place. Near him, the undernourished mare tore off grasses.

Past that, Boden could see or hear little. But they were out there—the wizard, the brigands, the juggler, all of them searching for Sara. But why?

He was in far over his head. Never had he planned to become so involved. Twas supposed to be a simple mission. Return Lord Haldane's spoiled mistress and child to the fold. Naught else.

But the mistress was dead, and the child was firmly held in the arms of the woman called Sara. Her name flowed through his mind like a soft summer breeze. She was sunshine and laughter, softness and hope. And yet, when cornered, this woman who was like heaven in his arms, had the courage of a tiger.

His eyes fell closed. He would be a fool to let her go. And yet what else could he do? Without his knighthood, he was nothing, and he would surely lose even that if he crossed Haldane. All he could hope for was these moments with her. To feel the warmth of her presence, the sweet touch of her kindness, the dulcet melody of her voice like sun-ripened—

"Boden."

He awoke with a start.

"Sara!"

"My apologies." She was there, so near him, her oval face pierced by her sky-blue eyes. "I did not mean to frighten ye."

"Nay. I am a knight," he said. His tone was breathless. She smiled.

Pain lanced his heart. Damn Haldane.

"The children," he said, trying to think, to keep his hands at his sides. "They are well?"

"They are well," she said. "But Tilly is acting strangely."

He rose to his feet. "And that seems unusual to you?"

"Well . . ." she began, but just then the goat tottered into view.

Her bleat sounded odd and she held her head at a peculiar angle.

"What happened to her?"

"I dunna know," Sara said. "I was sleeping when I heard her stumbling about."

"Do you suppose she ate something poisonous?" Boden asked. Reaching out a hand, he approached the nanny slowly, but there was little need for his caution, for their past misunderstandings seemed to have been forgiven. The goat stood in a stupor.

Boden touched her neck, then ran his hand across the bumps of her ribs and onto her belly. "Did you see her eat anything?"

"She eats everything," Sara said, wringing her hands.

"Then mayhap . . ." he began, but just then Tilly turned toward him and burped.

Boden reared back at the onslaught of her breath, blinking for a moment. "Sara?"

"Aye?"

"Did you drink the ale I gave you?"

"Nay. I forgot it."

Boden nodded. "And the goat found it."

Tilly belched again, sending him another wave of fermented breath. He grimaced and turned away.

"I dunna know if I should be relieved or worried," Sara said.

Boden straightened. "It looks as if Thomas will have his first taste of ale."

Sara turned toward the knight as Tilly tottered away toward Mettle. "I am sorry to have awakened ye."

"'Tis you that should be sleeping."

She glanced away, into the darkness. "I wished to thank ye anyway."

In profile, she looked very like he imagined an angel might. God, he was sappy. "Thank me?" he asked.

She glanced back. "For saving Margaret."

Why did she take his breath away? He was a knight. All right, so he was a tanner's son, knighted because of some ungodly accident of nature. Still . . .

"The girl bites," he said.

"She's been wounded."

"And she stinks."

"'Tis probably the marten that smells. She's a beautiful child, is she not?"

Boden raised his brows in the darkness. The child was missing both her front teeth. Her arms were as thin as pale willow switches and her hair was tangled to a mass of snarls so dense he was certain they could not be undone. "Aye," he said. "Beautiful."

Sara smiled at him. And he knew she read his thoughts—again. If he had the sense of a squirrel that disconcerting thought alone would keep him at bay. But the fact that their thoughts melded seemed no more unnatural than the unearthly blue of her eyes. "Inside," she whispered. "Inside she is beautiful."

The child still bites, he thought, but . . . "With you to guide her . . ." He hadn't meant to speak his thoughts aloud, and although he stopped them before they were complete, he couldn't help but reach out to touch her face.

And suddenly, somehow, certainly against his will, she was in his arms. Her kiss was like magic, so soft, so sweet, so breathtakingly surreal, that for a moment he thought he must be dreaming.

"What can I do?" she murmured, realizing she was probably hurting his leg.

"Don't stop," he pleaded, and kissed her again.

Heat was building like a blaze out of control. Her skin felt like velvet beneath his touch and in his mind he remembered every moment he had spent in her arms, every word, every thought, every touch. And he yearned for more, to feel welcomed into her inner core, to press past the boundaries of their minds and . . .

"What was that?" she asked, pulling away.

Nothing! It was nothing! Nothing! Oh, God, let it be nothing! "I think the babe is crying," he said. How was it that his words always betrayed his body?

She glanced at him regretfully, breathing hard, her eyes wide with something he could only hope was desire.

"I must see to him," she said.

He was going to kill himself. "Aye," he said, and she slipped from his arms.

He let his head bang back against the tree behind him, but the concussion was as nothing in comparison to the throbbing in his nether parts.

In a moment he had caught up with Sara. She stood near an elder tree, just peeking round the trunk to stare out at their small fire.

Thomas lay not far from it. His arms were waving and now and then he squawked unhappily. But that was not what she watched, for beside him, crouched like a frightened tree frog, was the girl.

What was she planning? Boden wondered, and was just about to barge into the firelight and chase her away, when Sara caught his arm. He scowled down at her, but remained where he was, hidden in the shadows until a small noise issued from the girl.

"Shhh. Shhh," the child whispered, and glanced furtively toward the woods.

The babe cried again.

"Shh," she said and reached out one grubby hand.

Boden tensed, ready to lunge forward.

But he saw that Margaret's touch was feather soft on the babe's head, stroking him with such tender care that it made his heart lurch.

"Shhh," she whispered again, but the baby would not be hushed, and wailed louder still.

Her eyes looked frantic now as she scanned the woods, but just as she reached out with both hands, Sara stepped forward.

Margaret gasped and cowered away.

Sara stopped. "Thank you," she said, "for soothing him. He is hungry."

Margaret lunged to her feet and scampered toward the brush where she stopped and turned to stare at them. Above her sagging neckline the weasel's tiny head popped out, his dark eyes bright as beads in the firelight.

"I will milk the goat," Sara said.

The tone of her voice was as soothing as a spring breeze. Boden took a single step forward. Margaret's gaze snapped to him, but he stopped there and leaned against the tree.

"Sir Boden has been keeping watch," Sara said. "So that none come to harm us."

Aye, he had been keeping watch, before he fell asleep and began dreaming of Sara. Before she had walked right up to him without him hearing. Before he had let her distract him as if he were a callow youth. St. Rupert's rump. He was a sad excuse for a warrior.

"I will be awake now," Sara said, her tone still ultrasoft as she turned to him. "And Margaret will help watch. Get some sleep, Sir Blackblade. Please?"

He didn't want to sleep. He wanted to hold her, kiss her, make love to her. Barring that, he just wanted to stare at her. He was pathetic. But there was little he could do but pretend he was not.

"You'll wake me if there is any sign of danger?" he asked.

"Aye."

He forced himself to toss his cloak on the ground, but in a moment, he straightened. "You won't do anything foolhardy will you?"

It seemed a silly question now, for she was so small, so slim, so genteel, holding a baby near her breast, her heavenly eyes serene.

"Such as?" she asked, and it was the spark of laughter in her eyes that worried him.

"If there is any sign of danger, call me."

"I will."

"A cracking twig, a lumpy shadow, a fearful thought—"

"I'll wake ye," she said and watched him as he lay down.

In all honesty and knightly good manners, he tried not to grimace as he lowered himself to the ground, but his leg hurt and other things hurt too. Less knightly things, that ached in direct proportion to her nearness.

He felt her gaze on him as he wrapped himself in his cloak, but the baby cried again, drawing her away, and despite everything, he slept.

Sara didn't bother to try to lead Tilly. Instead, she led Mettle into the firelight, and Tilly followed. Still, even in her intoxicated state, the nanny wasn't fun to milk and managed to knock the kettle over twice. Righting the pan, Sara glanced toward Sir Boden, hoping he hadn't been awakened. He had not. For a moment, she studied his face. It was lean, too lean, she thought, and wished suddenly that she could let him rest indefinitely. That he could sleep on one of the poster beds at Glen Creag and wake to a fine, leisurely meal. She would serve him herself, and they would sit and tell stories to the children and . . .

She was doing it again, she realized. Pretending things that could never be.

After the milking, she loosed Tilly and poured the warm milk carefully into the bladder. Still there was some left over, so she set the kettle aside and turned her gaze to Margaret, who crouched in the shadows some distance away.

"You're welcome to it," she said, "if ye've a taste for milk."

The child didn't answer, and since the babe was not so silent and apt to wake Sir Boden, Sara lifted Thomas onto her lap.

He nursed greedily. For a while Sara was absorbed in the beauty of his innocence, the rapt attention on his face, the darling tilt of his nose. But soon she felt Margaret's gaze on her, and looked up.

Terror! It was there, felt as well as seen in the child's wide eyes. But why? Did she fear Sara would hurt the child just as Leoma had hurt Margaret? Or did she think Sara would harm the babe just as she had wounded Leoma? After all, Sara had hit the girl's mother—struck her with all the force she could, and had not even waited to see if she would recover. Of course the child would fear her.

Remorse flooded her. Moving slowly, she settled Thomas back onto his blanket.

"Margaret." She spoke quietly to the shadowed figure, yearning to do more, to pull her into her arms, to make things right. "'Tis sorry I am. So sorry. I did not wish to harm yer mother. Twas just . . ."

But the shadow was suddenly gone, the darkness

empty, and there was nothing she could do but wait and pray she would be back in the morning.

Sara settled onto the grass, putting her shoulders to a tree and listening to the darkness. But no untoward sounds disturbed her peace.

Her mind wandered and spun until the sun rose and the world turned light and Sara rose to her feet. Much to her surprise, Margaret was standing only a few feet from her, silent as the dawn, her grubby hands wrapped firmly round the weasel she held before her.

Hope slashed across Sara's mind, and after that came a silent thanks for Sir Boden's quick ploy that had kept the girl close at hand. But she was careful to show no expression on her face and remain still.

"'Tis time for his tonic," Sara said.

The child neither affirmed nor denied the statement. Instead, she stood perfectly still as if afraid to move closer, but determined to remain.

Tilly wandered over to Boden, and lowering her nose, bleated in his ear.

Boden lurched to his feet. Margaret squawked, Sara jumped, and Tilly, affronted, ran to Mettle for protection.

"Timothy's sainted toes, that goat's going to be the death of me," Boden growled, and trying to look forbidding, stumped off into the woods to relieve his bladder and his peace of mind.

Short of running the girl down and forcing her into the saddle, Margaret could not be convinced to ride with Boden, and so she rode with Sara. Even then, she didn't go willingly, but sat perched stiffly behind her, where she could tumble from Mettle's back and flee at the first sign of trouble.

Sir Blackblade sighed. What had happened to him? There had been a time when he was respected. Feared even. But now his charger was ridden by a woman whose presence made him sweat, and two children who smelled rather like an overused barnyard. As for his own knightly self, he had been relegated to riding an aged, bony mare of uncertain heritage. But probably better that than riding Mettle, because ever since the mare had joined their ranks, the gray charger had been prancing about like a half-witted colt. That jarring gait was likely to kill Boden.

But if that was not enough, he feared the goat was infatuated with his bold destrier. Dear God, things couldn't get any more humiliating, he thought.

Unfortunately, he was wrong, he realized, for just then he noticed Tilly had eaten Mettle's tail.

During the day Boden managed to shoot a trio of hares with his crossbow. Near noon, they roasted one of them.

By nightfall, his leg was stiff and painful. Apparently, riding bareback put added strain on it. He all but fell from the mare's sharp back.

"Boden."

Sara rushed over to him. He should, of course, have some pride, but when she touched him, there seemed little purpose.

"You are hurting," she said. "Let me see to your wound."

Reality flooded back. "Nay," he said. "You do evil things to wounds." She was so close he could feel her warmth. "However, you are exceptionally good with other parts of my anatomy."

She blushed, but her tone was not so demure. "Sit down," she ordered.

Why did he constantly forget her nasty side? "The light is fading," he said. "And I would catch our meal afore tis too late."

She raised her brows and propped her fists on her narrow hips. "Are ye thinking of running down a stag, mayhap?"

"I thought I might just catch a few fish instead. Give my leg a rest," he said, and with that, he managed to turn away.

Surprisingly enough, she let him go. Sometime later, he was at the stream with a hook tied to a string and the string tied to a branch. He found a comfortable spot with his back to a maple and let the evening fall down upon him as clouds gathered overhead.

In less than an hour he had caught and cleaned three graylings and an eel.

Sara had a small blaze burning and the kettle boiling water above it. Thomas was lying nearby, gurgling and blowing bubbles.

Margaret was nowhere to be seen, Boden noticed, but suddenly her furry friend launched himself from the shadows, scrambled up Boden's leg, and onto the nearest fish. In a moment he was scurrying away, the fish flapping behind him.

Boden watched him go. "And not a word of thanks," he said.

Sara turned from the fire with a laugh, and taking the remaining fish from him, dropped them into the kettle to boil. "Take off yer hose, Sir Blackblade," she said.

Boden raised his brows at her. "Lady, I am shocked."

"Somehow I doubt it. Margaret, please fetch another bowl of water from the burn."

Boden saw the girl now, little more substantial than a shadow as she stood at the edge of the campfire.

"The burn," Boden said. "Tis our Sara's endearing way of saying stream."

Margaret remained motionless for a moment, then, stashing the weasel, fish and all, into her bodice, she crept forward to retrieve the bowl from Mettle's pouch. Nervous as a cat, she scampered away a moment later.

"So you have a need to torture me again?" Boden asked, feeling strangely content.

"I've a need to see ye healed," she countered.

"Ahh."

"Roll down yer hose."

"Leave me some little pride," he said. "I'm a knight and—"

"And ye look good with two legs."

"You think so?"

Her gaze caressed his face. "Aye, Sir Blackblade. I do indeed. Now sit down and lie back."

He did so, because he was weak and could not help himself when she flattered him or teased him or looked at him. Pathetic. He loosened his lacing points with some effort.

Sara's hands felt warm and soft against his thigh as she rolled down his hose. He felt her untie the bandage and his body tightened. But a sudden noise behind him made him yank himself to a sitting position.

Margaret squeaked and jumped back, splashing water down the front of her gown.

"You've scared her again," Sara said.

"*Her*?" His heart was contemplating jumping from his chest. "Couldn't we put a bell around her neck?"

"Dunna worry, Margaret," Sara said, looking over his head as he lay down again. "'Tis enough water still in the bowl. Can ye bring it here?"

Apparently not, Boden thought, for she remained absolutely still.

"Better yet," Sara said, barely missing a beat, "add that to the kettle. But have a care not to burn yerself."

The child did so, giving them both a wide berth as she moved toward the fire.

Sara rose and fetched water she had boiled and left to cool. Dunking a cloth in the bowl, she raised it above Boden's thigh. He tensed, but when the cloth settled against his bandage there was no pain. Even when she pulled the binding away, there was only slight discomfort.

Still, he didn't look, being one to distinctly dislike the sight of his own blood.

Thunder rumbled overhead.

"How does it look?" he asked finally, as much to keep his mind off her work as to gain an answer.

"Ye are a fast healer, Sir Knight."

"Indeed?"

"Aye. Already it is knitting together nicely."

Well it hurt like hell . . . except when she was touching him.

"But I fear riding without a saddle has added undue strain."

"There is little to be done about it," he said, thinking himself quite chivalrous to utter the words. After all, she was now packing gunk in his thigh wound.

"Ye could ride in a cart."

He raised his gaze to hers. "Your pardon?"

"If we could obtain a pony trap, ye could ride in it. Surely twould be better for yer leg."

"I am a knight," he said slowly. "And knights do *not* ride in pony traps." But neither should they feel like swooning every time a woman touched him. And yet he did. Pathetic.

Chapter 21

❧━━━━━∽∞∾━━━━━❧

Luck, Boden found, hadn't abandoned him completely, for the rain held off. Late the next day, when the first fine drops were just beginning to fall, he saw a small spiral of smoke against the evening sky.

Carefully, they approached it and found that there, amidst the verdant hills, was a wattle and daub cottage and a number of sheds made from the same substances.

Boden confined everyone to the shelter of the trees for a while, and finally, when all looked safe, they ventured forth.

A dog barked as they rode up to the low house. A woman stepped out, wiping her hands on her apron. Her face was plump and her graying hair was bound on top of her head and partially covered with a white coif.

"Mistress." Boden nodded to her. "We have been traveling a long while and have nowhere to spend the night. I wondered if we might make use of your barn to shelter from the rain."

Two small children trailed after her to hide in the folds of her generous skirt. Behind them, a stout man stepped out into the light drizzle.

"Who are you?" he asked, his eyes narrowed suspiciously.

"My name is Michael Briar, a leather wright by trade," Boden said. "And this be my wife, Mary." He

nodded to Sara. Mayhap there was no need for such sub-
terfuge, but mayhap there was.

The farmer's gaze skimmed over the motley crew.
"Where might you be heading?"

"My sister died some months back, leaving her daughter orphaned," Boden lied, and quite well, he thought.
"We traveled to London to bring her home with us."

All eyes turned to the wild girl who perched so stiffly
behind Sara.

Silence stretched forever.

"We ain't got much to eat," said the farmer.

His wife pulled her gaze from Margaret with an effort.
"We surely have enough to share with hungry travelers,"
she argued softly.

It was settled.

Boden gave the hares to the farmer's wife. Then they
rode to the stable and dismounted. Mettle had to duck
his head to step inside, but once there the stone building
was large enough for all of them with room to spare.

Sara milked Tilly as Thomas lay on a pile of chaff and
cooed. Margaret remained near the door, ready to make
a dash for freedom if necessary.

But soon footsteps were heard outside, forcing the girl
to duck around the corner and hide. A gangly boy of
twelve or so appeared in the doorway. His legs seemed
endlessly long and his elbows poked through the holes
in his tunic.

"Mother says I'm to fetch you in," he said, barely
able to make eye contact.

It was no easy task to convince Margaret to accompany
them to the cottage, but they finally did so. The hut was
crowded, but the meal was filling and hot. Even Margaret, who stole morsels from her plate and fed them into
her gown, seemed comparatively content after a few
minutes.

It was dark when they trooped back toward the barn,
carrying a horsehide blanket and lantern loaned by the
farmer's wife. Glancing behind the building, Boden

thought he caught a glimpse of a broken wooden wheel. They stepped inside, lantern in tow. The place was cozy and snug. The rain fell soft and quiet on the tile roof. Two goats bleated from the corner where they were tied. Tilly turned up her nose and resolutely ignored them as she chewed her cud near Mettle.

Hay was piled on the loft overhead. Sara nodded toward it. "You may sleep up yonder, lass," she said softly.

But the girl didn't move.

"Nothing will harm you," Sara assured. "Sir Blackblade will be here to watch over us."

The words were said with quiet confidence, and sent a shiver of painful pride through Boden, but it seemed to do little for the girl. She remained motionless, her gaze stuck on the babe in Sara's arms.

Silence for a moment, then, "I will put Thomas to sleep there. Mayhap, if tis not too much trouble, you might watch over him for me."

Still, the girl didn't move, but Sara stepped toward the ladder. Once on top, she rustled about, making a bed for the babe.

Margaret backed toward the horses and flickered her gaze between Boden and the loft.

He made no move, lest she fly like a panicked starling over his head, and soon Sara was back at his side.

"He is already asleep," she said to the disheveled child, "and will not need us for a while. There is a burn just the other side of the house. Mayhap ye would like to bathe."

A fine idea, thought Boden, remembering her distinctive odor, but the girl didn't respond.

"Well, tis up to ye," said Sara. "But I will make use of the water while I may." She turned toward the door. "Sir Blackblade, might ye come along and make certain the burn is safe?"

Caught off guard, Boden raised his brows at her, but she only smiled and stepped into the darkness.

There was little Boden could do but turn down the lantern he'd hung on the wall and follow her outside.

They stood near the door in silence. Moments later they heard Margaret scramble, quiet as a woods creature, up the ladder to the loft.

Boden cleared his throat. "I suppose I can hardly return immediately now that your ploy worked."

Their gazes met in the darkness. "Twould surely frighten her," Sara agreed, and suddenly found that her breath had been stolen away, for he was close, within inches of her.

"Come, then, I'll walk you to the stream."

When they reached the water's edge, Sara turned and found him tense and silent as he looked down at her. A thousand wayward thoughts sparked between them, a thousand steamy images. He cleared his throat and looked away. "There's something I would speak to the farmer about," he said, and turning quickly on his heel, headed back to the house.

Sara watched him go. Disappointment lodged in her throat, but she refused to acknowledge it. He was Lord Haldane's knight. He was not for her, she knew, but as she undressed in the dark, she felt the fingers of desire slip like smooth satin across her skin.

The water felt soft as lily petals as it rose up her legs. She waded in farther, then swam, letting the waves float over her. Her hair streamed across her back, caressing, teasing. Overhead, the beleaguered moon shone for a moment between tattered clouds, causing silvered images to dance on the rippled surface of the water. And there it seemed she saw Boden's face. His eyes were half closed, his lips curled up in that expression that was distinctly his. Hair as black as midnight seemed to move across the face of the stream.

But suddenly a movement caught her eye. She glanced toward shore and he was there in the flesh, as if summoned by her desire, his face shadowed, his body shrouded in darkness. She knew it was him, could feel it in the beat of her heart.

And suddenly nothing mattered. Life was short. Her time with him was shorter still. Soon they would part. Too soon. The words echoed in her mind, and without thought, without volition, she rose from the water.

Sweet Saint Stephen! Boden tried to turn away—to think. But all his blood had suddenly drained from his brain into other regions that demanded it more. So he lowered his expectations and simply tried to keep breathing as he watched her approach.

The moon, three quarters full, shone bright as a silver penny, gilding her face, caressing her breasts, falling like fairy dust on the freckles across her nose and cheeks.

And suddenly she was there, before him, like an angel.

He opened his mouth to speak, but she placed a finger to his lips.

"I know ye are a knight and vowed to loyalty," she whispered. "I know ye are true and strong and disciplined. But tonight. Just tonight, I need ye."

"A damsel in distress!" he murmured. "I can hardly refuse."

With a smile, she kissed him. Her touch was like a spark on dry tinder, burning up any hope of resistance. So he would lose his knighthood. So he would be ostracized. So he would be drawn and quartered. There were worse things.

He swept her into his arms, kissing her, caressing her, no more able to stop the embrace than he could stop the beating of his heart.

Her hands were warm and impatient, pulling, prodding, slipping the clothes from his body, and suddenly he was naked, too. Her breasts pressed against his chest. He moaned at the impact and deepened the kiss, savoring, loving, melting in her heat, in her desire.

"Boden!" Her tone was throaty, driving him wild. "Boden."

He drew away a fraction of an inch.

"'Tis raining,'' she said.

And so it was. But who cared?

He kissed her again, but she slipped out of his arms, grabbed his hand, and pulled him into the water. It rose up to his knees. Fear coiled around his throat. He hated the water, but she was going deeper, and he could not stay behind. The stream lapped at his thighs, rose to his waist. Panic welled up, but still she went on. Waves washed across his ribs, and now he noticed that her breasts were nearly hidden beneath the surface.

"No farther,'' he said, pulling her into his arms. "I cannot bear to have your beauty hidden from me.''

Their lips met. Panic faded. Desire roared within him. Her hands were everywhere, caressing, smoothing. Hot pleasure touched him where her hands ventured. Ecstasy waited.

He skimmed his fingers down her back, over her buttocks. She shivered beneath his touch and suddenly her legs were wrapped about his waist and he slipped inside her.

She enveloped him like a warm, velvet sheath. He tilted his head back, feeling as if he might explode, and pulled her more tightly against him. He heard her moan of pleasure, felt her nipples press hard and warm against his chest. The next moan was his own.

"Ahh, lass, what magic do you work here?''

She arched against him. "'Tis ye that is the magician,'' she murmured. Her eyes were closed, her beauty surreal.

"Then let me make our worries disappear, if only for a moment,'' he said, and pressed into her. Their rhythm increased. Desire had built to a crashing cascade, driving them on. She rocked against him. He pushed back. She moaned louder, pressed again, arched hard and tight against him.

He watched her face as ecstasy took her, and thus his own release could not be delayed.

For a moment, he thought his legs would give way, but the buoyancy of the water and his own freed spirit kept him upright. Her thighs loosened from around his waist. Her feet slipped to the sand, but he couldn't bear to be parted from her, and so he lifted her into his arms and bore her to shore.

The rain was still falling, not cold or unfriendly, but warm and soft, caressing them, binding them. He kissed her lips, and then, when the river water no longer cradled her hips, he let her feet slip to the earth.

They stepped out of the water, but when Sara reached for her clothes, he couldn't bear to be separated from her even by a layer of cloth.

Retrieving his cloak from beneath the shelter of the tree, he wrapped it about them both, then grabbing their clothes, he steered Sara toward the barn.

The door creaked quietly open. They stepped into the soft circle of light. Mettle nickered. Tilly bleated, the mare munched hay—the quiet sounds of contentment.

Boden led Sara beneath the hayloft and spread the horsehide onto a corner of the floor where they could not be seen from the perch up above. No words were spoken as they lay down upon its soft warmth. And in the shelter of his cloak, he kissed her.

The tiny flame from the lantern offered them little light, and yet Boden's pleasure was not dimmed, for he could feel every curve of her delicate body, could taste the sweetness of her lips, and when her fingers brushed feather light across his chest, he let the feelings shiver into his soul. Finally there was nothing to do but love her again, soft and slow, bringing them both to ecstasy until she fell asleep in his arms.

He watched her from inches away, memorizing her every feature, etching every detail in his mind, her hair drying to golden glory, her face pale and soft, caressed by butterfly lashes.

She was his. If only for this moment, she was his. And regardless of the outcome—regardless of everything, he would keep her safe. Thus, he would do what he could to make the journey more pleasant for her.

Quiet as morning, he rose from her side.

Sara slipped through her dreams on gossamer wings. Boden's hands were warm and strong against her skin. Raindrops, water-lily soft, kissed her face as waves sloshed against her backside. Pleasure washed gently across her. She was safe, she was warm, all was right with the world.

The baby cried again from above. Sara sat up with a start. Reality hit her hard. She was naked and alone, covered with nothing but Boden's abandoned cloak.

And Thomas was crying sporadically from the loft. Glancing quickly about, she scampered from her nest to find her clothes hung to dry on a nearby peg. She snatched them down and donned them with all due speed. The mare was still munching hay, she noticed, as she hurried up the ladder.

Thomas grinned at her from his bed, but she realized suddenly that Margaret was gone.

Panic washed over Sara. Snatching up Thomas, she rushed back down the ladder. Where was she? Had she run? Boden would find her. Sara pushed open the door, ready to call his name.

Mettle was there, tied to a ring in the wall. On the far side was Tilly and . . .

"Margaret." She breathed the name in relief.

The child lurched to her feet, spilling a few drops of milk she'd been pouring into the bladder.

"Margaret," she said, realizing immediately what was happening. Hearing the baby cry, the girl had hurried down the ladder, tied Mettle just so to keep Tilly happy, and made certain the mare was out of sight so that the nanny wouldn't feel threatened by her presence. "Ye meant to hurry and feed Thomas," she said. "Why?"

The girl stepped backward, her eyes wide.

"Do ye think we'll be angry if the babe cries? Do ye think we'll hurt him?" she whispered.

Margaret swallowed, her eyes wider still.

"We'll not hurt him, lass, as we'll not hurt ye." Sara took a step forward.

Margaret spun away.

"Please," whispered Sara, coming to a halt. "Can ye not trust me?" she asked. But now memories swooped in. The girl had little reason to think herself safe with Sara. Not after what she had seen. "I had no wish to hurt your mother." The girl turned back. "I am sorry. But I could not bear to see ye bartered off like . . ." She shook her head. Painful emotions tightened her throat. "I meant only to help."

The girl turned away again, but Sara called her back. "Please, dunna go. I need help feeding the babe."

The child stopped, chewing her lip and debating. But Sara knew better than to wait for an answer. Striding back into the barn, she sat down on the horsehide where she'd slept and settled Thomas onto her lap. The spot was still warm.

The door creaked open. A tangled mass of hair appeared, and then a face, wide-eyed with fear.

Sara remained very still. Margaret crept forward, her small hands clutching the fat milk bladder.

"Sit down," Sara urged. It took Margaret a moment, but she did so, looking cautious and flighty.

"I must go find Sir Boden, if you're able to feed Thomas."

The girl chewed her lip. Sara rose slowly to her feet. The weasel peeked his nose above her neckline, then disappeared back under for an extended nap.

Every step Sara took, the child looked more nervous, but finally Sara was able to place Thomas in her lap. The tiny girl hunched her shoulders as if expecting a blow, but remained seated.

"You've seen me feed him," Sara said, indicating the milk bladder. "Do ye need my help?"

Margaret shook her head frantically and set the bladder to the baby's mouth.

He gurgled with glee and fell to feeding.

Sara's heart lurched. Her children. Her babies.

The door opened again. Margaret gasped in fear and glanced toward the noise as Boden stepped inside.

Sara's heart wrung with longing. Her family, if just for the moment.

"Good morningtide." Boden's husky voice felt as soft as darkness against her ears.

"Good morningtide," she said, unable for the life of her to think of anything else.

For a moment they were both speechless, and then, "The mistress sent this to break the fast." He lifted a basket covered with a loose weave woolen.

"We are in her debt," Sara said, and taking the basket, motioned to the straw some yards from Margaret and Thomas.

They dined on dark bread and honey, washed down by fresh goat's milk. The marten, ever hungry, slunk from Margaret's sleeve and darted over to steal a crust. Although Sara wanted nothing more than to sit in peace with her family, Boden soon rose, saying he would see to the horses.

Thomas fell asleep in a short while. Gathering the remainder of the meal, Sara brought it to Margaret and reached for the baby in exchange. For a moment, she thought the child might not give him up, but finally, she drew her small hands back and let Sara take him as she sat stiff as a board upon the chaff.

Though Sara was careful to keep busy and not look directly at Margaret, she knew the child ate as Sara strapped the baby to her back.

"Are we ready?" Boden asked, stepping into the barn.

"Ye must ride the saddle this day," said Sara.

"Aye," agreed Boden, "and you shall drive the cart."

"Cart?" She stepped outside into the uncertain morning sunshine and stared in surprise as she saw Mettle hooked up to a humble, wooden tumbrel. "However did ye come upon that?"

"I found some wheels behind the shed. The farmer

had no objections to me using it so long as I could salvage the parts.''

''And the harness?'' she asked.

''The harness I bartered for.''

''But, why Mettle?'' she asked, eying the huge destrier bound to the humble cart. ''Why not the mare?''

''She took objection to the idea.''

Sara slanted her gaze up at him. ''He is yer charger, sir, ye should not have to sacrifice him for us.''

''Tis of little regard if it makes your journey more pleasant.''

Pleasant? She skimmed her gaze to his. She had not expected this journey to be anything but arduous and yet, with him beside her, it was more than pleasant at times.

''My thanks,'' she murmured, and though she knew she was a fool, she hoped he would kiss her.

They stood unmoving. The barn door opened. Margaret stepped out.

Boden tore his attention away. ''Mistress Maggie,'' Boden said, bowing slightly toward her. ''Today you will ride in comparative comfort.''

Margaret flicked her gaze nervously from him to the cart.

''Tis safe enough,'' he assured her. ''Lady Sara and the babe will accompany you.''

Still she seemed uncertain, but Tilly was not. Trotting up to the cart, she nibbled the straw that littered the floor and then hopped in, happy as a clam.

This must surely be the depths of humiliation, Boden thought. His sword had been broken. He couldn't walk without limping, and his noble steed had been reduced to cart horse status.

He watched in silence as Margaret finally scrambled aboard and Sara settled the babe in the child's eager arms.

Aye, the depths of humiliation—so why did he feel such elation?

Chapter 22

❧

The morning slid slowly toward noon. Near a stream, Sara spied a wandering patch of dewberry bushes. While Boden unhitched the cart, she laid wee Thomas on a blanket in the shade and showed Margaret how to gather the fruit.

After a drink of sparkling water, the horses rolled in the sandy soil, then ambled onto the grass to graze.

Twas a lovely morning. The sun shone on a world of color so bright it all but hurt Boden's soul. Untamed flowers grew in bunches of whites and yellows. The grass was green, the water silvery blue and the sky, a spotless expanse of azure. Evil seemed a million miles away, and Sara, laughing as she wiped juice from the corner of her mouth, shone like a jewel in this perfect setting.

Boden knew he should stay away, but the sight of her thus was too much to resist. Thus he wandered like a small, lonely boy to her side.

"Boden." She smiled up at him. "Here. Taste." Reaching up, she popped a berry into his mouth.

It was seedy and sweet, but the sight of her smiling face was far sweeter still.

"Another," she said, and fed him again.

It seemed only right, somehow, that he pick a few and feed her. It was sensual and soft, nearly touching, but not

285

quite, until he felt he could not go another minute without pulling her into his arms.

"Sara." His voice was throaty when he reached for her, but she slipped away, turning her gaze to Margaret and thus warning him to be good.

"Hungry?" she asked, and picking another berry, tossed it at his mouth.

He caught it in his hand, and she laughed.

"Tis not how the game is played," she said. "Open yer mouth."

Foolery. And he was a knight. But God, her eyes were so blue. He opened his mouth. She tossed another berry. It grazed his ear.

"Very good," he said.

She laughed. "I am out of practice."

"Ahh, so this is an art that you must practice for."

"Aye, long hours by the banks of the Burn Creag with my cousins," she said. "Open again."

He did so, because he was a fool and she was enchanting.

The berry hit him squarely on the nose.

Her giggle was infectious. "You're too far away."

"That I can agree with," he said, and strode quickly around the brambles to reach for her again.

She pushed his hand away and skipped back, just out of reach. "There now. Stay. Open, and . . ." She tossed the berry. It hit his mouth dead center. He chewed.

"Tis my turn," he said.

"Have ye practiced this?" she asked doubtfully.

"Nay." He hoisted the berry. "But don't forget, I'm a knight."

"Ahh, well then . . ." She smiled. "Fire away."

It missed her by a half a foot. She laughed, nearly doubled over, not like a lady at all, but like a guileless child.

His own chuckle sounded rocky beside it.

"Here. Let me try again," he insisted.

"You are certain you're a knight?" she asked.

"Aye. Sir . . . No-blade," he said. "Straighten up and open your mouth."

She did as ordered. The berry shot from his hand in a beautiful arch, soared through the air and landed, dead center, down her bodice to lodge firmly between her breasts.

Her eyes went wide. Her mouth fell open. Boden remained frozen dutifully to the earth while a thousand wild thoughts rampaged through his head. He cleared his throat.

"I've never been quite certain what knighthood entails, but surely tis my duty to remove that seedy projectile from its lodging," he said and took a single step forward. Twas then he realized Margaret was laughing. He and Sara turned in unified shock.

For a second no noise was heard but the silvery sound of childish laughter. But just as quickly as it started, it stopped. The girl's eyes went wide. Fear sparked there again, but in a desperate attempt to hold it at bay, Sara spoke.

"So ye think tis funny do ye?" she asked, and turning, fetched the berry out of her bodice and tossed it lamely at Margaret.

It arched well away from the child, who looked nothing but startled.

"A pathetic attempt," Boden scoffed. "Here." He opened his mouth, then gestured to the child. "Teach Lady Sara how to make a decent throw, Maggie."

Margaret's startled expression turned to shock. He ignored it. "Come on then, toss away."

She stood frozen in place.

"Hit him in the nose," Sara said in a stage whisper.

Boden sent her a scornful look. "She would do no such thing. Right here," he repeated.

And to everyone's amazement, the tiny girl actually threw one. It wobbled a short distance through the air and landed halfway between them.

"Not a bad attempt," said Sara.

"Not bad? The marten could do better," said Boden. "Come on, right here," he goaded.

Margaret bit her lip, scowled, and obviously drawing forth every whit of her courage, threw the next berry.

It was sheer luck that made it career into his mouth to land in his throat. He started, coughed, and then coughed again.

Sara laughed. Margaret still looked surprised.

He coughed again, grabbed his throat, and then, seeing Sara was still laughing, staggered about.

"Boden?"

There was a smidgen of worry in her voice. Twas good to know she wasn't entirely without a conscience.

He staggered some more and fell to his knees.

"Boden!" Sara ran to him, slapping him on the shoulder with a good deal of force.

He fell to his palms.

"Boden!" Her voice was panicked now, and he took mercy.

Slipping onto his back, he caught her in his arms and rolled her with him.

"Now that was a good throw," he said and winked at Margaret.

There was a moment of petrified silence.

"Ye were teasing!" Sara gasped.

He nodded.

"I thought ye were a gentleman."

He laughed. "Twas but a rumor."

"Spread by ye."

"True enough," he said and moved to kiss her.

But she was out of his arms in an instant and pelting him with dewberries.

A wild fray followed, with no one being entirely free from the barrage. Even Margaret threw a few. The marten hid in the bushes, and finally, after a brief but exhausting battle, Boden and Sara removed themselves to wash up in the stream.

Although Margaret at first resisted the suggestion, the

marten's enthusiasm for the water finally drew her in.

The adults settled back on the shore to watch her timid first attempts at play by the edge of the stream.

Finally, when even the marten tired of the water, Sara tried to convince the girl to remove her gown and let her wash it. But to no avail.

Early afternoon found them traveling again, a kettle full of berries tucked in the back of the cart.

Evening came with cooler temperatures. They camped by the same stream near which they had found the dewberries, nestled deep in the woods and far from sight or sound of the road they had followed.

With no questions asked, Margaret milked Tilly. Twas amazing how little fuss the goat made when parked between Mettle and the mare. While the girl fed Thomas, Sara built a fire, and Boden saw to the horses. Then, digging out his hook again, he found two likely branches and tied a string to each.

"Let's have at it then, Maggie," he said.

She stood up quickly, her eyes typically wide.

Sara stopped in the process of changing the babe's swaddling.

"The way the marten eats, you'd best do your part in catching the fish," he said.

The girl turned her wild stare to Sara. But Sara only smiled. "Go on then, lass."

Boden set off toward the stream as if assuming the girl would follow.

"Ye wouldn't want Marten to miss his chance to play in the water," Sara added.

Margaret chewed her lip. Marten popped his sleek head out near her neck as if agreeing with the fact, and finally, very slowly, the girl made her way toward the stream.

Boden was already seated on a rock with his impromptu pole stretched out over the water. "Yours is there," he said, motioning toward the branch he'd left several rods away.

Marten rushed out of her gown and down her skirt to slap at the water with his sharp-clawed toes, and finally Margaret picked up her pole and sat on the bank.

Twas nearly an hour later that they returned to camp together.

"Just in time ye be," Sara said, dropping a wild scallion into the boiling kettle. "What did ye catch?"

Boden held up two scrawny fish, none exceeding three inches in length.

Sara laughed. "Judging by their size, ye must surely be a knight," she said.

He grimaced at her. "I was busy training."

"Truly, and how did the wee trainee do?" she asked, turning to the girl.

Shy as a kitten, Margaret drew forth her stringer. Five handsome fishes hung there, each more than a foot in length.

Sara clapped her hands in glee. "Well, ye've certainly earned yer supper, lass."

One corner of Margaret's mouth turned up, just showing the wide gap where her front teeth were missing.

"However, the knight did not do so well," Sara said, taking the fish from Margaret. "Shall we let him eat anyway?"

The shabby child hunched her shoulders and turned her wide solemn eyes up to Boden's face. He watched her watch him.

"Aye," she lisped in a nearly soundless whisper. " 'e tried 'is best."

"So how did ye get her to talk?" Sara asked, turning the last piece of fish she was smoking over the fire.

The moon was very bright. Far off, a wildcat shrieked, but it did nothing but make this spot seem cozier, for near the fire, the children slept, and not far away, Sir Boden Blackblade rested with his back to a bent elder as he watched her.

She approached him slowly, memorizing his face, the

slant of his jaw, the tilt of his head. "I would like to know your trick."

He shrugged "I'm a knight, you know."

How could he thrill her so? How could such simple things seem so important? "So knighthood enables ye to heal the mute?"

"Of course. Tis but one of the many remarkable but necessary skills."

"For knighthood," she said and sat down next to him.

"Aye. That and a thousand other things," he said airily.

"And what things are those, Sir Knight?" she asked.

His gaze caught hers. The playful moment was ended.

"Sara." His voice was soft and low, suggesting a hundred tortured thoughts.

"What?"

He reached out slowly and touched her face. The feelings flashed like lightning from his fingertips. "We have almost reached Knolltop." He paused. She watched a muscle dance in his lean jaw. "Soon you'll be with Lord Haldane."

She couldn't look at him any longer, couldn't face him. She turned to stand, but he tugged her back down.

"How will I let you go?"

"Shh." She whispered the sound and pressed her fingers to his lips. "We mustn't talk about it."

He pulled her hand away. "I cannot let you go."

"Please!" She jerked to her feet, terror and pain ripping through her heart. Facing away from him, she squeezed her eyes closed. "We will do what we must."

"What we must? Even if that means giving yourself to one man while yearning for another?"

She drew in a deep breath. She would not make him an exile. She would not let him deny his vows to his lord. "Aye," she said. "I will bear what I must." Pain ticked away. Silence lingered. "I can bear anything, so long as I have these moments with ye," she whispered and turned.

He looked at her for a long, painful moment then he stood and walked away.

Morning dawned thick with fog, but it was no darker than Boden's mood. They traveled in relative silence, only the wheels of the cart and the muffled clop of the horses' hooves disturbing the stillness.

They stopped only for a short time in the afternoon, then moved on again. Margaret said nothing, and despite her laughter and speech of the previous day, seemed little changed from when they had first found her. She huddled against the goat in the back of the cart, cradling Thomas in her lap. Tilly chewed her cud in utter content, seeming to be the only one unmoved by the pervasive gloom.

Clouds, thick as curdled cream settled in. It began to drizzle. They clopped on down the road, their hearts growing heavier by the moment until Boden finally stopped the mare and turned back.

"Sara?"

"What?" Her tone was high and tight, and when she lifted her face, he saw the fear that reflected his own. It set a warning bell clanging in his mind.

"Turn off here. Quickly," he said.

She did so, urging Mettle into the woods. Margaret glanced anxiously at the road they left behind, then huddled even lower in the cart as if hiding from something unseen. So she felt it too.

"Hurry!" Boden ordered.

Sara slapped the lines against Mettle's back. He broke into a trot.

"Faster!" Boden said, for it seemed as if the clouds themselves were lowering on them, closing in.

She slapped the lines again, but the forest was no place for a cart. Wood creaked against wood. The cart jerked to a halt, lodged against a bent tree.

Boden slid from the saddle, grabbed a branch from the forest floor, and pried upward at the cart. It creaked away from the tree that bound it.

He heard hoofbeats thundering down the road on the wings of evil. Boden cowered, terror smothering him.

But the noise thundered past and his breathing eased. "Go!" His voice was barely audible.

They moved through the woods like haunted wraiths, barely daring to breathe. The terror slipped a notch, leaving a bitter residue. But they did not stop, even to feed Thomas, though the going was heavy and hard and swamps often clogged their wheels.

Daylight finally faded into dusk. Darkness followed. Still they traveled on until they came to a river. It was loud and raucous, white capped and wild.

Boden stopped the mare, glancing to his right and left. Little could be seen except for a fading ribbon of silvery waves and the dark mask of trees overhead. He turned to Sara. She looked tired but alert as she too gazed off along the river.

"I dunna feel anything," she said.

It was, mayhap, a strange comment, and yet he knew what she meant. The evil could be as tangible as a wall of stone, but now it was gone.

"We'll pass the night here," Boden said, and dismounted.

They didn't attempt to light a fire. Inside a thicket of blackthorn bushes, Boden found a spot that was relatively dry. Stomping down the undergrowth, he laid a blanket down, and after feeding Margaret a bit of dried fish, they put the children down to sleep.

The night was long and oppressive, disturbed by hunting beasts and accented by lingering vestiges of fear. In the darkness, Boden roamed the banks of the river, searching for a place to cross.

Morning finally dawned. The clouds had broken up a bit. Smoked fish was getting tiresome, but he had no wish to chance a fire.

Even Thomas seemed affected by the gloom and cried more than normal. The sharp sounds seemed to pierce the air around them.

"We must be moving," Boden said finally.

"Do ye ken where we are?" Sara asked.

She looked worried, he thought, and would have given the world to take that worry from her, to give her a place where peace was the norm, and laughter was as common as speech.

"I know this area a bit," he said. "There should be a bridge some miles to the east of here, but it's on the open road."

"We dare not risk it," she said and he nodded, remembering the direction the riders had been traveling.

"Downstream, a half a league or so, there's a place we might cross."

They loaded into the cart. The going was even slower along the river, for the earth was boggy and the underbrush thick. Still, they reached the predetermined place before noon.

Much to Boden's dismay, the river looked no less intimidating in the bright light of day. It was a good furlong wide, bedeviled with rocks and rapids. Boden stared at it queasily, watching the water roll over itself in its wild exit to the sea. He would be glad to let it go without disturbing it.

"This is the place?" Sara asked. She was staring into his face.

Boden scowled and looked down at her. Exactly what could she read in his expression? Could she see the memories of his brother's drowning? "Aye. This is it." His tone sounded no more enthusiastic than he felt.

They sat in silence for a moment, then, "Shall I and the children cross first?" she asked.

"Aye. That's a good idea. You and the goat and the baby and the child—just to make certain the water's safe for me."

She lifted the reins to drive Mettle forward, but he stopped her.

"St. Peter's pate! I jest, Sara. I will test the depth first. Find the best place to cross."

With that, he dismounted, took a deep breath, and stepped into the water. It swirled around his feet like hungry carrion. His stomach turned at the same rate. He stepped back out, tried to think of a reason to change his mind, and finally satisfied himself with a short sojourn from the water's edge to find a long, stout branch.

Finally, he could think of no more excuses and stepped back into the water. It swirled and threatened and bullied, making it difficult to keep his feet in the rapid waves. He ignored it like a true warrior, until it rose nearly to his waist. Then he pushed down the bile that curled into his throat and refused to look. But finally he was back on shore.

"Twill be safest to take the cart across empty," he said, his tone harsh. "The floor is uneven and rocky, but if we're careful all should be well."

In a matter of minutes he was mounted bareback on Mettle. Tilly was left in the box to fend for herself.

To Boden's eternal amazement, they reached the other side with all parties still alive.

Breathing hard, he unhooked the cart. Mettle turned a disgusted look on him. "Unless you'd like me to tell the mare about your fear of thunderstorms, I'd suggest you keep quiet," he said. The stallion flicked his ears back irritably. Boden mounted the gray bareback and turned him into the water again. Nausea was becoming the norm. Reaching the opposite side was not. Nevertheless he did just that.

He sat soaking wet on his destrier and thanked God for continued survival. But they had no time to spare, for his fear of the water paled in comparison to the fear he had felt at the sound of the riders that followed them. He glanced at Margaret. She drew in her breath sharply and scampered away. He scowled, thinking, mayhap it was best if he didn't take the girl with him anyway, seeing as how his seat was less than perfect with a wounded leg and a bare-backed horse.

"Can the three of you ride the mare?" he asked.

But Sara was already gathering the reins and stepping into the near stirrup. Even while carrying a babe she had an amazing fearlessness and grace.

It took little enough coaxing to convince the girl to mount behind her.

Unhitching one of the long lines from Mettle's bit, Boden clipped it to the mare's headstall for extra support lest she lose her footing.

Again the water swirled. Thomas slept peacefully in his sling against Sara's bosom while Margaret sat very still behind her. Only Marten seemed nervous as he poked his pointed head from his mistress's bodice. He disappeared and reappeared again moments later. Yes, only the rodent and the knight were nervous. Wonderful, Boden thought. He was now in the same category as the weasel. But where he sat very still, with a white-knuckled grip on the reins, the marten twitched and chattered, climbing up on Maggie's shoulder only to scurry down her arm and back up to perch on her head.

Mettle tripped once on a submerged rock. Boden's stomach streaked to his throat, but the stallion righted himself and seemed to chuckle as he did so.

They had nearly reached the safety of the shore when Boden heard a squeal of dismay. Panicked, he jerked about just in time to see Marten hit the water.

Margaret shrieked again and nearly launched herself from the mare's back.

"Nay!" Sara cried and yanked the child back just in time. "Boden. Help!"

Help? Help? Boden thought. It was a weasel! Just a weasel. It was a pest. It stunk . . . and it was going under. And the girl was crying and fighting Sara's hold.

"Jesus!" he swore and without another thought dove from Mettle's back.

Chapter 23

He hit the water like a flat board, spraying foam in every direction. But the weasel was there, in his hand—for an instant. And then it was gone, swept beneath the current again.

Panic spewed up. It was just a weasel, Boden remembered and turned back. A wave hit him square in the face, knocking his feet out from under him. The undercurrent rolled him down. His head went under. Water filled his nose, sharp and cold as death. His feet hit bottom and he shot to the surface, gasping for air. But he was only there an instant before he was rolled under again. Terror roared in his head. With fingers like claws he grasped for anything to hold onto. There was nothing but frothing water and the memory of his brother's cold, limp body.

His leg banged against something. Agony pierced him, threatening unconsciousness. But he twisted and grabbed. Too late. His lungs burned and his head throbbed. Something brushed against his arm. He snatched at it. It was slick and narrow and twisted wildly in his hand, but he held on with chill desperation, trying to pull himself upward. Out of hell. Back into the sweet air. But suddenly something sharp and wicked sank into his thumb.

He let go of the marten with a shriek of pain. Water filled his mouth, his lungs, and the world went gray.

Something clawed at his neck, his ear, his head, and suddenly, like a miracle, he cleared the water.

Air spurred into his lungs. He flailed again. His feet struck the bottom. He grabbed wildly, and there, at the end of his reach, he found a branch. He grasped it like a lifeline, gulping air that seared his lungs with sweet agony.

His arms shook, but he pulled himself along the partly submerged log until he was in the center. It stretched almost all the way to the opposite shore, but right now he didn't care. Closing his eyes, he managed one single prayer, and then, like so much laundry on the line, he draped his body over the slick wood and vomited into the water.

An eternity later, he lifted his head and found, to his dull surprise, that there were scratches up his neck and a weasel clinging to his back.

For a moment, he was tempted almost beyond control to drown the damned thing. But he lacked the strength, and so, pulling himself hand over hand, he yanked himself clumsily toward shore.

Finally, less than two yards from the bank, the branch ended. He stopped as his stomach churned. He wasn't about to venture through those last deadly few feet of water. He wasn't going to. He'd simply rather stay where he was and die.

"Boden! Boden!"

He lifted his head. It was heavy and dull, but even so, he could see Sara, splashing into the water as if there was no great danger. And behind him, like a tiny water nymph, galloped Margaret.

Why couldn't they let him die like a proper hero? Self-disgust spurred through him. Snatching the weasel from his shoulder, he let go of the branch and splashed into the water. It washed against his thighs, but no higher. And soon, somehow, he was in Sara's arms.

"Boden!" She kissed his face, half dragging him from

the water. "Boden! Dear God, ye could have been killed. Ye could have died!"

"That thought crossed my mind," he rasped. But he hadn't died and here he was, in her arms, her tears warm against his face. The roiling water receded from his mind. She kissed him again, sweeping the hair from his face, kissing his ear where Marten had scratched it.

"Why did you do it?" she whispered.

Maggie stepped forward. They turned to her in unison. Her brown, solemn eyes were bright with unshed tears. She was breathing hard through her parted lips, and her small, grubby hands were shaking. Against her pale skin, the scar on her forehead showed up with vivid contrast.

Boden drew a deep steadying breath. There seemed very little to say, barring a hysterical, "That damned weasel nearly killed me," which didn't seem very heroic. So, "Here's your rodent," he said and then handed him to the girl.

They didn't delay by the river. In truth, Sir Boden Blackblade, the brave knight, had little desire to linger by the noisy waters, even though Sara was wont to fuss over him, so they tacked up the horses and journeyed on.

By nightfall, fatigue weighed like a millstone on his back. But he refused to stop.

"Sara," he said, turning in the saddle to look past his stallion at the menagerie pulled by the charger, "crawl into the cart and rest. Mettle will follow the mare."

Surprisingly, she did as requested, and so they traveled forth.

At some point during the night Boden felt the evil creep over him. Despair rode him, and every shortcoming he possessed seemed in that moment to be amplified a hundredfold, but it passed, leaving him tense with fear.

He pressed the horses onward.

Sometime far after midnight, they came to a road. Boden halted the horses and stared into the darkness, waiting, listening, feeling. But all seemed safe. And so they turned, and picking up their pace, hurried toward the northeast.

Sara's dreams ranged across a broad scope, through laughter and tears and into the years beyond, but in every image, against every backdrop, was a knight—dark, loyal, true. He was beside her at every turn, holding her in his arms, loving her against all odds.

''Blackblade!''

Sara awoke with a jolt at the sound of a strange man's voice. Beside her, Tilly quit chewing her cud long enough to rise to her feet in the cart. Margaret slept on, curled up like a bundle of rags beside Thomas.

''Blackblade! What the hell happened to you?''

Sara sat up, pushing wayward strands of hair from her face as she tried to get her bearings.

''Tis a long story, David.'' Boden sat relaxed atop the bony mare. ''Are you considering letting us in or should we travel on?''

''Travel on?'' Laughter. Sara turned toward it, realizing finally that they had come somehow to a castle. They were now on its drawbridge. ''I don't think you could travel on, my friend. Not on that nag.''

''You might be surprised what one can do when sufficiently motivated,'' said Sir Boden dryly.

''Ahh. So that's the way of it,'' said the other, then, ''I cannot bear to miss this tale. Raise the portcullis, lads.''

The iron gate lifted amidst the creak and rattle of chains. Feeling ridiculous, Sara crawled from the cart bed onto the seat, trying to press her hair into some semblance of order. Obviously this man was an acquaintance of Sir Boden, and the thought of her disheveled appearance made her cheeks flame. But there was little she could do about it. A half a lifetime in the wilderness had not improved her sense of style.

In a matter of moments, they had traveled beneath the portcullis and were encased by high brownstone walls.

"I hadn't thought it possible, old boy, but you look even worse close up," said the man who approached them. He was not a particularly handsome fellow, nor tall, nor brawny, but he had a bearing that suggested he knew none of those things. His gaze skimmed over the makeshift cart, the diapers drying on the back, the goat that perused him with baleful eyes, the bundle of children, and finally Sir Boden's scarred and wounded body. "Tell me the tale."

"I see your manners haven't improved with the inheritance of Avian," Boden said. "The lady is weary and hungry. Might we not break the fast before I satisfy your bloodthirsty curiosity?"

"Ahh, the lady," said David, skimming his gaze to Sara before approaching the cart. "And who might the lady be?"

He bowed at the waist, then straightened and reached for her hand.

Sara felt her blush deepen, but restrained from trying to press her hair into place, for there was little hope. "Sara," she said, raising her hand to his. "Of the Forbes."

"And Blackblade's wife?" he asked.

"Nay." The blush deepened, and she felt the fool.

"How glad I am to hear that, Sara of the Forbes." He kissed her knuckles. "Might you be of the Forbes that rule Glen Creag Castle?"

"My uncle is the laird," she said.

"Truly?" He seemed delighted to hear it. "'Tis said the women of Glen Creag are the most beautiful in all the world."

She tugged gently at her hand, but he didn't relinquish his grip. "I am sure you are thinking of my cousins."

His gaze didn't travel from her face. "I am certain I am not," he said.

"David!" Boden's voice was sharp.

"Aye?" Still he didn't look away.

"About that food . . ."

"Tell me, sweet Sara, whose daughter are you?" David asked, still intent on holding her hand.

But now Margaret awoke and narrowed her eyes at David.

"Colin Forbes was my father," Sara said, glancing at Margaret.

"Was?"

"He died some months back."

"My sincerest condolences," said David. "I've heard many good things about—"

But now Margaret sat up. Marten crawled from her gown and onto the seat of the cart where he leaned from the wooden plank to sniff at David's sleeve.

Releasing Sara's hand, David turned his gaze first to the weasel and then to Margaret, his expression startled as he searched for words. "And who might this be?"

"Give us a meal and a bath and I'll tell you the tale," said Sir Boden.

"A deal then," said David, laughing. "And my apologies, lady, for making you wait. Please. Let me help you dismount," he said, and reached for her hand again. But just then, Margaret grabbed Marten and scrambled over the seat holding the weasel before her like a shield.

Sara glanced at her in surprise, then dismounted on her own before walking to the back to lift out Thomas.

David widened his eyes even further. "The tale gets more and more interesting, I see."

"It's worth the wait," said Boden, and lifting his leg over the cantle, grimaced as pain shot through his thigh.

Sara was beside the mare in a heartbeat, cradling Thomas in one arm and reaching for him with the other.

"Careful," she said. "Please." Their gazes met. Warmth flooded her like morning sunshine. "Or ye'll break open your thigh wound yet again."

"More and more interesting," said David.

Both Sara and Boden raised their gazes to their host.

"Please," he said, indicating the open doors of the nearby hall with a flourish. "Enter."

The hall was large, capped by huge beams overhead and protected from winter drafts by colorful tapestries that lined the walls. It was empty now, but for a few soldiers who lingered at the trestle tables.

"Phoebe," David called to a woman across the room.

She hustled toward him, her broad hips wiggling madly. "Yes, m'lord." Her tone was gruff and her scowl suggested she had other things to do than his bidding. But suddenly her expression changed to one of ecstatic joy.

"Sir Boden!" she cried, wrapping him in dimpled, white arms.

"Phoebe." Boden smiled nervously down at her. "'Tis glad I am to see you."

"Glad to see me? Is that all you've to say after this long time? But I would hardly recognize you. What have you done to yourself? Have you been going off to battle without breakfast again?"

Boden's laughter was sweet and low. "Nay, Phoebe. But I fear I've had a bit of trouble."

"A bit!" She looked him over from head to toe. "'Twould appear you've been living in trouble. And a couple stone too thin you be." Propping her hands on her generous hips, she continued. "And I had such hopes you would straighten up once you got shed of Sir David here."

"Phoebe," David said, nodding to Sara. "The lady has brought a babe into our midst."

The big woman's jaw dropped, then she clapped her hands in sudden joy, apparently just recognizing the bundle Sara carried. "A babe," she crooned. "Ohh, and such a wee little fellow, too. Might I hold 'im?"

Sara flicked her gaze indecisively to Boden.

"Not to fear, Sara," he said. "Phoebe is Avian's official mother hen. Chicks come from the country round about to gather beneath her sheltering wings. Do they not, Phoebe?"

"I've been waiting half my life to hold one of you

rogues' babes,'' Phoebe said, nodding toward David, but reaching for the babe. Sara placed Thomas in her arms. The older woman reverently spread the blanket back from his face. "Ohhh, what a beauty. What a bonny babe. How I've been longing. But 'is lordship 'ere won't give me a single one to spoil.''

"Well, Phoebe, if that's all you wish for . . ." David began, but the old lady interrupted with a snort even as she crooned to the bundle in her arms.

"I want you wed right and proper's what I want. Like our Boden here,'' she said, beaming up at the battle-scarred knight.

Boden cleared his throat. "I'm afraid that's not quite—'' he began, but David cut him off.

"Well, until that happy eventuality, mayhap you could see to the lady's comfort instead of wearing her ear off with your chatter,'' said David.

"Your pardon, lady,'' said Phoebe, sending her master an evil look. "But what good is a man that scatters his seed like chaff to the wind?''

"I . . .'' Sara searched hopelessly for a response.

"Ahh, but you're the smart one, you are, Lady Sara, landing yourself our Blackblade. Not everyone could see his worth. Tis said takes a lady of quality to see through the rust to the kettle below.''

"I fear—''

"And here you be, a baby already in your arms. Lord David, you should be ashamed for not—''

"The child's not mine,'' Boden said abruptly.

Phoebe's mouth fell open. Her brows rose. She settled her gaze on Boden, then on Sara, then on Boden.

"The lady is not my wife, Phoebe, though . . .'' He stopped. Sara stood in breathless anticipation, every nerve taut. "The lady is not mine,'' he repeated, softer now. "I am but delivering her to her master.''

"Oh.'' Phoebe could not have looked more crestfallen had he declared the king of England was a wart-covered frog. "But the babe . . .''

"Lord Haldane's," Boden said, his tone curt.

"Haldane!" David said. "You're still loyal to that—"

He stopped abruptly and glanced at the men in the hall. "We shall talk later. Phoebe, take care of the babe, and mayhap you could see to the . . ." He paused as he tried to determine what to call Margaret, who half hid behind Sara's back. "The . . . girl?"

"Margaret shall stay with me," Sara said. "Please, if you would be so kind as to care for Thomas that would be more than gracious. There is a goat in the bailey that gives the milk he is accustomed to."

"A goat?" Phoebe began, skimming her gaze over Sara's modest bosom.

"You'll find the nanny and the milk bladder in the cart the lady arrived in," Boden said, his tone and expression brooking no more comment.

"In the cart. Aye m'lady. Twould be my pleasure," said Phoebe, and bobbing a curtsy, hurried off.

They were shown to the table set on a dais in the center of the hall. David pulled out his own padded chair at the end of the trestle. "For you, my lady," he said.

Sara sat, but before David could commandeer the chair to her right, Margaret had rushed into it, her eyes wide as she kept the stranger from sitting next to Sara. David raised his brows. Boden smiled, just the corner of a grin.

The girl met his gaze, and then, like a tiny coy fox, she smiled too. Sara couldn't help but notice the exchange and as Boden seated himself on Sara's left, she felt her heart rip. So the girl had found a champion, and insisted on protecting him.

"Lord David," Sara said, diverting his attention from Margaret's obvious ploy, "how do you know Sir Blackblade?"

"From more battles than I can recall," he said. "I would happily regale you with the tales, but I see you are hungry and I am outmaneuvered." He nodded toward a server who appeared from the kitchen with a tray. "Eat now, sweet Sara,'' he said, and lifting her hand, kissed it again. ''I will speak with you later.''

''You owe me a tale,'' he said to Boden before exiting the hall.

Breakfast was heavenly—warm barley meal cooked with honey, dark bread with butter, and a sweet wine. Even Margaret ate her fill, though she kept careful watch of everyone in the hall.

Eventually, sated and tired, they were led up the curving stone stairs to a small anteroom.

The serving girl pushed the door open. ''Lord David asked me to prepare you a bath.''

And there it was—a large wooden tub. A conduit ran from the wall, spilling water into the basin. Beside it, two women emptied buckets of hot water into it.

Sara sighed. ''You've my everlasting gratitude.''

The girl smiled. ''If you'll but test the water, we'll fetch what is needed.''

Sara entered the room. Margaret followed cautiously behind, and Boden, nearly as large as the doorway, leaned against the jamb and watched as she dipped her fingers into the water.

A thought flashed through her mind—two people in a similar tub, their hands roving . . . She blushed, refusing to look at the knight who filled the doorway.

''M'lady?''

''Tis perfect,'' she said, straightening quickly. ''Sir Boden will bathe first.''

''Nay.'' His tone was low, drawing her gaze against her will.

Memories flashed between them, hot and torrid. She felt suddenly as if she had been struck with something broad and flat, stealing her breath and her thoughts.

''Please.'' Twas a word spoken out of context, and suddenly even she didn't know what it meant. The world faded to nothing. There was only him and her and a tub of perfect water.

"M'lady?" asked the maid.

"Please!" she said, drawing from her trance with a jolt. "Sir Boden, ye must bathe first."

For a moment she thought he would not respond, but finally he lifted his weight from the door. "I will await your pleasure," he said, and left her to her raging thoughts.

The room seemed strangely silent.

"Would you like me to stay and assist you while you bathe, lady?" asked the girl.

He awaited her pleasure. What did that mean? Sara's mind felt boggled. Her body weak. And for a moment, she was tempted almost beyond control to go after him.

"M'lady?"

"Ohh. Nay!" She had said the word sharply and drew a breath now to try again. "Nay. That will not be necessary. Thank ye."

"As you wish. There are soaps and towels beside the basin."

Sara thanked her again, and soon the room was empty but for herself and Margaret.

She turned to the girl. Margaret watched her, and suddenly Sara wondered what the child could read in her flushed face.

"Well," she said, turning away, feeling flustered. "Shall we bathe?"

No answer. She turned back to the child, who shook her head rapidly.

"No bath?" She dipped her fingers in the water. "'Tis warm."

Margaret shook her head again.

Sara reached for the bar of soap and lifted it to her nose. "Ahhh," she sighed, "lavender." She lifted the next, then closed her eyes as a thousand memories rushed through her mind. "And heather," she whispered, remembering the wild hills of her homeland.

The girl's eyes were as wide as goose eggs. Sara drew

herself back to the present. "Come, Margaret, smell. Which scent do ye prefer?"

The child took a scant step forward, then another, until finally she was close enough for Sara to lift the soap to her dirt-streaked nose.

Sara smiled. "And this is the scent of my hills," she said, lifting the other soap for the girl's inspection. "'Tis heather."

Margaret smelled that one too. Marten slithered out of her gown and down her arm to test the scents, then scratch insultingly at his nose. In a moment, he crawled down her skirt and up the wooden tub to dip his paws in the water.

"So which do ye think?" Sara asked, watching the girl and feeling a thousand tender thoughts touch her. "Or would ye like to soak whilst ye consider it?"

The girl glanced at the tub and gnawed at her lip.

Sara waited in silence, and finally the words were spoken in whispered reverence.

"Which is Sir Boden's favorite?" Margaret asked.

Chapter 24

The detangling process must have hurt, Sara thought, for the snarls in Magaret's hair went clear to the scalp. Still, the child sat in the cooling water, not voicing a complaint as Sara wrestled with the knots. Finally the job was finished.

Sara shampooed her own hair and Margaret mimicked the task, choosing the heather-scented bar. Then they washed thoroughly while Marten walked round and round the edge of the tub, testing the water at regular intervals. Finally, trying to overreach, he fell in with a splash.

In the end, Marten, too, got a thorough scrubbing. The three of them emerged from the tub, squeaky clean and sweet-smelling.

Their clothing had been taken away by the maid-servants, and so, uncertain what else to do, they wrapped in the linen towels supplied and wandered sleepily through the arched doorway to the adjacent room given for their use.

And there was the bed. Twas six feet wide if it was an inch. Covered with a fine velvet counterpane, it was topped and curtained in the same rich, green fabric.

Sara turned her attention from the bed to the girl. Margaret glanced at Sara in disbelief, and then they smiled.

It was impossible to guess how long they slept. But finally Sara opened her eyes. The bright light from the narrow window had faded a bit, and her stomach felt empty.

"M'lady." A light knock sounded at the door, making Sara realize twas the same noise that had awakened her.

"Aye," she called, then cleared her voice and tried again. "Aye."

"I was told to bring your clothes."

"Oh." They must have slept for quite some time indeed if their clothing had already been washed and dried. Glancing across the bed, Sara saw that Margaret still slept at the far side of the wide mattress. "Come in," she called, not wanting to wake the girl.

The maid entered, but instead of carrying the much-abused gowns surrendered to the laundress, she bore something else entirely—gayly colored attire complete with undergarments.

Sara lifted her gaze to the servant's. "Either ye have a wonderfully talented laundress or these be not our gowns."

The girl smiled shyly. "Your lord sent these."

Sir Boden, Sara thought. But he was not her lord. He was not her husband. He was only her love. Her heart ached, and there was nothing to do but accept the gifts.

"He asked that I suggest you wear these when you come down to sup."

"Is it that time already?" Sara asked.

"Nearly so," answered the maid.

A moment later, the door closed behind the serving girl.

Sara touched the sleeve of the largest gown. Had Boden chosen it himself? And if so, where and how had he obtained it? Had he imagined how she would look in it? And what was he doing now?

Sara shook the thoughts from her head and turned to Margaret.

The girl slept curled into a tiny ball, all but the top of

her head hidden beneath the covers. The weather was warm, but she was so thin, mayhap it took a good deal to keep her from becoming chilled.

Reaching out gently, Sara touched a wayward strand of the girl's hair. Much to her surprise it had proven to be the color of late summer wheat—a somewhat darker version of her own. In truth, she could have been Sara's own child. Her heart twisted. If only she could find a place of peace apart from the world they knew, a place where she could nurture the people she loved, where she could feed them and caress them, where they could laugh and love and trust.

Carefully pressing the blanket lower, Sara examined the child's face. The scar on her temple was still red, but the bruising around it had faded to a tannish brown.

Sara touched it gently, smoothing her fingers from the brow into the silky hair. If only life were different. There were few things love and blackberry scones couldn't cure. But right now she could only think of staying alive, of protecting Thomas as she had vowed to do. She sighed again and pulled the blanket higher.

Twas then the girl awoke.

There was not an instant of time between sleep and wakefulness, not a sigh, not a blink, not a twitch. One moment she slept, the next she was out of bed and backed against the wall, her eyes wild, one hand clutching the marten, the other holding up her sagging towel.

Dear Lord, what had this child endured that a few hours of sleep would return her to such a wild state, make her forget that Sara meant her no harm?

Seconds ticked painfully away as Sara tried to marshal her senses, tried to find something to say.

''Tis nearly time to sup,'' she said, her heart twisting at the sight of the terror in Margaret's face.

The girl bit her lip, breathing hard and glancing toward the door.

''And my hair is all atangle,'' Sara said, running her fingers through her disarrayed locks and praying time would heal the child's wounded soul. "We'd best not dawdle. Tell ye what," she added, shifting her gaze to the gowns on the bed. "Ye dress whilst I plait my hair, then I'll see to yours."

Margaret shifted her gaze to the gowns. Her eyes grew wider and she pressed even harder against the wall behind her.

Pain and regret felt hard and bitter, and for one evil second, Sara hoped the girl's mother had not only died, but had died painfully.

"There is nothing to fear, lass," she said softly, no longer able to pretend all was well and normal. "I will not hurt ye. Indeed, had my greatest wish been fulfilled I would have a daughter of mine own." Silence filled the room. Sara's throat grew tight with the force of her emotions. "She would be just like you," she whispered. "With all your goodness and beauty and spirit."

The girl's lips parted slightly and she blinked as if confused by the other's words. Then she scowled. "I am evil," she lisped. "A witch."

"Who told ye that?" Sara demanded, lurching from the bed.

Margaret cowered against the wall.

Sara stopped, drawing a deep breath and shaking her head in an effort to calm her emotions. "Listen to me, lass," she said softly. "It does not matter who told ye that lie, for a lie it surely is. Twas the speaker who was evil. Twas the speaker who did not know good when she saw it." It took all her strength to keep from reaching out to draw the child into her arms. "For ye are good, lass. Naught but good."

Still the girl didn't move. But mayhap her eyes had lost a bit of their frantic hopelessness.

"Ye are good," Sara repeated, then smiled. "Sir Boden knows it. See, twas he who sent ye the gown."

The hall was crowded with soldiers and servants. The day had passed quickly for Boden for he'd done little but sleep. Exhausted, he had fallen onto the first available cot and passed out. Then, finally awakening far past noon, he had bathed and dressed, but his thoughts never left her. What else was there to consider but how she looked, how she felt, how she laughed?

Where was she?

David had somehow managed to obtain suitable clothing to replace their own tattered ones. The garments had subsequently been sent to the master chambers.

So where was Sara and the child? Maybe Boden shouldn't have allowed them to use the master's room, for David was hardly above reproach when it came to women.

Blackblade glanced toward the stairway. Trenchers were being delivered to the high table by rushing servants, and the hall was louder than ever.

"Sir," said a young man at his elbow, "will you have wine or ale?"

Boden glared at the stairway again. Where the devil were they?

"Sir—"

"What?" Boden asked, irritably turning his attention to the server.

"Will you have wine or—"

He stopped in mid-sentence, his eyes going wide and his jaw dropping slightly as he stared into the distance.

Boden deepened his scowl. "What?" he said again, but suddenly he realized that the hall had gone silent and that every face had turned toward the stairs.

He whipped his head around and caught his breath. There at the bottom of the steps stood a pair of delicate angels. He stood without realizing it, drawn inexorably toward them.

The taller of the angels was adorned in a gown of rich, mauve brocade. The neckline was square and low, revealing pale, perfect skin, as cool and regal as the lace in her slashed sleeves, as soft as the velvet of the gown.

Her hair, plaited and wound about her skull, looked like a delicate circlet of gold.

And Margaret . . . She was clean. Her hair was adorned in exactly the same manner as Sara's, and her mint-green gown was graced by tiny bows in the center of the bodice and at the top of her softly puffed sleeves.

A pair of angels—of princesses—of goddesses, come to grace lowly man.

But suddenly Boden's poetry came to a grinding halt, for he realized the angels' eyes were wide and bewildered and that they were holding hands. It made a sweet effect, and yet, when he looked closely, he realized their knuckles were white with the strain as they stared at the sea of unknown faces before them.

They were afraid—the two of them—his ladies.

All but sprinting from his spot, Boden raced across the floor toward them. But just then he saw another figure bearing down on them from the right.

"Sweet Sara," said David, somehow reaching them first. To Boden's growling anger, the other knight raised her knuckles to his lips. "I knew you were beautiful. But I was a fool, for I didn't know you would challenge the very sun with your radiance."

St. Bernard's butt, thought Boden, give him two seconds alone with David and the man would think the sun had *burst* in his head.

But in that instant Sara lifted her gaze. In her eyes Boden saw a thousand thoughts, a thousand emotions, a thousand yearnings. Then her gaze shifted worriedly to the girl who tried to hide behind her skirts.

It was all very clear.

Boden stepped around David. Margaret went absolutely still. Her eyes met his. Her breath stopped in her throat.

"Margaret," he said softly. "But nay, it cannot be my Maggie for she has no marten on her neck."

The girl bit her lip, then, slipping her hand from Sara's, dipped it into her opposite sleeve to pull out the rodent.

Boden could do nothing but laugh.

The girl cowered away, seeing now that in that instant, Sara had left her. Her eyes went wide, but Boden squatted down and smiled, stilling his laughter to a quiet chuckle.

"Tis a true lady who remembers her friends in the good times as well as the bad. Come," he said, leaning closer to whisper. "This night I will need your bold assistance to keep the jackals from our Sara."

Rising to his feet, he reached out his hand.

Maggie stood like a misplaced wood sprite lost in a sea of humans, her eyes so wide they seemed to swallow her somber little face. Moments ticked by, and then, with shaking trepidation, she reached out and took his hand.

Warmth spurred through Boden at the feel of her tiny fingers in his, and for a moment, he felt his eyes sting with tears. If he started crying, suicide would be the only honorable thing to do, he realized, and turning, followed David to the center table.

It wasn't much later that Boden realized the truth. He hated David—probably always had. He just hadn't noticed before, Boden thought as he stared across the table at the man who sat far too close to Sara. His shoulder was nearly touching hers, and his hands seemed forever wont to stray to her fingers where they shared a trencher. Damn him! If he touched her pinky once more Boden was going to have to—

Twas then he noticed that Margaret was plucking at his sleeve. He looked down in surprise. She'd been absolutely silent the entire meal, even saying nothing when he had insisted on feeding Marten under the table instead of in her gown where he usually ate. The whole while she had sat very close to him, her eyes panicked in her somber face as she skimmed the crowd. But now her gaze was trained on Sir David as he leaned close to Sara.

"What is it, Maggie mine?" asked Boden, carefully

keeping his gaze diverted from the couple across the table.

She was silent for a moment, but finally she whispered, ''A shrew.''

''What?'' he asked.

Margaret's gaze flicked to Boden's, then back to David. '' 'e looks like a shrew.''

It was the kindest thing she could have said. For a moment, Boden sat in silent surprise, and then he laughed and leaned close to the child.

''You are astute beyond your tiny years,'' he said, smiling at her.

Her lips, stained red from the watered wine she drank, curled up just the tiniest bit. But her eyes were not so shy. They danced, and Sir Boden the brave knight was smitten.

This, he thought, was how Sara must have looked, like a tiny rose, not quite in bloom, like a baby swallow, not out of its down, but showing the soaring promise of its grace to come.

''And tell me, wee Maggie,'' he said, suddenly terrified that he would lose the wild light in her eyes. ''What beast do I look like?''

Her expression went utterly sober, though her eyes were just as wide and shining.

''You,'' she whispered in that voice that was hers alone, ''are a charger.''

He reared back slightly, utterly surprised. ''A horse?''

She bit her lip, but managed to go on. ''Aye. Like Mettle . . . But black . . .'' Her voice lowered to the tiniest of whispers. ''. . . and handsome, and very, very brave.''

God! Something ripped in his heart. His eyes watered. He turned away, but there, across the table, as steady as stone, were Sara's eyes, reading his soul like the letters in a book. Her lips curved up slightly, her expression so gentle it made him want to . . .

No! Dammit all! He was *not* going to cry.

"Blackblade," said David. "Have you swallowed something amiss? Your eyes are watering."

"Oh." Boden cleared his throat and lowered his voice an octave. "Nay. I am fine. Tis just the child's wit. Tis sharp as a Welshman's dagger. I am but trying not to laugh."

"Right." David said, but looked as if he knew far better. "Well, as much as I am loathe to leave such charming company, I would hear your tale. Might we find someplace quiet so we can talk?"

"But Lady Sara . . ." Boden began.

"I am quite finished," she said, "if Margaret is."

The girl glanced regretfully at Boden, then nodded jerkily.

"Then we will have some time," David said. "If you wish to retire, Lady Sara, I would be honored if you and the girl would use my chambers again. But if you are not ready to sleep, please, feel free to visit the solar." He laughed. "Although Avian has no lady, Phoebe insists that it have a ladies' solar. The nest to bait the wren, I believe she said. Ask any servant where it is. Or feel free to explore on your own."

"Thank you, sir." Sara rose to her feet. "We may do that," she said, and rounding the table, took Margaret's hand in her own.

Boden watched them go. Like sunshine at the end of day, they were.

"That bad is it, old boy?" David asked.

"What?" Boden said, narrowing his eyes.

But David only laughed. "Care for a linen to wipe off the drool."

Boden employed his best scowl. "You've never made a lick of sense, man."

He laughed again. "Nay. And you've never been smitten. Not until now. But come," he said before the other could protest. "There are too many ears here."

Closeted away in a small room that overlooked the

courtyard, Sir Boden told his story, leaving out nothing but his desire for his master's mistress.

"Then you don't know why you're being plagued by these brigands?" Sir David finally said.

"Nay." Boden took another drink from his horn mug. "I only know that they mean great evil."

"Already they have done that," David said, "if twas they that killed the babe's mother."

"But I don't know that!" Boden countered. He jerked to his feet to pace irritably. "I don't know who killed her or why. I don't know if the same brigands now bedevil us." He turned to stare out the smoky glass of the narrow window. Below, the courtyard seemed far away and very dark. "What are they after?" he murmured.

"Twould seem they are after the babe, if they did the mother harm and were still not satisfied," David surmised.

Silence settled in. Twas then the first silvery notes of the harp floated to them.

"So your lady has found the solar," David said, but now a voice joined in, so dulcet and melodic that they remained in absolute silence, spellbound as the music wrapped them in its enchanted tendrils, driving everything from their hearts but the ability to feel.

Time passed unnoticed until the last note soaked into the night.

David took a deep breath as if drawing himself from another world.

The silence seemed almost unbearable now.

"How will you give her back?" David asked, his tone low. "And to *Haldane*!"

Boden turned abruptly from the window. "What do you mean, to *Haldane*?"

"He's a noble ass. You've never cared much for the nobility."

Boden let out his breath and forced his muscles to relax. Twas clear enough he was looking for an excuse, any excuse, to avoid his mission, but he must be realistic, honest. "An ass he may be," he said. "But he's also the babe's sire."

"But not the lady's husband."

Boden turned away again. "She'll not abandon the babe. Even discounting her feelings for the duke, she wouldn't leave the child."

"Have you asked?"

"I know her well."

"In a biblical sense?"

Boden swung back, fists clenched, anger sparking through him. "She's a lady! Lest you forget!"

David raised a brow. "Nay, I don't forget. But neither do I forget a man I once knew. Little use did he have for courtly love, or any other noble foolishness. Neither was he above being a confidante to the jaded second son of a penniless baron."

"I am still your confidante," Boden said, relaxing a bit. "Or I wouldn't have told you half of what I have."

"And because I am your friend I tell you to think," David said, slamming down his tankard. "If the babe is in danger, the lady is too. Would you trust her to Haldane?"

"Who better than a duke to protect her?" Boden asked, frustration spurring through him.

"Who better than the champion who cherishes her?" David asked.

Boden clenched his fists. "Look at me! What have I? Not even a sword," he said. "Certainly not a home or holdings or wealth. Haldane has all those things. And power to protect her from every evil force that clamors to harm her."

"And what if the evil comes from within?" David asked.

Silence smothered the room.

"What do you mean?"

David paused, his expression strained. "Not all evil seems evil. Some looks sweet and fair, even melancholy at times."

"The confidante I once knew didn't mince words," Boden said, feeling dread build in him like water behind a dam.

David turned, clasped his hands behind his back and paced to the far wall. There he stopped to finger a faded tapestry. "How well do you know Haldane?"

"I knew him when he was still in his full health, before he started weakening. He is a duke." Boden shrugged, letting those words imply what they would. "I fought for him for most of a decade," said Boden, "as did you."

"Aye. His best knights we were. Loyal, though mayhap those other preening peacocks would seem more so."

"Until you left him." Boden said the words as an accusation, but knew it was childish. There was no reason a knight shouldn't take the opportunity to serve another.

"Have you never wondered why I left so abruptly?" he asked.

Boden scowled. "I assumed it was because Lord Bevier offered more—"

"I was betrayed!"

"What?"

David turned abruptly away, but even from behind, Boden could see his tension.

"What are you saying?" Boden asked again.

"By the saints," David groaned. "I don't know what I am saying."

"Who betrayed you?"

"What do you know of Lady Haldane?"

"My lord's wife?"

"Of course your lord's wife!" stormed David, swinging about. "Do you know her?"

"In a biblical sense?" Boden asked.

The corner of David's mouth twitched. "So I was not the only one."

It was Boden's turn to tense now. Perhaps he would be not only a cad, but a foolish cad to share the truth with this man he'd not seen for half a year. "What are you speaking of?"

"She offered herself to you, didn't she?"

"This is my lord's wife we are speaking of," Boden said, keeping his tone careful.

"Aye. Elizabeth, your lord's wife—still beautiful, and noble, with hair like shining sable and skin so soft it all but melts your soul." He paused and drew a deep breath. "She knows."

"Knows what?"

"She knows about Haldane's . . . indiscretions. And it hurts her. Or so I thought."

"Holy saints, man!" growled Boden. "You're making me daft with your hooded suggestions. What are you saying?"

"I bedded her!" David stormed. "Dear God I knew it was foolish. But she was so sad, so alone, and so . . ." He blew out his breath and cocked the corner of a smile. "Damn, I will never forget how her skin felt against mine."

Boden's jaw dropped. "You slept with the duke's wife?"

"We didn't actually sleep."

"David, you're daft!"

The other snorted. "Don't bother to tell me you weren't tempted."

"I may have been tempted. But I have no wish to die with my wick hacked off and my head on a pike!"

"And what do you think will happen if Haldane learns you humped his favorite concubine?"

Boden lunged across the floor and grabbed David's tunic like a dog gone mad. "If you wish to live out the day you'll not use such language when speaking of her."

David's jaw dropped. His eyes went wide, and then he laughed, throwing back his head in glee and finally managing to brush off Boden's grip. "So I was right."

"If you tell a soul, I swear I'll feed your heart to the crows."

"Smitten was hardly the word for you, Blackblade. Whipped like a cur might be more apt."

Boden reached for him again, but David snorted. "Think on it, Blackblade. I've just admitted to bedding Haldane's wife. Are we not in the same vessel?"

"Nay, we are not," Boden said softly. "You did not love her."

David was silent for a moment, then, "Mayhap I did. She was sweet and soft and kind. Or so she seemed. In fact, twas not just once we loved, but many, until finally, in tears, she met me and said that she could not bear the guilt. She was going to her husband to tell him the truth."

"About your indiscretions?" Boden stared in absolute amazement. "But she surely would have lost everything, possibly her very life."

David smiled, but the expression was cynical. "Did I not tell you she was noble? Twas the right thing to do, she said."

"And so you fled!"

He shrugged. "I had grown rather found of my balls by then. Mind you I have no regrets about my exodus; my service to Lord Bevier gave me Avian. But did it not weaken Haldane's power with me gone? The other knights . . ." He shrugged. "Who were they faithful to? I've had much time to think. Mayhap too much time."

"And you think Lady Haldane seduced you for her own purposes?"

"That much is obvious," David said. "'Tis said I am an exceptional lover."

"'Tis also said the moon is made of green cheese. I am not wont to believe it."

David laughed and paced again before becoming serious. "Do you know how many times Lady Elizabeth has given birth?"

Boden shrugged. "Four times, maybe five."

"And each babe has died."

"Surely you cannot blame the woman for her loss."

"And Haldane's mistresses—how many babes did they bear?"

"I'm not privy to the intimate details of my lord's life."

"He was not a faithful man, regardless of his affection for his wife. And despite his age, neither was he impotent. There were many babes—and each of them dead."

Boden watched him, dread a full-blown hurricane in his chest. "You're suggesting terrible things, Sir David."

"I'm suggesting you watch your back, Sir Boden."

Chapter 25

Knolltop was set high on a verdant slope where the wind blew fresh and clean.

And there, just down from the hill—Sara, sitting with a babe on her lap and children running round about her.

Sara! Boden's heart ached at the sight of her, at the memories of her touch, her nearness. For a while, for a short bit of heaven, she had been his. No more. Never again. But she was safe now. She was safe.

Boden lifted his gaze, and there at the top of the next hill, stood Haldane, watching her.

Rage and bitterness welled up. But she was safe, Boden told himself again. Safe.

And then, like a storm that bursts over the sea, a woman sprang from the woods.

Sara rose and spun toward her, but in slow motion, as if every moment was pulled along by the ancient strings of time.

The woman's ebony hair streamed behind her, and in her hand was a knife.

''No!''

Boden heard his own scream of terror like a distant death knell. He thumped his heels against Mettle's sides. The great horse lunged forward, but too slow. Far too slow, as if swimming against a violent tide.

The woman struck!

Blood sprayed from Sara's throat. Her eyes—so blue and stark with terror, turned to him. To him!

"Sara!"

He awoke with a start, clawing at the bedclothes as he sprang to his feet. But one glance about the room told him there was no one there. There were no anguished screams, only the harsh, raspy sound of his own breath, and the haunting memories of his dreams.

"Sara," he whispered, and reaching for the door handle, leapt into the hall.

"Boden!"

She was there—like magic, collapsing against him, shaking and cold and terrified.

He swept her into his arms and without a moment's thought, bore her into his room and shut the door behind them.

"Boden! Ye are well! Ye are whole!" Her fingers were like velvet against his face, her voice like music to his soul.

"Aye." He couldn't hold her close enough. Couldn't kiss her fast enough. "I am well, sweet Sara."

"I dreamt . . . I dreamt . . ." She pushed away enough to look into his face. Through the thin fabric of her nightrail, he felt her fine body tremble. "I dreamt that she killed ye," she whispered and shivered.

"Nay. Nay, lady. It was you that I saw wounded."

"So again we share our dreams," she murmured. "But what are they trying to tell us?" She shivered again. The room fell silent as she glanced toward the narrow window.

"All I know is that I must protect you, lady, that I would die to see you safe and happy."

Her face was pale as she turned her heavenly eyes to his, and in them he saw her terror at his words.

"How far are we from Knolltop?" she whispered.

"Perhaps two days journey to the north and east," he said. "But why?"

"Then Haldane could be here soon," she whispered.

"Aye." The word hurt his throat, and his fingers where they touched her, burned.

"Boden," she whispered, her lips inches from his, her breath soft and rapid against his face. "Love me. Please. Afore tis too late."

Sara had no choice but to leave, for she knew Boden had spoken the truth. He would die to keep her safe, and she could not bear to be the cause. Better to die herself. But she must try to survive. She would travel as fast as she could. Alasdair, her half brother, lived far up in the northern reaches of Scotland. He would keep her safe at Hartmore Castle for as long as she needed to hide.

Thomas was silent when Sara strapped him to her back. And there, only a few feet away, Margaret lay, her small body curled up in sleep, her golden plait still looped about her tiny head. Sara closed her eyes against the pain of abandoning her. She must leave before the child awoke, she thought and turned away.

But she could not abandon the child without even an explanation to soften the blow. Returning to the bed, she touched the girl's face.

She awoke with a start.

"Margaret." Sara whispered her name and felt her throat tighten with emotion. "I have to leave, tonight, while it is still dark, for I have promised a friend I would protect her babe. I have no choice but to go."

Margaret sat up quickly, but Sara touched her shoulder to keep her in bed.

"Ye must stay, wee one, for I cannot care for ye as I long to. But Sir Boden will." Her voice cracked. "He cherishes ye so. And someday mayhap we shall meet again. But for now I must escape to the Highlands."

"Nay," Margaret whimpered.

"Aye, I must, but I will be safe at Hartmore, and ye will be safe here. Ye must keep our secret between us."

Margaret tried to rise again, but Sara pressed her gently down.

"Please, lass, for me, dunna make this more difficult. Ye are all that is good, and I couldna bear to see ye hurt. I shall pray for ye every day that I live," she whispered, and turning stiffly away, Sara slipped from the room.

"What do you mean she's not in her chambers?" Boden kept his voice low. She could not be gone, for she had left his room only a few hours before. She could not be gone. He knew it in his mind, and yet his heart said otherwise, making his stomach roil with panic.

"I knocked at her door. No one answered. Hence, I took the liberty of going in." The maid caught her lower lip between her teeth. "Only the girl was there."

"The babe?"

"Gone also. But surely there is no need to worry, sir. We are safe here at Avian. Mayhap she but went for a walk."

"Aye," he said. "A walk it is." But even as he said it his heart was racing like a panicked charger and he was flying down the steps to the courtyard.

She wasn't there. Nor was she in the stable, or the chapel, or the hall.

The door to the master chamber banged hard against the wall as Boden strode in. Margaret jumped as she turned from the window.

Boden skimmed his gaze about the room. It was empty but for the child and the weasel.

"Maggie." His tone sounded strangled and hoarse. "Where is she?"

She didn't answer, but her eyes were wide.

"Maggie." He strode forward, his steps loud on the bare floor until he dropped to his knees to stare into her face. "Where is Sara?"

Her eyes gleamed like pools of amber, not quite able to cry.

"Where?" he shouted.

She cowered away. "Gone." The single word was barely audible.

"Nay! She cannot be gone! She cannot be!" he raved, and rising, slammed his fist against the wall. He swung about, fists clenched. Twas then he noticed the tear that had crept down her cheek. "Maggie." His voice broke as he swept the tiny body into his arms. Her arms entwined about his neck, soft as a butterfly's kiss, with a lifetime of loneliness in the embrace. "She could not have left you," he murmured. "She could not have left *me*."

But she had. Margaret's tears felt hot against his neck.

"I will find her for you," he promised, squeezing the child. "I will find her, and I will bring her back." But where had she gone? And why? Did she trust him so little that she would flee to Haldane?

But no! No! A thousand thoughts flashed through his mind, a thousand memories as bright as tomorrow. "She would not go there," he whispered. "She goes home— to the Highlands."

He unwound his arms from about the child and set her aside. His course was set. Drawing a deep breath, he pivoted on his heel and hurried toward the door.

Behind him, alone and small, Maggie squeezed the marten to her chest and whispered, "Don't leave me," but Boden was already gone.

Twas still morning when Boden found the spot where Sara had climbed the wall and disappeared into the forest. Only moments later he lost her trail, circled back, searched, and galloped on.

The day wore away. David had sent nearly fifty men out to look for her. But now they had spread into the distance, and Boden no longer saw them. Frustration gnawed at him. She was heading north, returning to the Highlands. He was certain of that. So why couldn't he find her? He must! Before it was too late. Before . . . But his mind refused to finish that thought.

Terror gripped him. Darkness swept in. But he couldn't stop! The night skimmed past in dark waves.

Surely they would find her. There were fifty of them, combing the woods, heading north.

But the others didn't know what they searched for. Perhaps they thought Sara was but a woman. Perhaps they didn't know she was an angel. The others hadn't been healed by her touch, soothed by her beauty. They hadn't held her in their arms, in their hearts, forming a bond that would forever draw him to her, regardless of time and distance.

Mettle turned to the west. Boden stopped him. The horse tossed his heavy neck, yanking at the bit and walking on. Boden tightened the reins and pulled the animal about, but in that instant he knew the truth.

Sara wasn't north of him. She was to the west. He felt it in his heart. And he would follow his heart.

On the third day Boden found a faint trail made by three horses and heading north. He was now more than five leagues west of Avian, and so his theory made no sense, and yet, somehow, he knew he was right; twas Sara's trail he followed.

She was close. He was certain of that, though he didn't know why. Perhaps it was the dragon that had somehow bound their thoughts. Perhaps it was truly magical. But it mattered little. All that mattered was Sara. She rode a horse. Where she'd obtained it or who she rode with, he couldn't say. All he knew was that he would find her, or he would die trying.

Danger followed her, just as he did, and he was determined to reach her first.

Night came again, surrounding him with its dark curtain. Slipping off Mettle's bridle and armor, Boden wrapped himself in his cloak and slept.

Dreams enveloped him, swirling, tantalizing, showing glimpses of Sara, her smile, her eyes. He chased her, breathing hard, needing to hold her, to learn the answers. But he lost her in the fog, and then he awoke! Cold sweat chilled him. She needed him! She needed him now!

Minutes later he was astride again, pushing Mettle re-
lentlessly through the darkness. Miles flashed beneath his
churning hooves, until finally Boden pulled the steed to
a halt.

"Sara." He whispered her name, for she was near. He
could feel her presence, just as he could feel her need.
But he could also feel the approaching evil. Sweat
slipped down Boden's back, but he pushed Mettle on.

Suddenly from up ahead, came the sound of galloping
horses. Fear froze the blood in his veins. Their hoofbeats
thundered in his heart. She was riding into danger, into
evil.

He must stop her. He set his spurs to Mettle. The horse
leapt ahead.

Terror stabbed Boden's heart.

"Sara!" he screamed, and then, as if through a haze,
he saw her. She was on the ground, trying to rise, to
escape, but someone stood over her.

"Sara!" Sweeping the sword from his scabbard, he
thundered toward them.

He saw her turn her hooded head toward him. He
could not fail her. He swung his sword at the man standing over her. The brigand screamed and fell. In an instant
Boden was off his horse.

"Sara!" He reached for her and she turned.

But it was Warwick who stared at him from the dark
hood.

Boden reared back in horror. The black haze fell from
his mind. Dear God, twas not Sara at all. He'd been
tricked. He spun away, but it was too late, for something
crashed with white hot pain against his skull, and the
darkness found him.

Boden awoke slowly. Cold fog filled his mind, and his
head throbbed. He felt sick to his stomach, and within
him there was a dread so deep it threatened his very
existence. Better surely to die than to awaken, he thought.
Better to die, but he could not. Not yet.

"So you are awake."

The voice sent a sliver of raw terror down Boden's spine.

"There is little need for you to feign sleep," the voice said. "Surely you must know that."

He did know it, for Warwick had captured him, and Warwick would realize the truth. Somehow he would know.

Boden lifted his head, then propped it against the tree behind him as he skimmed the area with his gaze. They were in the forest, that much he knew, though it was dark but for the fire that glared red and evil beneath the leaning branches. And then, right before him, out of thinnest air, Warwick appeared, nothing more than a narrow, dark shadow in the night.

Terror slapped Boden hard enough to make his head reel with it. But his hands were bound to the tree behind him, keeping him from escaping.

"Fear?" Warwick chuckled. "Already? And I have not yet begun. But what can one expect from a tanner's son?" The dark figure turned. Boden drew a breath, finding he could only do so when the wizard's back was turned. "You were not meant to be a warrior," he said. His voice was soft now, soothing. "You were not meant to be a knight." Boden's muscles relaxed as the wizard crooned on, his tone soothing, entrancing. He was not in danger. And no, he was not meant to be a knight. "You were meant to be a tanner. From this close distance I cannot fail to read your thoughts. You are a gentle man. A craftsman."

He was. He'd always been good with his hands, though his father had never known it.

"You want to return to your home, make useful things. Not . . ." The shadow turned.

Boden held his breath, but the wizard only chuckled. The sound was calming.

"You were not meant to kill, but to create," he said. "Is that not so?"

Boden nodded. They were alone, and he felt strangely small and helpless. But he was in no danger and the wizard was right.

"But of late, evil things have happened."

Yes, there had been evil. Boden scowled, trying to think. Hadn't the evil been somehow connected with this man, this wizard?

"I have tried to prevent them," Warwick said quickly. "I have done my best, but the woman . . ." His tone was suddenly harsh. Boden hunched his shoulders and pressed against the tree. "The woman is wicked. She is wicked. Do you see that?" Warwick asked, striding quickly to him. "She has taken your lord's babe. Your lord to whom you have vowed fealty. And she will do evil things to the child if we do not stop her."

Evil! Yes! He could feel it!

"So you must tell me where to find her," Warwick crooned. "You must tell me before tis too late—for the babe. For you," he whispered.

Yes. He would tell.

"Good lad," Warwick purred. "Where has she gone?"

Boden opened his mouth. But suddenly he remembered her eyes. Heavenly blue, they were, the window to a soul so pure that even now he could feel the soothing effect of her presence. "I don't know." The words came unbidden. He watched the wizard's blue-white hand clutch to a fist, but when he spoke his voice was still soft.

"Oh but you do, Boden my lad. You wished to protect the babe. Twas your vow, your task. But she would not have it. Tell me, Boden. Tell me, and I will help you find her. You want to find her, don't you?"

Boden scowled in confusion. His head throbbed and felt strangely disembodied, as if he were dreaming, as if his thoughts were not his own. Yes, he wanted to find Sara. *Needed* to find her, though he couldn't remember why. And Warwick could do anything he set his mind to. Surely he could locate her.

"She left," Boden said, but his own voice seemed to come from far away. "She left."

"Aye, but where did she go?"

"She went . . ." Boden began, but the niggling of a memory stopped his words. Her voice . . .

"Where did she go?" repeated the wizard, his voice rising.

"She would sing to the babe," Boden whispered.

"She lied to you," hissed the wizard, his white fingers curled into fists. "She made you believe she cared for you. She used your body as a shield. She's a witch, trying to steal your soul. But tis not too late for atonement, not if you tell me where she is."

Boden opened his mouth.

The wizard leaned closer, waiting, his face shadowed by his hood. The silence continued. He hissed with impatience. "She lied to you. Used you. Left you to die."

She had. Twas all true. "She went—" Boden began, but again the sound of her song rang in his head. Like silvery bells. Like the first light of dawn.

"Where?" asked Warwick.

And suddenly the song ended. Her fear slashed across Boden's soul. Reality warred with twisted confusion, goodness with evil. "She went . . . to Knolltop," he said. "To take the babe to his sire."

The wizard's fist clenched again, but he smiled, curling his lips above his teeth. "She did not go to Knolltop," he said patiently. "You are mistaken, Boden," he said, and stepped forward a pace.

Fear came again, but just a corner of it. Still, Boden felt his heart pick up speed. "Nay," he said, his gaze still riveted on the wizard. "She knew the duke could protect—"

"Lies!" Warwick screamed, and suddenly the mask of goodness was torn away. He was directly in front of Boden, his face twisted with hate. One long curved nail reached out to scrape his cheek, but when he spoke next he had gained his composure once more. "You are mistaken again, my dear Boden, but I will give you one more chance to make me happy. After that, I fear I may not be so pleasant."

He was a knight, controlled, disciplined. But dear lord, fear gnawed at his belly, threatening to spill his meal, to loosen his bladder. He marshalled his senses. He was a knight.

"I wouldn't lie to you." His voice was soft, sounding pathetically childish to his own ears. "She went to Haldane."

The wizard swung away with a scream of rage, and when he pivoted back around, he gripped a wooden staff. It glowed red at the end. "Have you ever wondered how it feels to have your eyes burnt from your head?"

Dear God! Oh, sweet Jesus! Terror erupted like a hurricane wave. The wizard stepped closer.

"It feels . . ." Warwick stopped.

Boden stared at the burning tip, mesmerized, terrified to immobility.

"It feels something like this," he said softly, and thrust the tip against Boden's arm.

Agony seared him. His scream shrieked through the night. The smell of his burning flesh twisted his stomach. He yanked at his bonds in wild desperation.

Warwick pulled the staff back a scant inch and smiled. A bit of charred wood crumpled from the end and fell out of Boden's sight. "It feels like that, Sir Knight," he sneered, then turned to thrust the staff back into the fire. "But worse. Much worse," Warwick said, approaching again, staff in hand. "Unless you tell the truth."

Sobs threatened. Pleading! What would work? He hurt, everywhere, as if his whole body burned.

"Where is she?" Warwick asked in his melodious voice.

Dear Jesus! The staff was coming closer. Boden

watched it, hearing his own breathing, harsh as a dying beast's as he struggled with the ropes.

"Where is she?"

"Haldane," he said.

"I wonder who would keep a blind knight?" Warwick said. The staff lifted, still glowing to wave before Boden's eyes.

His stomach knotted, rose, threatened, and suddenly spilled its contents forth. He wretched, fought for breath, then wretched again.

"Oh, knight," Warwick said, bending forward to stare eerily into Boden's face. "What an ignoble thing. And so soon into the proceedings. Your lady would be revulsed. But you need not worry, for she'll not want a blind knight anyway, and when I finish with her, you'll not want her either."

Rage roared suddenly through Boden like a windswept inferno. There was no longer any thought. He shrieked like a wild beast and yanked at his bonds. One hand slipped free and crashed into Warwick's face. The wizard screamed as he fell.

And then Boden's legs burst free. The rope had burned through from the fallen ember. He was almost loose. He yanked at his hand even harder.

"Seize him!" shrieked Warwick.

He was almost free. Men swarmed into view. Only his fingers were caught. And then the rope gave way. Boden launched himself from the tree, but something hit him.

He staggered back, swinging wildly. A man went down. He swung again, but suddenly something struck him in the face and he was flung backward.

Almost free, his mind said, but the thought was slow and foggy, and as he fell, just before the darkness took him, he saw the heaven-bright blue of Sara's eyes.

Chapter 26

〜〜✺✺〜

"**A**wake!" Warwick ordered.

But she was there! So near, her voice like music, her hands like magic. Boden struggled to hold the dream, to immerse himself in its cushioning blanket.

"Awake!" screamed the wizard. Pain seared through Boden's hand, jerking him into reality.

He was back at the tree. But daylight had come, suffusing the world with gray, hopeless light.

"Let us start anew, dear knight," Warwick said, his voice a soft hiss. There was a purplish bruise above his left eye. Had he had the balls of a squirrel, Boden would have smiled at the wounds the wizard had sustained last night. "Where is the maid?"

"Why do you want her?" Boden's voice didn't sound so good, muffled, as if his lips were swollen, as if his brain had swollen, but the fear had dulled, like stale beer.

The wizard smiled. "I do not want *her*, but I believe she has something I do want."

"Haldane's heir?"

The dark wizard laughed. "Nay, it is not I that wants *him*. But that is how I learned that the amulet had resurfaced. Find the babe and you'll find the dragon, I was told. Twas far too tempting for me to resist."

"You're after Dragonheart?" Boden asked, but Warwick only grinned, curling his pale lips up evilly.

"I have answered enough questions, Sir Knight," he said, stopping only inches away from Boden. "Now you will answer mine. Where is she?"

"I told you. She goes to Knolltop."

The staff burned into Boden's right hand. Jesus! All right, the fear was back. His mind was bright with it. He would tell! He would tell the truth.

"There's a lad!" Warwick crooned, drawing the staff away. "Where is she?"

Blue eyes. Dear God, so blue! "Go to hell!" he muttered, and screamed again.

Oblivion. It was a nice, safe place, but Boden could feel it withdrawing. He tried to pull it back, to slip into the soft folds, to ignore the voices that argued by the fire.

"He ain't about t' tell, little matter what we do."

"He will tell." Warwick's voice seared away the soft fog of Boden's unconsciousness.

"Then why ain't he spoke yet?"

"Because we have not used sufficient incentive. He passed out too quickly."

Thank God for a weak stomach. Darkness had come again, Boden noticed through closed lids.

"He'll be lucky t' live out the night," said another voice.

"He will live. If I allow it. In fact . . . he is awake now."

Boden hadn't opened his eyes, and yet he felt Warwick's approach. He tried to keep his lids closed, but there was no hope. The fear flooded back.

"He is awake, and he is prepared to tell all, is that not right, Sir Knight?"

Dear God, already he had the burning staff!

"Is that not right?" Warwick asked again, lifting the brand.

Nausea swept through Boden as he watched the burning stick. Yes! Yes! He would tell.

"Yes?" Warwick asked.

"Go to hell!" Boden muttered through swollen lips.

The wizard shrieked. The brand stabbed for Boden's eyes.

"I'll tell!" rasped a voice from the woods. The brand stopped. Warwick jerked around.

Boden jerked too, his stomach clenching. He was dreaming again. The voice had sounded small, like a child's, like Maggie's. But she couldn't be here. She had been left in the safety of Avian.

He skimmed the area within his sight, trying to find her, while hoping he would not. She wasn't there. He was dreaming. He *must* be. Dear God, don't let her be here!

"I know where she went," lisped the voice, soft and earnest in its childish intensity.

Warwick's gaze swept to his men, hard and searing, promising dire punishment for missing such a waif in their midst. But when he spoke his tone was soothing. "What a clever child to have found us. But how I wonder? And you say you know where the maid went?"

There was no answer.

"I'll not hurt you, child." Warwick's voice was mesmerizing again, crooning. "Come out into the light where I can see you. Do not fear. Come out."

"No, Maggie! Don't!" Boden tried to scream the words, but they came forth as no more than a raspy whisper.

"Come out, clever child," Warwick crooned.

The girl stepped forward, appearing magically from the woods like a fairy child. Her golden, coiled plait had come loose. There were streaks of dirt down her cheeks.

"Run," Boden yelled. She could get away. She had survived this long, had learned to be invisible. "Run, Maggie."

But she didn't. Instead, she turned her solemn gaze on him. "Let him go!" she whispered. "And I'll tell you."

"Will you now? Will you tell me if I set him free?" Warwick asked.

She nodded again.

"Then of course I will. Simon, cut the good knight free."

Simon stepped forward. A blade gleamed in his hand.

"Where did the woman go?" Warwick asked her.

Maggie caught her lip in her teeth as she watched Simon, for he had stopped, bare blade shining in the fire's glow.

"Why do you wait?" Warwick growled, not turning his gaze from the child. "Cut him loose."

Simon stepped forward and bent.

Boden felt the blood rush back to his feet as the bonds fell free, but he didn't look down.

"Run, Maggie. Run now!"

"Nay," said Warwick, stepping slowly forward. "She will not run. Will you, child? You know you can trust me, for we are kindred spirits, are we not? I will not hurt you, or Sara. Where is she?"

Maggie stood transfixed, her huge eyes caught on the wizard's. "She went to the high lands."

"To the Highlands? But where in the Highlands, little one?"

She paused, her small face scrunched in thought. "Deermore."

"Deermore?" Warwick shook his head. "Deer— Hart! Hartmore Castle! She has gone to Hartmore! Grab the child!" shrieked the wizard, but just then the fire exploded.

Maggie screamed and wheeled away. Boden kneed Simon in the groin. The villain fell with a gasp, dropping his dagger.

Off to the right hell boomed, and a man shrieked.

Boden tried to reach the dagger with his foot, dragging his bonds forward as far as he could. But the brigand had rolled to his knees. Boden kicked him in the head, and he went down again.

But in that moment, Warwick advanced with the flaming brand.

Boden strained again, trying to reach the knife. Fear was like an inferno, burning his senses.

"Warwick!" The name was screamed.

The wizard spun about, searching for the source. "Liam." He chanted the name as he skimmed the black curtain beyond the fire's light. "Show yourself."

The night was as silent as death.

"Show yourself!" Warwick ordered, reaching the brand back toward Boden.

Liam stepped into the light.

"You have come." The wizard's tone was quiet, almost reverent.

"Aye. I have."

"So you finally know the truth."

Silence again, deep and eerie.

The villain at Boden's feet groaned, and then, gentle as a field mouse, Boden felt a tug at his wrists. Someone was behind him.

Sara. He didn't turn, didn't speak, and yet he knew it was she, and his soul wept, for she'd been safe. Far out of Warwick's grasp.

Go away, run, hide, he wanted to plead. But it was too dangerous. He dared not speak. His hands were freed, but he remained as he was.

"Aye." Liam looked only at the old man, though a half score of men closed in behind him. "I know the truth."

"And have you come to join me . . . or to hinder me?"

Liam shrugged, still not acknowledging the men that moved closer. "You may think me a good deal of things, Warwick, but dunna think me such a fool as to underestimate your powers."

"Then you come to ally yourself with me."

The silence was as heavy as hell.

"It seems the past has written my future," said Liam, his expression grim.

"Tis the truth," said Warwick, and in that instant, the closest man grabbed for Liam.

But just as quickly, Liam ducked. "Run!" he screamed. The brigand closed his arms on nothing, stumbled to a halt, and turned.

Liam scrambled away, but a dozen others were after him.

Boden snatched the dagger from the ground, prepared to launch himself into the fray, but in that instant two horses burst from the darkness.

"Come!" Sara screamed from the first.

Warwick wheeled about as Boden lunged toward Mettle. His leg gave way and he stumbled, then managed to nab a stirrup. He was whipped forward with the charger's lunge. Warwick reached for him. Boden felt bony fingers graze his tunic, but he had his fist wrapped tight in the stirrup. Someone hit his back, dragging him down. He twisted wildly and bucked against him, and the brigand fell, screaming as Mettle's hooves struck him.

"Get up! Get up!" Sara yelled, and in that moment Boden realized they had stopped.

He scrambled to mount. The chargers leapt forward.

"Maggie!" Boden screamed. He pulled Mettle about as he remembered the girl, but at that moment he saw two riders ahead and knew she was safely astride.

"Hurry!" Liam yelled.

Boden spurred Mettle ahead. Darkness galloped past.

Behind them, men yelled and swore. A horse screamed, and hoofbeats thundered.

Dear God! They were after them, and the nightmare began anew. Terror pursued them like the hounds of hell. Branches slapped his face and scraped his burns. Boden wrapped his fingers in Mettle's mane, hoping with every dim wit that if he passed out he wouldn't fall, wouldn't slow them down.

They rode for an eternity. Morning came, then noon, hurting his head.

"We've lost them for now," Sara said. "Into the barn. Quickly."

The world moved. The daylight dimmed, and then they stopped.

"Here, Boden, here," Sara said, reaching up. Her hands felt like heaven against his skin. Liam's were not so gentle, but finally Boden was eased to the earth. "Boden." There were tears in her voice. One fell soft and warm against his face. So sweet. So nice to rest, but she was unhappy, and he was so content, just to lie there near her. "Boden, I am sorry."

"Aye," he said, sighing. "And well you should be. Couldn't you have rescued me sooner? Tis the duty of all good angels." He touched her face because he couldn't help himself.

The tears felt hot and seared his heart. "I'm fine, lass," he whispered.

She shook her head. "I know tis not true. You are not even complaining."

"I am a knight," he said, and stroked her cheek.

She smiled shakily. Silence settled in.

"I couldn't find you," he said, his voice barely audible. "Where were you? How could you leave . . . Maggie? The goat?"

She laughed, but the sound was nothing more than a warbled sob. "I could hardly escape you while dragging the goat about," she said. "But I had to leave. I promised Caroline, and I couldn't risk you any longer."

"Risk me?"

"Tis your duty to take me to Knolltop. Tis mine to see Thomas to safety. I took the babe and the milk bladder and went to Firthport. My cousin, Roman, owns a house there, but Liam was there instead. Twas he who found a nursemaid and horses."

"So my heart was right; you went west instead of north." Boden fell silent for a moment, and though he supposed his words sounded nonsensical, she didn't question them.

Her eyes were like heaven, her whisper soft as the dawn. "We rode as fast as we could. But finally I could go no farther." She paused. Her lips trembled with emotion.

"Why?"

"I could bear your pain no longer," she whispered. "I knew ye were in danger. I felt it in my soul, and I thought surely I would die if ye were hurt again. So I left Thomas and the nursemaid at this farm, for I could not live any longer without ye."

A thousand half-imagined possibilities sparked between them. But suddenly Margaret was beside them. Sara moved aside to give the girl room. The child stood back, terror in her eyes.

"Maggie mine," he whispered. "Angel child."

She refused to move. He lifted a wounded arm toward her, hoping she would come to him, needing some way to assure himself that she was well, but she spun away and bolted from the barn.

"Maggie," he called after her, trying to sit up, but Sara pressed him firmly back down. He turned his gaze to her.

"We abandoned her," Sara whispered.

"But you went back for her."

"Nay." Sara shook her head, her expression solemn. "I did not. She found you on her own."

"Nay."

"Tilly followed Mettle. Wee Maggie followed the goat."

"'Tis not possible," Boden rasped. Hot emotion seared his heart. "She could not have done that. Not for me."

"Love makes all things possible," she murmured, cupping his cheek.

"Love?" He whispered the word, but now she drew her hand from his face.

"Lie back now," she said. "Let me tend your wounds."

Boden grimaced. "They're not so bad," he murmured, and hoped he would faint.

*   *   *

Long before evening they were riding again, six of them, not counting the goat and the weasel.

The rolling green of Scotland surrounded them in silence. If he were a true knight, he would insist they turn around to return to Haldane, Boden thought, but he didn't. Instead, he rode with them, drugged, bandaged, scarred.

Night passed. Morning came and went, and then evening again. Twas that night that they felt the evil.

They stopped deep in the woods where they rode, huddled together like frightened rabbits. Liam had somehow obtained two swords. Boden now had one strapped to his hip, but the odds were against him defending them from anything more fierce than a field mouse. Far better to hide than to challenge powers he could neither understand nor defeat.

"Wh . . . What is that?" whispered the nursemaid named Tess.

Liam hushed her. "Don't think about it. All will be well."

And then, to keep their minds free, Sara sang. Her voice was low and as sweet as mountain water. Boden lay against a summer soft tussock of grass, letting the notes flow over him, taking what he could for as long as he might, and finally the deep dread passed.

On they rode again, more careful than ever to stay hidden. The terrain roughened.

"How far do you think?" Sara whispered.

Night had settled in.

"Less than two days travel if our luck holds," Liam said.

Luck! Not Boden's forte, and the feeling of dread was growing again. He drew his sword and sat awake in the darkness.

Morning dawned cool and foggy. They ate dry bread, shared a bit of Tilly's milk, and tightened their belts.

The day warmed rapidly. Fear rode with them. The

very air felt heavy with it, like an impending, inescapable storm.

Boden scanned the hills that seemed to close in around them and pushed Mettle up beside Sara's mare.

Her eyes looked wide, her face drawn. Their gazes caught.

"They are coming," she whispered and he nodded, wanting to reach out, to pull her to him, to hold her for these last few moments before the storm broke. "When do you think?"

"Soon," he said.

"We have tried," she whispered. "We have done our best."

"And you will succeed," he said, "but you must go now."

"Nay, I canna."

Their gazes clashed. "Please," he whispered. "I beg you. The dragon is with you. He will keep you safe. When they come, I'll hold them off for a time. Ride as fast as the mare will take you."

"Nay!" Her voice was fierce. "I will not—"

"You will not what?" he asked, desperation spearing through him. "You will not give the babe a chance at life?"

Tears filled her eyes, and he weakened still more, almost reaching out. But there was no time.

"And what of Maggie?" he asked softly. "Does she not deserve a life in your Highlands?"

"I canna live without ye," Sara whispered, and for a moment Boden thought his heart might rip in two, so sweet was the bitterness that seared it.

"You can," he whispered. "And you—"

The air was shattered by a scream from the woods beside them. Horses crashed out from every side.

"Ride!" Boden yelled. "Ride!" For one heart-stopping moment, he thought she would refuse, but she wheeled her mare away. Margaret froze, but Boden spun

Mettle toward her and whipped her mount, sending her after Sara.

There was no more time to think. A warrior's shriek filled his mind, and suddenly, like darkness in the dawn, fear fled and anger consumed him. They would not have Sara, not if he had to fight the powers of hell to keep her safe. Not if he had to give his very soul. He spun like a madman, spurring Mettle into the brigands as he slashed and hewed. Men screamed and fell before him.

Something sliced his arm, but he barely noticed. A destrier reared up in front of them. Mettle slammed into him, knocking his opponent off balance, and in a moment he was dead.

Satisfaction burned through Boden, but suddenly he realized the truth. Warwick was not there.

He spun Mettle about. In the distance, he saw the wizard thundering after Sara.

"No!" Boden screamed and slammed Mettle into a gallop. There was nothing now but evil and good. The distance between him and Warwick snapped away. There were only a few yards between him and his quarry when suddenly a black horse lunged toward him. A sword swiped at him.

Reflex made him answer. Steel rang against steel. Boden parried, but he was not fast enough, and blood spurted from his shoulder. Rage washed over him like a tide of blood. He spurred Mettle into the other horse, and the black crumpled beneath him, spilling his rider to the earth. The man rolled away. He was on his feet immediately, but he had no chance. Boden drew back his sword, ready to strike. But in that instant a scream split the air.

"Sara!" Boden yelled her name even as he wheeled Mettle away, exposing his back to the brigand behind him.

The world stood still. Only Warwick and Sara seemed to move, struggling against each other in the midst of the river.

There was only a breath of a moment, a split second of opportunity. But no thought was required. Boden aimed and threw. His sword spun from his hand in slow motion, end over end for an eternity to slice with predestined accuracy between Warwick's shoulder blades.

It took forever for the dark wizard to fall, like an old tree too long standing. But he did so, toppling silently downward with his fist clenched tight. Water sprayed up like smoke, then settled around him, dragging him under. Behind him, Sara lifted her gaze.

"Boden!" Her scream began the world anew.

Boden spun his horse back toward his opponent, but it was too late! Mettle shrieked in pain as blood sprayed like a geyser from his forearm and he fell, crumpling to his knees, spilling Boden off balance. From another world, Boden saw a sword swing toward him.

He heard the sharp hiss of an arrow, a shriek of agony. Pain descended, and death laughed as he fell beside Mettle's body.

Hoofbeats filled his head.

"Boden!" Sara screamed his name, and in a moment she was there beside him, her hands like cool heaven against his skin.

"Sara." He forced his eyes open. "Sara." It was all he could manage, though he wanted to lift his hand, to brush the tears from her cheek. "Don't cry. Not for me. My life is done."

"No." She sobbed the word. "Don't say that."

"It is," he said, "but I don't mind, for you will never be mine, and without you I do not care to live." He smiled. "What chivalrous love, aye? Mayhap I was a knight after all."

"Boden, do not leave me."

"Be happy, Sara," he whispered, and let the darkness take him.

Chapter 27

"**B**oden! Boden!" she sobbed, rocking back and forth. "Don't leave me. Please." But he lay still and limp, his eyes closed. "No!" she cried. "No."

"Lady! Lady!" screamed Tess, hugging Thomas to her. "Come! We must fly! They're coming."

Coming? The words soaked into her mourning. She lifted her face. Tears blurred her vision, but now she saw the riders galloping toward them. "Who?"

"Brigands. More brigands!" shrieked Tess and wheeled her horse away.

"No!" Sara stumbled to her feet, searching wildly for a weapon. The only sword nearby was clutched in a brigand's hand. She lurched forward to pry it from his fist and swing about to face the oncoming horsemen. "Stay back!" she shrieked, shielding Boden's body with her own. "You'll not have him."

Suddenly she was surrounded by horsemen. One leapt from his mount and banged her sword aside with his own.

She stumbled at the force of the blow, but righted herself and brought her blade back to center. "Stay back, I say!" she warned.

But he bent and felt for a pulse at Boden's throat. "He's dead," he said, rising.

"Nay!" Sara screamed, and slashed at him.

Shocked, he lifted his own blade, but fury lent her power, and his sword flashed from his hand. She swung again. He stumbled backward, tripped and fell. Panting and weeping, Sara pressed the sword to his throat.

"He's not dead!" she sobbed. "He's not."

"Sara, no!" Liam yelled.

"Sara! Sara, love!"

The words rang in her ears, the memory of a gentler time. Her killing rage dwindled. "Rachel?" she whimpered, glancing up.

"Sara!" called Rachel again, and suddenly she was there. "Don't kill him, cousin. He's my guard."

"Rachel," she whispered again, her hand shaking, causing the sword to tremble against her victim's throat. "Boden's not dead. He canna be dead."

"Then we'll take him to Mother," crooned Rachel. "She'll know what to do."

"To Fiona," Sara whispered, then, backing away, she waved her sword at the man on the ground. "Get up!" she ordered. "And you!" She motioned to the others. "Lift him up. Gently. Not a hair will be harmed. Do you hear me?"

"Aye!" murmured the man she'd nearly killed. "Aye, Lady!"

It had taken Boden long enough to get to heaven. It had felt like a long, grueling horse ride. But he had finally arrived. He hadn't expected it to smell so good. But he wasn't surprised by the music. It was lovely, angelic, floating over him in waves of dulcet peace, letting him sleep. Nay, encouraging him to sleep.

God was in his heaven and all was right with the world.

Quiet settled about him again.

Voices woke him, but they were hushed and soft, gentle, strangely familiar, soothing. Not like the orders he'd heard yelled as he lay dying.

Heaven was heavenly.

But then it came. Darkness. A flash of something. Evil? But he was dead. Nothing could harm him now. Surely he had earned some sleep.

But darkness flared up again.

Sara! Her face flashed through his mind.

He sat up with a start. Too fast. His head pounded. He reached a hand for his brow and was surprised to find it just where he'd left it, right above his eyes. Were angels supposed to have bodies? And if they did, would they hurt? Because his throbbed.

Good God! Where the hell was he? Had he been sent back to earth? He glanced painfully about. It was dark but for a single candle. He sat upon a narrow bed in a narrow room. Dried, indistinguishable plants hung from the walls and through an open window he could see the moon.

A pretty night, but—

"Sara!" He said her name aloud in a flash of panic. There was danger. He could feel it, but where?

His head reeled when he rose to his feet, but the door opened soundlessly beneath his hand and he was in the hallway. From the left, he heard voices. Something familiar there. But not Sara, not danger.

He turned to the right. His feet were bare, noiseless. The hall stretched on forever, and now his heart was pounding. He hastened his pace.

Dear God, please God, don't let him be too late. Surely as an angel he could not fail her, he thought. He began to run, staggering down the hall, the floor cold against his feet.

There! He felt her presence! Yanking a door open, he looked inside and found a loom, a harp, chairs set near the hearth. No Sara! But across the room another door stood open.

"So it was you." Sara's voice was melodious even in fear.

The laughter that followed was low and humorless.

"Why?" Sara asked. "Why would you wish to harm your own heir?"

Haldane! Boden thought. But why?

Boden reached for his sword. It wasn't there! No weapon! Barefoot, shirtless, barely standing upright! Jesus! What kind of guardian angel was he?

"My heir?" said the other voice. But it was not Haldane. It was a woman's voice.

"He could be!" Sara said. "He could be your son."

"You think I want that bitch's child to inherit what is mine? Nay!" said the woman. Footsteps sounded. "Nay. I want this child, no more than I want yours."

"I'm not Lord Haldane's lover. Never have I been."

The woman's laughter was as harsh as sin. "You imagine I care, do you? Tis a credit to my act then. But the truth is, I do not. I only want what I deserve. Which is . . . everything the duke thinks is his."

Boden flattened himself against the wall and glanced around the corner. The nursery was empty but for the two women and the babe. Lady Haldane stood with her back to him, a knife in her hand.

Sara was less than a rod away, between Elizabeth and the babe who rested in a cradle.

"He is dying you know. Aye." Elizabeth Haldane took a step forward. Her face, once beautiful, was twisted with hatred. Sara retreated. "Tis sad. But, of course, mayhap the henbane I feed him daily does not help his condition. I would have thought that long ago he would have had the decency to quit siring children. At least on me!" Her voice was bitter. "But nay! I've been obliged to rid myself of yet another."

"Nay!" Sara murmured breathlessly. "Surely ye did not kill your own babes."

"Did I not?" Elizabeth laughed. "I suppose you think I am too maternal? Mayhap you even think I will not kill this child?" She nodded toward the baby.

"Please." Sara's voice shook. "Let us go. I will take him away. Hide him. Lord Haldane will never find him."

"Perhaps he would not, for his men are far more loyal to me than to him. Tis amazing what you can convince a man to do if you use sex wisely. The one that killed Caroline was quite adept in bed. Unfortunately, he was not so good with a sword." She shrugged. "When I learned he was dead I called upon Warwick. He and I were old friends. And he had his own reasons to be rid of you. But even Warwick failed. And I am left again to do the deed myself."

"You will fail," Sara said. "They'll hear my screams—"

"Through these walls? No one will hear. And if they do and come running..." She shrugged. "I will be in the solar with my stitchery, like a good lady. So genteel, so wounded. They'll not suspect me." Her tone was utterly innocent, the sweetness that Boden remembered of old. "I fear you've no idea how much I've gotten away with already. But I must say goodbye now, for my beloved lord will be missing me soon," she said and lunged.

With a roar, Boden dove through the door, snatched a cradle from the floor, and flung it across the room. It glanced off Lady Haldane's shoulder, spinning her aside. But the effort pushed Boden against the wall, barely able to stand. In an instant Elizabeth was on her feet and racing toward him, teeth bared, blade drawn back.

He gathered his strength and pushed himself from the wall just as she pounced. He reached for her arms. The knife bit into his shoulder.

His wail echoed Sara's, and then she was there, ripping the madwoman from him. Elizabeth wheeled away, crouched, wild as a cat, her eyes gleaming.

Sara circled, hands empty, eyes wide. "You'll not get away, lady. You'll not."

"What a fool you are!" spat the other. Her dark hair had come loose, framing her face like a demon's halo. "You will die, then your champion. And then the babe."

She lunged. Sara leapt aside, but her toe caught on the leg of a chair and she fell.

Elizabeth leapt after her. Boden pounced forward, grabbing her arms. She twisted about, knife slashing.

"Elizabeth!" Haldane gasped from the doorway.

A growl ripped up from his wife's throat. She yanked her arm free and lunged, the knife drawn far back.

Sara rose from the floor, grabbed a chair, and swung it at Elizabeth's head. The wood cracked against the lady's skull. She stretched up on her toes. Her eyes went wide. Her mouth opened. Her fingers formed to claws, and then she fell. Toppling to the floor, she was dead in an instant.

Boden watched, and then, to his dismay, he too crumbled. St. Adrian's arse, even as an angel, he couldn't stay on his feet.

Boden lay in peace again. Sara's voice murmured gently, soothing. Soft hands touched him. Once or twice he felt himself being lifted, but it was neither painful nor worrisome. Darkness settled around him like a sun-softened blanket. He sighed. Time drifted past at an uncertain pace. Dreams sifted with reality, memories with hopes. This must be heaven, for she was at his side, loving him, touching him, her kiss endless, her touch infinite. Every moment was theirs to share, to float together, but something was not quite right, not quite complete, as if there was some thin, invisible barrier between them. He tried to reach through it, to draw her more firmly to him.

"Boden."

The dimness fell away by slow degrees. He opened his eyes with some effort. The room seemed inordinately bright, but he supposed the hereafter was like that sometimes.

"Sara?" he murmured. She seemed clearer to him suddenly, more tangible, as if he'd broken through the barrier, and now she was completely his.

"I'm here, Boden." She smiled, but the expression wavered slightly, and he realized she was clasping his hand between both of hers and that his fingers were wet with her tears.

"Don't cry," he said. His voice sounded strange, not angelic at all, but rough and coarse. He ignored it. Anything would sound coarse next to her voice. "You can't cry, my love," he whispered, "not in heaven." He smiled and, pulling her hand to his lips, kissed her knuckles, wanting nothing but to hold her against him, to feel her kiss, to hear her voice, soft in his ear. Strange, he needed her no less as an angel than as a man. But now she was completely his. His heart sang. "Come love." He urged her closer. "I've waited a lifetime for you and beyond. There is no sin here. Come lie with me again. Let me kiss you and hold you. Let me fill you with—"

"Sir Blackblade."

The duke's voice struck him like a sharp blow to the chest. Boden twisted his neck to find the speaker.

"Lord Haldane," he rasped.

"Aye." The duke took a step forward and placed a proprietary hand on Sara's shoulder. Boden dropped his own away. Reality sizzled through his veins, burning away the last remnants of soft dreams. He was not an angel. The world was not kind, and she was not his.

"Sir Blackblade," Haldane said again, "you have said some ignoble things in your delirium."

"Delirium?" The single word hurt his throat. Reality pounded inside his skull.

"Nearly a fortnight you've been unconscious. Lady Fiona says tis due to the blows to your head. But she suspected you would awaken today."

Boden's gaze slipped to Sara's face. She looked pale and tired. Nearly a fortnight of dreams . . . of her. Twas the best he could hope for on this earth, for she was another man's. His soul wept.

"I thought I could trust you," Haldane said, turning his gaze from Boden to Sara.

And suddenly Boden realized the truth. In his sleep, he had told their secrets, had revealed their sins. But she must not suffer for them. Without thought he reached for his sword. But his scabbard was gone, his love undefended.

"Twas not the lady's fault," Boden said, struggling to sit up. "Twas mine."

"Nay," said Sara, reaching for his hand. "Tis not true, my lord. Twas my own weakness that caused the sin, if sin it be. But ye see, I love him."

A lance of hot painful pleasure speared Boden's heart. She loved him.

"Love him!" Haldane snorted.

His words jerked Boden back to reality. "The fault is mine," Boden growled, trying to rise, and barely able to realize she was pinning him down with pressure on his shoulder. "And I'll not have you blame her!"

For a moment there was silence. "So you would be her champion, Sir Blackblade?"

"She'll not suffer for my sins!" he snarled.

The world was silent. "Were I a younger man I would challenge you for her hand. But mayhap I have sinned too much already in an attempt to call her mine." His expression looked strained.

Boden settled onto his elbows, saving his strength, and realizing suddenly that Haldane looked to be more like his former self, before the weakness took him. But wait. He frowned, fighting to clear the fog from his brain, to remember.

Sara had been in danger. He had stumbled down the hall as if called by a frantic bell. The image of Lady Elizabeth with a knife flashed through his mind. Haldane's weakness hadn't been natural at all, but a slow form of poison.

Taking his hand from Sara's shoulder, the duke paced the room. "I have little guilt over Stephen's death," he said.

"You killed him?" Boden asked, his body tense, his mind reeling.

Haldane watched him in silence for a moment. "The deer killed him. I but let him die. I had warned him not to strike his wife again. I had warned him, and so his death was justifiable. Twas not that I wanted her for myself." His gaze slipped to Sara, and in its depths, Boden saw that he lied. "But with his death there was that possibility." The room was silent. "But now there is you, Sir Blackblade. You, who I thought I could trust."

"It was not her fault," Boden repeated.

"Then you take the blame for betraying me?"

"Aye," Boden growled. His fist closed on nothing, but somehow, he would fight.

Haldane nodded stiffly, then relaxed slightly and exhaled. "Then you will suffer the consequences."

Silence settled in, tight and heavy.

Boden held his breath.

Lord Haldane paced back across the room to stand beside his bed. "You'll be given Cairn Heights."

No one spoke, as seconds ticked by. Boden scowled, his mind spinning. "What?" he asked cautiously.

"Tis a poor castle on rocky soil. The people are proud, stubborn Scots." Haldane paused, and looked at Sara. "Not unlike your lady.

"Sara." He spoke her name with a somber reverence. "You have saved my heir—in fact, you have saved my very life. I owe you much."

"You have given me everything my heart desires, Your Grace," she said.

There was a wealth of sadness in his expression. "Then you will not change your mind? You choose the knight?"

"I do," she said.

Boden scowled. Reality was blurring again, fuzzing around the edges. The dreams were creeping back in control. Part of him welcomed them, but in that world he could not hold her in his arms. "What?" he repeated.

Haldane straightened to his full height. "Cairn Heights," he repeated. "'Tis to the south and east of here and commands a wide view of the sea. An important post it is. I need a man there I can trust."

"Never will you find a man more loyal than Sir Blackblade," Sara said. "You will stay for the wedding, Your Grace?"

Confusion swirled in Boden's head like fruit bats in the darkness. "The wedding?" His words were barely heard above the beating of his own heart. "The wedding?" he said again.

"'Tis little choice ye've been given, I fear," Sara said. Her smile was tremulous as though she might cry again with the sheer weight of her emotions. "The festivities are already being planned."

"Festivities?"

"I would ask you one last favor," said Haldane.

"Favor?" It would seem Boden could do nothing but echo their words.

"My strength has not yet returned to its full. I must return to London, and that is no place to grow a lad. But at Cairn Heights where the wind blows fresh off the sea, Thomas would have a mentor to train him and a mother to love him."

Boden found no words. Dreams? Was he dreaming again? But no, tears stung his eyes, and his leg throbbed gently. He embraced the pain, reveling in the knowledge that it always came with life.

"The mentor will love him too, my lord," Sara said, gently squeezing Boden's hand. There were tears on her cheeks again. "We thank ye from the depths of our souls."

The duke nodded, then turned and left the room, closing the door behind him. The world fell into silence.

"You are mine?" Boden whispered the words, and she laughed shakily.

"Aye, yours, forever and eternity. But now ye must sleep."

"Sleep! Maybe I could fly, but sleep . . ." He laughed wildly, trying to rise. She pushed him back down as if he were no stronger than a wooly lambkin.

"Fiona will have my hide if I overtax ye," she said.

"Mine," he repeated, tugging at her hand.

"Lie back."

"Never when I can—"

"If I lie with ye?" she interrupted.

He exhaled sharply, but she gave him no time to answer. Instead, she slipped in beside him, pulling the blankets up over them both.

"Sara." He breathed her name, and touched her face.

She squeezed her eyes shut and kissed his fingers as they slipped across her lips.

"Mine," he whispered.

A lone tear slipped from the corner of her eye. "Forever," she repeated and buried her face against his chest.

He stroked her hair. A thousand tender emotions scurried through him, a thousand kind thoughts. The world was heaven. "I love you," he whispered.

She opened her eyes and smoothed her fingers across his cheek. "I know."

"Dragonheart?" he asked. "Did it tell you just as it told me when you needed me, where to find you?" But now he noticed that the dragon was gone.

"Lost." She raised her gaze to his. "Warwick tore it from my neck. It fell with him into the river."

Boden tightened his grip on her. His breath felt like gravel in his throat, but she kissed the corner of his mouth, his cheek, his hairline until the memory faded into the pleasure of her touch.

"Mayhap there was some magic in it," she whispered. "Some magic that melded our souls. But mayhap it was just our love."

"You knew I loved you?"

She smiled. "You said so a hundred times in your delirium."

Her touch was heaven on earth. "Had I known . . ."

His words fell into silence. She was his, forever. "Had I known you would be mine, I would have awakened sooner."

Stroking his hair away, she kissed his brow. "You were unconscious."

Every touch of hers felt wonderful, velvet soft. Forever. The word echoed in his mind. He let his eyes fall closed. "You should have kicked me awake," he said.

She laughed, but there was a tear in the sound. Her touch was a warm balm against his face, his chest, his arm, caressing, soothing, lulling. "I could never hurt you. Never."

He sighed. "I remember a knife. In my arm, I think."

"Shh," she kissed the corner of his mouth. "Never again."

"You are mine," he murmured.

"Sleep now," she crooned.

"Can't," he said, but her fingers were doing delectable things against the small of his back. "Well, maybe just for a bit," he said, and fell asleep like a babe in her arms.

Chapter 28

Boden opened his eyes. Something flashed at the corner of his sight. He sat up part way and grimaced as a hundred different muscles complained.

From across the room, Margaret gasped. "You're hurt," she said, rushing forward a few paces before stopping. There was a smudge of dirt on her cheek and a stain on the sleeve of her blue gown. A small, grubby angel who held a weasel in both hands.

Memories rushed back to Boden. Memories of hope, of happiness. "Maggie," he murmured. "You are well?"

"You're hurt," she repeated, wide-eyed.

"Nay. I am healing quickly, and what of you?"

She chewed her lip, then glanced toward the door and back. Her eyes looked strangely bright suddenly. "Don't die," she whispered.

A lump settled in his throat. He swallowed it with an effort. "I've no intention of dying. I will wed Sara."

Her brown eyes were somber and wide. She was a tiny imp, alone in the world, and so sad that he felt his heart had been ripped in two.

"And me?" Her words were barely audible, forced out at the edge of all her bravery.

"You, Maggie mine," he said, his voice husky. "You will be our daughter."

Her mouth formed a small o, and suddenly, like a flurry of wind, she flew into his arms.

The weasel dropped to the bed, then scurried up Boden's pillow. A hundred myriad places ached as she squeezed her arms around his chest, but Boden closed his eyes and smiled at the wonderful crush of pain.

"Carefully, lass," said a voice. "Lest you break open the stitches."

Boden opened his eyes. In the doorway stood a small woman with eyes of amethyst and a sunlight smile.

"Lady Fiona," Maggie whispered, her tone awestruck as she loosened her grip a bit. "The healer."

Boden stared at Fiona. She exuded kindness and caring. So this was the woman Sara had spoken of with such reverence. This was the woman who had brought him from the brink to find love. "You have my thanks," he said, his tone low.

"Tis I that thank you," she said, stepping forward, "for saving our Sara."

"I fear it was she who saved me."

"Nay," said Sara, stepping inside to take his hand in her own. Feelings as potent as wine coursed through him at the touch of her skin, the warmth of her gaze. "Twas ye that saved my heart, Sir Knight, and Shona that saved ye."

"Shona?"

"My cousin," Sara said, turning slightly to glance toward the door. "Shona of the Forbes. Sir Boden Blackblade."

With some difficulty, Boden forced his gaze from Sara, and there, near the door, he saw a tall woman with hair that swept down to her hips in red waves of fire.

So David had been right; Glen Creag boasted the world's most beautiful women. He heard Maggie's small gasp of admiration, but as for himself, he could not keep his gaze from the warmth of Sara's smile, the brightness of her presence.

Even so, dim memories crowded in on him—green

eyes—a woman carrying a bow, many small, gentle hands lifting him, carrying him, their bright hair washing over him as one shouted orders.

Sara? Had his sweet Sara been shouting? Something about gentle—and horses?

He shook his head, trying to remember, then turning his eyes to Shona, "So twas you who felled the man who . . ." His voice broke, but he was past caring that he showed weakness. Surely they all knew the truth by now. "Who killed my steed?"

"Kilt yer steed?" said Shona. "Sara, surely ye've not allowed him to think his stallion be dead."

"There's been little time for talk," she said.

"Mettle . . ." Boden said, refusing to believe there was a catch in his voice. "He is . . ."

"He is alive," Shona said. "Resting until his leg heals."

Tears threatened, but that was going too far. Boden held them back with manly effort.

Shona saw his expression and smiled. "Our Sara would not allow him to die. The soldiers were wont to leave yer steed behind. But she took offense. I believe her words were, leave the horse and ye might as well leave yer heads."

He squeezed her hand. *His* Sara, soft as an angel, tough as hell.

"It was Fiona who saved him," Sara said.

God, he loved her so much it hurt.

"Come," she urged, gently tugging on his hand. "Lady Fiona says you can walk for a wee bit. Ye can see him from the window."

He eased to a sitting position. His head swam, then steadied. The floor felt cool against his feet. He glanced down, then sat abruptly.

"Sara!" he gasped, seeing he wore nothing more than a rude loincloth. "I'm indecent."

"Oh." Her face flamed.

"Here. Wrap this around your waist," Fiona said, tugging a blanket about his body. Her voice was steady, but he wondered if there was laughter somewhere behind it as she helped him back to his feet.

Now would be a fine time to faint, Boden thought, but there was little hope of that, for he was being led to the window like a sheep on a string.

"There," Sara said.

Looking out the window, Boden saw the courtyard below, and there, hanging from a timber braced between the stone wall and an oak tree, hung Mettle upon a sling. Tilly stood guard nearby, and feeding him from her hands was a taller replica of the woman named Shona.

He stared in amazement. His throat tightened. "You have my thanks again, Lady Fiona."

"'Tis Flanna who nurtures him most," said the older woman, pressing up beside him.

"Flanna?"

"My mother," said Shona, "the Flame of the MacGowans. You'll be lucky if she lets you have the steed back once she becomes attached."

"I owe her a great . . ." Boden began, but just then his blanket began slipping downward.

He grabbed it. Pain speared through his arm, his back, his thigh.

"Here," said three women, all reaching to help him wrap the thing back around.

Gentle fingers brushed his flesh in quite intimate places, and though twas all done in the most casual way, embarrassment seared him.

"There now," said Fiona softly, but the laughter seemed closer to the surface of her voice now. "There's no need for embarrassment." She shrugged, looking out the window with a twinkle in her eye. "I've seen all there is of you."

Saint Judas!

"And?" whispered Shona, the same diabolical gleam in her eyes.

"Quite impressive," said Fiona.

And Boden hoped for oblivion.

Boden's days passed in flashes of soft laughter and gentle kisses, introductions to an endless stream of relatives and servants, and long afternoon naps. Although Sara refused to lie with him again before the wedding, she would sit at his bedside and talk of her childhood, or sing as she fed Thomas.

On one particular afternoon, a tall, fair-haired man stepped into the infirmary. Sara glanced up, still laughing at Boden's jest.

"Roddy," she gasped, and launching from her stool, flew into the man's arms. He hugged her tightly to him and stroked the back of her head as one might do to a precious child.

"My sunshine," he whispered, closing his eyes for a moment as if he would absorb the feelings deep into his soul. Pushing her to arm's length finally, he smiled into her face. "Returned to light the Highlands."

Propped against the pillows at his back, Boden watched the exchange. The newcomer was perhaps a score of years older than himself. He wore a plain saffron tunic and a plaid of greens and browns that crossed over his chest and was pinned by a brooch in the shape of a cat's face. He was built rugged and lean, with the smile of a rogue and the confidence of a champion. It would be simple enough to be jealous of Sara's obvious affection for him, had it not been for the stark family resemblance.

"Roddy," she repeated and taking his hand, tugged him toward the bed. "I wish for ye to meet my betrothed, Sir Boden Blackblade.

"Boden, this is . . ."

"Sara's favorite uncle," Roderic said, and reaching out, clasped the younger man's hand in his own. There was a moment of silence as they weighed each other, then, "I am told we have ye to thank for returning our wee lass to us," he said.

For a while Boden was tempted to tighten the handshake and prove himself, but the foolishness passed. "Aye. She had to save my hide so many times that finally she thought twould be best if she brought me here for safekeeping."

There was a pause, and then Roderic threw back his head and laughed as he released the other's hand. "Tis not quite the tale I was told. Well met we are, Sir Blackblade." His expression sobered, becoming almost, but not quite, somber. "Ye have my thanks, sir. Sara is like a daughter to my heart."

"I feared ye might not return from France before the wedding," Sara said.

Roderic laughed again. The sound seemed as common as speech to him. "Even had I not learned of your betrothal, I couldna have left Dun Ard so long."

"No trouble there I hope," Sara said.

"Nay, na now," Roderic said and grimaced, "for Shona is here and is bound to have brought the trouble with her. It follows her like flies to a dung heap."

Sara laughed. "You've not found a suitable match for her yet?"

"Who could be suitable for my Shona, when she has her mother's spirit and my own marvelous charm." His words stopped as he turned his head toward the door. "And who might this be?"

Boden glanced sideways.

"Margaret," Sara said softly. "Come here. There is no need to fear."

The girl slunk forward, shy as a fawn with a stranger around. There was a smudge of dirt on her nose, and her grubby hand was wrapped about a bundle of pungent shrubbery that bore tiny white blossoms.

Boden watched her advance toward his bed with the bouquet hugged to her narrow chest. "White heather,"

she whispered, shifting her gaze quickly to Roderic.
"Lady Fiona said twill bring good luck."

Boden's heart twisted slightly. How had his world become so full? "I need no more good luck, Maggie mine," he said. "For I have you."

"So ye are Sara's lass," Roderic said, watching the child with a light in his eyes, "if not by nature, then by love." He smiled. "I remember when she was na bigger than ye. A mother hen she was even then. My Shona had entered the world na more than two months hence and was wont ta fuss sometimes during the night. There was a maid in the nursery to watch the babe, but Sara awoke first and decided the woman was not seeing to her duties near well enough. So she took the babe from her cradle." He shook his head. "In the morn when Flanna went to check the babe, the maid was sound asleep and Shona was gone. I think twas the first time I saw her mother truly frightened."

Maggie's eyes were as round as silver groats as she waited for him to continue. The silence stretched away, until, able to wait no more, she bit her lip and whispered, "Where was the babe?"

"Sara had taken her to the burn. We found them wrapped in a blanket fast asleep. She said the singing water soothed the child."

Boden shifted his gaze to Sara's angelic face, and the day passed by with tales and laughter and satin-soft kisses.

Finally, seeing Boden could no longer bear to be confined inside, Fiona allowed him to venture from the hall.

It had rained the night before and the clouds still hung low over the courtyard, but the air was fresh and Sara was at his side. Though his head felt light and his leg weak, he was not about to call a halt to their walk.

After a brief stop in the kitchens they visited Mettle. His sling had been lowered slightly so that his giant hooves just reached the ground, allowing him to bear a bit of his own immense weight. He'd learned to push off so that he could sway from side to side, and did so now, stretching his neck and his upper lip as he plucked a few select grasses from Maggie's hand.

The little girl giggled, looking no bigger than a gosling as the destrier lowered his huge, bowed nose for the girl to stroke.

''He'll be as round as a barrel if you keep feeding him,'' Boden chided.

Mettle tilted his ears forward at the sound of his voice and swung lazily toward him, already nuzzling him for treats. ''Here then,'' Boden said, keeping his tone gruff as he offered him a chunk of stolen bread.

The marten slipped from Maggie's sleeve, sniffed madly and dashed up her arm to try to reach the bread. Stymied, he finally leapt from her elbow, landed on Mettle's mane and dragged himself onto the stallion's crest to perch between his ears.

The picture was ridiculous, the laughter contagious.

''He's never had a scrap of pride,'' Boden said with a chuckle, ''but how does Lady Fiona confine him to the sling?''

''Magic,'' said a voice from behind.

Boden turned. Liam stood less than a dozen rods before him. They stared at each other like wary hounds.

''The Lady Fiona has a magic for healing,'' Liam said, breaking the silence.

''Aye,'' Boden agreed, glad to find something they could agree on, for Sara's sake, then, ''I didn't know you had remained here at Glen Creag.''

''I've had things to see to and have been here and there.'' Liam's gaze settled on Sara for a moment. ''Tis good ta see ye rested and well, lass.''

She smiled, seeming to be the only one at ease. ''I am well, Liam. Where have ye been? Surely not searching for Dragonheart again.''

He shrugged. The corner of his mouth lifted into a

sheepish grin. "Mayhap. I was quite distraught that ya'd lose my gift."

"I am sorry," she said, "but I had other things on my mind."

"Such as staying alive," said a dark-haired woman who approached from Boden's right.

He nodded at her, remembering he had met her some days past. With eyes as amethyst bright as her mother's, she was not an easy woman to forget. "Lady Rachel," he said by way of greeting.

She smiled at him, then raised a dark brow and turned her attention to Liam. "You forget that some people value things above jewels," she said.

"Speaking of jewels," Liam said. "What's that by your ear?" He frowned and stepped forward with an outstretched hand. "A pearl. Oh. No," he said, drawing his hand back and seeming to pull something from her ear as he did so. Between his fingers, a fat toad squirmed.

Rachel arched a brow at him, looking unimpressed and unsurprised. "Still trying to turn toads into jewels, Liam?"

Liam scowled and waved his hand with a quick snap. The toad disappeared. Boden stared.

"The amulet was far more than a jewel," the magician said, sounding cross, either because of her disbelief or her lack of reaction to his trick. What an odd place this was, Boden thought. "Twas a magical charm to keep our Sara safe."

"A poor job it did then," said Rachel. "For she was nearly killed."

"But she was not," Liam reminded her.

"Neither was I," said Rachel. "Shall we attribute that to your all-powerful amulet?"

"Nay," he said. "'Tis not all-powerful, for I asked the dragon to strike ye mute."

"Luckily it had far more sense than ye," Rachel said, "and it sent Shona and myself to seek out Sara."

"So you were there too?" asked Boden.

"Aye," Rachel said, catching his gaze. "Shona and I took an escort to go to London. Worried we were for Sara's well-being. Do ye not remember us lifting ye up, Sir Blackblade."

"I remember angels," he said softly. "Angels with hair of every hue."

"Angels," Liam scoffed, "and one she-devil. I warn ya, dunna let her near the wedding or she will surely jinx it."

"I will be at the nuptials," Rachel said, "but mayhap I should find the amulet and implore it to keep ye away."

"The dragon is gone. Though I searched I could not find it," Liam said.

Rachel snorted. "Ye could not even find Warwick."

"Shhh!" Liam interrupted sharply. "Dunna speak his name."

Silent surprise surrounded them as all turned their gazes to Liam.

He cleared his throat, looking embarrassed at his own skittishness. "I found no body."

Sara laughed. "When did ye become such a worrier? He is dead. Boden killed him. I saw him fall."

Liam took a deep breath and chuckled, seemingly at his own foolishness. "Aye, he is dead. There is naught to delay your wedding." He paused. The courtyard was silent but for the sound of the windlass as someone hauled water from the well. "Ya have my best wishes."

Silence again.

"And?" Rachel said, staring at him.

Liam cleared his throat. "And my apologies for wounding ya, Sir Boden. Twas not my intent, I assure ya. I but tried to protect Sara. I thought ye were the dark wizard. And when I saw twas you, I thought her safer in your care than in mine."

"Not to mention you feared that Boden would part your head from your body," Rachel said.

Liam grinned like a satyr. "Aye. Not to mention that."

Boden forced himself to relax marginally. Perhaps he

would never like this man who was so different from himself, and yet held a piece of Sara's heart. But he could, at least, understand his desire to protect her.

"You are forgiven," he said.

"Good." Liam stepped forward and thrust out his hand. "Ya have my congratulations, Sir Knight."

Boden reached out, momentarily wondering where the toad had gone before their hands clasped. Nothing repulsive touched his skin. Their gazes clashed, but then Liam leaned forward slightly, looking over Boden's shoulder.

"Ye know she's the best woman in all of Christendom." Liam said the words softly, for Boden's ears alone.

"Aye. That I know."

"And if ye mistreat her . . ." He paused. "I'll turn ye into a frog."

"You can put your mind at ease," Boden said, offering Liam a smile. "I've never much liked the water."

The day of the wedding finally arrived. Not a cloud marred the autumn sky. The trees were etched in colors so bright it all but hurt the eyes to look upon them—golds, crimsons, russets, and the last, stubborn remnants of green.

Glen Creag's great hall was festooned with bunches of heather and sweet-smelling sprays of purple thistle. But most of the throng of visitors reveled outside.

Children ran foot races, walked on stilts, and played blindman's buff. Little Margaret sat atop Mettle and watched the revelry with wide-eyed wonder. Her hair was plaited, wound around her skull, and adorned with wildflowers. Her small face, although solemn, seemed aglow. Her gown was made of fine yellow satin. There was a stain on the collar and from the sleeve, a weasel poked his head.

Tilly escaped her pen and wandered at will through the throng, lapping up any unguarded spirits, until she disgraced herself a number of times and they were forced to tie her to the tree next to Mettle's.

Liam entertained the crowd with magic tricks and argued with Rachel.

Shona charmed half the male assemblage and won the archery contest, defeating even her father, who swore he had allowed her to win.

And just after the vows were completed Boden and Sara slipped away.

"Explain it to me again," Boden said, turning Sara in his arms.

Her gown was bell-shaped, made of soft, russet satin that was cinched at her tiny waist and squared at the neckline. But it was her smile that stole his attention. "Explain what, my lord?"

"How I have found heaven on earth?"

She laughed, the sound silvery light. "Luck?" she suggested.

He shook his head and leaning forward, kissed her lightly. "Nay. Nothing so wondrous could be from simple luck."

She sighed as his kisses slipped down her throat. "Mayhap Liam is right, then, maybe the dragon brought us together. Mayhap twas its intent to bring me my one true love."

He leaned back slightly, studying her, the blue of her eyes, the warmth of her smile. "I have never believed in magic," he said, "until I saw you."

The comment gained him a kiss.

"Then you think twas the amulet that drew you to me when I was fleeing north with Liam, twas the amulet that gave me my dreams?"

He shrugged. "Stranger things have happened, I suppose."

"But I worry then," she said, narrowing her eyes and stepping away from him. "If twas Dragonheart that drew you to me, mayhap ye will lose interest now that it is gone."

"Lose interest?" He breathed the words. "In you?"

She watched him through her lashes as she nodded, but suddenly she was in his arms again, held tight against the power of his chest.

"Never. Not as long as the sun rises and the seasons change. Forever and always you will be my heart," he swore.

Their lips met in a vow as solid as stone, and far away, in the icy depths of the Burn Creag, Dragonheart smiled.

Dear Reader,

If you've just finished this Avon romance title and are looking for more of the best in romantic fiction, then be on the watch for these upcoming romance titles—available at your favorite bookstore!

Affaire de Coeur says Genell Dellin is " . . . one of the best writers of ethnic romances starring Native Americans." And her latest, AFTER THE THUNDER, is Native American romance filled with sensuality and emotion. When a young Shaman falls for a scandalous young woman he must decide if he will fulfill the needs of the spirit—or the body.

For lovers of Scotland settings, don't miss the luscious A ROSE IN SCOTLAND by Joan Overfield. When a desperate young woman marries the handsome, brooding Laird of Lochhaven, she expects nothing more than a marriage of convenience. But what begins as duty turns into something much more.

Maureen McKade's A DIME NOVEL HERO is a must-read for those who like their heroes tough and their settings western. This tender romance about a woman who writes dime novels, her adopted son and the man she's turned into an unwilling hero—and who is unknowingly the boy's father—is sure to touch your heart.

Contemporary romance fans are sure to love SIMPLY IRRESISTIBLE by debut author Rachel Gibson. A sassy charm school graduate is on the run—from her own wedding. She's rescued by a sexy guest but never dreams that, nine months later, she'll have a little bundle of joy—proof of their whirlwind romance. And when he barges back into her life, complications ensue—and romance is rekindled.

Remember, look to Avon Books for the very best in romance!

Sincerely,
Lucia Macro
Avon Books

AEL 1197

Avon Romances—
the best in exceptional authors
and unforgettable novels!

Avon Romantic Treasures

Unforgettable, enthralling love stories,
sparkling with passion and adventure
from Romance's bestselling authors

EVERYTHING AND THE MOON *by Julia Quinn*
78933-7/$5.99 US/$7.99 Can

BEAST *by Judith Ivory*
78644-3/$5.99 US/$7.99 Can

HIS FORBIDDEN TOUCH *by Shelley Thacker*
78120-4/$5.99 US/$7.99 Can

LYON'S GIFT *by Tanya Anne Crosby*
78571-4/$5.99 US/$7.99 Can

FLY WITH THE EAGLE *by Kathleen Harrington*
77836-X/$5.99 US/$7.99 Can

FALLING IN LOVE AGAIN *by Cathy Maxwell*
78718-0/$5.99 US/$7.99 Can

**THE COURTSHIP OF
CADE KOLBY** *by Lori Copeland*
79156-0/$5.99 US/$7.99 Can

TO LOVE A STRANGER *by Connie Mason*
79340-7/$5.99 US/$7.99 Can